Dear Friends,

As youngsters, long before there were such things as computer games or videos, my friends and I played a game we called "make believe." My favorite of those "make believe" sessions were the times we pretended we were secretaries. We would take dictation, type up reports and complain about the unreasonable demands of our bosses.

In retrospect it makes perfect sense to me now that some of my earliest novels involved secretaries, or what we usually call administrative or executive assistants these days. *Love in Plain Sight* brings back two books I wrote in the late 1980s, which was early in my writing career. I read them over recently and did my best to update terminology and attitudes. Much has changed in the past thirty years, mostly for the better. You could call these books "vintage Debbie Macomber" and while they are traditional romance novels, I believe the stories are as readable today as they were all those years ago.

Feedback from my readers has been invaluable to me through the years. You can reach me through Facebook at Debbie Macomber World or at my website at DebbieMacomber.com. You can download my app on your cell phone, too. (I'm so technologically connected I hardly know where I am any longer.) Or you can reach me at my P.O. Box 1458, Port Orchard, WA 98366.

Warmest regards,

Debbie Macomber

DEBBIE MACOMBER

LOVE in
Plain Sight

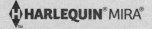

ISBN-13: 978-0-7783-1413-4

LOVE IN PLAIN SIGHT

Copyright © 1987 by Harlequin Books S.A.

The publisher acknowledges the copyright holder
of the individual works as follows:

LOVE 'N' MARRIAGE
Copyright © 1987 by Debbie Macomber

ALMOST AN ANGEL
Copyright © 1989 by Debbie Macomber

Recycling programs
for this product may
not exist in your area.

For questions and comments about the quality of this book, please contact us
at CustomerService@Harlequin.com.

HARLEQUIN®

Printed in U.S.A.   www.Harlequin.com

To
Doris LaPort
and
Teresa Colchada
for helping me keep my life sane
and
my home beautiful

Also by Debbie Macomber

Blossom Street Books

The Shop on Blossom Street
A Good Yarn
Susannah's Garden
Back on Blossom Street
Twenty Wishes
Summer on Blossom Street
Hannah's List
The Knitting Diaries
   "The Twenty-First Wish"
A Turn in the Road

Cedar Cove Books

16 Lighthouse Road
204 Rosewood Lane
311 Pelican Court
44 Cranberry Point
50 Harbor Street
6 Rainier Drive
74 Seaside Avenue
8 Sandpiper Way
92 Pacific Boulevard
1022 Evergreen Place
A Cedar Cove Christmas
   (*5-B Poppy Lane* and
   Christmas in Cedar Cove)
1105 Yakima Street
1225 Christmas Tree Lane

Dakota Series

Dakota Born
Dakota Home
Always Dakota

The Manning Family

The Manning Sisters
The Manning Brides
The Manning Grooms

Christmas Books

A Gift to Last
On a Snowy Night
Home for the Holidays
Glad Tidings
Christmas Wishes
Small Town Christmas
When Christmas Comes
   (now retitled *Trading*
   Christmas)
There's Something About
   Christmas
Christmas Letters
Where Angels Go
The Perfect Christmas
Angels at Christmas
   (*Those Christmas Angels*
   and *Where Angels Go*)
Call Me Mrs. Miracle

Heart of Texas Series

VOLUME 1
(*Lonesome Cowboy* and
   Texas Two-Step)
VOLUME 2
(*Caroline's Child* and
   Dr. Texas)
VOLUME 3
(*Nell's Cowboy* and
   Lone Star Baby)
Promise, Texas
Return to Promise

Midnight Sons

VOLUME 1
(Brides for Brothers and
    The Marriage Risk)
VOLUME 2
(Daddy's Little Helper and
    Because of the Baby)
VOLUME 3
(Falling for Him,
    Ending in Marriage and
    Midnight Sons and Daughters)

This Matter of Marriage
Montana
Thursdays at Eight
Between Friends
Changing Habits
Married in Seattle
    (First Comes Marriage and
    Wanted: Perfect Partner)
Right Next Door
    (Father's Day and
    The Courtship of
    Carol Sommars)
Wyoming Brides
    (Denim and Diamonds and
    The Wyoming Kid)
Fairy Tale Weddings
    (Cindy and the Prince and
    Some Kind of Wonderful)
The Man You'll Marry
    (The First Man You Meet and
    The Man You'll Marry)

Orchard Valley Grooms
    (Valerie and *Stephanie)*
Orchard Valley Brides
    (Norah and *Lone Star Lovin')*
The Sooner the Better
An Engagement in Seattle
    (Groom Wanted and
    Bride Wanted)
Out of the Rain
    (Marriage Wanted and
    Laughter in the Rain)
Learning to Love
    (Sugar and Spice and
    Love by Degree)
You...Again
    (Baby Blessed and
    Yesterday Once More)
Three Brides, No Groom
The Unexpected Husband
    (Jury of his Peers and
    Any Sunday)
I Left My Heart
    (A Friend or Two and
    No Competition)

Debbie Macomber's
    Cedar Cove Cookbook
Debbie Macomber's
    Christmas Cookbook

CONTENTS

LOVE 'N' MARRIAGE

One

Stephanie Coulter sauntered into the personnel office at Lockwood Industries, the largest manufacturer of airplane parts in North America, carrying a brown paper bag. Her friend Jan Michaels glanced up expectantly. "Hi. To what do I owe this unexpected pleasure?"

In response, Stephanie placed the sack on Jan's desk.

"What's that?"

Stephanie sat on the corner of her friend's desk and folded her arms. "Maureen sent books. It seems I've been allotted the privilege of delivering your romances."

"I take it Potter is still sick?"

"Right." The entire morning had been a series of frustrations for Stephanie. Her boss was out with a bad case of the flu for the third consecutive day. For the first couple of days Stephanie had been able to occupy herself with the little things an executive assistant never seemed to find the time to do. Things like clearing out the filing cabinets, updating the on-line calendar and reorganizing her desk. But by the third morning she'd run out of ideas and had ended up writing a letter to her parents, feeling guilty about doing it on company time.

"Old Stone Face is out, as well," Jan informed her.

The uncomplimentary name belonged to the executive assistant to the company's president, Jonas Lockwood. In the two years Stephanie had been working for the business, she'd never known Martha Westheimer to miss a day. For that matter, Stephanie had never even visited the older woman's domain on the top floor and doubted that she ever would. Martha guarded her territory like a polar bear protecting her cubs.

The corner of Jan's mouth twitched. "And guess who's working with Mr. Lockwood in the interim? You're going to love this."

"Who?" Stephanie mentally reviewed the list of possible candidates, coming up blank.

"Mimi Palmer."

"Who?"

"Mimi Palmer. She's been here about a month, working in the mail room, and—get this—she's Old Stone Face's niece."

"I can just imagine how that's working out."

"I haven't heard any complaints yet," Jan murmured as she opened the paper bag. "But then, it's still early." She took out the top book and shot a questioning glance in Stephanie's direction. "Are you sure you don't want to read one of these? The stories are great, and if you're looking to kill time…"

Stephanie held up both palms and shook her head adamantly. "That would look terrific, wouldn't it? Can you imagine what Potter would say if he walked in and caught me reading?"

"Take one home," Jan offered.

"No, thanks. I'm just not into romances."

From the look Jan was giving her, Stephanie could

tell that her friend wasn't pleased with her response. She knew that several of the other women at Lockwood Industries read romances, and often traded books back and forth. To be honest, she didn't see why they found the books so enjoyable, but since she hadn't read one she felt she didn't have any right to judge.

"I wish you wouldn't be so closed-minded, especially since—" Jan was interrupted when the door burst open and Mr. Lockwood himself stormed into the room like an unexpected squall. He was tall and broad-shouldered and walked with a cane, his limp more exaggerated than Stephanie could ever recall seeing it. She remembered the first time she'd seen Jonas Lockwood and the fleeting sadness she'd felt that a man so attractive had to deal with the twisted right leg that marred the perfection of his healthy, strong body. His appearance was that of a cynical, relentless male. As always, she couldn't take her eyes away from him. His dark good looks commanded her attention any time he was near.

He paused only a second while his frosty blue gaze ran over her in an emotionless inspection, dismissing her. She wasn't accustomed to anyone regarding her as though she were nothing more than a pesky piece of lint. His attitude infuriated her. She hadn't exactly been holding her breath waiting for the company president to notice her. Still, she found him intriguing, and subconsciously had expected some reaction from him once they met. He revealed nothing except irritation.

"Michaels, couldn't you find me a decent replacement for even one day?" he roared, completely ignoring Stephanie.

"Mr. Lockwood, sir." Clearing her throat, Jan got to her feet. "Sir, is there a problem?"

"I'd hardly be standing here if there wasn't," he gritted. "Why would you send me that nitwit woman in the first place?"

"Sir, Miss Westheimer recommended Miss Palmer. She told me that Mimi Palmer is highly qualified—"

"She's utterly incompetent."

He certainly didn't mince words, Stephanie mused.

"I specifically asked for a mature executive assistant. Certainly that shouldn't be such a difficult request."

"But, Mr. Lockwood..."

"Older, more mature women approach the office with businesslike attitudes and are far less emotional."

That had to be one of the most unfair cracks Stephanie had ever heard. She bristled involuntarily. "If you'll excuse me for interrupting, I'd like to point out that a qualified executive assistant is able to adapt to any situation. I sincerely doubt that age has anything to do with it."

His sharp eyes blazed over her face. "Who are you?"

"Stephanie Coulter."

"Miss Coulter is Mr. Potter's executive assistant."

"Do you always speak out of turn?" He eyed Stephanie with open disapproval.

"Only when the occasion calls for it."

"Can you type?"

"One hundred words a minute."

"Computer skills?"

"Of course."

"Follow me."

"But, Mr. Lockwood..." Stephanie felt like a tongue-tied idiot for having spoken out of turn.

Ignoring her, he imperiously addressed Jan. "I'm sure Ms. Coulter is willing to prove just how qualified she is. She can work for me today. What you tell Potter is no concern of mine." He turned abruptly, obviously expecting Stephanie to trot obediently after him.

Her gaze clashed with her friend's. "I guess that answers that."

Grinning, Jan pointed in the direction of the elevator. "Good luck."

Stephanie had the distinct feeling she was going to need it.

Walking briskly down the wide corridor, she arrived just as the elevator doors parted. She stepped inside, holding herself stiffly.

Jonas Lockwood moved forward and pushed the appropriate button, then stepped back. Stephanie noted that he leaned heavily on the cane. She had trouble remembering the last time she'd seen him use one. More often than not, he walked without it.

The elevator rode silently to the top floor, and the doors swished open to reveal his huge office, which occupied the entire top floor. Half of the area was taken up by an immense reception area with a circular desk in the center.

"This way," he said.

Speechless, she followed him, taking in the plush furniture in the gigantic office. The view of Minneapolis was spectacular, but she didn't dare stop to appreciate it. Mimi Palmer was sitting at the large circular desk, sniffling. A man Stephanie didn't recognize was pacing the area near the desk. He glanced up when Jonas and Stephanie approached, and frowned. He was ruggedly built and of medium height. She guessed his age to be around forty-five, perhaps a bit older.

"Jonas, I'm sure the young lady didn't mean any harm," the other man said, gesturing toward Mimi.

Jonas ignored the other man the same way he'd ignored Stephanie only moments earlier. He stepped in front of Mimi and shot a furious glance in her direction. "She may have ruined six months of negotiations with her incompetence."

"I'm sorry, s-so sorry," Mimi said, still sniffling. "I didn't know."

"Not only does she keep an important call on hold for fifteen minutes while she makes a pot of coffee, she insults the company president by demanding to know the nature of his business, and then claims I'm not to be bothered and hangs up on him."

Mimi covered her face with her hands. "I was only trying to help."

Jonas snorted, and Mimi let out a sob.

Stephanie moved forward. "Mimi, stop crying. That's not doing anyone any good. Unless you can help here, I'd suggest you go to the ladies' room and compose yourself." She turned to Jonas. "Tell me whom to contact and I'll do whatever is necessary to smooth matters over."

"Phinney," he said, not sounding at all pacified. "Edward Phinney."

"I tried to call him back, but I couldn't find his phone number," Mimi said on her way out of the office.

Jonas Lockwood glared at Mimi's departing back.

Stephanie had a fairly good idea what might have happened. "Under pressure, she might have had trouble spelling it." Sitting at the desk, she went through the Rolodex until she located the *Ph*'s. Within seconds she located the card. "I'll return Mr. Phinney's call and explain."

"I would prefer do it myself," he barked.

"Fine." She pulled the card free and handed it to him.

"Now, how can I help you?" She directed her question at the middle-aged man who stood in the center of the room with his mouth hanging open.

"I'm Adam Holmes."

"Mr. Holmes," Stephanie acknowledged briskly. "As I'm sure Mr. Lockwood explained, his executive assistant is ill for the day, but I'll be happy to help."

He opened his leather briefcase. "I'm here to drop off a few papers for Jonas to read over."

Stephanie took them from his outstretched hand. "I'll see to it that he receives these as soon as he's free."

"I don't doubt that for an instant," he said with a low chuckle. "Tell Jonas to contact me at my office if he has any questions."

"I'll do that."

The phone beeped, and Stephanie reached for the receiver. "Mr. Lockwood's office," she said in a crisp, professional voice, then wrote down the message, promising that Mr. Lockwood would return the call at his earliest convenience.

While she was writing down the information, Adam Holmes raised his hand in salute and sauntered toward the elevator. She watched him go. There was a kindness to his features, and the spark in his dark blue eyes assured her that he was far from over the hill.

The phone rang twice more while she sorted through the mail. She wrote down the messages and put them in a neat stack, waiting for Jonas to be off the line so she could give them to him.

Mimi reappeared dabbing at the corner of her right eye with a tissue. "I made a mess of things, didn't I?"

"Don't worry about it." Stephanie offered the younger woman a warm, reassuring smile. "This job is just more than you're used to handling."

"I'm really not very good at this sort of thing."

"It's all taken care of, so don't worry."

"Aunt Martha said I wouldn't have any problems for one day."

"I think your aunt seems to have underestimated the demands of her position."

"I...think so, too," Mimi said. "Would it be all right if I went back to my job in the mail room? I don't think I'll be any good around here."

"That'll be fine, Mimi. I'll tell Mr. Lockwood for you."

At the mention of their employer's name, Mimi grimaced. "He's horrible."

Stephanie watched the young blonde leave, furious with Old Stone Face for having put her niece in such an impossible position. An hour later, however, Stephanie found herself agreeing with Mimi's assessment of their employer. He *was* horrible.

A couple of minutes after Mimi's departure, Jonas had called her into his office. She had taken the phone messages and the mail with her.

"Take a letter," he said, without glancing up from his huge rosewood desk.

She was too stunned by his cool, unemotional tone to react quickly enough to suit him.

"Do you plan to memorize it?" he said sarcastically.

"Of course not..." Stephanie didn't fluster easily, but already this arrogant, unreasonable man had broken through her cool manner. "If you'll excuse me a moment, I'll get a pad and pen." She hadn't used her shorthand skills in a very long while. But apparently this was the method he used with Martha and was most comfortable with, so she would adjust—just as she'd told him a good executive assistant would do.

"That's generally recommended."

No sooner had she reappeared than her employer began dictating his daily correspondence. He barely paused to breathe between letters, obviously expecting her to keep pace with him. When he'd finished, he handed her a pile of financial reports and asked her to update the computer records.

"How soon will you have the letters ready?" His expressionless blue eyes cut into her. The impatience in his gaze told her that as far as he was concerned, half the day was gone already, and there was business to be done.

"Within the hour," she replied, knowing she would have to draw on every skill she'd learned on the job to meet her own deadline.

"Good." He lowered his gaze in a gesture of dismissal, and she returned to the other office, disliking him all the more.

Her fingers fairly flew over the keys, her concentration total. Jonas interrupted her three times to ask about one thing or another, but she was determined to meet her own deadline. She would have those letters ready on time or die trying.

Precisely an hour later, smiling smugly, she placed the correspondence on his desk. She stepped back, awaiting his response. Meeting the deadline had demanded that she stretch her abilities to their limits, and she anticipated some reaction from her employer.

"Yes?" He raised his head and glared at her.

"Your letters."

"I see that. Are you expecting me to applaud your efforts?"

After all the effort she'd gone to, that was exactly what she had expected. After his derogatory remarks, she felt that her superhuman effort had shot holes in his chauvinistic view of the younger assistant's abilities, and she wanted to hear him say so.

"Listen, Miss Coulter, I'm paying you a respectable wage. I don't consider it my duty to pat you on the back when you merely do what you're paid to do. I have neither the time nor the patience to pander to your fragile ego."

Stephanie felt her face explode with color.

"If you require me to sing your praises every time you complete a task, you can leave right now. Is that understood?"

"Clearly," she managed, furious. This was a rare state for her; she thought of herself as even-tempered and easygoing. Never had she disliked any man more. He was terrible. An ogre. She pivoted sharply and marched into the reception area, so angry that she had to inhale deeply to control her irritation.

Rolling out her chair, she sat down and took a moment to regain her composure.

She hadn't been back at her desk more than fifteen minutes when the intercom beeped. For one irrational instant she toyed with the idea of ignoring him, then decided against it.

"Yes, Mr. Lockwood?" she said in her most businesslike tone.

"Take lunch, Miss Coulter. But be back here within the hour. I don't tolerate tardiness."

Stephanie sincerely doubted that this man tolerated much of anything. Everything was done at his convenience and at someone else's expense.

Grabbing her purse, she took the elevator down to the floor where Human Resources was located. Jan was at her desk, and she raised questioning eyes when Stephanie walked in the door.

"Hi, how's it going?"

Slowly shaking her head, Stephanie said, "Fine, I think." The lie was only a small one. "Is he always like this?"

"Always." Jan chuckled. "But he doesn't push anyone half as hard as he drives himself."

Stephanie wasn't entirely sure she believed that. "He gave me an hour for lunch, but I think I'm supposed to show my gratitude by returning early."

"I'll join you." Jan called a coworker to say she was taking her lunch hour, then withdrew her purse from the bottom drawer and stood.

Although Stephanie hated to admit it, she was full of questions about her surly employer, and she hoped that Jan would supply the answers. For two years she'd only seen him from a distance, and she had been fascinated. From everything she knew about Jonas Lockwood, which wasn't much, she wouldn't have expected him to be so surly. Those close to him were intensely loyal, yet she had found him rude and unreasonable.

By the time they arrived, the cafeteria was nearly

deserted. Stephanie doubted that many employees took lunch this late.

They decided to share a turkey sandwich, and each ordered a bowl of vegetable-beef soup. Jan carried the orange plastic tray to a table.

Stephanie tried to come up with a way of casually introducing the subject of Jonas into their conversation without being obvious. She couldn't imagine any executive assistant, even Martha Westheimer, lasting more than a week. Finally she just jumped right in. "Why does Mr. Lockwood find young assistants so objectionable?"

"I haven't the slightest idea."

"You know—" Stephanie paused and took a bite of the sandwich "—he'd be handsome if he didn't scowl so much of the time."

Jan answered with a faint nod. "I think he must be an unhappy man."

That much was obvious, Stephanie thought. "Why does he walk with a limp?" The problem with his leg couldn't be age-related, since she guessed that he was probably only in his mid-thirties, possibly close to forty. Figuring out his age was difficult, since he'd worn a perpetual frown all morning.

"He had an accident several years ago. Skiing, I think. I heard the story, but I can't remember the details. Not that he'd ever let anyone know, but I'm sure his leg must ache sometimes. I can tell because he usually goes on a rampage when it hurts. At least that's my theory."

From the short time she'd spent with him, Stephanie guessed that his leg must be causing him excruciating pain today. She'd noted the way he'd leaned heavily on the cane while in the elevator. Maybe there was a chance that his temperament would improve if the pain eased. But at this point she doubted it would make any difference to her feelings toward the man.

Part of the problem, she realized, was that she was keenly disappointed in him. For two years she'd been studying him from a distance. Perhaps she'd even romanticized him the way that Jan and others romanticized men in the books they read. Whatever it was that had fascinated her from afar had been shattered by the reality of what a hot-tempered, unappreciative slave driver he was.

Jan finished off her soup. "Will you stop by after work?"

"So you can hear the latest horror stories?"

"He's not so bad," Jan claimed. "Really."

"He's the most arrogant, insufferable man I've ever had the displeasure of knowing."

"Give him a day or two to mellow out."

"Never."

Finished with lunch, Stephanie deposited their tray and refilled her coffee cup to take with her to the top floor. When she arrived, the door between the two offices was closed, and she hadn't the faintest idea if Jonas Lockwood was inside or not. Setting the coffee on the desk, she read over a stack of financial reports and cost sheets he'd left on her desk, apparently wanting her to update them. Taking a sip of coffee, she turned one sheet over, her eagle eyes running down the columns of figures.

"Welcome back, Miss Coulter." The gruff male voice came from behind her. "I see that you're punctual. I approve."

She bristled. Everyone who worked with the man

seemed to think he was wonderful, but that certainly wasn't the impression she had. He made her furious, and she struggled to disguise it.

"I would suggest, however, that you stop wasting time and get busy."

"Yes, sir." She tossed him an acid grin. For just an instant she thought she caught a flicker of amusement in his electric-blue eyes. But she sincerely doubted that someone as cold as Jonas Lockwood knew how to smile.

As the afternoon progressed, the one word that kept running through Stephanie's mind was *demanding*. Jonas Lockwood didn't ask, he demanded. And when he wanted something, he wanted it that instant, not so much as one minute later. He tolerated no excuses and made no allowances for ignorance. If he needed a dossier, she was expected to know what drawer it was filed in and how to get to it in the most expedient manner. And she was to deliver it to him the instant he asked. If she was a moment late, he didn't hesitate to let her know about his disapproval.

The phone seemed to ring constantly, and when she wasn't answering it, she was tending to his long list of demands.

Just when she got back to updating the financial report, the buzzer rang.

"Yes." If she didn't get this finished before the end of the day, he would certainly comment. He didn't want a mere executive assistant, he required Wonder Woman. Her low estimation of Martha Westheimer rose quite a lot.

"Bring me everything you can find on the Johnson deal."

"Right away." She moved to the cabinet and groaned

as her gaze located three files, all labeled Johnson. Not taking a chance, she pulled all three and set them on his desk. She noted that he was rubbing his thigh, his hand moving up and down his leg in a stroking motion. His brow was marred by thick lines. He seemed to be in such pain that she paused, not knowing what to say or do.

He glanced up, and the steely look in his eyes grew sharper. "Haven't I given you enough to do, Miss Coulter? Or would you like a few more tasks that need to be completed before you leave tonight?"

Rather than state the obvious, she returned to her desk. Sitting at the computer, she couldn't get Jonas out of her mind. There was so much virility in his rugged, dark features, yet for all the emotion he revealed, he could have been cast in bronze. No matter what, he wasn't a man she would be able to forget.

Five o'clock rolled around, and she still had two short reports to finish. It didn't matter how much time it required, she was determined to stay until every last item he'd given her was completed.

"Hi," Jan said, stepping off the elevator at five-thirty and greeting her. "I've been waiting for you."

"Sorry." Stephanie rested her hands in her lap. "I've only got a bit more to do."

"Leave it. I'm sure Old Stone Face doesn't expect her desk to be cleared when she comes in tomorrow morning."

"It isn't what she expects, it's what Mr. Lockwood demands. I've never met anyone like him." She lowered her voice. "Everything has to be done at his convenience."

"It *is* his company."

Stephanie shook her head. "Well, listen, I'll trade you bosses any day of the week."

"Is that a fact, Miss Coulter?"

Stephanie managed to swallow a strangled breath. She turned and glared at Jonas, despising him for eavesdropping on a private conversation.

"That will be all, Miss Coulter. You may leave."

She opened her mouth to argue with him but decided she would be a fool to give up the opportunity to escape when it was presented to her. "Thank you. And may I say it was a memorable experience working for you, Mr. Lockwood."

He'd already turned and didn't even acknowledge her statement.

"However—" she raised her voice, determined that he hear her "—I'd prefer working for a more mature male." She wondered if he even remembered his earlier derogatory comments about executive assistants. "A man over forty is far less demanding, and a thousand times more reasonable and patient."

"Stephanie…" Jan hissed in warning.

"Good day, Miss Coulter." He'd turned to look at her, and if possible, the icy front he wore like an impenetrable mask froze all the more.

"Goodbye, Mr. Lockwood." With that, she retrieved her purse and marched out of the office, Jan following in her wake.

"Wow, what happened this afternoon?" Jan asked the minute the elevator doors closed, her eyes sparkling with curiosity.

"Nothing."

"I can tell."

"He wasn't any less objectionable after lunch than

he was before. Mr. Jonas Lockwood is simply impossible to work with."

"Obviously you two didn't start off on the right foot."

"I'm a fairly patient person. I tried to work with the man. But as far as I'm concerned, there's no excuse for someone to be so rude and arrogant. He has no right to take out his bad mood on me or anyone else. There's simply no call for such behavior."

"Right." But one side of Jan's mouth twitched as though she were holding in a laugh.

"You find that amusing?"

"No, not really. I was just thinking that you could be just the woman."

"Just the woman for what?"

"For ages the female employees of Lockwood Industries have been waiting for a woman exactly like you, and for the last two years you were right here under our noses."

"What are you talking about?"

"Jonas Lockwood needs a woman with nerves of steel who can stand up to him."

"Martha must be able—"

"Not in the office."

"Then what are you talking about?"

"Someone to bring him down amongst us mortals. A few of us feel what he really needs is to fall in love."

Stephanie couldn't help herself. She snickered. "Impossible. Rocks are incapable of feeling, and that man is about as emotional as marble."

"I'm not so sure," Jan commented. "He works so hard because this business is his life. There's nothing else to fill the emptiness."

"You don't honestly believe a mere woman is capable of changing that?"

"Not just any woman, but someone special."

"Well, leave me out of it."

"You're sure?"

"Absolutely, positively, sure." Although the thought of seeing Jonas Lockwood humbled was an appealing one, Stephanie was convinced it would never happen. He was too hard. A man like that was incapable of any emotion.

"Oh, I forgot to tell you."

"Tell me what?" From the look on Jan's face, Stephanie could tell she wasn't going to like her friend's next words—and that Jan hadn't forgotten at all.

"Martha Westheimer telephoned this afternoon...."

"And?" Already Stephanie could feel the muscles between her shoulder blades tightening in anticipation.

"And she's apparently recovering."

"Good."

"But, unfortunately, not enough to return to work. It looks like you'll be working with Mr. Lockwood another day."

"Oh, no, you don't," Stephanie objected. "I'll quit before I'll work with that man for another minute."

Jan didn't speak for a moment. "In other words, you're willing to let him assume everything he said about younger assistants is true?"

Two

"Good morning, Mr. Lockwood." Stephanie looked up from her desk and smiled beguilingly. After a sleepless night, she'd decided to change her tactics. Her mother had always claimed that it was much easier to attract flies with honey than with vinegar. In working with Jonas Lockwood that first day, she'd been guilty of giving him a vinegar overdose. Today, she'd decided, she would fairly ooze with charm and drive the poor man crazy. With that thought in mind, she'd been humming happily as she'd dressed for work.

"Morning." He showed no reaction at all to her good-natured greeting.

"There's coffee, if you'd like a cup." She'd arrived an hour early to organize her desk and her day, and making coffee had been part of that.

"Please." He carried his briefcase into his office.

She realized that his limp was barely noticeable this morning. Jan's theory about his leg tying in with his disposition could well be proven within the next ten hours.

He was already seated at his desk, going through his mail, by the time she brought in his coffee. He didn't look up. "I would have thought you'd consider making coffee too menial a task for a woman in your position."

"Of course not. A good executive assistant is responsible—"

"I get the picture, Miss Coulter." He cut her off and continued to scan the mail, his concentration centering on the neat stack of letters she'd previously sorted. "I'll need you to accompany me to a luncheon meeting and take notes."

"Of course," she replied sweetly. "Are there any files I should read beforehand to acquaint myself with the subject?"

"Yes." He listed several names and businesses, but for all the notice he gave her, she could have been a marble statue decorating his office. "One last thing." For the first time he raised his eyes to hers. "Contact personnel and find out how much longer Ms. Westheimer will be out." His tone told her that day couldn't come soon enough to suit him.

It was on the tip of Stephanie's tongue to tell him that his precious "mature" executive assistant couldn't be back soon enough to suit her. "Right away." Her tone dripped honey.

The piercing blue eyes narrowed fractionally. "I think I liked you better when you weren't so subservient. However, I'm pleased that you finally realize the nature of the position."

She was so furious that she wanted to explode. Instead, she smiled until the muscles at the sides of her mouth ached with the effort. "It's my pleasure."

His eyes sharpened all the more if that was possible. "Good to know, Ms. Coulter."

It took every ounce of self-control Stephanie possessed to disguise her irritation. She'd never before had to deal with such a difficult man. But with everything that was in her, she was determined not to give in to his dislike of her.

They worked together most of the morning, dealing with the mail first. If Jonas spoke to her, it was in the form of clipped requests. They had a job to do, and there was no room for anything else. Not a smile. Not a joke. No unnecessary communication. He seemed to look at her as a necessary piece of equipment, like the computer. She was there to see to the smooth running of his business—nothing else. She hated to sound egotistical, but that puzzled her. She knew she was reasonably good-looking, and yet Jonas treated her with as much emotion as he would his briefcase. She was both amused and insulted.

In every other office where she'd been employed, she'd seen herself as part of a team. With Jonas, she was keenly aware that she was only a small spoke in a large wheel, and Jonas Lockwood was the wagon.

Once back at her desk, she took a minute to contact Jan before tackling the long list of requests Jonas had given her.

"Jan? Stephanie here. I won't be able to meet you for lunch."

"Do you want me to bring you back something?"

"No, I'm attending a meeting with Mr. Lockwood."

"Hey, that's great. He's never taken Old Stone Face with him before. You must have impressed him."

"I sincerely doubt that. I don't think a rock could make an impression on him."

"Don't be so sure," Jan said, a smile evident in her

voice. "By the way, did you give any thought to what I said yesterday?"

Stephanie could only assume Jan was referring to the challenge of making Jonas Lockwood fall in love. The idea caused her to smother a small laugh. "Yes, I did. You're nuts if you even think I'd attempt anything so crazy."

"He doesn't need to be put in his place as much as to find it. And from what I saw yesterday, you're just the woman to help him with that."

"Maybe." However, Stephanie sincerely doubted that someone as unemotional as Jonas Lockwood was capable of falling in love. Part of her wanted to rebel at the way he treated her. Rarely had a man been so indifferent toward her. With her even features, smooth ivory skin and soft golden hair, she was aware that men found her attractive. Jonas's blatant indifference was a surprise. When he looked at her, all she felt was a chill that cut straight through her bones.

"Steph? Are you there?"

"Oh, sorry, I was just thinking."

"I hope that means what I think it does. Listen, I'd like to get together with you soon. There's something we—I—want to talk over with you."

"If it has to do with you-know-who, forget it!"

Chuckling, Jan said, "I'll see you later."

"Right."

Replacing the receiver, Stephanie wheeled her chair to face the computer. She worked with only a few interruptions for the next two hours. Forty minutes before the scheduled luncheon, she read through the files Jonas had recommended in order to familiarize herself with the people she would be meeting, and tucked her tablet computer in her purse so she would be ready to take notes.

She felt mentally prepared and alert when he appeared. She stood wordlessly and followed him into the elevator. Well aware that he was a man who didn't appreciate unnecessary conversation, she kept her comments and questions to herself. She would have her answers eventually.

A limo and driver waited outside the building, and the driver held open the door for them as they approached.

She climbed inside, her fingers absently investigating the smooth leather interior of the limo. Almost immediately, Jonas opened his briefcase and took out a file.

She eyed him curiously. She might have a low opinion of him as a human being, but his knowledge and business acumen were beyond question. He was a man born to lead. In working with him these two days, she had witnessed his swift, decisive nature. When he saw something, he went after it by the most direct route. Life had no gray areas for a man of his nature—everything was either black or white, with no middle ground.

She found her gaze wandering to his hands. They were large, with blunt nails, and short wisps of dark hair curled out from the French cuffs of his shirt. He could be gentle—his hands told her as much. The thought of his large hands stroking her smooth skin did funny things to her breathing. The ridiculousness of the notion made her shake her head. A funny sound slid from the back of her throat, and he glanced up momentarily.

Quickly, she turned to look out the side window, wondering what was happening to her. She didn't even like this man.

As the limo pulled up to a huge skyscraper, Jonas announced, "As I said earlier, I want you to take notes during the meeting. When we return, format them for me and give me your impressions of what happened."

Stephanie opened and closed her mouth in surprise. She was his assistant, not his analyst. But she knew better than to question the mighty Jonas Lockwood. She would do as he asked and accompany it with a smile. She would give him no reason to find fault with her.

They rode the elevator to the twenty-first floor of the Bellerman Building. The heavy doors slid open, and Jonas directed her into the meeting room at the end of the long hallway. Ten chrome chairs upholstered in moss green were strategically placed around a long rosewood table. He claimed the seat at the end and motioned for her to take the chair at his side. She was faintly surprised that he wanted her so close at hand. Since she was an assistant and only there to take notes, she had expected to sit in a corner and observe the proceedings, not find herself right in the middle of them.

Lunch was served, and what followed was a lesson in business unlike anything she had learned in her four years as an executive assistant. There was a layered feel to the meeting. She took meticulous notes of everything that was said, but several times she wondered at the underlying meaning of the words. She was impressed by the role Jonas played. He appeared to be in complete charge of the subjects that were discussed, though he rarely spoke himself, determining the course of the meeting with a nod of his head or a small movement of his hand. At first glance, anyone looking in would assume that he was bored by the entire proceedings. The man was unnerving.

At precisely two, it was over. She looked up from her tablet and flexed her tired shoulder muscles. As the other men stood, the sounds of briefcases opening and closing filled the spacious room.

"Good to see you again, Lockwood." As the man sitting on Jonas's right spoke, his gaze slid over Stephanie with a familiarity that left a bad taste in her mouth. "Leave it to you to have the most beautiful woman in Minneapolis as your executive assistant."

Jonas's cutting blue gaze shifted to rest momentarily on her. "She's only a substitute. My regular assistant is ill this week." He didn't give her a moment more of his attention as he stood and reached for his cane, leaving her to follow him.

Fuming that he had treated her so dismissively, she reached for her purse. He hadn't noticed anything about her but her secretarial skills. She was a woman, and if Jonas Lockwood didn't recognize that, it was his problem, not hers. Even so, she was offended by his comment, and she stewed about it all the way back to Lockwood Industries.

The phone rang ten minutes after she was seated back at her desk. "Mr. Lockwood's office."

"Steph, it's Jan. I talked with Martha Westheimer this afternoon, and I have good news."

"I could do with some," Stephanie grumbled.

"She'll be back Monday morning."

"And not a minute too soon."

"How'd the luncheon meeting go?"

"I...I don't know." She hadn't yet sorted through her notes deeply enough to analyze what had transpired. "It was interesting."

"See, he's already having an effect on you."

"He?" she said, teasing Jan. "I can't possibly believe you mean who I think you do."

Jan's answer was a smothered giggle. "Don't forget to meet me at five-thirty. On second thought, I'll come up for you."

"Fine. And thanks for the very *good* news. I could do with a lot more."

The remainder of the afternoon was surprisingly peaceful. Stephanie fleshed out her notes and added her observations, then printed everything out and placed it on Jonas's desk.

He was writing something, but he paused and glanced up when she didn't immediately turn and walk away. "Yes?"

"I just wanted to tell you that Ms. Westheimer will be back on Monday morning. It's been an education working with you for the past couple of days."

He leaned back in his chair and looked at her steadily. "Not a pleasure? You filled in nicely. Quite a surprise, Miss Coulter."

She supposed that this was as much of a compliment as she could expect from such a man. "Now that's something I'm pleased to hear," she said, smiling despite the effort not to.

"I'm convinced you'll do well at Lockwood Industries."

"Thank you." She felt obligated to add, "And if ever you need a replacement for Ms. Westheimer…"

"I'm hoping that won't happen again any time soon."

Not as much as I am, Stephanie mused. "Good day, Mr. Lockwood."

He'd already returned to his work. "Good evening, Miss Coulter."

Her heart was pounding by the time she met Jan. For an instant there, she could almost have liked Jonas Lockwood. Almost, but not quite.

"I take it the afternoon ran smoothly."

"Relatively so," Stephanie confirmed.

"Are you ready to talk?"

"It depends on the subject. Jonas Lockwood is off-limits."

"Unfair," Jan objected. "You know I want to discuss our infamous boss. Come on, I'll buy you a drink and loosen your tongue."

"That's what I'm worried about."

"Stop complaining. Don't check the olive in a gift drink."

"What?" Stephanie asked, laughing.

"Oh nothing, I was just trying to make a joke. You know the old saying about checking the teeth in a gift horse? It's Friday, and it's been a long week." Folding her jacket over her arm, Jan led the way down the elevator and through the wide glass doors of the Lockwood Industries building. The Sherman Street traffic was snarled in the evening rush hour, and Jan wove her way to a small lounge a couple of blocks from the building.

Three women waved when they entered. Stephanie recognized one, but the other two were strangers.

"Hi, everyone. This is Stephanie."

"Hi." Stephanie raised her hand in greeting.

"Meet Barbara and Toni," Jan continued. "You know Maureen." She sat down and looked at the others. "Well, what do you think, ladies?"

"She's great."

"Perfect."

"Exactly what we want."

Taking a chair, Stephanie glanced around the small group, shaking her head in confusion. "What are you guys talking about?"

"You!" All four spoke at once.

"Does this have something to do with Jonas Lockwood?" Already she didn't like the sound of this.

"You didn't tell her?" Toni, a brunette, asked Jan.

"I think we'd better order her a drink first."

Still shaking her head, Stephanie glanced from one expectant face to the other. Barbara had to be over forty, Toni in her mid-thirties, Maureen younger, and Jan, Stephanie guessed, was near her own age of twenty-four.

The waitress returned with five glasses of sparkling wine.

"Now, what's this all about?" Stephanie asked, growing more curious by the minute.

"I think we should start at the beginning," Jan suggested.

"Please," Stephanie murmured.

"You see, we all read romances. We're hooked on them. They're wonderful."

"Right. And Jonas Lockwood makes *the* perfect hero, don't you think?" Barbara added.

"Pardon?" To Stephanie's way of thinking, he made *the* perfect block of ice.

"Haven't you noticed his chiseled leanness?"

"And those craggy male features?"

"I suppose," Stephanie muttered, growing more confused by the minute. To ease some of the dryness in her throat, she took a long swallow of her wine. It was surprisingly refreshing.

"He's got that cute little cleft in his chin."

Now that was something Stephanie hadn't noticed.

"The four of us have decided that Mr. Lockwood is really an unhappy man," Maureen, who was a redhead, continued. "His life is empty."

"He needs a woman to love, and who will love him," Barbara said.

"That's an interesting theory," Stephanie said, reaching for the wine for a second time. She had to watch how much she consumed, or the four of them would soon be making sense.

"It's obvious that none of us can be his true love," Toni added.

"What about you, Jan?" Stephanie pointed her drink in her friend's direction.

"Sorry, but you know I'm in a serious relationship. I'm expecting Jim to propose within the next year."

"Only Jim doesn't know it yet," Maureen piped in. Everyone laughed.

"But what has all this got to do with me?" Stephanie had to ask the question, even though she was sure she already knew the answer.

"You're perfect for him—just the type of woman he needs."

"The quintessential heroine. Attractive and bright."

"Spunky," Jan tossed in.

"I can't believe what I'm hearing," Stephanie protested. "I don't even like the man."

"That's even better. The heroines in the novels seldom do, either. Not at first, anyway."

"I think you ladies are confusing fantasy with reality."

"Of course we are. That's the fun of it. We're all incurable romantics, and when we see a romance in the making it's simply part of our nature to want to step in and help things along."

"We've even thought about writing one," Toni informed her.

"But why me?"

"You're perfect for Mr. Lockwood, in addition to being exceptionally attractive."

"Thanks, but…"

"And you don't seem to lord it over those of us who aren't," Barbara murmured.

"But that doesn't explain why you chose me to weave your plot around."

"Mr. Lockwood likes you."

"Oh, I hardly think—"

"All right, he respects you. We all noticed that this afternoon when you left for the meeting. He wouldn't take you along if he didn't value your opinion."

Stephanie shook her head wildly. "Do you know what he said? A man commented on what an attractive executive assistant he had, and your hero Lockwood told him I was only a substitute, as though he'd had to scrape the bottom of the barrel to come up with me." Finding the situation unbelievably hysterical in retrospect, she giggled. It took her a moment to notice that the other four were strangely quiet.

"What do you think, Maureen?" Jan asked.

"I'd stay he's definitely noticed her. He's fighting it already."

"Oh, come on. You've blown this all out of proportion."

"I don't think so." Jan reached for her purse, and withdrew a copy of Stephanie's employment application. "I did a bit of checking. You had two employers in the two years before you came to us. Right?"

"Right." Stephanie's hand tightened around her wineglass as she shifted uncomfortably.

"Why?"

"Well." She paused to clear her throat. "I've had some problems with the men I've worked with."

"What kind of problems?"

"You know." Embarrassed, she waved her hand dismissively.

"Men making advances?" Toni suggested.

"They all seemed to think I must be interested in off-duty activities, if you catch my drift."

"We do," Jan said. "Stephanie, there are laws against such behavior."

"I know, and I probably could have filed a lawsuit but it was easier to look for another job and avoid the hassle." She felt bad about that, but at the time it had seemed the more practical solution.

"It's always hard to know how to handle something like that," Jan said giving her shoulder a squeeze.

"I did make sure my replacement understood the reason I was leaving."

"Good move," Maureen said.

"Yes, she's heroine material, all right," Toni added with a nod.

Unable to hold back a laugh, Stephanie said, "You ladies don't honestly believe all this, do you?"

"You bet we do," all four concurred.

"But why does it matter to you if Jonas Lockwood is married or not? Maybe he's utterly content being single. Marriage isn't for everyone."

Jan answered first. "As I explained, we're all incurable romantics. We've worked for Mr. Lockwood a lot longer than you. He needs a wife, only he doesn't realize it. But we're doing this for selfish reasons, too. It would help the situation at work for everyone if Mr. Lockwood had a family of his own."

"Family?" Stephanie nearly choked on her wine. "First you have me falling in love with him, then we get married, and now I'm bearing his children." This conversation was going from the ridiculous to the even more ridiculous. To be honest, she was half tempted to practice her feminine wiles on Jonas Lockwood just for the pleasure of seeing if he would crumble at her feet. Then she would have the ultimate pleasure of snubbing him and walking away. But this clearly wasn't what Jan and friends had in mind.

"You see," Barbara inserted, "we feel that Mr. Lockwood would be more agreeable to certain employee benefits if he walked in our shoes for a while."

Dumbfounded, Stephanie shook her head. These women were actually serious. "I think a union would be the more appropriate way to deal with this."

"There isn't one. So we're creating our own—of sorts."

Stephanie still didn't understand. "What kind of benefits?"

"More lenient rules regarding maternity leave."

"Extra days off at Christmas."

"Increased health benefits to include family members."

Lifting the blond curls off her forehead, Stephanie looked around the table at the four intense faces studying her. "You're really serious, aren't you?"

"Completely."

"Utterly."

"We mean business."

"Indeed we do." Jan raised her hand and called for the waitress, ordering another round.

"I'm really sorry, but despite what you might think I'm not heroine material." The waitress delivered another round of sparkling wine, and Stephanie waited until the woman had left before going on. "A man like Mr. Lockwood needs a woman who's far less opinionated than I am. In two days, we barely said a civil word to each other."

"The woman who loves him will need a strong personality."

"She'll need more than that." Stephanie couldn't imagine any woman capable of tearing down Jonas's icy facade. He was too hard, too cold, too unapproachable.

"Say, I didn't know you spoke French." Jan glanced up from Stephanie's application, her eyes growing larger by the minute.

"My grandmother was French. She insisted I learn."

"Then you're bilingual?"

"Right."

All four women paused, regarding Stephanie as though she had suddenly turned into an alien from outer space. "Hey, why are you all looking at me like that?"

"No reason." Barbara lowered her head, apparently finding her drink overwhelmingly interesting.

"So your grandmother was French?" Toni asked.

"Yes, I just said so. And why do I have the feeling that you four have something dangerous up your sleeves?" She glanced from one grinning face to the other. "What does the fact that I speak French have to do with anything?"

"You'll see."

"I don't like the sound of this," Stephanie muttered.

"Be honest. What do you think of our idea?" Barbara asked bravely.

"You mean about finding a woman for Mr. Lockwood?"

The others nodded, watching her expectantly.

"Great. As long as that woman isn't me."

"I think it's fate," Jan said, ignoring Stephanie's words. "This couldn't be turning out any better than if we'd planned it."

"Planned what?"

"You'll see," all four echoed.

Monday morning Stephanie arrived for work early. She'd spent a peaceful weekend planting a small herb garden in narrow redwood planters and placing them on her patio. Living in a small apartment didn't leave much room for her to practice her gardening skills. The year before she'd rented a garden space through the parks department. This year she'd decided to try her green thumb on herbs.

Jan was at her desk when Stephanie arrived at coffee-break time. As much as possible, she had tried to blot out Friday evening's conversation with Jan and her friends. It appeared that the four had some hideous plot in mind. But she'd quickly squelched that. Even imagining Jonas Lockwood in love was enough to amuse her. It would never happen. The man had no emotions. That wasn't blood that ran through his veins—it was ink from profit-and-loss statements. He wasn't like ordinary humans.

"Oh, I'm glad you're here," Jan said.

"You are?" Already Stephanie was leery. "Ms. Westheimer's fully recovered, isn't she?"

"Yes, she's here. At least, I assume she is. I haven't heard any rumblings from above."

Stephanie felt a sense of relief. The less she saw of Mr. Jonas Lockwood, the better.

"I've made arrangements with your boss for you to be gone next week."

"Arrangements?" Stephanie repeated surprised. "What are you talking about?"

"Do you want to get together at lunch?" Jan asked, ignoring Stephanie's question.

"Jan, what's going on?"

"You'll see."

"Jan!"

"I'll talk to you later." She glanced at her watch. "I'd tell you, honest, but I can't...yet."

Disgruntled, Stephanie returned to her office, pausing on the way to question Maureen, who gave her a look of pure innocence. Stephanie didn't know what her friends had up their sleeves, but she was certain it involved Jonas Lockwood.

The remainder of the morning ran so smoothly that Stephanie was surprised to note that it was lunchtime. Truthfully, working for anyone other than Jonas Lockwood was a breeze. Mr. Potter, her grandfatherly boss, was patient and undemanding, a pleasant change from the man who'd barked orders at her as though she were a robot. And Mr. Potter was free with his praise and approval of her efforts. Getting a compliment from Jonas Lockwood was like pulling teeth.

She had lunch with Jan, Maureen and the two others she'd met Friday evening, so there wasn't an opportunity to corner Jan and ask her to explain her comment about arranging for her to be out of the office the following week.

The group was fun-loving, quick-witted and personable. Stephanie was grateful when no mention of their infamous employer entered the conversation. In fact, she was more than grateful. Despite all her intentions to the contrary, she had been thinking a lot about Jonas.

Later that afternoon, on her way back up to her office after delivering a file to accounting, she unexpectedly ran into the big boss himself. She was waiting for the elevator, checking her makeup with a small hand mirror, when the doors opened and she found herself eye to eye with him.

"Good day, Miss Coulter."

Caught entirely by surprise, she didn't even lower the tube of lipstick, her mouth open as she prepared to glide the color across her bottom lip. She was too stunned to move.

"Are you or are you not taking the elevator?"

"Oh, yes," she mumbled, hurrying in next to him. She quickly stuck her mirror and lipstick inside her purse, pressing her lips together to even out the pale summer-rose color.

He placed both hands on his cane. "And how are you doing, Miss Coulter?"

"Exceptionally well. Everyone I've worked with *lately* has appreciated my efforts."

"Perhaps your skills have improved."

She felt like kicking the cane out of his hands. The man was unbearable. "As you suggest," she said with a false sweetness in her voice, "things have definitely improved."

His mouth quirked upward in something resembling a smile. "I admit to missing your quick wit. Perhaps we'll have the opportunity to exchange insults again sometime soon."

A joke from Jonas Lockwood—all right, an almost joke. She couldn't believe it.

"Don't count on it." The elevator came to a halt at her floor, and the door swooshed open. As she stepped out she said, "Perhaps in another lifetime, Mr. Lockwood."

"You disappoint me, Miss Coulter. I was looking forward to next week." The doors glided shut.

Next week.

She'd let Jan get away without explaining earlier, but she wasn't waiting another minute. She hurried to Jan's office.

"All right, explain yourself," she demanded, placing both hands on the edge of her friend's desk.

"About what?" Jan was the picture of innocence, which was a sure sign she was up to something.

"I just saw Mr. Lockwood, and he said something about next week. I don't like the sound of this."

"Oh, I guess I forgot to tell you, didn't I?"

"Tell me now!" Stephanie straightened, a strange sensation, akin to dread, shooting up and down her spine.

"Mr. Lockwood's traveling to Paris on business."

Crossing her arms, Stephanie glared at Jan suspiciously. "That's nice."

"The interesting part is that he would like a bilingual assistant to accompany him."

Knowing what was coming, Stephanie tightened her jaw until her teeth ached. "You can't possibly mean..."

"When Mr. Lockwood first approached Human Re-

sources about it, we couldn't think of anyone appropriate, but since that time I've gone through our personnel
records, and when I found your application..."

"Jan, I refuse to go. The man and I don't get along."

"When I mentioned you to Mr. Lockwood, he was
delighted."

"I'll just bet."

"Your flight leaves Sunday night."

Three

The jet tilted its wings to the right, slowly beginning its descent. Stephanie stared out the small window, fascinated by the breathtaking view of the River Seine far below. Her heart pounded with excitement. Paris. How her grandmother would have envied her. As a young French war bride, Stephanie's grandmother had often longed to revisit the charming French city. Now Stephanie would see it for her.

"If you would tear your gaze from the window for a minute, Miss Coulter, we could get some work done," Jonas Lockwood stated sarcastically.

"Of course." Instantly she was all business, reaching for a pad. This was obviously the only level on which she could communicate with him. Not once since they'd taken off from Minneapolis-St. Paul International Airport had her employer glanced at the spectacular scenery. No doubt he would have considered it a waste of valuable time.

"I've reserved us a three-bedroom suite at the Château Frontenac," he informed her coolly.

She silently repeated the name of the hotel. "It sounds lovely."

He glanced down at the report in his lap and shrugged one muscular shoulder. "I suppose."

It was all Stephanie could do not to shout at him to open his eyes and look at the beauty of the world that surrounded him. At times like these she wanted to shake him. The mere thought of anyone—much less her—even touching him produced an involuntary smile. He would hate being touched.

She looked across the aisle at Adam Holmes, who had accompanied them. His role in Jonas's plans had been left to conjecture, but she suspected that he was an attorney.

"It's looks like we're in for pleasant weather," he said conversationally. His dark eyes narrowed fractionally as he gazed out at the ground below. For most of the trip he had carried the conversation. He was both friendly and articulate, a blatant contrast to the solemn, serious Jonas.

A little surprised, Stephanie glanced up, unsure whether Adam was addressing his comment to her. Jonas didn't respond. Of course, she would have been shocked to learn that any type of weather interested her employer.

"I would guess early summer is the perfect time to visit Paris." In reality, she wondered how much of the city she had any chance of seeing. Her one hope was that she would be able to visit the Champs de Mars and view the Eiffel Tower, built for the 1889 World's Fair. High on her list were the twelfth-century cathedral of Notre Dame, and the Arc de Triomphe. She'd spent a year in France as an exchange student in high school, but apart from a quick trip through the airport, she hadn't seen anything of Paris.

The plane began its final descent, and she clicked her seat belt into place. Casually Jonas put away his papers and closed his briefcase. As soon as they landed they would be going through customs and she would be expected to step into her role as translator. Although she spoke fluent French, it had been a while since she'd had the opportunity to use it, and she hoped she was up to the task.

To her surprise, everything went without a hitch at customs, and her confidence grew. They moved from the terminal to the waiting limo with only minimal delay.

The driver held the door open, and she climbed inside the luxurious automobile. Jonas and Adam followed her, and they were soon on their way.

At the hotel they were escorted to their rooms and their luggage was delivered promptly. While she unpacked her clothes, she heard Jonas and Adam discussing the project. Apparently they would be meeting a powerful financier in the hope of obtaining financial backing for a current project. Lockwood Industries, the largest North American manufacturer of airplane parts, was apparently ready to buy out their French counterpart. If the deal progressed as expected, Lockwood Industries would become the largest such manufacturer in the world. There also seemed to be the possibility of Lockwood establishing branches in several European cities.

"Miss Coulter."

"Yes." Responding instantly to the command in

Jonas's voice, Stephanie stepped into the doorway of her room.

"We have a lunch reservation downstairs in ten minutes."

"I'll be ready. I just need a few minutes to freshen up."

"Of course."

He was already turning away, and she doubted that he'd even heard her. He'd often given her that impression. Returning to her assigned room, she glanced in the mirror. Several tendrils of soft blond hair had escaped from the coil at the base of her neck. Rather than tuck them back, she pulled out the pins and reached for her brush. Unbound, her hair curled naturally to her shoulders. Normally when she was working she preferred to keep her hair away from her face. It gave her a businesslike look, and she felt that was particularly important around Jonas.

"Miss Coulter."

Jonas again.

Her brush forgotten in her hand, she moved into the large living room, where Jonas and Adam were waiting.

"Yes?"

For a moment the room went still as Jonas caught her gaze. Their eyes met and locked. His narrowed, and an expression of surprise and bewilderment flickered across his face. Something showed in his eyes that she couldn't define—certainly not admiration, perhaps astonishment, even shock. His mouth parted slightly, as if he wanted to speak, then instantly returned to a stern line.

Adam's face broke into a spontaneous smile as his lingering gaze swept her appreciatively from head to toe. "I don't think I realized earlier how attractive your assistant is, Jonas."

The muscles in Jonas's jaw looked as though they were frozen solid. He ran an impatient hand through his hair and turned to reach for his briefcase.

"You wanted me?" It was hard to believe that breathless voice was hers. She sounded as though she'd been running a marathon. She couldn't be attracted to Jonas. He was the last person in the world she wanted to have any romantic feelings for. Normally she was a level-headed person, not the sort who let her emotions carry her away. Not that Jonas Lockwood was worthy of a moment's consideration. He was arrogant and...

"We'll meet you downstairs." He interrupted her thoughts, his voice cool and unemotional.

"I'll be there in a minute."

"Take your time," he said dismissively, clearly doing his best to avoid her.

She turned to go back into her room, but not before she caught the look Adam directed at them both, disbelief etched clearly on his smooth, handsome features.

After closing the door, Stephanie sank onto the edge of her bed. There must be some virus in the air for her to be thinking this way about Jonas Lockwood. For a moment she'd actually found him overwhelmingly, unabashedly appealing. She'd been genuinely physically attracted to him. She shook her head at the wonder of it. She was playing right into Jan's and the other women's hands.

The amazing thing was that Jonas had noticed her, as well—really noticed her. At least when Adam had complimented her, Jason hadn't told him that she was "only a substitute." A small smile tugged at the corners of her mouth. Maybe, just maybe, Jonas Lockwood didn't have a heart of ice, after all. Perhaps under that glacial exterior there was a warm, loving man. The thought was so incongruous with the mental picture she held of him that she shook her head to dispel the image. Without wasting further time inventing nonsensical fantasies about her employer, she finished styling her hair and changed clothes, then went downstairs to the restaurant.

Lunch passed without incident, as did the first series of meetings.

In bed that evening, Stephanie's thoughts spun. They'd called it an early night, but she wasn't able to sleep. The most beautiful city in the world lay at her doorstep, and she would be tied up in meetings for the entire visit. Sitting up, she wiped a hand across her face. She was undecided. They would only be in Paris another two nights. If this was to be her only opportunity, she was going to take it.

Dressing silently, she slipped the hotel key into her purse and carefully tiptoed across the carpet, letting herself out.

Since their hotel was in an older section of the city, she caught a taxi and instructed the friendly driver to take her to several points of interest. He escorted her through Les Halles, the mammoth central food market, which had once been located on the north of the river, but had been moved to Rungis, in the suburbs of Paris.

From there he drove her past Notre Dame cathedral, pointing out landmarks as he went. But she barely heard him. Her thoughts were focused on that moment in the hotel room earlier in the afternoon when Jonas had looked at her for perhaps the first time. Her hands grew clammy just thinking about it. At the time she'd been flippant. Now she was profoundly affected. Just remembering it caused her pulse to react. In those brief seconds he had seen her as a woman, and, just as importantly, she'd viewed him as a man. She was intensely attracted to him and had been for weeks, she just hadn't been ready to admit it.

The driver, chatting easily in French, pointed out the sights, but instead of seeing the magnificent beauty in the buildings that surrounded her, Stephanie's thoughts revolved around Jonas. She wondered about what he'd been like as a child, and what pain had snuffed out the joy in his life.

Straightening, she shook her head and said to him in French, "Please take me back to the hotel."

The driver gave her a funny look. *"Oui."*

Stephanie had hoped to see the Louvre, but it wouldn't have been open at this time of night, anyway. As it was, she didn't seem to be able to view any of the sights without including Jonas in what she saw. It was useless to pretend otherwise.

Back at the hotel, she gave the driver a generous tip and thanked him. The lobby was quiet, and the soft strains of someone playing the piano sounded in the distance. She briefly toyed with the idea of stopping in the lounge for a nightcap but quickly rejected the idea. She needed to get some sleep.

Being extra-cautious not to make any unnecessary noise, she silently slipped into the suite. She was half-way across the living room when a harsh voice ripped into her.

"Miss Coulter, I didn't bring you to Paris so you could sneak out in the middle of the night."

She reacted with a startled gasp, her hand flying to her breast.

"Just who were you meeting? Some young lover?" The words were spoken with a cutting edge, mocking and bitter.

"No. Of course not." She could barely make out Jonas's form in the shadows. He sat facing her, but his features were hidden by the darkness.

"Surely you don't expect me to believe that. I understand you spent a year in France. Undoubtedly you met several young men."

The words to tell him what to do with his nasty suspicions burned on the tip of her tongue. Instead, she shook her head and replied softly, "I don't know anyone in Paris. I couldn't sleep. It may sound foolish, but I decided that I might not get the opportunity to see the sights, so I—"

"You don't honestly expect me to believe you were out sightseeing?" The shadow began to move, and as her eyes adjusted to the darkness she noted that he was massaging his thigh.

Against her will, her heart constricted at the pain she knew his leg must be causing him. With everything that was in her, she yearned to ease that pain. She took a tentative step in his direction, claiming the chair across from him. In low, soft tones, she told him about the historic buildings she'd visited and the chatty taxicab driver who had given her a private tour of the older sections of Paris, along with a colorful account of his own ancestry.

She watched as the cynical quirk of his mouth gradually relaxed. "It's really an exceptionally lovely city," she finished.

"Holmes is attracted to you."

"Adam?" Stephanie couldn't believe what she was hearing and quickly dismissed the suggestion. "I'm sure you're mistaken."

"Do you find it so surprising?"

"Yes…n-no."

"It's only natural that he thinks you're lovely. As you said, you're in one of the most beautiful cities in the world. It's springtime. You're single, Holmes is single. What's there to discourage a little romance?"

"I hardly know the man."

"Does it matter?"

"Of course it does." She sighed and dropped her gaze, sorry now that she'd made the effort to turn aside angry words and be friendly. The man was impossible.

"You could do worse. Adam Holmes is a bright attorney with a secure future."

"If I were buying stock in the man, I might be interested. But we're talking about *people* here. I find him friendly and knowledgeable, but I have no romantic interest in him. I'm simply not attracted to him."

"Who *does* attract you?"

Stephanie swallowed uncomfortably as she battled back the instinctive response. Jonas attracted her. She was still shocked by the realization, but she wasn't willing to hand him that weapon. "I don't believe my private life is any of your affair," she informed him crisply.

"So there *is* someone." Impatience surged through his clipped response.

"I didn't say that." Bounding to her feet, she stalked over to the window and hugged her waist. "There's no use even trying to talk to you, is there?" Her voice revealed her distress. "We seem incapable of maintaining even a polite conversation."

"Does that disappoint you?"

She could feel his gaze as it ran over her; it seemed to caress her with its intensity—and to demand an answer.

"Yes," she admitted gently. "Very much. I feel there's so much locked up inside you that I don't understand."

"I'm not a puzzle waiting to be solved."

"In some ways you are."

He rubbed a hand over his face. "I can't see that this conversation will get us anywhere."

She couldn't, either. She was tired, and he was unreasonable and in pain. The best thing she could do now would be to leave the conversation for a more appropriate time. "Good night, Mr. Lockwood." She didn't wait for his acknowledgement before she headed for her room.

"Good night, Stephanie."

It wasn't until she had changed into her cotton pajamas that she realized that for the first time since they'd met, he'd used her first name. No longer was she a robot who responded to his clipped demands. Somehow, in some way, she had become a woman of flesh and blood. The realization was enough to send her spirits soaring. Hugging the extra pillow beside her, she drifted into a sound sleep, content with her world.

"Good morning," Adam greeted her early the following morning. From the looks of the table, he and Jonas had already been working for hours.

"Morning." She walked across the room and poured steaming coffee into a dainty cup, then held it to her mouth with both hands.

"I trust you slept well, Miss Coulter," Jonas said.

So they were back to that. "Thank you, *Mr. Lockwood*, I slept very well."

He glanced up momentarily, and she recognized the glint of amusement in his eyes. A brief smile moved across his mouth.

"Would you like a croissant?" Adam asked, preparing to lift the flaky pastry onto a china plate with a pair of metal tongs.

"No, thanks." Actually, she might have liked one, but she was afraid that something as simple as accepting a breakfast pastry would encourage him. She hadn't noticed it the day before, but the eagerness glinting in his gaze revealed the truth of Jonas's statement. Adam Holmes really was interested in her.

As it turned out, it was just as well that she hadn't accepted the croissant, because she barely had time to down the coffee before Jonas stood. "We have a lot of ground to cover today."

He limped to the door without his cane. She knew that he preferred not to use it and did so only when absolutely necessary. His leg had kept him up last night and would soon be aching again without the cane.

"In that case," she said, "you'll want your cane."

Jonas expelled his breath. "Miss Coulter, I require an executive assistant and a translator, not a mother."

"Your leg was bothering you yesterday." She knew she was on dangerously thin ice. Not once had she ever mentioned his limp before. "I see no reason to aggravate it further."

He didn't answer her, but she noted triumphantly that he reached for his cane before they left the suite.

What followed was a day she was not likely to forget. The first meeting that morning was a marathon exchange of proposals and counterproposals. They adjourned briefly for lunch, then were at it again before she had the opportunity to take more than a bite or two of her salad.

The afternoon was just as jam-packed. No sooner had she finished translating one statement than Jonas gave her another. Much of the conversation went completely over her head, but in the weeks since meeting him, she had gained valuable insight into her employer. She could see that he was tense, although she was certain no one else noticed it. For the meeting, he almost seemed to wear a mask that revealed none of his feelings or emotions. This, like most of his life, was business, with no room for fun and games. If she had accepted what she saw on the surface, he would have frozen her out completely. But she'd seen a rare glimpse of the man inside, and she'd been intrigued.

Though the afternoon session was both complicated and challenging. She noticed that he was cool to the point of being aloof, as though what they were discussing was of little consequence to him. She suspected that, like a gambler, he placed his money on the line for the pleasure of tossing the dice. He enjoyed the thrill, the excitement, and had poured his whole life into pursuing it.

Throughout the afternoon Adam drifted in and out of the room, returning with one document and then another.

It was early evening when the meeting came to an end. Jonas and his French counterpart stood and shook hands.

"We're breaking until morning," Jonas informed

Adam outside the conference-room door. "Did you locate that report on the export tax I asked about earlier?"

"I have it with me," Adam responded, tapping the side of his briefcase.

"I'll want to look it over tonight."

For her part, Stephanie was exhausted and hungry. After no breakfast and virtually no lunch, her stomach was protesting strenuously.

Once they were back in the suite, she immediately slipped off her shoes. They were new, and pinched her heels. Sitting on the sofa, she crossed her legs and rubbed the tender portion of one foot, suspecting a blister.

On the other side of the room Jonas was drilling Adam about one thing or another. She couldn't have cared less. Then she noticed his gaze resting on her slender legs. When he realized she'd caught the direction of his glance, he turned his head. He looked tired, worn down. She wanted to suggest that he take this evening to rest, but after her comment that morning about his cane, she realized she would be pressing her luck. She was too weary to fight with him now.

"I'll get that statement for you as quickly as possible," Adam said, rising to his feet.

"Thanks."

The room seemed oddly quiet after Adam left.

"Miss Coulter, order a car."

She couldn't believe it. The man was a slave driver. Reaching for the phone, she contacted the front desk and asked that they have a car available. "How soon do you want it?" she asked, holding the receiver to her breast.

"Immediately."

She glared angrily at him. Not everyone was accustomed to his pace. She was tired, hungry and not in the most congenial mood.

"Will you be requiring my services?" She didn't bother to hide the resentment in her voice.

"Naturally, I'll need you to translate for me."

"Would you mind if I ate something first?" she asked as she reached for her shoes.

"Yes, I would."

Her gaze narrowed with frustration. "What is it with you? Maybe you can work all hours of the night and day, but others have limitations."

His mouth thinned, revealing his irritation; he picked up his cane. "Then stay here."

As much as she would have liked to do exactly that, she knew she couldn't. Reluctantly she followed him out of the suite. "Miss Coulter—" she mimicked his low voice sarcastically "—you've done a wonderful job today. Let me express my deepest appreciation. You deserve a break." She paused to eye him. The stone mask was locked tightly in place. "Why, thank you, Mr. Lockwood. Everyone needs a few words of encouragement now and then, and you seem to know just when I need them most. It's been a long grueling day, but those few words of appreciation seem to have made everything worthwhile."

"Are you through, Miss Coulter?" he asked sharply as they stepped into the elevator.

"Quite through." Her back was stiff and straight as they descended. She was tired, her feet ached, and she was hungry. For the last eleven hours she'd been at his beck and call. What more could he possibly expect from her now?

The driver was waiting outside the hotel when they

approached. He held open the door, and she climbed inside. Jonas paused to speak to the driver, but what he said and whether the driver understood him didn't concern her at the moment. If he needed her to translate, he would tell her. "Telling" was something Jonas had no problem doing.

They'd gone only a few blocks when the driver pulled to the curb and parked. They were in front of an elegant restaurant. Tiny tables were set outside the door, and white-coated waiters with red cloths draped over their forearms stood in attendance, watching for the smallest hint of a request. Stephanie blinked twice. Exhausted and dispirited, she didn't know if she could bear another meeting now. And at a restaurant! Her stomach would growl through the entire affair.

"Are you coming, Miss Coulter?" Jonas said, climbing out of the car. "I did hear you say you were hungry, right?"

Stunned, she didn't move. "We're having dinner here?"

"Yes. That is, unless you have any objections?" He suddenly looked bored with the entire process.

"No...I'm starved."

"I believe you've already stated as much. Luckily I have a reservation—unless you'd prefer eating in the car?"

"I'm coming." This was almost too good to be true. Eagerly she made her way onto the pavement. As they walked into the plush interior, her gaze fell longingly on an empty table outside on the sidewalk.

Jonas surprised her by asking, "Would you prefer to dine outside?"

"Yes, I'd like that."

Jonas spoke to the maître d', who led them to the table and politely held out Stephanie's chair for her, then handed each of them a menu. She was so hungry that she quickly scanned the contents. "Oh, I do love vichyssoise," she said aloud, biting her lower lip.

Before she knew what was happening Jonas had attracted the waiter's attention. "A bowl of vichyssoise for the lady."

"Jonas," she said, shocked. "Why did you do that?"

"From the way you were acting, I was afraid you were about to keel over from hunger."

"I am," she admitted, her gaze going up one side of the menu and down the other. "Everything looks wonderful."

"What would you like?"

"I can't decide between a huge spinach salad or a whole chicken."

The waiter returned, hands behind his back as he inquired courteously if they would like to place their orders. Jonas asked for the bouillabaisse, and raised questioning eyes to Stephanie.

"I'll have one of those," she said, pointing to the meal another waiter was delivering and indicating a huge salad that was piled high with fresh pink shrimp. "And one of those." Her gaze flew to the dessert cart, which was laden with a variety of scrumptious, calorie-laden goodies.

"Will that be all?" Jonas asked wryly.

"Oh, heavens, yes." She felt guilty enough already. "This is what you get for depriving me of nourishment," she joked. "I'm a grouch when I get too hungry."

"I hadn't noticed." One side of his mouth lifted in an aloofly mocking smile.

"I guess I owe you an apology for what I said earlier."

Her soup arrived, and she eagerly dipped her spoon into it and tasted, closing her eyes at the heavenly flavor. "Oh, this is absolutely wonderful. Thank you, Jonas."

His eyes smiled into hers. "You're quite welcome."

"I really am sorry."

"My dear Stephanie, I've stopped counting the times you've let your mouth outdistance your mind."

She was so shocked that she stopped with her spoon poised halfway between the bowl and her mouth. Jonas joking? Jonas calling her *dear?* It was almost more than her numbed mind could assimilate.

No sooner had she finished the soup than her salad was delivered. The top was thick with shrimp. "I think I've died and gone to heaven."

"Then you're relatively easy to please. It was my understanding that women were more interested in jewels and other luxury items."

She eagerly stabbed her fork into a shrimp. "Personally, I prefer shrimp and lobster." She smiled. "I haven't eaten this well in months."

Jonas arched his eyebrows expressively. "So a man could win you over with cheesecake."

"Tonight he could." Unable to wait any longer, she ate the fat shrimp and closed her eyes at the scrumptious flavor. When she opened them, she discovered that Jonas was watching her. Tiny laugh lines fanned out from his eyes.

He was so handsome that she couldn't take her eyes from him. "Are you wooing me?" It seemed overwhelmingly important that she know where she stood with him.

"I will admit that you're the cheapest date I've had in a long time."

"Is this a date?"

"Think of it more as a token of appreciation for a job well done."

She pressed her hand dramatically to her forehead, and her bright blue eyes grew round with feigned shock. "Do my ears deceive me? Jonas Lockwood of Lockwood Industries has deigned to pay an employee a compliment? An employee who's a relatively young woman, at that—admittedly one with minor faults."

"I won't disagree with you there."

Despite herself, Stephanie laughed. "No, I don't suppose you will."

"You did very well today."

"Thank you." She felt inexplicably pleased.

"Where did you learn to speak French?"

He seemed eager to keep the conversation going, and she was just as eager to comply. For the first time since meeting the man, she didn't feel on guard around him.

"My grandmother was a French war bride, and she taught my mother the language as a child. Later, Mom majored in French at the University of Washington. I've been bilingual almost from the day I was born."

"You're from Washington State?"

"Colville. Ever hear of it?"

"I can't say that I have."

"Don't worry, most people haven't."

"I imagine you were the town's beauty queen."

"Not me. In fact, I was a tall, skinny kid with buckteeth and knobby knees most of my life. It wasn't until I was in my late teens and the braces came off that the boys started to notice me."

"I have trouble believing that."

"It's true." She reached for her purse, and took out her cell phone. "I carry this picture because people don't believe me." She brought it up and was about to show him when they were interrupted by the waiter, who was bringing a bottle of wine.

Jonas looked up and spoke briefly with the other man.

Stephanie's blue eyes widened with astonishment and surprise. The waiter nodded and stepped away.

"You speak French."

"Only a little."

"But very well."

"Thank you." He dipped his head, accepting her compliment.

A clenching sensation attacked her stomach. "You didn't really need me here at all, did you?"

Four

"I brought you along as a translator," Jonas answered simply.

Stephanie lowered her fork to her plate. Her thoughts were churning like water left to boil too long, bubbling and spitting out scalding suggestions she would have preferred to keep in her subconscious. He'd tricked her into accompanying him on this trip. The meal that had tasted like ambrosia only seconds before felt like a concrete block in the pit of her stomach. "You speak fluent French."

"My French is adequate," he countered, reaching for his wineglass.

"It's as good as my own."

"My linguistic abilities are not your business."

"But I don't understand. Why…?" She couldn't understand the man. One minute he was personable and considerate, and the next he became brusque and arrogant. The transformation was made with such ease that she hardly knew how to respond to him.

"That I required a translator is all you need to know."

Rather than argue with him further, she stabbed another plump shrimp. She ate it slowly, but for all the en-joyment it gave her she might as well have been chewing on rubber. "Letting the French company we're negoti-ating with believe you don't speak the language is all part of your strategy, isn't it?"

"Wine?" He lifted the long-necked green bottle of pinot noir and motioned to her with it.

"Jonas? Am I right?" she asked as he filled her glass.

He cocked his head to one side and nodded. "I can see you're learning."

She ate another shrimp and discovered that some of the flavor had returned. "You devil!"

"Stephanie, business is business."

"And what is this?" The wine was excellent, and she took another sip, studying him as she tilted the narrow glass to her lips.

He stiffened. "What do you mean?"

"Our dinner. Is it business or pleasure?"

The crow's-feet at the corners of Jonas's eyes fanned out as if he were smiling, yet his mouth revealed not a trace of amusement. "A little of both, I suspect."

"Then I'm honored. I would have assumed that you'd prefer to escort a much more *mature* woman to dinner." She felt the laughter slide up her throat and suppressed it with some difficulty. "Someone far less emotional than a *younger* woman."

"I believe it was you who commented that age has little to do with maturity."

"Touché." She raised her glass in salute and sipped her wine to toast his comeback. She felt light-headed and mellow, but she wasn't sure what was to blame: Jonas, her fatigue or the excellent wine.

She couldn't believe this was happening. The two of

them together, enjoying each other's company, bantering like old friends, applauding each other's skill. As little as two hours ago, she would have thought it impossible to carry on a civil conversation with the man. She imagined that Jonas was about as relaxed as he ever allowed himself to be.

"I'll admit that the pleasure part comes from the fact that I knew you wouldn't be simpering at my feet," he commented, breaking into her thoughts.

"I never simper."

"You much prefer to challenge and bully."

"Bully? Me?" She laughed a little and shook her head. "I guess maybe I do at that, but just a bit." She didn't like admitting it, but he was right. She was the oldest of three girls, and did have a tendency to take matters into her own hands. "While we're on the subject of bullies, I don't suppose you've noticed the way *you* treat people?"

"We aren't discussing me," he said dryly.

"We most certainly are." She flattened her palms on either side of her plate and shook her head. "I've never known anyone who treats people the way you do. What I can't understand is how you command such loyalty."

He arched his eyebrows expressively, and his gaze swept her with mocking thoroughness.

She ignored him and continued. "It's more than just money. You pay well, but the benefits leave a lot to be desired." She felt obligated to mention that, since it had come up the other day and, she had to admit, the point was a good one.

"Is that a fact?"

"You're often unreasonable." She knew she was pressing her luck, but the wine had emboldened her.

"Perhaps others see it that way," he admitted reluctantly. "But only when the occasion calls for it."

For all the heed he paid her comments, they could have been discussing the traffic. "And I've yet to mention your outrageous temper."

"I wasn't aware that I had a temper."

Despite the fact he didn't seem to find their conversation the least bit amusing, Stephanie continued. "But by far, the very worst of your faults is your overactive imagination."

His gaze flew to hers and narrowed. "What makes you suggest something so absurd?"

She knew she'd trapped him, and she loved having the upper hand for the first time in their short acquaintance. "You actually believed I was meeting someone last night."

"With your own mouth you admitted as much."

She nearly choked on her wine, but she recovered and challenged his gaze with her own. "I most certainly did no such thing."

"You mentioned the taxi driver—"

"That's so farfetched, I can't believe you'd stoop that low."

"Perhaps, but you seemed to have enjoyed yourself. You sounded quite impressed by the sights you'd seen."

"If you want the truth, I hardly saw a thing. I was thinking about—" She stopped herself in the nick of time from admitting that her thoughts had been filled with him.

"Yes?" Jonas prompted.

"I was preoccupied with the meeting today. I was worried about how I'd do."

"Your French is superb. You needn't have been anxious, and you know it. What *did* occupy your thoughts? Or should I say who?"

Stephanie was saved from answering by the waiter, who reappeared to take their plates. She gave him a grateful smile and finished the last of her wine before the man returned with two steaming cups of coffee and her cheesecake.

A little while later Jonas asked for the bill, paused and looked at her. "Unless you'd like something more? Another dessert, perhaps?"

"No." She shook her head for emphasis and placed her hands over her stomach. After downing half of everything on the menu, she felt badly in need of exercise.

The sun had set, and the sky was darkening in shades of pink by the time they finished the last of their coffee.

"Shall we go?"

She nodded and stood. "Everything was wonderful. Thank you." The food *had* been marvelous—she freely admitted that—but it was this time with Jonas that had made the dinner so enjoyable. She didn't want the evening to end. For the first time since they'd begun working together, she felt at ease with him. She feared that once they arrived back at the hotel, everything would revert to the way it had been before. Jonas would immerse himself in the documents Adam was preparing for him, and everything would be business, business, business.

The maître d' was about to gesture for their waiting limousine when Stephanie placed her hand on Jonas's arm. "Would you mind if we walked a bit?"

"Not at all." He turned toward the maître d', who nodded and wished them a pleasant evening.

"I ate so much that I feel like a stuffed turkey at

Thanksgiving. I'm sure a little exercise will help." She was conscious of his leg, but hoped that if it pained him, he would say something. His limp was barely noticeable as they strolled down the narrow sidewalk. "I see there's a park across the way."

"That sounds perfect."

They crossed the street and sauntered down the paved walkway that led them into the lush green lawns of a city park. Black wrought-iron fences bordered flower beds filled with bright red tulips and yellow crocuses. Row upon row of trees welcomed them, proudly displaying their buds with the promise of new life.

"I've always heard Paris in springtime couldn't be equaled," she said softly, musing that anyone happening upon them would think they were lovers. Paris in the spring was said to be a city meant for lovers. For tonight she would pretend—reality would crowd in on her soon enough.

They followed the walkway that led to the center of the park, where a tall fountain spilled water from the mouths of a ring of lions' heads.

"Shall we make a wish?" she asked, feeling happy and excited.

He snorted softly. "Why waste good money?"

"Don't be such a skeptic. It's traditional to throw a coin in a fountain, any fountain, and what better place than Paris for wishes to come true?" She opened her purse, digging for loose change. "Here, it's my treat." She handed him a dime, since she had only a few Euros with her.

"You don't honestly expect me to fall victim to such stupidity?"

"Humor me, Jonas." She noted the amusement in

his blue eyes, and she ignored his tone, which sounded harsh and disapproving.

"All right." Without aim or apparent premeditation, he tossed the dime into the water with as much ceremony as if he were throwing something into the garbage.

"Good grief," she muttered beneath her breath. "I don't know of a single fairy in the entire universe who would honor such a wish."

"Why not?" he demanded.

"You obviously haven't given the matter much thought."

One corner of his mouth edged upward slightly. "I was humoring you, remember?"

"Did you even make a wish?"

He shrugged. "Not exactly."

"Well, no wonder." She shook her head dolefully and looked at him in mock disdain. "Try it again, and this time be a little more sincere."

His eyes revealed exactly what he thought of this exercise. Nonetheless, he reached inside his own pocket and took out a quarter.

Stephanie's hand stopped him. "That's too much."

"It's a big wish." This time his look was far more thoughtful as he took aim and sent the coin skipping over the surface of the water. The quarter made a small splash before sinking into the frothy depths.

She gave him a brilliant smile as she found another dime. "Okay, my turn." She turned her back to the fountain, rubbed the dime between her palms to warm it, closed her eyes and, with all the reverence due magical wish-granting fairies, flung it over her shoulder and into the fountain. "There," she said, satisfied.

"How long?" Jonas demanded.

"How long for what?"

"How long," he repeated with exasperation, "must one wait before the wish comes true?"

"It depends on what you wished for." She made it sound as though she had accumulated all the knowledge there was on the subject. "Certain wishes require a bit of manipulating by the powers that be. However, I'm only familiar with wishes made in American fountains. Things could be much different here. It could be that the wish fairies who guard this fountain work on a slower time scale than elsewhere."

"I see." It was clear from the frown that dented his brow that he didn't.

"Maybe you should just tell me what you wished for," she suggested, "and I can give you an estimate of the approximate time you'll have to wait for it to come true."

"It's my understanding that one must never reveal one's wish."

"That's not true anymore." She laughed, enjoying the inanity of their discussion. "Science has proved that theory to be inaccurate."

"Oh?"

"Yes, I'm surprised you didn't read about it in the papers. It was all over the news."

"I must have missed that." He reached for her hand, and they resumed their walk. "But if that's the case, then perhaps you'd be willing to share *your* wish with *me*."

Color instantly flooded her cheeks. She should have known he would turn the tables on her when she least expected it.

"Stephanie?"

It was completely absurd. With everything that was

in her she'd wished that Jonas would take her in his arms and kiss her. It was silly and hopeless and, as he'd pointed out earlier, a waste of good money.

When she didn't respond immediately, he stopped and turned, standing directly in front of her so that he could look into her eyes.

She felt the color rise in her face.

"I would think that a self-proclaimed expert on the subject of fountains and wishes would have no qualms about revealing her own wish, especially after sharing that latest scientific newsflash." He placed his finger under her stubborn chin, elevating her gaze so that she couldn't avoid his.

"I…"

"You still haven't answered my question."

"I wasted the wish on something impractical," she blurted out. The whole park seemed to have gone quiet. A moment ago wind had ruffled the foliage around them and hissed through the branches, but now even the trees seemed to have paused, as though they, too, were interested in her reply. She swallowed uncomfortably, convinced that he could read her thoughts and was silently laughing at her.

"I fear I wasted my wish, as well," he informed her softly.

"You did?" Her eyes sought his for the first time.

He placed his hands on the gentle slopes of her shoulders and bent toward her. "I'm seldom impractical."

"I…know."

His mouth descended an inch closer to hers, so close that she could feel his warm breath fanning her face. An inch more and their lips would touch. Stephanie moistened her lips, realizing all at once how very much she wanted to taste his mouth on hers. Her breath froze in her lungs; even her heart felt as though it had stopped beating.

"Could your wish have been as impractical as mine?" There was an unmistakable uncertainty in his voice.

She levered her hands against his chest, flattening one palm over his heart. His heartbeat was strong and even. "Yes." The lone word was breathless and weak, barely audible.

His arms went around her, anchoring her against him. Gently, he laid his cheek alongside hers, rubbing the side of his face over her soft skin as though he feared her touch, yet craved it. She closed her eyes, savoring his nearness, his warmth and the vital feel of him. A thousand objections shot through her mind, but she refused to listen to even one. This was exactly what she'd wished for, fool that she was.

Jonas turned his head and nuzzled her ear, and she noticed that his breathing was shallow. His arms tightened around her, and he whispered her name, entreating her—for what, she was afraid to guess.

It was at the back of her mind that she should break free, but something much stronger than the force of her will kept her motionless. He was her employer, she reminded herself. They argued constantly, battling with each other both in and out of the office. Jonas Lockwood was an arrogant, domineering chauvinist. But all her arguments were burned away like deadwood in a forest fire as his lips moved to her hair. He kissed the top of her head, her cheek, her ear, and then moved back to her hair. He paused, holding her to him as though it were the most natural thing in the world for them to be wrapped in each other's arms.

"Tell me, Stephanie," he asked in a hoarse whisper. "Did you wish for the same thing I did?"

Their eyes met hungrily and locked. She nodded, unable to answer him with words.

He caught her closer and lowered his mouth to hers, finally claiming her lips in a greedy kiss that left her weak and clinging. She felt herself responding as her arms slid around his neck. Their lips clung, and his tongue sought and found hers. Against her will, she arched against him, seeking to lose herself in his arms for all time.

Abruptly they broke apart, both of them moving of their own accord. She was trembling inside and out. She dared not look at Jonas. Neither of them spoke. For a moment they didn't move, didn't breathe. The world that only seconds before had been silent now burst into a cacophony of sound. Wind whistled through the trees. Car horns blared from a nearby street. An elderly couple could be heard arguing.

"Jonas, I…"

"Don't say anything."

She wouldn't have known what to say, anyway. She was as stunned as he was.

"It was the wine, and this silly wishing business," he said stiffly.

"Right."

"I told you wasting your money on wishes was foolish."

"Exactly," she agreed, though not very strenuously. Their wishes had come true; now they both wanted to complain.

She noticed on the way out of the park that he seemed to be keeping his distance from her. His steps were rushed. In order to keep up with him, she was forced into a half run. The instant they hit the main thoroughfare, he raised his hand and hailed the limo, which drove them directly back to the hotel.

"Well, how was Paris?" Jan asked the first day Stephanie was back at the office. They were sitting in the employee cafeteria. Jan had purchased the luncheon special, and Stephanie had brought a sandwich from home.

"Fine."

"Fine?"

"I was held captive in a stuffy room for most of the four days. This wasn't exactly a vacation, you know."

"How'd you get along with Mr. Lockwood?"

"Fine."

"Is that the only word you know?" Disgruntled, Jan tore open a small bag of potato chips and dumped them on her tray.

"I have an adequate vocabulary."

"Not today, you don't. Come on, Steph, you were with the man day and night for four days. Something must have happened."

The scene by the fountain, when Jonas had held her and kissed her, played back in Stephanie's mind in 3-D. If she were to close her eyes, she might be able to feel the pressure of his mouth on hers. She strenuously resisted the urge. "Nothing happened," she lied.

"Then why are you acting so strangely?"

"Am I?" Stephanie focused her attention on her friend, trying to look alert and intelligent, even though her thoughts were a thousand miles away in an obscure Paris park.

"Yes, very."

"What did you expect would happen?"

"I don't know, but the others thought you might have fallen in love with him."

"Oh, honestly, Jan, you're mistaking jet lag for love."

Disappointment clouded Jan's eyes. "This isn't going well."

"What isn't?"

"This romance. The girls and I had it all planned. We felt it would work out a whole lot easier than it is."

"How do you mean?"

"Well, in the books, the minute the hero and heroine are alone together for the first time, something usually happens."

"What do you mean, something happens?"

"You know, an intimate dinner for two, a shared smile, a kiss in the dark. Something!"

"We weren't exactly alone; Adam Holmes was with us." She avoided Jan's eyes as she carefully cracked a hard-boiled egg. If Jan could see her eyes, she would figure it all out. The egg took on new importance as she peeled the shell off piece by piece.

"At any rate," Jan continued, "we'd hoped that things might have taken off between you two."

"I'm sorry to disappoint you and the others, but the trip was a working arrangement, nothing else." Stephanie sprinkled salt and pepper on the egg.

"Well, I guess that's it, then."

"What do you mean?"

"If Mr. Lockwood was ever going to notice you, it would have been last week. You were constantly in each other's company, even if Adam Holmes was playing the part of legal chaperone. But if Mr. Lockwood isn't attracted to you by now, I doubt he ever will be."

"I couldn't agree more." Stephanie's heart contracted with a pang that felt strangely like disappointment. "Now can I get on with my life? I don't want to hear any more of your ridiculous romance ideas. Understand?"

"All right," Jan agreed, but she didn't look happy about it. "However, I wish you'd start reading romances. You'd understand what we're talking about and play your role a little better."

"Would you stop hounding me with those books? I'm not in the mood for romance."

"Okay, okay, but when you *are* ready, just say the word."

Stephanie took a look at her untouched egg, sighed and stuffed it in the sack to toss in the garbage, her appetite gone.

She couldn't decide how she felt about Jonas. Part of her wished the kiss had never happened. Those few minutes had made the remainder of the trip nearly intolerable. They had both taken pains to pretend nothing had happened, going out of their way to be cordial and polite, nothing less and certainly nothing more. It was as if Adam Holmes was their unexpected link with sanity. Neither Jonas nor Stephanie could do without him as they avoided any possibility of being trapped alone together. On the long flight home Jonas had worked out of his briefcase, while she and Adam played cards. For all the notice Jonas had given her, she could have been a piece of luggage. They'd separated at the airport, and she hadn't seen him since. It was just as well, she told herself. The incident at the fountain had been a moment out of time and was best forgotten.

"Steph?"

She shook her head to free her tangled thoughts. "I'm sorry, were you saying something?"

Jan gave her an odd look. "I was asking if you'd like to meet Jim's cousin, Mark. I thought we might double-date Saturday night. Dinner and a movie, maybe."

It took Stephanie a moment to remember who Jim was. "Sure, that sounds like fun." Anything was better than spending another restless weekend alone in her apartment.

"I knew Mark was interested, but I've held him off because I wanted to see how things developed between you and Mr. Lockwood."

Stephanie stared at her blankly and blinked twice, carefully measuring her words. She was saddened by the reality of what she had to say. "It isn't going to work between Jonas and me. Nothing's going to happen." The crazy part was that she was of two minds on the subject of the company president. He intrigued her. There wasn't a single man who interested her more. He was challenging, intelligent, pigheaded, stubborn and completely out of her league. Ah, well, she thought, sighing expressively, you won some and you lost some. And she'd lost Jonas without ever really having known him.

"Saturday at seven, then?"

"I'll look forward to it." She wasn't stretching the truth all that much. A date really did have to be better than staying home alone and moping.

"The three of us will pick you up at your apartment. Okay?"

"That sounds fine."

Jan groaned and laughed. "You're back to that word again."

* * *

Saturday evening, Stephanie washed and curled her hair, and spent extra time on her make-up. She dressed casually in slacks and a bulky knit sweater her mother had made for her last Christmas. The winter-wheat color reminded her of the rolling hills of grain outside her hometown.

The doorbell chimed, and she expelled her breath forcefully as she went to answer. She wasn't looking forward to this evening. All day her thoughts had drifted back to Jonas and their time in Paris, especially their stroll in the park. If she went out with anyone tonight, she wanted it to be with him. Wishful thinking, and not a fountain in sight. She wasn't especially eager to meet Jim's cousin, either. Jan had tried to build him up, but Stephanie knew from experience the pitfalls of blind dates. If she'd had her wits about her and been less concerned about revealing her attraction to Jonas, she would have declined the invitation. But it was too late now.

She needn't have worried about Mark, she quickly realized. He looked nice enough, although it came out immediately that he was newly divorced. Miserable, too, judging from the look in his eyes.

The vivacious Jan carried the conversation once the introductions were finished.

"Would anyone like some wine before we leave?" Stephanie asked. She'd set a tray with wine glasses on the coffee table, waiting for their arrival. "It's a light white wine."

"Sounds marvelous," Jan said, linking her fingers with Jim's. The two claimed the sofa and sat side by side. Mark took a chair, leaving its twin for Stephanie.

Still standing, she poured the wine. "What movie are we seeing?"

"There's a new foreign film out that sounds interesting," Jan said.

The doorbell chimed, and Stephanie got up to answer it. "I'm not expecting anyone," she said. "It's probably a neighbor looking for a cup of sugar or something."

She opened the door and stopped cold. It wasn't a neighbor who stood on the other side of her door. It was Jonas Lockwood.

Five

"Jonas!" Stephanie experienced a sense of joy so strong she nearly choked on it. Just when she'd given up any hope of seeing him again, he'd come to see her. But her joy quickly turned to regret as she heard the others talking behind her. "What are you doing here?" she whispered fiercely.

He stood stiffly on the other side of the door, his expression impossible to read. His grip on his cane tightened. "I came to see you. May I come in?"

"Yes…of course. I didn't mean to be rude." She stepped aside, still holding the doorknob. His timing couldn't have been worse, but she was so pleased to see him that she wouldn't have cared if he'd arrived unannounced on Christmas Eve.

"Mr. Lockwood, how nice to see you again," Jan said, tossing Stephanie a knowing look that was capable of translating entire foreign libraries.

Both Jim and Mark stood, and Stephanie made awkward introductions. "Jim, Mark, this is Mr. Lockwood."

"Jonas," he said, correcting her and offering them his hand.

"Would you care for a glass of wine?" Jan offered.

"Yes, of course," Stephanie hurried to add, her face filling with color at her lack of good manners. "Please stay and have some wine." Before he could answer, she walked into the kitchen for another glass, then came back, filled it and handed it to Jonas, who had claimed the chair next to Mark.

Resisting the urge to press her cool hands against her flaming cheeks, she took a seat on the sofa beside Jan, the three of them crowding together. The men were asking Jonas questions about the business as though it was the most interesting topic in the world. While they were occupied, Jan took the opportunity to jab Stephanie in the ribs with her elbow. "I thought you said he wasn't interested," she whispered under her breath.

"He isn't," Stephanie insisted. Glancing around, she wanted to groan with frustration. Although the small, one-bedroom apartment suited her nicely, she was intensely conscious that most of her furniture was secondhand and well-worn. She hadn't been the least bit ashamed to have Jan and her friends view her mix-and-match arrangement, but entertaining Jonas Lockwood was another matter entirely. Oh, for heaven's sake, what did she care? He hadn't stopped by to check out her china pattern.

"I can see that I've come at a bad time," Jonas said, standing. He set his glass aside, and Stephanie noted that he hadn't bothered to taste the wine.

She stood with him.

"We were about to leave for dinner," Jan explained apologetically. "But if you needed Steph for something at the office, we could change our plans."

"That won't be necessary." He shook hands with Jim and Mark again. "It was a pleasure meeting you both."

"I'll walk you to the door," Stephanie offered, locking her fingers together in front of her. He'd stopped in out of the blue, and she wasn't about to let him escape without knowing the reason for his impromptu visit.

Instead of stopping to ask him at her front door, she stepped into the hall with him. For a moment, neither spoke. She was trying to come up with a subtle way of mentioning that she'd only met Mark a few minutes earlier, that the blind date had been Jan's idea, and that she'd only accepted the offer because she didn't think that Jonas wanted to see her again. But she couldn't explain without sounding foolish.

"I apologize for not calling first," Jonas said finally.

"It...doesn't matter. I'm almost always home."

He cocked his brow as though he didn't quite believe her.

"It's true."

He glanced at his wristwatch. "I should be going."

"Jonas." Her hands were clenched so tightly that she was sure she'd cut off the blood supply to her fingers. "Why did you come?"

"It isn't important."

It was terribly important to her. "Is it something to do with work?"

"No."

"Then...why?"

"I believe there's someone in there waiting for you. It's not very polite of you to stand here with me, discussing my motives."

"What is this? Do you want to play twenty questions?"

He frowned.

"All right, you obviously want me to guess the reason you stopped by. Fine. Since that's the way you want it, let's start with the basics. Is it animal, vegetable or mineral?"

"Ms. Coulter." He closed his eyes, seemingly frustrated by her tenacity.

"I'm not going back inside until you tell me why you're here."

"This is neither the time nor the place to discuss it." His gaze hardened.

The look was one she knew all too well. "It's common courtesy to tell someone why you stopped by."

"The only manners you need concern yourself with are your own toward your friends. I suggest that you join them. We can discuss this later."

"When?" She wasn't about to let him off as easily as that.

"Monday."

She didn't want to agree, but she could hear the others talking and knew they'd long since finished their wine. "All right. Monday."

His gaze rested on her for a long moment. "It would be far better if you forgot I was ever here."

"I'm not going to do that." How could she? She hadn't been so pleased to see anyone in months.

"I didn't think you would. Enjoy yourself tonight." He said it with such sincerity that she wanted to assure him that she would, even though she knew the entire evening was a waste.

"Goodbye, Jonas."

"Goodbye." He hung the end of his cane over his forearm and turned away from her.

Stephanie watched him go, biting into her lower lip to keep from calling him back. If there had been any decent way of doing so, she would have sent Jan, Jim and Mark on their way without her. Reluctantly, she went back inside her apartment.

As she had known it would be, the evening was time misspent. Mark's conversation consisted of an account of how misunderstood he was by his ex-wife and of how terribly he missed his children. Stephanie tried to appear sympathetic, but her thoughts were centered on Jonas. They wavered between quiet jubilation and heart-wrenching disappointment. More than once she had to resist the urge to tell Mark to be quiet and go back to his wife, since it was so obvious that he still loved her. A thousand times over she wished she'd never agreed to this blind date, and she silently vowed she wouldn't do it again, no matter how close the friend who arranged it. She hoped Jan appreciated what she was going through, but somehow she doubted it.

After the movie the four of them returned to Stephanie's apartment for coffee. Jan offered to help as an excuse to talk to her alone.

"Well, what do you think?"

"Mark's nice, but he's in love with his wife."

"Not about Mark. I'm talking about Mr. Lockwood," she said. "I knew it from the first. I knew he was hooked!"

"Oh, hardly. Mr. Lockwood has no feelings for me one way or the other." Stephanie filled the basket with coffee and slipped it into place above the glass pot with unnecessary force.

"Don't give me that," Jan countered sharply. "I saw the way you two looked at each other."

"I don't even know why he came." Stephanie busied herself opening and closing cupboards, and taking down four matching cups.

"Don't be such a dope. There's only one reason he showed up. He wanted to see you again. He's interested with a capital *I*." Jan crossed her arms and leaned against the kitchen counter. "He's so into you that he can't look at you without letting it show."

"You're exaggerating again." Stephanie prayed her friend was right, but she sincerely doubted it. Jonas Lockwood wasn't the kind of man to reveal his emotions as easily as that.

"I'm not exaggerating."

"Come on," Stephanie said, refusing to argue. "The guys are waiting."

"Just do me a favor."

"What now?" Stephanie asked, desperate to change the subject. It was bad enough that Jonas had dominated her thoughts all evening. Now Jan was bringing him up, as well.

"Just think about it. Jonas Lockwood wouldn't have stopped by here for any reason other than the fact that he wanted to see you."

Jan's logic was irrefutable, but Stephanie still wasn't sure she could believe it. "All right, I'll think about it, but for heaven's sake, don't tell anyone. The last thing I need is for the rest of your Gang of Four to find out about this."

"I won't breathe a word of it." But Jan's eyes were twinkling. "I'll give you some time to think things through. You're smart. You'll figure Lockwood out." She held the door open for Stephanie, who carried the tray with the four steaming cups of coffee into the living room.

After a half hour of strained conversation, mostly about Mark's ex-wife, Jan and the men departed. Stephanie sighed as she let them out the door. It was only eleven, but she hurriedly got ready for bed. Amazingly, for all her doubts and uncertainty regarding Jonas, she slept surprisingly well.

Sunday morning Jan was at Stephanie's front door, smiling broadly and carrying a large stack of romances under one arm.

"What are those for?" Stephanie asked, letting her friend into the apartment. She was still in her housecoat, fighting off a cold with orange juice and aspirin, and feeling guilty for being so lazy.

"Not what—who."

"All right. *Who* are those for?" Stephanie's sore throat had taken a lot of the fight out of her.

"You."

"Jan, I've told you repeatedly that I'm not interested. You can't force me to read them."

"No, but I thought you might be interested in a little research." Jan paused, noticing Stephanie's appearance for the first time. "What's the matter—you look sick."

"I'm just fighting off a cold." And maybe a touch of disappointment, too.

"Great, there's no better time to sit back and read."

"Jan…"

Her friend held up a hand to stop her. "I refuse to hear any arguments. I want you to sit down and read. If I have to, I'll stand over you until you do."

Muttering under her breath, Stephanie complied,

sitting on the sofa with her back against the armrest and bringing her feet up so she could tuck them under a blanket. Jan picked up the book on the top of the pile, silently read the back cover and nodded knowingly. "You'll like this one. The circumstances are similar to what's happening between you and Mr. Lockwood."

Stephanie bolted to her feet. "Nothing's happening between me and Mr. Lockwood."

"You called him Jonas the other day," Jan said, ignoring Stephanie's bad mood. "The funny part is, until then I'd never thought of him other than as *Mr.* Lockwood."

To the contrary, Stephanie had almost always thought of him as Jonas, but she wasn't about to add ammunition to her friend's growing arsenal.

"But I don't think we need to worry about his name."

"Thank heaven for that much," Stephanie muttered, sitting back down.

"Promise me you'll read these?"

"I would never have taken you for such an unreasonable slave driver." Stephanie fought back a flash of rebellion and shook her head. "All right, I'll read one, but I won't like it."

"And I bet you a month's pay you'll end up loving them the way the rest of us do."

"I'm reserving judgment."

Jan left soon after Stephanie opened the cover of the first book. To be honest, she was curious what the other women saw in the novels that they read with such fervor. What was even more interesting was the fact that they did more than just read the books; the whole group talked about the characters as though they were living, breathing people. Stephanie had once heard Barbara comment that she wanted to punch out a certain hero, and the others had agreed wholeheartedly, as though it were an entirely possible option.

The next time Stephanie glanced at the clock it was afternoon and she'd finished the book, astonished at how well-written it was. All along she'd assumed that romance heroines were sappy, weak-willed women without a brain in their heads. From tidbits of information she'd heard among the others, she couldn't imagine anyone putting up with some of the things the heroines in the books did. But she was wrong. The heroines in the first romance she'd read and the one she reached for next were strong women with realistic problems. Although she might not have agreed completely with the way they handled their relationships with the heroes, she appreciated why they acted the way they did. With love, she realized, came tolerance, acceptance and understanding.

First thing on Monday morning Stephanie stopped at Jan's desk. She dutifully placed three romances in Jan's Out basket, willing to admit that she had misjudged her friend's favorite reading material.

"What's that for?"

"I read them."

"And?" Jan's eyes grew round.

"I loved them, just the way you said I would."

Laughing, Jan nodded, reached for her phone and punched in Maureen's extension. "She read the first three and she's hooked." Once she'd made her announcement, she replaced the receiver and sat back, folding her hands neatly on top of the desk and sighing. "I'm waiting."

Stephanie groaned and shook her head lightly. "I

knew I wasn't going to get away this easily. You want to hear it, so…all right, all right—you told me so."

Jan laughed again. "You look especially nice today. Any reason?"

Stephanie considered a white lie but quickly changed her mind. Like the heroines in the romances, she was a mature woman, and if she happened to be attracted to a man, it wasn't a sin to admit as much. "I'll be talking to Jonas later, and I wanted to look my best."

"You'll keep me up to date, won't you?"

Stephanie secured the strap of her purse on her shoulder. "I don't know that there'll be anything to report. Our relationship isn't like those romances."

"Maybe not yet, but it will be," Jan said with the utmost confidence.

"I'm not half as convinced as you are. Just keep this under your hat. I don't want the others to know."

"My lips are sealed."

But Stephanie wondered if Jan was capable of keeping anything a secret. Her coworker was much too friendly, and much too eager to see something develop between Stephanie and Jonas to keep the news to herself.

The day went smoothly although Stephanie was constantly on edge, expecting to hear from Jonas. Each time her phone rang she felt certain it would be him, issuing a request to join him in his office. He didn't call, and by five o'clock she felt both disappointed and frustrated. He'd said he would talk to her on Monday, and she'd taken him at his word.

Jan, Toni, Maureen and Barbara sauntered in together at quitting time. "Well? What did he say?"

Stephanie glared at Jan, who quickly lowered her

eyes. "I couldn't help it," she murmured, looking miserable. "Toni guessed, and I couldn't lie."

"You didn't have any problem promising me your lips were sealed."

"She had to tell us," Maureen insisted. "It was our right. We're the ones who got you into this."

Stephanie straightened the papers on her desk. "I'm not sure I can find it in my heart to thank you. Jonas Lockwood has been a thorn in my side from the moment we met."

"Perfect," Barbara announced.

"Enough of that," Toni said. "We want to know what he had to say today."

"Nothing." Stephanie tried unsuccessfully to hide the disappointment in her voice.

"Nothing!" the others echoed.

"I haven't seen him."

"Why not?"

"Good grief, how am I supposed to know?"

Toni paused, and pressed her forefinger to her temple. "I was thinking about what happened Saturday night, and in my opinion it wasn't necessarily such a bad thing that Jan's friend was there. It lets Mr. Lockwood know he's got competition."

"It might have been enough to scare him off, though," Barbara disagreed.

"Then he isn't worth his salt as a hero."

"Would you four stop!" Stephanie demanded, waving her arms for emphasis. She returned her attention to Jan. "Are they always like this?"

Jan shrugged. "It doesn't matter. What are you going to do?"

Stephanie had no idea. Jonas had said that he would

talk to her on Monday, and there were still several hours left in the day. Maybe he intended to contact her at her apartment. No, she quickly dismissed the notion. He wouldn't be back; she'd seen it in his eyes.

"Steph?"

She looked up to notice that all four of her coworkers were studying her expectantly.

"I'm going up to his office," she said, the announcement shocking her as much as it did the others. The upper floor belonged to Jonas and was well guarded by his Martha Westheimer, who was reputed to have slain more than one persistent dragon.

Jan grinned. "Didn't I tell you she was heroine material?"

"The perfect choice," Maureen agreed.

The four of them followed Stephanie out of her office and to the elevator. Barbara pushed the button for her. Toni and Maureen stood behind her, rubbing her shoulders as though to prepare her for the coming confrontation. For a moment Stephanie felt as if she was getting ready for the heavyweight boxing championship of the world.

"Don't take any guff from Old Stone Face."

"Just remember to smile at Mr. Lockwood."

"And it wouldn't hurt to bat your lashes over those baby blues a time or two."

Armed with their advice, Stephanie entered the waiting elevator. Jan gave her the thumbs-up sign just before the heavy metal doors closed.

Now that she was alone, Stephanie felt herself losing her nerve. She sighed and leaned against the back of the elevator. The others had lent her confidence, but standing alone in the chilly, dimly lit elevator gave her cause to doubt. If there had been any way of disappearing from a moving elevator, she would have been tempted to try it.

The doors opened, and Martha Westheimer raised her eyes to frown at Stephanie's approach. A pair of glasses were delicately balanced at the end of the older woman's nose. She was near sixty, Stephanie guessed, tall and slender, with a narrow mouth. Just looking at the woman inspired fear.

"Do you have an appointment?" Martha asked stiffly, giving Stephanie a look that was not at all welcoming.

Stephanie stepped off the elevator and thrust back her shoulders, prepared for this first encounter. "Mr. Lockwood asked to see me." That was only a partial white lie.

"Your name, please?" With the eraser end of her pencil, Martha flipped through the appointment schedule.

"Stephanie Coulter."

"I don't see your name down here, Ms. Coulter."

"Then there must be some mistake."

There was challenge in Martha's dark brown eyes. "I don't make mistakes."

"Then I suggest you contact Mr. Lockwood."

"I'll do exactly that." The woman flipped on the intercom. "There's a Ms. Coulter here to see you. She claims she has an appointment." Her tone made it clear that she was certain Stephanie had lied.

"I said," Stephanie corrected her through clenched teeth, "that Mr. Lockwood had asked to see me." The hand clenching her purse tightened. "There's a difference."

The silence on the other end of the intercom stretched

out uncomfortably, and Stephanie was convinced she was about to be dismissed.

"Mr. Lockwood?"

"Send her in, Miss Westheimer."

Stephanie flashed Jonas's guardian a brilliant smile of triumph as she waltzed past her desk. The older woman had to know that Stephanie had stepped in while she was ill, yet she gave no indication that she was aware who Stephanie was, or even that she was employed by Lockwood Industries.

Stephanie let herself into Jonas's office and was instantly met by a rush of memories. She liked this room, just as she respected the man who ruled from it.

He was busy writing, his head bowed, and didn't bother to acknowledge her presence. She stood awkwardly as she waited for him to finish, not enough at ease to take a seat without being asked.

When he'd finished, Jonas put the cap on his pen and set it aside before glancing in her direction. "Yes?"

His crisp tone made her all the more uncomfortable, but she pushed on. "You said you would talk to me on Monday."

"About?"

He was making this difficult, and she drew a deep breath before continuing. "About Saturday night. You told me we'd talk."

"I don't recall committing myself to that."

"Please, don't play games with me. You stopped by my apartment on Saturday, and I want to know why."

The lines around his mouth deepened, but he wasn't smiling. "I happened to be in the neighborhood."

"But…"

"Leave it at that, Ms. Coulter. It was a mistake, and one best forgotten."

"But I don't think it *was* a mistake." He was closing her out; she could see it by the way he sat, his back stiff with determination. His eyes looked past her as though he wanted to avoid seeing her.

The silence was broken by Jonas. "Sometimes it's better to leave things as they are. In my opinion, this is one of those times."

Her hands trembled slightly but she stood her ground. "I disagree."

His mouth twisted in a cynical smile. "Unfortunately, you have little say in the matter. Now, if you'll excuse me, I have several reports to read over."

It was clearly meant to be a dismissal, and she wavered between stalking out of the office and trying to forget him, and staying and admitting that she was attracted to him and that she would like to know him better. But for all the attention he was giving her now, she might as well have been a stack of signed papers on his desk. Out of sight, out of mind, she mused ruefully. Her pride told her that she had better things to do than allow Jonas Lockwood to poke holes in her fragile ego.

Finally her pride won, and she gave him a small, sad smile. "You don't need to be rude, Jonas. I get the message."

"Do you?" He focused his gaze on her.

"Thank you for that wonderful night in Paris. I'll always remember that—and you—fondly."

His hard blue eyes softened. "Stephanie, listen…"

He was interrupted by the phone. "I'm waiting for a call," he said, almost apologetically, as he reached for the receiver.

She turned to leave, but he stopped her as he reverted to French. She could tell that he was speaking to a government official regarding his negotiations with Lockwood Industries' French counterpart, but the conversation quickly became too technical for her to understand fully.

A few minutes later Jonas hung up the telephone. His eyes revealed his excitement.

"Congratulations are in order," he said, standing. "Our trip to France was a success. Our bid has been accepted."

"Congratulations," she whispered. His happiness was contagious; it filled the enormous room, encircling them both.

He walked around the front of the large rosewood desk, his eyes sparkling. "It seemed for a while that this deal could go either way."

Stephanie noticed that his limp was less pronounced now than at any time she'd seen him walk.

"Do you know what this means?" He walked to the other side of the room, as though he couldn't contain himself any longer.

She nodded eagerly, pretending she did know, when in actuality she was ignorant of nearly all the pertinent information.

He came back over to her and locked his hands on her shoulders. "I can't believe it's falling into place after all the problems we've encountered." His arms dropped to her waist and circled her. With a burst of infectious laughter, he lifted her off the plush carpet and swung her around.

Caught completely off guard, she gasped and placed

her hands on his shoulders in an effort to maintain her balance. "I'm so happy for you."

As if suddenly aware that he was holding her, he relaxed his grip. Her feet found the floor, but her hands remained on his shoulders, and her eyes smiled warmly into his.

He tensed, and the exhilaration drained from him as his gaze locked with hers. His hand slid beneath her long hair, tilting her head to receive his kiss. She had no thought of objecting. Since that night in Paris, she'd longed for him to hold and kiss her again. But she hadn't admitted how *much* she'd wanted it until now. He kissed her a second time, and his mouth was hungry and demanding. His lips moved persuasively over hers, hot and possessive. She was equally hungry and eager for him. A slow fire burned through her, and she melted against him. "Oh, Jonas," she whispered longingly.

He brushed his lips over hers again, as though he couldn't get enough of the taste of her. She opened her mouth to him, drugged by the sensations he aroused.

His mouth ravaged the scented hollow of her throat and began a slow meandering trail to her ear. He paused, took a deep breath, and waited a moment longer before releasing her. "Forgive me." He brushed the wisps of hair from her temple. "That shouldn't have happened."

She felt like a fool. She'd savored the feel of his arms, lost herself in the taste of his kiss and the rush of sensations that flooded her, and he was apologizing.

"No apology necessary," she murmured stiffly. "Just don't let it happen again."

Jonas hesitated, as though he wanted to say something more but then decided against it. He turned sharply and stalked back to his desk.

Six

"Well?" Maureen was at Stephanie's desk early the following morning. "Don't keep me in suspense. What happened?"

"Nothing much." Stephanie kept her gaze lowered, doing her best not to reveal her emotions. She'd been depressed and out of sorts from the minute she left Jonas's office.

"'Nothing much'? What does that mean?"

"It means I don't want to talk about it."

"You had an argument?" Toni joined her friend. The two of them placed their hands on the edge of Stephanie's desk and leaned forward, as if what she had to say was a matter of national importance.

"I wish," Stephanie muttered, sighing heavily. "No, we didn't argue."

"But you don't want to talk about it?"

"Very perceptive, ladies." Stephanie searched for something to do and finally settled for inserting a pencil in the sharpener. Despite the loud grinding sound, neither Toni nor Maureen budged.

"I think we need to talk to the others," Toni said.

"You'll do no such thing," Stephanie insisted, her tone determined.

"Hey, come on, Steph, we're all in this together. We want to help. At least tell us what happened," Maureen said.

It was apparent to Stephanie that she wouldn't have a minute's peace until she confessed everything to her romance-loving friends. "Meet me at ten in the cafeteria," she told them. "I'll get it over with all at once, but only if you promise never to mention Jonas Lockwood's name to me again."

Toni and Maureen exchanged meaningful glances. "This doesn't sound good."

"It's my final offer." Replaying her humiliation was going to be bad enough; she didn't want it dragged out any more than necessary.

"All right, all right," Toni muttered. "We'll be there."

After that Stephanie's morning went smoothly. Her boss, George Potter, was on a two-day business trip to Seattle, but there was enough work to keep her occupied for another week if need be.

When she arrived in the cafeteria promptly at ten she found the four women sitting at the table closest to the window, eagerly awaiting her arrival. A fifth cup of coffee was on the table in front of an empty chair.

"From that frown you're wearing, I'd say the meeting with Mr. Lockwood didn't go very well," Jan commented, barely giving Stephanie time to take a seat.

"There are no adequate words to describe it," Stephanie said by way of confirmation, reaching for the coffee. "I'm sorry to be such a major disappointment to you all, but anything that might have happened between me and Jonas Lockwood is off."

"Why?"

"What happened?"

"I could have sworn he was hooked."

"To be honest," Stephanie said, striving to be as forthright as possible, "I think he may be attracted to me, but we're too different."

"That's what makes you so good together," Barbara countered.

"And I saw the way he looked at her," Jan inserted thoughtfully. "Now tell us what happened and let *us* figure out the next step."

Stephanie swallowed and shrugged. "If you must know, he kissed me."

"And you're complaining?"

"No, *he* was!"

"What?" All four of them looked at her as if she'd been working too much overtime.

"He kissed me, then immediately acted like he'd committed some terrible faux pas. The way he was looking at me, anyone seeing us would have assumed that *I'd* kissed *him* and he didn't like it in the least. He was angry and unreasonable, and worse, he insulted me with an apology."

"What did you say?"

"I told him never to let it happen again."

A chorus of moans and groans followed.

"You didn't!" Jan cried. "That was the worst thing you could have said."

"Well, it was his own fault," Stephanie flared. She'd been furious with him *and* with herself. She'd enjoyed his kisses—in fact, she'd wanted him to continue.

"Did you like it—the kiss, I mean?" Toni looked at her hopefully.

Stephanie pretended to find her black coffee enthralling. "Yes."

"How do you feel about Mr. Lockwood?"

"I...I don't know anymore."

"But if he'd asked you to dinner, you would have accepted?"

"Probably." She remembered the exhilaration in his eyes when he'd found out his bid had been accepted. He'd worked so hard, and given so much of himself to the business, that she'd experienced a sense of elation just watching him. She'd been happy for him and pleased to have played a small part in his triumph.

"Then you can't give up."

"It was Jonas who did that," Stephanie said sharply.

"But he hasn't. Don't you see?" Toni asked, and the others nodded in agreement.

Stephanie glanced around the table, thinking her co-workers must be kidding. "No. Not at all."

"She hasn't read enough romances yet," Jan said, defending her friend. "She doesn't understand."

"Mr. Lockwood is definitely attracted to you," Barbara claimed with all the seriousness of a clinical psychologist. "Otherwise he wouldn't have reacted to kissing you the way you described."

"I'd hate to see how he'd react if he *didn't* like me," Stephanie said sarcastically. "I'm sorry, but this is getting just too complicated to understand. I'll admit to being disappointed—he's not so bad once you get to know him. In fact, I might even have enjoyed the chance to fall in love with him." She admitted this at the expense of her own pride.

"It's hardly over yet," Maureen told her emphatically.

"Whose move is next?" Jan asked, looking around the table, seeking an answer from her peers.

"Mr. Lockwood's," Toni and Maureen said together, nodding in unison. "Definitely."

"Then I'm afraid we've got a long wait coming," Stephanie informed them, finishing her coffee. "A very long wait."

"We'll see."

That same afternoon Stephanie was on the computer at her desk when Jonas entered her office. He leaned heavily on his cane, waiting for her to notice him before he spoke.

She was aware of him the second he entered, but she finished the line she was typing before she turned her attention to him. Ignoring her pounding heart, she met his gaze squarely, refusing to give him the satisfaction of knowing the effect he had on her.

"Good afternoon, Mr. Lockwood," she said crisply. "Is there something I can do for you?"

"Miss Coulter." He paused and looked into Mr. Potter's office. "Is your boss available?"

Jonas had to know that he wasn't.

"Mr. Potter's in Seattle."

"Fine. Take a letter." He pulled up a chair and sat beside her desk.

She reached automatically for her steno pad, then paused. "Is Miss Westheimer ill again?"

"She was healthy the last time I looked."

"Then perhaps it would be better if she took your dictation." She raised her chin to a defiant angle, thinking as she did that her behavior would upset her friends. But she didn't care. She wouldn't let Jonas Lockwood boss her around, even at the cost of a good job. Her hold on the pencil was so tight that it was a miracle it didn't snap in half.

"Address the letter to Miss Stephanie Coulter."

"Me?"

"Dear Ms. Coulter," he continued, ignoring her. "In thinking over the events of last evening, I am of the opinion that I owe you an apology."

As fast as her fingers could move the pencil, Stephanie transcribed his words. Not until her brain had assimilated the message did she pause. "I believe you already expressed your deep regret," she said stiffly. "You needn't have worried. I didn't take the kiss seriously."

"It was an impulse."

"Right." She felt her anger flare. "And, as you say, best forgotten." But she couldn't forget it, even though she wanted to banish it to the farthest reaches of her mind. He'd held her and kissed on two different occasions, and each time was engraved indelibly on her memory. She wondered if she would ever be the same again.

He scowled. "You're an attractive woman."

"I suppose I should thank you, but somehow that didn't sound like a compliment."

His frown deepened. "You could have any man you want."

She gave a self-deprecating laugh. "You clearly have an exaggerated opinion of my charms, Mr. Lockwood."

"I don't blame you for being offended that someone like me would kiss you."

"I wasn't offended." She was incensed that he'd even suggested such a thing. "If you want the truth, which you obviously do, I happened to find the whole experience rather pleasant."

"In Paris?"

"It was exactly what I wished for, and you know it." Even as she said it, she knew how true it was. Since leaving his office the night before, she'd been in a blue funk, cranky and unreasonable, and all because of him. As much as she'd disliked him those few days she'd spent filling in for Martha Westheimer, she admitted to liking him now. What she couldn't understand was why everything had changed. For days, angry sparks had flown every time they were in the same room. Sparks were still apparent, but now they set off an entirely different kind of response.

"What about my limp?"

"What about it?" Deliberately, she set the pencil aside.

"Does it trouble you?"

She noticed the way his hand had tightened around the handle of his cane. His knuckles were stark white, and some of her outrage dissipated. "Of course not. Why should it?"

"Some women would be repelled." He wouldn't look at her; his gaze rested on the filing cabinet on the opposite wall. "I want neither your sympathy nor your pity."

"That works out well, since you don't have either one." Her voice was crisp with impatience. She hated to believe that he had such a low opinion of her motives, but he gave her no choice but to think that.

"You could have your pick of any man in this company."

"Listen," she countered, her patience having long since evaporated. "It isn't like I've got a tribe of men seeking my company, and even if I did, what would it matter?"

"You're attractive, bright and witty."

"Such high praise. I don't know how I should deal with it, especially when it comes from you."

Jonas was still studying the filing cabinet. "I can see that our little talk has helped clear away some misconceptions," he said.

"I certainly hope so."

"Have a good day, Ms. Coulter."

"You, too, Mr. Lockwood."

Jonas had been gone for five minutes before Stephanie fully accepted the fact that he'd actually been in her office. It took her another ten minutes to react. Her fingers were poised over the computer keyboard, ready to resume her task, when she realized she was shaking. She closed her eyes and savored the warm feelings that washed over her in waves. Then she felt chilled; nerves skirted up and down her spine. Jan and the others had been right about him. He was attracted to her, although he wore that stiff, businesslike facade like a heavy coat, not trusting her or the attraction they shared. He didn't have faith in her feelings for him, but she hoped that eventually he would realize they were genuine.

Unable to contain her excitement, she reached for her phone and dialed Jan's extension.

"Human Resources," Jan said when she answered.

"He was here."

"Who?"

"Guess," Stephanie said, laughing excitedly. "You were right. It was his move, and he made it."

"Mr. Lockwood?"

"Who else do you think I'm talking about?"

"I'll be right there."

Jan arrived a minute later, followed by Barbara, Toni and Maureen. "What did I tell you?" Jan said excitedly, slapping Barbara's open hand with her own.

"There isn't time for you to read more romances," Toni murmured, looking worried.

"The only thing she can do now is follow her instincts," Maureen said brightly. "He's interested. She's interested. Everything will follow its natural course."

"What do you mean 'natural course'?" Stephanie asked, concerned. This was beginning to sound a lot like kidney stones.

"Marriage." They said the word in unison, and looked at her as though her elevator didn't go all the way to the top floor. "It's what we're all after."

"Marriage?" Stephanie repeated slowly. Everything was happening too fast for her to take in.

"You like him, right?" Toni challenged.

"Hey, wait a minute, you guys. Sure, I like Jonas Lockwood, but liking is a long way from love and marriage."

"You're perfect together." Maureen sounded incredulous that Stephanie could question her fate. The four romance-lovers had everything arranged, and her resistance obviously wasn't appreciated.

"Perfect together? Jonas and me?" Stephanie frowned. The two of them did more arguing than anything. They were barely beginning to come to an understanding.

"You have to plan your strategy carefully."

"My strategy?"

"Right." Barbara nodded.

"You'll need to make him believe that love and marriage are all his idea."

"Don't you think we could start by holding hands?"

"Very funny," Jan said, placing her fist on her hip.

"I feel it's more important to let this relationship take its own time." Stephanie looked up at the four women who were standing around her desk, arms crossed, staring disapprovingly down at her. "That is, if there's going to *be* a relationship."

Together, they all shook their heads. "Wrong."

"So tell us, what are you planning next?" Jan asked.

"Me?" Stephanie held her hand to her breast. "I'm not planning anything. Should I be?"

"Of course. Mr. Lockwood made his move, now it's your turn."

This romance business sounded a lot like playing chess, or perhaps tennis. "I...hadn't given it any thought."

"Well, don't worry, we'll figure out something. Are you doing anything after work?" Jan asked.

"Depositing my check and picking up the bookcase I've had on layaway."

"Well, for heaven's sake, what's more important?" Jan gave her an incredulous look.

"You want the truth?" Stephanie glanced around at her friends. It didn't matter if she was with them or not; they were going to plot her life to their own satisfaction. "I'm going with the bookcase. If you four come up with something brilliant, phone me."

Several pieces of polished wood lay across Stephanie's carpet, along with a bowl full of screws. The screwdriver was clenched between her teeth as she struggled with the instructions, turning them one way and then another. The phone rang, and she absently reached for it, forgetting about the screwdriver.

"Hebbloo."

"Stephanie?"

"Jonas?" Her heartbeat instantly quickened as she grabbed the screwdriver from between her lips. For one crazy second she actually wanted to tell him he couldn't contact her—it was her move!

"I hope this isn't a bad time."

"No...no, of course it isn't. I wasn't doing anything." She stared at the disembodied pieces of the bookcase scattered across her carpet and added, "Important."

"I know it's short notice, but I was wondering if you were free to join me for dinner."

"Dinner?" She knew she sounded amazingly like an echo. She quickly toyed with the idea of contacting Jan before she agreed to do anything with Jonas, then just as quickly rejected that thought. Her coworkers were making her paranoid.

"If you have company or..."

"No, I'm alone." She picked up the instructions for assembling the bookcase and sighed. "Jonas, do you speak Danish?"

"Pardon?"

"How about Swedish?"

"No. Why?"

At that point she was so frustrated she wanted to cry. "It's not important."

"About dinner?"

"Yes, I'd love to go." Never mind that she had a pot roast in the oven, with small potatoes and fresh peas in the sink ready to be boiled.

"I'll pick you up in a few minutes, then."

"Great." She glanced down at her faded jeans, ten-year-old sweatshirt and purple Reeboks, and groaned. She picked up the receiver to phone Jan, decided she didn't have enough time and hurried into her room. The sweatshirt came off first and was flung to the farthest corner of her small bedroom. She found a soft pink silk blouse hanging in her closet and quickly slipped it on. Her fingers shook as she rushed to work the small pearl buttons.

She had the jeans down around her thighs when the doorbell chimed. She closed her eyes and prayed that it wasn't Jonas. It couldn't be! He'd only phoned a couple of minutes ago. She jumped, hauling her jeans back up to her waist, and ran to the door, yanking it open.

"Listen, I'm sorry if I sound rude, but I don't have the time to buy anything right now—" She stopped abruptly, wishing the earth would open up and swallow her. Her breath caught in her throat, and she closed her eyes momentarily. "Hello, Jonas."

"Did you know your pants are unzipped?"

She whirled around, sucked in her stomach and pulled up the zipper. "I didn't expect you so soon."

"Obviously. I called on my cell from across the street."

"Please come in. I'll only be a few minutes." If he so much as snickered, she swore, she would find a way to take revenge. Some form of justice fitting the crime, like a pot roast dumped over his head.

He glanced around at the pieces of wood strewn across her carpet. "You're building something?"

"A bookcase." She'd hoped to have that cleaned up before he arrived, but that had been her second concern.

She'd wanted to be dressed first. He gave a soft cough that sounded suspiciously like a smothered laugh.

"Did you say something?" Her hands knotted at her sides, and she eyed the oven where the pot roast was cooking.

"I don't believe I've ever seen you flustered before." His look was amused, and his voice soft and gruff at the same time. "Not Stephanie Coulter, the woman who defies and challenges me at every turn."

"Try answering the door with your underwear showing. It has a humbling effect."

He chuckled, and the sound had a musical quality to it. Despite her embarrassment, she laughed, too, feeling completely at ease with him for the first time since Paris. "I'll only be a few minutes."

"Take your time."

She was halfway to her bedroom when she stopped, realizing that she'd forgotten her manners in her eagerness to escape. "Would you like something to drink while you wait?"

"No, thanks." He picked up the assembly instructions for the bookcase, which were on the end table by the phone. "Danish?" he asked, cocking both brows.

"I guess. It may be Swedish or Greek. I can't tell."

His gaze scanned the pieces on the floor. "Would you like a little help?"

"I'd like a lot of help." A wry smile curved her mouth. She'd spent the better part of two hours attempting to make sense of the diagrams and the foreign instructions.

"Do I detect a note of resignation in your voice, Ms. Coulter?"

"That's not resignation, it's out-and-out frustration, disillusionment, and more than a touch of anger."

"I'll see what I can do."

She started to leave, but when she saw him take off his suit jacket and reach for one long piece of shelving to join it to another, she paused. "That won't work." Soon she was kneeling on the floor opposite him. She began to feel like a nurse assisting a brain surgeon, handing him one part after another. In frustration, he paused to study the diagram, turning it upside down and around, just as she had done, but he still couldn't figure out which pieces linked together, either.

"Wait," Jonas said, shaking his head. "We've been doing this all wrong."

Stephanie, kneeling close to his side, groaned, then mumbled under her breath, "The man's a genius."

"If I was such a whiz, these bookcases would have books in them by now," he grumbled, his brow knit in a thoughtful frown. "Give me the screwdriver, would you?"

"Sure." She handed it to him.

He turned to thank her. Their eyes met, and they stared at each other for an endless moment. She blinked and looked away first. Never before had she been so aware of Jonas as a man. He looked different than any time she'd seen him in the office. Younger. Less worried. Almost boyishly handsome. He made no move to touch her, yet she felt a myriad of sensations shoot through her as though he had. He was so close that she could smell the spicy scent of his aftershave and feel the warmth of his hard, lean body chasing away the chill of her insecurities. She could feel his breath against her hair, and she welcomed it, swaying toward him.

She didn't know who moved first. It didn't matter. Before she was aware of anything, they were on their knees with their arms wrapped around each other. She closed her eyes and let the warm sensation of his touch thread through her limbs. His hands gripped her upper arms as he moved his mouth to hers. His kiss was tentative, exploring, as though he expected her to stop him. She couldn't. She'd been wanting him to hold and kiss her again from the moment he'd last released her and then apologized. His lips were warm as they covered hers. The tip of his tongue traced her lips, and she eagerly opened her mouth to his exploration.

Stephanie's fingers moved from his hard chest, and she slid her arms up and around his neck, flattening her torso to his. His hands were splayed across her back, drawing her as close as humanly possible. His kiss grew greedy, hungry and demanding.

She reveled in the feel of the hard muscles of his shoulders and the softness of the thick hair at the base of his neck. A delicious languor spread through her.

Jonas buried his face in the hollow of her throat and shuddered. "Stephanie?"

"Hmm." She felt warm and wonderful.

"I don't know what it is, but something smells like it's burning."

Her eyes flew open. She let out a small cry of alarm and jumped to her feet.

Seven

"Oh, Jonas, the roast!" She grabbed two pot holders and pulled open the oven to retrieve the pot roast. Black smoke filled the small kitchen, and Stephanie waved her hand to clear the air. "So much for that," she said, heaving an exasperated sigh.

"What is it?" He joined her, examining the charred piece of meat.

"What does it look like?" she said hotly, then stared at the crisp roast and slowly shook her head. "If you have any kindness left in your heart, you won't answer that."

Chuckling, he slipped his arm around her shoulders. "There are worse disasters."

"I imagine you're referring to an unassembled bookcase with instructions in a foreign language."

Amusement glinted in his blue eyes at the belligerent way her mouth thinned.

She couldn't help pouting. She was furious with herself for ruining a perfectly good piece of meat, and what was even worse was having to face the disgrace in front of Jonas.

"Come on," he prompted. "There's a fabulous Chinese restaurant near here. The kitchen can air out while we're gone, and when we get back, I'll finish putting that bookcase together."

"All right," she agreed, and her mouth curved into a weak smile. He was right. The best thing she could do was to draw his attention away from her lack of culinary skill. If he continued to see her, at least she would know for certain that it wasn't her talent in the kitchen that had attracted him.

It was not until she had buckled the seat belt in Jonas's Mercedes that she realized she was still wearing her faded jeans and tennis shoes. "This restaurant isn't fancy, is it?" She placed her hand over the knee that showed white through the threadbare blue jeans.

His gaze followed hers. "Poor Stephanie." He chuckled. "You're having quite a night, aren't you?"

She folded her hands in her lap and crossed her legs. "It's an average night." Better than most. Worse than some. It wasn't every day that Jonas Lockwood took her in his arms and kissed her until her world spun out of its orbit. Just thinking about the way he'd held her produced a warm glow inside her until she was certain she must radiate with it.

"You do enjoy Chinese food?"

"Oh, yes."

"By the way, do you often wear purple tennis shoes?"

She glanced down at her feet and experienced a minor twinge of regret. "I bought them on sale—they were half price."

Jonas chuckled. "I think it was the color."

"I usually only wear them around the apartment,"

she said, only a little offended. "They work fine for *The Twenty-Minute Workout.*"

"The what?"

"*The Twenty-Minute Workout.* It's on every morning at six. Don't you ever watch it?" She wasn't sure the neighbor in the apartment below appreciated her jumping around the living room at such an ungodly hour, but Mrs. Humphrey had never complained.

"I take it you're referring to a televised exercise program."

"Yes. Have you heard of it?"

"No, I prefer my club."

"Oh, the joys of being rich." She said it with a sigh of feigned envy.

"Are you complaining about your salary?"

"Would it do any good?"

"No."

"That's what I thought." Her gaze slid to him, and again she marveled at the man at her side. The top buttons of his starched white shirt were unfastened, exposing bronze skin and dark curly hair. The long sleeves were rolled up, a sign of the eagerness with which he'd helped her with the bookcase. He stopped at a red light and seemed to feel her watching him. His gaze met hers, and she noted the fine lines that feathered out from the corners of his eyes. The grooves at the side of his mouth, which she had so often thought of as harsh, softened now as he smiled. Jonas Lockwood was a different man when he grinned. It transformed his entire face.

Stephanie was astonished how much his smile could affect her. Her pulse slowed, then started up again, sending the blood pulsing hotly through her veins. If given the least bit of encouragement, she would have impulsively eliminated the small space that separated them and pressed her mouth to his, revealing with a kiss how much being with him had stirred her heart.

She reluctantly dragged her gaze from his and glanced down at her hands folded neatly in her lap. In that instant, as brief as it was, she'd recognized the truth. She was falling in love with Jonas Lockwood, and she was falling hard. Up to this point in their non-relationship, she had considered him an intriguing challenge. Jan, Maureen and the others had piqued her interest in their domineering, arrogant employer. The trip to Paris, and their time at the fountain in the park, had added to her curiosity. She'd glimpsed the man buried deep beneath the gruff exterior and had been enthralled. Now she was caught, hook, line and sinker.

Long after they'd returned from dinner and the finished bookcase stood in the corner of her living room, Stephanie recalled the look they'd exchanged in the car on the way to the restaurant. Briefly she wondered if Jonas had recognized it for what it was. Certainly the evening had been altered because of that glance. Before that they had been teasing each other and joking, but from the moment they entered the restaurant, they had immersed themselves in serious conversation. He'd wanted to know everything about her. And she had talked for hours. She told him about growing up in Colville, and what living in the country had meant to a gawky young girl. When he asked how she happened to move to Minneapolis, she explained that her godparents lived nearby, and had encouraged her to move to the area. There were other relatives close by, as well, and clinching the deal was the fact that there were precious few job positions in the eastern part of Washington State.

It wasn't until their plates were cleared away and the waiter delivered two fortune cookies that she realized that while she'd been telling him her life story, he had revealed very little about himself. She felt guilty about dominating the conversation, but when she mentioned it, he brushed her concern aside, telling her there was plenty of time for her to get to know him better. For hours afterward she was on a natural high, exhilarated and happy. She enjoyed talking to him, and for the first time since Paris, they'd been at ease with each other.

When Stephanie arrived at work the following morning, there was a message on her desk from Jan. The note asked Stephanie to join her and the others in the cafeteria on their coffee break. All morning she toyed with the idea of telling her friends about the evening she'd spent with Jonas, but she finally decided against it. The night had been so special that she wanted to wrap the feelings around herself and keep them private.

At midmorning she found the four women gathered around the same table by the window that they'd occupied earlier in the week. Again her coffee was waiting for her.

"Morning."

"You're late," Jan scolded, glancing at her watch. "We've got a lot of ground to cover."

"We do?" Stephanie glanced around the table at her friends and wondered if the Geneva peace talks had held more somber, serious faces.

"It's your move with Mr. Lockwood," Maureen explained. "And we've been up half the night discussing the best way for you to approach him."

"I see." Stephanie took a sip of her coffee to hide an amused grin.

"Subtlety is the key," Barbara insisted. "It's imperative that he doesn't know that you've planned this next *chance* meeting."

"Would it be so wrong to let him know I'm interested?" Stephanie let her gaze fall to the table so that her friends couldn't read her expression.

"That comes later," Toni told her. "This next step is the all-important one."

"I see." Stephanie didn't, but she doubted that her lack of understanding concerned her friends. "So what's my next move?"

"That's the problem—we can't decide," Jan explained. "We seem to be at a standstill."

"It's a toss-up between four different ideas."

One from each romantic, Stephanie reasoned.

"I thought you could wait until Old Stone Face has left her guard post for the day and then make up an excuse to go to his office. Any excuse would do—for that matter, I could give you one," Jan said eagerly. "You'd be on his turf, where he's most comfortable. Of course, you'd need to find a way to get close to him. You know, bend over the desk so your heads meet and your fingers accidentally brush against his. From there, everything will work out great."

"I don't like that idea," Maureen muttered, slowly shaking her head. "It's too obvious. Besides, Mr. Lockwood's too intelligent not to see through that ploy."

"George Potter is always taking one thing or another up to Jonas's office. I could volunteer to do it for him.

I'm sure he wouldn't mind," Stephanie said, defending Jan's idea.

"Yes, but from everything I've read, it would be better if you force his hand."

"Force his hand? What do you mean?" Stephanie glanced at Maureen.

"Let him see you with another man."

"But that's already happened, with disastrous results," Jan argued. "Besides, where are we going to come up with another man?"

"My husband's brother is available."

"Ladies, please," Stephanie said, raising both hands to squelch that plan. "I've got to agree with any scheme you come up with, and that one is most definitely a *no*."

"Sympathy always works," Barbara said thoughtfully. "I've read lots of romances where the turning point in the relationship comes when either the hero or the heroine gets sick or is seriously hurt."

For a moment Stephanie actually believed her friends were about to suggest she came down with the mumps or chicken pox just so she could garner Jonas's sympathy.

"I've got a cousin who works for an orthopedic surgeon. He could put a cast on Stephanie's leg so Mr. Lockwood would think she had broken it." Again Barbara glanced around the table, gauging the others' reactions.

Stephanie could just see herself hobbling to and from work for weeks in a plaster cast up to her hip while she carried out a ridiculous charade. After all, she couldn't very well arrive one day later without the cast and announce to everyone that a miracle had occurred.

"No go." She nixed that plan before anyone else

could endorse it and she ended up in a body cast without ever knowing how it happened. "What's wrong with me inviting him over to my apartment for dinner?"

"It's so obvious," Barbara groaned.

"And the rest of your ideas aren't?"

"Actually, something like that just might work," Jan said thoughtfully, chewing on the nail of her index finger. "It's not brilliant, but it has possibilities."

"There's only one problem," Stephanie informed her friends, remembering the charred pot roast from the night before. "I'm not much of a cook."

"That's not a problem. You could hire a chef to come in. Mr. Lockwood would never have to know."

"Isn't that a bit expensive?" Stephanie could visualize the balance in her checkbook rapidly reaching the point of no return.

"It's worth a try." Barbara rapidly discounted Stephanie's concern.

"What was your idea, Toni?" Everyone had revealed their schemes except the small brunette.

Toni shrugged. "Nothing great—I thought you might 'accidentally on purpose' meet Mr. Lockwood by the elevator sometime. You could strike up a casual conversation and let matters follow their natural course."

"But Steph could end up spending the entire day hanging around the elevator," Barbara said, her voice raised at what she considered an unreasonable plan.

"Not only that," Jan added, "but who's to say that the elevator will be empty? She'd look ridiculous if there were other people aboard."

Stephanie's gaze flew from one intent face to the other. "Actually, I like that idea best."

"What?" Three pairs of shocked eyes shot to Stephanie.

"Well, for heaven's sake! With the rest of your ideas, I'm either going to have to subject myself to Martha Westheimer's scrutiny, date Barbara's brother-in-law, sheath my body in plaster or deplete my checking account to hire a chef to cook for me. Toni's idea is the only one that makes any sense."

"But *you* suggested inviting him to dinner," Jan informed her.

Maureen folded her hands on the table top and studied Stephanie through narrowed eyes. "You know, it suddenly dawned on me that you're not fighting us anymore, Steph."

"No," she said and reached for her coffee, curving her fingers around the cup. She took a drink and when she set it back down, she noted that the others had all fallen silent.

"In fact, if you've noticed, she's even contributing her own ideas." Jan's look was approving.

"Could it be that you've developed feelings for Mr. Lockwood?" Barbara asked.

"It could be that I find the man a challenge."

"It's more than that," Toni said, pointing a finger at Stephanie. "I noticed when you first joined us this morning that there was something different about you."

So it shows, Stephanie mused to herself, a bit irritated.

"What do you feel for Mr. Lockwood?"

"I'm not completely sure yet," she admitted honestly. "He makes me so angry I could shake him."

"But…"

"But then, at other times, he looks at me and we share a smile, and I want to melt on the inside." Stephanie knew her eyes must have revealed her feelings, because the others grew quiet again.

"Could you see yourself married to him?" Maureen asked.

Stephanie didn't need to think twice about that. "Yes." They would argue and disagree and challenge each other—that was a given—but the loving between them would be exquisite.

The unexpected shout of joy that followed her announcement nearly knocked her out of her chair. "Good grief, be quiet," she said, her hand over her heart. "We're a long way from the altar."

"Not nearly as far as you think, honey," Barbara said with a wide, knowing grin. "Not nearly as far as you think."

Stephanie left the cafeteria a couple of minutes later. In spite of everything, she had to struggle not to laugh. Her four romance-minded friends seemed to believe that a couple of dinners—one of which they knew nothing about—and a few stolen kisses in the moonlight practically constituted a proposal of marriage.

When she got back to her desk Stephanie placed her purse in the bottom drawer, sat down and turned on her computer, preparing to type a letter. She paused, her hands poised over the keyboard, trying to analyze her feelings for Jonas. The words on the screen blurred as she remembered his kisses. From the way he'd looked, he'd been as surprised as she was. The minute they'd met, she had disliked the man. He was so dictatorial and high-handed that he infuriated her. He enjoyed baiting her and challenging her. In some ways, Jonas Lockwood was the most difficult man she'd ever known. But at the same time, she suspected that the rewards of his love would be beyond any worldly treasure she could ever hope to accumulate.

At five that evening Stephanie cleared off the top of her desk, preparing to head home to her apartment. It had been so late by the time Jonas finished assembling the bookcase that she hadn't had the energy to fill it with the books that were propped against her bedroom wall. She'd learned as the evening progressed that he was an avid reader, and they'd had a lively discussion on their favorite authors. When he'd left her apartment, it had been close to midnight. She'd thanked him for dinner and his help, and had been mildly disappointed that he hadn't kissed her good-night. Nor did he arrange for another meeting. At the time she had been in such a happy daze that she hadn't thought too much about it. Now she wondered how long it would be before she saw him again. She was a bit discouraged not to have heard from him yet. All day she'd been half expecting him to pop in unannounced and dictate another letter to her. The entire afternoon had felt strangely incomplete, and she realized that she'd been wanting to hear from him since the minute she arrived that morning.

On her way to the elevator, she spotted him talking to Donald Black, head of the accounting department. Her pulse quickened at the virile sight Jonas presented. He was tall and broad-shouldered, and—she freely admitted it—a handsome devil. Her heart swelled at the sight of him, and when his gaze happened to catch hers, she smiled warmly, revealing all the pleasure she felt at seeing him again.

Jonas didn't respond. If anything, he almost looked right through her, as if she were nothing more than a piece of furniture. If any emotion showed on his taut features, it was regret. She swallowed, feeling as if she had a pine cone lodged in her throat.

When he did happen to glance in her direction, she read the warning in his eyes. What happened outside the office was between them, but inside Lockwood Industries she was nothing more than George Potter's executive assistant, and she would do well to remember that.

Humiliated and insulted, she stiffened and looked past him as though he were a stranger, pretending she had neither the time nor the energy to play his infantile games. She thrust her shoulders back in a display of anger and pride, and held them so stiffly that her shoulder blades ached within seconds.

From the minute he had left her the night before, she had been happy and content. Now her spirits plummeted to the bottom floor at breakneck speed and landed with a sickening thud. She turned her gaze to the front of the elevator and refused to look at him another moment.

She heard the two men walking behind her, but she ignored them both.

"Good evening, Miss Coulter," Jonas said in passing.

"Good evening," she responded tightly, her tone professional and crisp.

The elevator arrived, and without another word, Stephanie joined the others in the five o'clock rush. Five minutes later she caught Metro bus #17, which dropped her off a block from her apartment.

Affronted by his attitude, chagrined at how much she had read into the simple evening they'd shared, and upset that she'd allowed Jan and her friends to talk her into believing Jonas Lockwood had a heart, Stephanie quickly changed clothes and decided to weed her miniature herb garden.

She hadn't been at it more than thirty minutes when the doorbell chimed. Glaring at her front door, she continued pulling up the weeds in the small redwood planters, then stared down at her garden gloves and realized she'd uprooted more basil than weeds.

She didn't need to answer the door to know it was Jonas who stood on the other side. When the doorbell rang sharply a second time, she impatiently set her trowel aside and stood up.

She muttered under her breath as she marched across the living room floor, and swore that if he commented on her purple tennis shoes one more time she would slam the door in his face. She jerked off a dirt-covered glove and pulled open the door.

"Hello, Stephanie."

"Mr. Lockwood," she responded tautly. "What an unpleasant surprise."

"May I come in?"

"No." She avoided his eyes. It took all her willpower not to close the door and be done with him. But she'd decided to play out this little charade. She might not come from a rich, powerful family like his, but she didn't lack pride. "As you can see, I'm busy," she finished.

"This will only take a minute."

"I'm surprised you're lowering yourself to come here," she said waspishly. "Your message this afternoon came through crystal clear."

"I'd like to explain that." Disregarding her unfriendly welcome and her unwillingness to allow him into her apartment, he stalked past her and into the living room.

"It seems I have no say in the matter. All right, since you're so keen to explain yourself, do so and then kindly leave."

"I honestly *would* like to explain—"

"Go ahead," she said. "But let me assure you, it isn't necessary."

Jonas leaned heavily on his cane as he walked to the center of the room. Stephanie stubbornly remained at the front door. She'd closed it but stood ready to yank it open the minute he finished.

He turned to face her and placed both hands on the curve of the polished oak cane, using it for support.

When long moments passed without him saying anything, she spoke into the heavy silence. "I realize the name Coulter may not cause a banker's heart to flutter, but it's a good name. My father's proud of it, and so am I."

"Stephanie, you misunderstood my intentions."

"I sincerely doubt that." Her voice trembled with the strength of her emotion. "I understood you perfectly."

His eyes were blue and probing as they swept her tightly controlled features. She wondered if a splattering of mud was smeared across her cheek but wouldn't give him the satisfaction of running her fingers over her face to find out. No doubt he would view that as a sign of weakness. She *was* weak, she realized, but only when he held her and kissed her, and she wouldn't allow that now.

"It wouldn't matter to me if your name was Getty or Buffet, or Gates, for that matter. Don't you understand that?"

"Obviously not," she returned stiffly. "You put me in my place this evening—and you did a good job of it, I might add. I'm a lowly assistant, and you're the big, mighty boss, and I shouldn't confuse the two. Since I'm not the mature woman you prefer, I would do well to bow low whenever your shadow passes near me. Isn't that what you meant to say?"

"No. I should have known you'd be unreasonable."

"Me? Unreasonable? That's a laugh. I've worked for Mr. Potter for nearly two years, and we've never exchanged a cross word. Two seconds in your company and I'm so angry I can hardly think."

"Would you stop with this lowly assistant bit? I wouldn't care if you were the first vice president," he said. "Anything that's between you and me has to stay out of the office!"

"Of course it does," she simpered. "It would do your reputation considerable harm if anyone knew you'd lowered yourself to actually date an employee."

"It's not me I'm thinking about."

"You could have fooled me."

"Stephanie, if you'd get off your high horse a minute, you'd see that it's good business. The fact is, I shouldn't even be seeing you now. I'm supposed to be at a meeting."

She jerked open the door. "Don't let me stop you." She recognized the flash of anger in his eyes and experienced a small sense of triumph.

He ran a hand over his face, wiping his expression clean as he fought for control of his considerable temper. "Don't you understand that I'm doing this for your own protection?"

"Forgive me for being dense, but quite frankly, I don't."

He continued as though she hadn't spoken. "Some no-good busybody is going to drag your name through the mud the minute they learn we're seeing each other. The next thing either of us knows, you'll be the subject of jealous, malicious gossip. You won't be able to walk into a room without people whispering your name."

Stephanie swallowed convulsively. "I hadn't thought of...that." Her friends were supportive, but they were only a tiny fraction of the staff at Lockwood Industries.

"A thousand times I told myself that seeing you would only lead to trouble." A dark, brooding look clouded his eyes. "Even now, I'm not convinced it's right for either of us."

She had to swallow down the words to argue with him, because being with him felt incredibly right to her.

"If you're seeking my apology for what happened earlier," he said in a gruff, low-pitched voice, "then you have it. It has never been my intention to offend you."

She swallowed tightly, and nodded, embarrassed. "*I* owe *you* an apology, as well." With her hands clasped in front of her, she took a step toward him. "You're right about the office, Jonas, only I was too much of an idiot to see it."

He smiled one of those rare, rich smiles of his, a smile that she was convinced could melt stone. "I'm pleased we cleared up this misunderstanding," he said, and glanced at his watch, frowning. "Now I really must be going."

"Thank you for coming." Knowing that he'd found it important to explain meant a great deal to her.

He walked to the door, then suddenly turned to her. "Do you sail?"

"Sure." She'd never been on a sailboat in her life. "At least, I think I can, given the chance."

"How about this weekend?"

"I'd like that very much."

"I'll call you later," he said on his way out the door.

Then he muttered something about her not making bankers' hearts flutter but doing a mighty fine job with his own.

She closed the door after him and leaned against it, grinning with a warmth that beamed all the way from her heart.

Eight

A stiff breeze billowed the huge spinnaker, and the thirty-foot sailboat heeled sharply, shaving the water-line with a razor-sharp cut. Stephanie threw back her head and laughed into the wind. The pins holding her hair had long ago been discarded, and her blond tresses now unfurled behind her like a flag, waving in the crisp air. "Oh, Jonas, I love this."

His answering smile was warm. "Somehow I knew you'd be a natural on the water."

"This is so much fun." She crossed her arms over her breasts as though to hug the sense of exhilaration she felt.

"You've really never sailed before?"

"Never." She noted the way he steered the boat from the helm, his movements confident, sure. "Can I do that?"

"If you'd like."

She joined him and sat down at his side. "Okay, tell me what to do."

"Just head her into the wind."

"Okay." She placed both hands on the long narrow

handle that controlled the rudder and watched as the boat turned sharply. Almost immediately the sails went slack, but one guiding touch from Jonas and they filled with wind again.

"This isn't as easy as it looks," she complained with a smile. The day was marvelous. There wasn't any other way to describe it.

Jonas had arrived at her apartment early that morning, bringing freshly squeezed orange juice, croissants still warm from the oven and two large cups of steaming coffee. She had always been a morning person, and apparently he was, as well.

She had prepared her own surprise by packing them a picnic lunch. Included in her basket were two small loaves of French bread, a bottle of white wine, a variety of cheeses and some fresh strawberries that had cost her more than she cared to think about. But one look at the plump, juicy fruit and she couldn't resist.

The journey into Duluth was pleasant, as Jonas spoke of his family and their home on Lake Superior. His mother lived there now, and he said they would be joining her later that afternoon.

"You're quiet all of a sudden," Jonas mentioned as he reached over to correct her steering once again. "Is anything troubling you?"

"How could anything possibly be wrong on a glorious day like this one?"

"You were frowning."

"I was?" Stephanie glanced out over the choppy water. There wasn't another boat in sight. It was as though she and Jonas alone faced the mighty power of this astonishing lake. "I was thinking about meeting your mother. I guess I'm nervous."

"Why?"

"Jonas, look at me. I could be confused with a fugitive from justice in these old jeans. I only wish you'd said something earlier, so I could have brought a change of clothes along."

"Mother won't care."

Perhaps not, Stephanie mused, but *she* certainly did. If she was going to come face-to-face with Jonas's mother, she would have preferred to do it when she looked her best. Not now, with her hair in tangles and knots from the wind, and her face free of makeup and pink from a day in the sun. On the other hand, Mrs. Lockwood would be seeing her at her worst and would no doubt be pleasantly surprised if she met her again later. Her lazy smile grew and grew, and she glanced at Jonas.

His look was thoughtful. "Stephanie, I don't want you to fret about meeting my family."

"She must be an amazing woman."

"As a matter of fact she is, but you say that as if you know her, and that isn't possible."

Stephanie momentarily scanned the swirling green water in an effort to avoid meeting his intense gaze. "You're right. I could pass her on the street and not know who she is, but I'm sure she's a special person." The woman who'd born and raised Jonas would have to be.

Jonas placed his arm around her shoulder, and she leaned her head back against the solid cushion of his chest. Gently, he kissed the top of her head.

She turned so that her lips touched his throat where his shirt opened. His skin was warm, and she both felt and heard his answering sigh. His large hand was splayed against the back of her head, and he directed her mouth to his. She didn't need any more encouragement, and their mouths met in a gentle brushing of lips. She moved away from the helm and slipped her arms around his neck. He kissed her again, longer this time, much longer, but still he was infinitely gentle, as though he feared hurting her. He finally released her when the sails began to flap in the wind, but he did it with such reluctance that her heart sang.

"Are you hungry?" she asked, more for something to do than from any desire for lunch.

"Yes," he admitted hoarsely, but when she went toward the wicker picnic basket, he caught her hand, delaying her.

She raised questioning eyes to his. "Jonas?"

In a heartbeat, he gently pulled her back to him, his hand slipping around her waist. "It isn't food that tempts me." He kissed her again, his mouth moving on hers with an urgency as old as mankind itself. She threaded her fingers through his hair and held his head fast until she was so weak that she slumped against him.

"Jonas," she breathed

He brought her down so that they were sitting side by side. He put his arms around her and fused his mouth to hers. Again and again he kissed her, tasting, nipping at her lower lip, until she thought she would go mad with wanting him. Her hand crept up his hard chest and closed around the folds of his collar. The kiss was long and thorough. This day with Jonas was the sweetest she had ever known.

With his arms wrapped securely around her shoulders, she swayed with the gentle rocking of the boat, lulled by the peace that surrounded them. He had somehow lowered the sails without her even knowing it. He continued to hold her, staring out over the rolling water. Not for the first time she noticed that his eyes were incredibly blue. As though sensing her scrutiny, he gazed down at her. For a long moment they stared at each other, lost in a world that had been created just for them and for this moment.

Sometime later Jonas reached for the picnic basket. He brought out a plump red strawberry, plucked the stem from the top and fed it to Stephanie. She bit into the pulp, and a thin line of juice ran down her chin. As she moved to wipe it away, his hand stopped hers. He bent his index finger, and with his knuckle rubbed the red juice aside. Then, very slowly, as though he couldn't resist, he lowered his mouth to hers. Their lips met and clung. His grip tightened as his tongue sought and found hers. When he lifted his mouth from her lips, he smiled gently. Moisture pooled in her eyes, and a tear slipped from the corner of her eye and rolled down her cheek.

A puzzled frown furrowed his brow. "You're crying."

"I know."

"Did I hurt you?"

"No."

"Then why?"

She turned her head into his shoulder, convinced he would laugh once he knew.

"Stephanie?"

"It was so beautiful. I always cry when I'm this happy." Feeling foolish, she rubbed her hands against her eyes. "It's a family curse. My mother cries every Christmas."

Jonas reached for the wine, opened it and poured them each a glass.

"Alcohol won't help," she said, sniffling, but she didn't refuse the glass Jonas offered her.

"Are there any other family curses I should know about?"

"I have a bit of a temper."

Jonas chuckled. "I've encountered that."

Laughing lightly, she straightened and took her first sip of wine. It felt cool and tasted sweet, reminding her that she was hungry. "Some cheese and bread?" she asked, looking at him.

He leaned forward to reach for it, and as he did, a look of pain shot across his face, widening his eyes. He sat back quickly.

"Jonas?" Concerned, she turned to him. "What is it?"

"It'll pass in a moment."

"What will pass?"

"The pain," he managed, his voice grating, stroking the length of his thigh in an effort to ease the agony. He closed his eyes and turned away from her.

She bent in front of him, nearly frantic. "Tell me what I can do."

"Nothing," he said through clenched teeth. "Go away."

"No," she said. "I won't...I couldn't." Because she didn't know what else to do, she put her hand on his, kneading the knotted flesh that had cramped so viciously. She could feel the muscles relax when the spasm passed.

"What happened? Did I do something?"

"No." He moved away from her, reaching for the ropes, preparing to raise the sails.

"Talk to me, for heaven's sake," she demanded, grabbing his forearm. "Don't close up on me now. I care about you, Jonas. I want to help!"

His hard gaze softened, and he tenderly cupped her cheek. Relieved, she turned her face into his palm and kissed it.

"Did I frighten you?" he asked her softly.

"Only because I didn't know what to do to help you." She sighed, feeling weak and emotionally drained. "Does that happen often?" The thought of him enduring such pain was intolerable.

"It happens often enough to make me appreciate my cane."

In spite of the circumstances, she bowed her head to hide a smile.

"You find that amusing?"

Her head shot up. "No, of course not. It's just that everyone in the office claims they know when your leg is hurting, because you're usually in a foul mood."

"They say that, do they?"

"It's true, isn't it?"

He shrugged. "To be honest, I hadn't given it much thought."

She reached inside the picnic basket for the two loaves of bread. She set them out, along with a plate of cheese, avoiding looking at Jonas as she asked him the question that had been on her mind since Paris. "How'd it happen?"

"My leg?" His gaze sharpened.

"You don't have to tell me if you'd rather not."

He hesitated, and when he finally spoke, she realized that telling her the story was an indication that he trusted her. "It happened several years ago, in a skiing accident. I was on the slopes with a…friend. There isn't much to say. She got in trouble, and when I went to help her, I fell."

"Down the slope?"

"No, off a cliff."

"Oh, Jonas." She felt sick at the thought of him being hurt. She closed her eyes to the mental image of him lying in some snow bank in agony, waiting for help to arrive.

"The doctors say I'm lucky to still have my leg. In the beginning I wished they had amputated it and been done with it. Now I'm more tolerant of the pain. I've learned to live with it." He grew silent, and Stephanie sensed that there was a great deal more to the story that he hadn't revealed, but she accepted what he had told her and didn't press him further.

"Thank you, Jonas," she said softly.

"For what?"

"For bringing me with you today. For relating what must be a difficult story for you to tell. For trusting me."

"No, Stephanie," he whispered, lifting her mouth to his. "Thank you."

Later that day, when Jonas pulled up to the large two-story brick mansion overlooking Lake Superior, Stephanie's breath caught at the sight of his magnificent family home. "Oh, Jonas," she said, awed. "It's beautiful." Imposing, as well, she thought, attempting to subdue her nervousness. Her hand went to her hair, and she ran her fingers through the tangled mass.

"You look fine," he told her.

She lowered her arm and rested her clenched hand in her lap. "Just you wait," she threatened. "I'm going to introduce you to my father. He'll be in mud-spattered coveralls, sitting on top of a tractor. You'll be in a thousand-dollar pin-striped suit, and you'll know what it feels like to be out of your element."

To her amazement, Jonas laughed. He parked the car at the front of the house, or perhaps the back—she couldn't actually tell which—and turned off the engine. "I look forward to meeting your family."

"You do?"

He climbed out of the car and came around to her side, opening her door for her. "One thing, though."

"Yes?"

"Don't introduce me to your mother at Christmas. I have a heck of a time dealing with crying women."

Stephanie got the giggles. They were probably a result of her nervousness, but once she started it was nearly impossible to stop. He laughed with her, and they were still laughing as, with his arm linked around her waist, he led her through the wide double doors of the house.

The minute they were inside her amusement vanished. The marble floor of the entryway had probably cost more than her family's farm in Colville. Marble that was probably imported from Italy. Maybe Greece. A large winding stairway angled off to the right, its polished mahogany balustrade gleaming in the sun.

"Jonas, is that you?" An elegantly dressed woman appeared. She was tall and regal-looking, with twinkling blue eyes that were the exact image of Jonas's. Her hair was completely gray, and she wore it in a neatly coiled French roll. She held her hands out to her son. He claimed them with his own and kissed her on the cheek.

"Mother."

They parted, and his mother paused to greet Stephanie. If she disapproved of Stephanie's attire, it wasn't revealed in the warmth of her smile. "You must be Stephanie."

For one crazy second Stephanie had the urge to curtsy. "Hello, Mrs. Lockwood." Even her voice sounded awed and a bit unnatural.

"Please call me Elizabeth."

"Thank you, I will."

"I can see you've had a full day on the lake." Elizabeth glanced at her son.

"It was marvelous," Stephanie confirmed.

"I hope you're hungry. Clara's been cooking all day, anticipating your arrival."

Jonas placed his hand along the back of Stephanie's neck and directed her into the largest room she had ever seen in a private home.

"Who's Clara?" she asked under her breath.

"The cook," he whispered. When his mother turned her back, he kissed Stephanie's cheek.

"Jonas," she hissed. "Don't do that!"

"Did you say something, Stephanie?" Elizabeth turned around questioningly.

"Actually...no," she stuttered, glowering hotly at Jonas, who coughed to disguise a laugh. "I didn't say anything."

"Would either of you care for a glass of wine before dinner?" Elizabeth asked, taking a seat on an elegant velvet sofa.

Stephanie claimed the matching chair across from her, and Jonas stood behind Stephanie.

"That would be fine, Mother," he said, answering for them both. "Would you like me to serve as bartender?"

"Please." Elizabeth folded her hands on her lap. "Jonas has spoken highly of you, Stephanie."

"He...has?" she sputtered.

"Yes. Is there something unusual about that?"

Jonas delivered a glass of wine to his mother before bringing Stephanie hers. He sat beside her on the arm of the chair and looped his arm around her shoulder.

"Clara will never forgive you if you don't say hello, Son," Elizabeth informed him. "While you do that, I'll show Stephanie my garden. It's lovely this time of year."

"I'd like that," Stephanie said, standing. She continued to hold her wine, although she had no intention of drinking it. All she needed was to get tipsy in front of Jonas's mother.

"I'll be back in a minute," he whispered as he left the room.

A small, awkward silence followed. Stephanie looked down at her soiled jeans and cringed inwardly. "I feel I should apologize for my attire," she began, following Jonas's mother out through French doors that led to a lush green garden. Roses were in bloom, and their sweet fragrance filled the air.

"Nonsense," Elizabeth countered. "You've been sailing. I didn't expect you to arrive in an evening gown."

"But I don't imagine you expected jeans and purple tennis shoes, either."

Elizabeth laughed; the sound was light and musical. "I believe I'm going to grow fond of you."

"I hope so." Stephanie studied her wine.

"Forgive me for being so blunt, but are you in love with my son?"

Stephanie raised her eyes to Jonas's mother's and nodded. "Yes."

Elizabeth placed her hand over her heart and sighed expressively. "I am so relieved to hear you say that."

"You are? Why?"

"Because *he* loves *you,* child."

Stephanie opened her mouth to argue, but Elizabeth stopped her.

"I don't know if he's admitted it to himself yet, but he will soon. A few minutes ago, when you came into the house, I heard Jonas laugh. It's been years since I've heard the sound of my son's laughter. Thank you for that."

"Really, I didn't do anything...I—"

"Please forgive me for interrupting, but we haven't much time."

Stephanie's heart shot to her throat. "Yes?"

"You must be patient with my son. He's been hurt, terribly hurt, and he is greatly in need of a woman's love. He probably hasn't told you about Gretchen. He loved her deeply, far more than the wretched woman deserved. She left him after the accident. She told him that she couldn't live with a cripple, even though it was she who had caused the accident with her carelessness."

Jonas's mother didn't need to say a word more for Stephanie to hate the fickle, faceless woman.

"That was nearly ten years ago, and he hasn't brought another woman to meet me until today. Knowing my son the way I do, I'm sure he'll battle what he feels for you. He's reluctant to trust again, so you must be patient and," she added, gently touching Stephanie's hand, "very strong. He deserves your love, and although he may be stubborn now and again, believe me, the woman my son loves will be the happiest woman alive. When Jonas loves again, I promise you it will be with all his heart and his soul."

Stephanie felt moisture gather in her eyes. "I don't know if I deserve someone as good as Jonas."

"Perhaps not," Elizabeth Lockwood said, her soft voice removing any harshness from her words. "But *he* deserves *you*." She glanced over her shoulder. "He's coming now, so smile, and please don't say anything about our conversation."

"I won't," Stephanie promised, blinking back tears.

"There you are," Jonas said as he joined his mother and Stephanie. "Did mother let you in on any family secrets?"

"Several, as a matter of fact," Elizabeth said with a small laugh.

"Clara wants me to tell you that dinner is ready any time you are."

"Wonderful," Elizabeth replied with a warm smile.

"She cooked my favorite dessert," Jonas said, sharing a secret smile with Stephanie. "Strawberry shortcake."

Stephanie could feel the heated color seep up her neck, invading her cheeks.

"I don't recall you being particularly fond of strawberries," Elizabeth commented as she led the way into the dining room.

"It's a recent addiction, Mother," Jonas said, reaching for Stephanie's hand and linking her fingers with his. He raised her knuckles to his mouth and lightly kissed them.

The meal was one Stephanie would long remember, but not because of the food, though it could have been served in a four-star restaurant. Jonas was a different person, chatting, joking, teasing. He insisted that Clara join them for coffee so Stephanie could meet her. Although Stephanie liked the rotund woman instantly, she could feel the older woman's distrust. But by the end of the evening all that had changed, and Stephanie knew she could count Clara as a friend.

When it came time to leave, Elizabeth hugged Stephanie and whispered softly in her ear, "Thank you, my dear, for giving me back my son. Remember what I said. Be patient."

"No. Thank *you*," Stephanie whispered back. They joined hands, and Stephanie nodded once. "I'll remember."

It was dark by the time they left Duluth, and Stephanie was physically drained from the long day. She yawned once and tried to disguise it. "I like your mother, Jonas."

"She seemed to be quite taken with you, too."

They talked a bit more, and she began to drop off, giving way to her fatigue. He woke her when they reached the outskirts of Minneapolis.

"I'm sorry to be such terrible company," she said, yawning.

"You're anything but," he said, contradicting her. He eased to a stop in front of her apartment building and parked the car, but he kept the engine running.

"Do you want to come in for coffee?" she asked.

"No, you're exhausted, and I have some work that I need to look over."

"Jonas, don't tell me you're going to work on a Saturday night." She glanced at her wristwatch, shocked to find that it was after eleven.

He chuckled, and leaned over to press his mouth lightly to hers. "No, but it was the best excuse I could come up with to refuse your invitation."

"Good, I was worried there for a minute. You work

too hard." She yearned to tell him how much the day had meant to her, how much she'd enjoyed the time on the sailboat, and meeting his mother and Clara. But finding the right words was impossible. "Thank you for everything," she said when he helped her out of the car. "I can't remember a day I've enjoyed more."

"Me, either," he murmured, his gaze holding hers.

"We've got it!" Jan announced Monday morning, as she, Maureen, Toni and Barbara circled Stephanie's desk like warriors surrounding a wagon train.

"Got what?" Stephanie looked up blankly. She'd only arrived at the office a few minutes earlier and hadn't even turned on her computer. "What are you talking about?"

"Your next move with Mr. Lockwood."

"Oh, that," she returned with a sigh. She hadn't told her friends about the weekend sailing jaunt, but then she'd been keeping quite a few secrets from them lately.

"We've got it all worked out."

"Answer me this first," Stephanie said. "Will I need to wear a cast? Date someone's brother-in-law? Hire a French chef?"

"No."

"It's working out great. We've got a contact in the janitorial department."

"A what?"

"All you have to do," Maureen explained excitedly, "is get in the elevator alone with Mr. Lockwood."

"Yes?" Stephanie could feel the enthusiasm coming from her coworkers in waves. "What will that do?"

"That's where Mike from maintenance comes into the picture," Toni explained patiently.

"He'll flip the switch, and the two of you will be trapped alone together for hours."

"Isn't that a marvelous idea?" Barbara said.

"It works in all the best romances."

"It's a sure thing."

"You're game, aren't you, Steph?"

Nine

"No, I'm not game for your crazy schemes," Stephanie informed her friends primly. It wasn't that she objected to being alone with Jonas for hours on end—in fact, she would relish that—but to plot their meeting this way went against everything she hoped for in their relationship.

Jan, Maureen, Toni and Barbara exchanged an incredulous look.

"But it's perfect."

"Jonas and I don't need it," Stephanie said, knowing that the best way to appease her friends was with the truth.

"What do you mean, you don't need it?" Jan asked, her eyes narrowing with suspicion.

"You been holding out on us, girl?" Maureen barked, her hand on her hip.

"I do believe she has been," Barbara said before Stephanie had a chance to answer.

"Let's just say this," Stephanie said with a conspiratorial smile. "The romantic relationship between Mr. Lockwood and me is developing nicely."

"How nicely?" Jan wanted to know. "And put it into terms we understand."

"Like on a scale of one to ten," Barbara added.

"What's a ten?" Stephanie glanced up at her friends, uncertain.

"If you need to ask, we're in trouble."

"Right." Hot color blossomed in Stephanie's cheeks.

"If he phoned once or twice and showed up at your apartment—that's a four, a low four."

"But if you shared a couple of romantic evenings on the town, I'd call that a six."

"I'd say meeting his family is an eight," Toni murmured thoughtfully, her index finger pressed against her cheek. "Maybe a nine."

The four romantics paused expectantly, waiting for Stephanie to locate her relationship with Jonas on their makeshift scale. "Well?" Jan coaxed.

"An eight, then, maybe a nine," she admitted softly, waiting for her friends to break into shouts and cheers. Instead, she was greeted with a shocked, dubious silence.

"You're not teasing, are you?" Barbara murmured. "You really aren't joking?"

"No. Jonas introduced me to his mother this weekend. She's a wonderful woman."

"It's going to work," Maureen whispered in awe, her face revealing her surprise. "It's really going to work!"

"Speaking of work…" Stephanie said reluctantly, glancing at her watch. She was relieved not to be subjected to an endless list of questions from her coworkers, but she was so grateful to her romance-loving friends that she wanted them to share some of her happiness.

As though in a daze, Jan, Maureen, Toni and Barbara turned and walked away as if in a trance.

"Do you think the janitor will give us a refund?" Barbara asked no one in particular as they moved out the door.

"Who cares?" came the reply from the others.

Stephanie's boss, George Potter, arrived at the office a couple of minutes later, his first day back from Seattle. They exchanged a few pleasantries, and he handed her some notes from his briefcase. "If you get the chance, could you take these receipts to Donald Black?"

He said the name stiffly; Stephanie knew from experience that there was little love lost between the two men. She couldn't imagine her amiable boss disliking anyone, so she was quite certain he had a good reason for his animosity.

"I'll do it as soon as I finish this report," she said with a welcoming smile. There was so much to be happy about that she felt like humming love songs. She wondered briefly how Jonas's day was going, her thoughts wandering naturally to the man who just happened to be in sole possession of her heart.

The morning whizzed past. Stephanie was so close to finishing the report that she skipped her midmorning coffee break. Five minutes later, with the floor all but deserted and Mr. Potter in a meeting, she walked down the hallway to give the receipts to Donald Black.

"Good morning, Mr. Black," she said, knocking politely on his open door. "Mr. Potter asked me to bring these over."

"Put them over there," he said, indicating a table on the other side of the room.

Stephanie placed the envelope where he'd requested

and turned to leave, but the middle-aged, potbellied man stood and blocked her way.

"You and Jonas Lockwood seem to be seeing a great deal of each other."

A plethora of possible answers crowded her mind. Jonas had mentioned that he would prefer to keep their personal relationship out of the office, but she wasn't in the habit of lying. Nor was it her custom to discuss her personal relationships with a stranger.

"We're…friends," she said, since apparently Jonas himself had mentioned her to the other man.

"I see." With slow, deliberate movements, Mr. Black placed his pencil on the edge of his desk. "How willing are you to be…friends with other Lockwood employees?"

She stiffened at the insulting way he uttered the word *friends*. "I'm not sure I understand the question."

"I'm quite certain you do."

She didn't know what game this middle-aged Don Juan was playing, but she had no intention of remaining in his office. "If you'll excuse me."

"As a matter of fact, I won't. We're having an important discussion here, and I'd consider it a desertion of your duties to this company and to me personally if you left."

She wasn't much into office gossip, but she was starting to understand why George Potter had no respect for Donald Black. As the head of the accounting department, Black had been through three assistants in the two years Stephanie had been employed by Lockwood Industries. From her own dismal experience with her former employers, she could guess the reason why he had trouble keeping a decent employees.

"I'll desert my duties, then," she replied flippantly. She turned to go, but didn't make it to the door. He reached out and gripped her shoulder, spinning her around. She was so shocked that he would dare to touch her that she was momentarily speechless.

"Everyone in the company knows you're being generous with Lockwood. All I want is a share in the goods."

Still breathless with shock, she slapped his hand aside. "You sicken me."

"Give me time, honey, I promise to improve."

"I sincerely doubt that."

He drew her closer, obviously intent on kissing her, but she managed to evade him. With everything that was in her, she pushed against his chest with both hands and was astonished at the strength of the man.

Her eye happened to catch the clock, and she realized it would be another five minutes before anyone returned to the department. Crying out would do no good, since there wasn't anyone there to answer her plea for help.

"All I want is a little kiss," Mr. Black said coaxingly. "Just give me that and I'll let you go."

"I'd rather vomit!" she cried, kicking at him and missing.

"You stupid—"

"Let her go."

The quietly spoken words evidenced such controlled anger that both Stephanie and her attacker froze. Black dropped his arms and released her.

With a strangled sob she turned aside and braced her hands against the edge of the desk, weak with relief. Her neatly coiled hair had fallen free of its restraining pins and hung in loose tendrils around her flushed face.

It took her several deep breaths to regain her strength. She didn't know how or why Jonas was there, but she had never been so glad to see anyone.

"Clear out your desk, Black." The emotionless, frigid control in Jonas's voice sent a chill up her spine. She'd never heard a man sound more angry or more dangerous. Acid dripped from each syllable. An unspoken challenge hung over the room, almost as if Jonas was hoping for a physical confrontation.

"Hey, Jonas, you got the wrong idea here. Your lady friend came on to me." Black raised both hands in an emotional plea of innocence.

Stephanie spun around, her eyes spitting fire.

"Is that true?" Jonas asked evenly.

"No!" she shouted, indignant and furious. "He grabbed me—"

"You didn't hear her crying out, did you?" Black shot back, interrupting Stephanie. "I swear, man, I'm not the kind of guy who has to force women. They come to me."

"I said clear out your desk." Jonas pointed the tip of his cane at the far door. "A check will be mailed to you tomorrow."

Donald Black gave Stephanie a murderous glare as he marched out of the office. "You'll regret this, Lockwood," he muttered on his way past Jonas.

Stephanie could see the coiled alertness drain from Jonas the minute Black was out of the room. "Did he hurt you?"

"No...I'm fine." She closed her eyes. She was too proud to allow a man like Donald Black to reduce her to tears.

Jonas's arm slipped around her, comforting and warm, chasing away the icy, numbing chill that had settled over her. "I'm fine," she whispered fiercely, burying her face in his shoulder. "Really," she insisted as she shuddered against him.

"Let's get out of here." He led her into the hallway and toward the elevator. She didn't recall anything of the ride to the top floor, but when the thick door glided open, Jonas called to Martha Westheimer.

"Bring me a strong cup of coffee, and add plenty of sugar."

"Jonas, really," Stephanie said, her voice wavering slightly. "I'm fine, and I'm certainly not in shock."

He ignored her, leading her into his office and sitting her down in a heavy leather chair. He paced the area directly in front of her until the ever-efficient Martha appeared with the coffee, carefully handing it to Stephanie. The older woman gave her a sympathetic look that puzzled her. She couldn't understand why the other woman would regard her with such compassion, but then she remembered her hair, which was certainly evidence of a sort. She smiled back as Martha quietly left the room, softly closing the door behind her.

"I won't ever have you subjected to that kind of treatment again," Jonas seethed, still battling his rage.

She stared up at him blankly as he paced. He marched like a soldier doing sentry duty, going three or four feet, then swiftly making a sharp about-face. She realized his irritation wasn't directed at her.

"We're getting married," he announced forcefully.

Her immediate response was to take a sip of the syrupy coffee, convinced she'd misunderstood him.

"Well?" he barked.

"Would you mind repeating that? I'm certain I heard you wrong."

"I said we're getting married." He said it louder this time.

She blinked twice. "If I wasn't in shock before, I am now. You can't possibly mean that, Jonas."

"My name will protect you."

"But, Jonas—"

"Will you or won't you be my wife?" he demanded.

"Stop shouting at me!" she cried, jumping to her feet. The coffee nearly sloshed over the edges of the cup, and she set it down before she ended up spilling it all over the front of her dress.

"Anything could have happened down there," he continued. "If I hadn't arrived when I did…" He left the rest to her imagination.

She went still, her gaze studying this man she loved. "Isn't marriage a little drastic?"

"Not in these circumstances." He looked at her as though she were the one being unreasonable.

"Jonas, do you love me?" She asked the question softly, almost fearing his response.

"I'd hardly be willing to make you my wife if I didn't."

"I see."

He hesitated, looking uneasy. "How do you feel about me?"

"Oh, Jonas, do you really need to ask?" Her gaze softened, and her heart melted at the pride and doubt she read in his hard expression. He was more vulnerable now than at any time since she'd begun working for him. "I've been in love with you from the moment we stood in front of the fountain in Paris—only it took me a while to realize it."

His eyes looked deeply into hers, and when he spoke,

the burning anger had been replaced by tenderness. "Stephanie, I love you. I never expected to fall so hard, and certainly not for a woman who is so proud and forthright. But it's happened, and I'll thank God every day of my life if you'll agree to marry me."

"Oh, Jonas." She battled back the tidal wave of emotion that threatened to engulf her. Then she sniffled and turned around, desperately seeking a tissue.

He handed her one and paused to cup her face in his hands, smiling at her gently, lovingly. "We're going to have a wonderful life together," he said as he lowered his mouth to hers. His kiss was tender and sweet. The wonder of being in his arms, knowing he loved her, made her knees grow weak.

She locked her arms around his neck as his mouth meandered over her lips to her ear. "You're a crazy woman."

"Crazy about you," she admitted, loving the feel of him rubbing against her, knowing that their lovemaking would be exquisite.

"A man attacks you and you're a fireball. I ask you to marry me, and you burst into tears."

"I'm happy."

"You will, won't you?"

"Marry you? Oh, Jonas, yes. A thousand times yes."

"Do you want children?"

"A dozen, at least," she said with a happy laugh. Fresh tears misted her eyes at the thought of their raising a family together.

"A dozen?" He cocked his brows and grinned sheepishly. "I'm willing, but you may change your mind after three or four." Still holding her, he flipped the switch to the intercom. "Miss Westheimer?"

"Yes," came the tinny-sounding reply.

"Contact Mr. Potter and tell him that Miss Coulter won't be in for the remainder of the day."

"Jonas," Stephanie whispered. "I told you, Black didn't hurt me. I'm fine, really."

He ignored her, but his grip on her shoulder tightened. "And cancel my appointments for today, as well."

"Yes, of course," Martha said, but the reluctance in her voice was evident even to Stephanie.

"Is that a problem, Miss Westheimer?"

"Adam Holmes is scheduled for four-thirty, and he'll be leaving town this evening."

Jonas closed his eyes and sighed with frustration. "All right, I'll make a point of being back before four-thirty, then."

When he'd finished speaking, he released the switch and turned Stephanie into his arms. "We have some shopping to do."

"Shopping?" For some reason her mind flashed to the grocery store. She hadn't eaten breakfast and had hoped to pick up something on her coffee break, but she'd been so involved working on the report for Mr. Potter that her plan had fallen by the wayside.

"Shopping for a ring. A diamond, preferably, and so large anyone looking at it will know how special you are and how much I love you."

"Jonas," she said slowly, measuring her words carefully, "a plain gold band would do as long as I'm marrying you."

"I can afford a whole lot more, and I have every intention of indulging you from this minute to the end of our lives."

She swallowed her objections. She loved Jonas, and

not for the material wealth he could give her. She remembered Elizabeth Lockwood's words. His mother had told her that when Jonas admitted that he loved her, he would make her the happiest woman alive. For now he equated bringing her joy with adorning her with riches. And diamonds *were* wonderful, but her happiness came from being loved by Jonas and nothing more. It wouldn't matter to her if he made sandwiches at the corner deli; she loved the man. In time he would learn that her happiness was linked to his. He was all she would ever need to be content and whole.

His look grew sober and thoughtful. "What do you think about making Potter a vice president?"

Stephanie was both stunned and thrilled. She was surprised and complimented that he had asked her opinion. "George Potter is a wonderful choice."

"Then consider it done," Jonas said with a decisive nod. "Now that I'm going to be a married man, I don't want to spend nearly so much time at the office. Not when I have more important matters to concern myself with."

"Right," she said with a wide grin, thinking of all the years they would have to build a life together. She could see them thirty-five years from now, teaching their grandchildren to sail. "Jonas," she said suddenly, remembering her own happy childhood. "I want you to meet my parents and my sisters."

"We can fly out next week," he answered matter-of-factly.

"When do you want to have the wedding?" she asked. He was moving so fast he was making her head spin.

"Is next month too soon?"

"Oh, Jonas," she said, wrapping her arms around

his neck and hugging him fiercely. "I wonder if it will be soon enough."

From that point the afternoon took on the feel of a circus ride. Their first stop was the jewelers, where Jonas bought a lovely diamond solitaire. When he slipped it on her finger, she felt emotion tighten her chest. She bit into her lower lip to keep her feelings at bay, not wanting to embarrass either of them with a display of tears. From the jewelers, Jonas drove to an exclusive French restaurant in memory of their trip to Paris. They dined on veal, sipped champagne and shared secret glances with eyes full of love.

At four, he glanced irritably at his watch. "I may be tied up with Holmes for several hours, and then I've got a dinner engagement."

"Not with another woman, I hope," she teased.

He looked startled for a moment. "There will never be another woman for me, Stephanie. Never."

"Jonas, I was only joking."

"You need never doubt me on this. All my life I've been intensely loyal. I'm sure my mother can give you several examples from my boyhood, if you want to hear them."

"Jonas, please, I didn't mean to imply…"

"I know, love." He paused to caress the side of her face tenderly. "I knew I was falling in love with you, too, you know—perhaps even as early as Paris—but I fought it. I thought I was in love once before, and I was thoroughly disgusted with myself, given how things turned out. But this morning, when I saw Black pawing at you—I've never experienced such overwhelming rage. I knew in that moment that the feelings I hold for you could be nothing less than love."

She found his hand and squeezed it gently.

His blue eyes darkened by several shades, and she realized that had they been anywhere other than a restaurant, he would have taken her in his arms and kissed her until she begged him to stop.

From the restaurant they drove back to the office. She was about to burst with happiness, and if she didn't share it with Jan and the others soon, she was convinced she would start screaming that Jonas Lockwood loved her from the top floor for all of Minneapolis to hear.

Her first stop after they parted at the elevator was Human Resources. Jan looked up from her desk and blinked.

"Hey, where were you at lunchtime? I have a feeling you were trying to avoid questions. You can't do this to us, Steph. We're all dying to find out what's happening."

"I wasn't avoiding anyone."

Jan looked at her more intently. "You've got that saucy grin again. Would you care to tell me the reason you look like a contented cat with feathers in his mouth?"

In response, Stephanie held out her left hand. The large diamond solitaire sparkled in the artificial light.

Jan gasped, and her eyes shot to Stephanie's. "Mr. Lockwood?"

"Who else would it be?"

Jan's hand flew to her breast. "I think I'm going into cardiac arrest. You did it! You actually did it!" Even as she spoke, she was reaching for the phone.

"Tell the others to meet us at that place you took me to that night. The drinks are on me this time," Stephanie said happily. "I owe all of you at least that."

An hour later the five of them were gathered around

a table, sipping wine and munching on an assortment of appetizers,.

"How did you get him to propose?" Barbara wanted to know.

"I didn't do anything. I was more surprised than any of you."

Jan refilled Stephanie's glass, and they all raised their drinks in a silent salute to their illustrious boss.

"To years and years of happiness," Maureen said.

"And romance," Stephanie added, a believer now. She recalled the first time she'd met with her coworkers and how they'd claimed to have recognized her as the perfect match for Jonas. At the time she had been shocked, even appalled. She wouldn't have given the man a free bus ticket. Now, at the very mention of his name her knees turned to butter, she was so much in love with him. Truly head over heels in love, for the first time in her life.

"Who guessed today?" Toni asked.

"No one," Jan answered.

"Today? What are you talking about?" Stephanie glanced around the table at her friends. True, they'd all had their share of wine—and she'd had a bit more than her share, since she'd also had champagne at lunch with Jonas. But until this moment, everything her friends said had made perfect sense.

"Have you decided on a date for the wedding yet?"

Stephanie noticed how intense their faces became as they awaited her reply. "I'm not answering your question until you answer mine," she said, crossing her arms stubbornly. "What's all this about guessing the day?"

"The marriage pool."

"The what?" Stephanie cried.

"You know, like a football pool, only we had a bet going on when Lockwood was going to pop the question."

Stephanie took another swallow of her wine. "I can't believe I'm hearing this."

"A lot of people bet that you wouldn't be able to carry this off. They lost out big time." Jan and Maureen slapped hands high above the table.

"Money?"

"Three hundred dollars is riding on your wedding date."

Stephanie placed her elbows on the table and cradled her head in her hands. "So that's how Black heard about me and Jonas," she mumbled under her breath.

"Say, do you know what happened to him today?" Jan asked.

"How would I know?" Stephanie didn't look her friend in the eye. She hoped that by asking the question she could avoid lying outright.

"I got a call from Old Stone Face shortly after I returned from break this morning. She told me that Donald Black had been terminated, and to arrange for his check to be mailed to him at his home."

"How unusual," Stephanie commented, struggling not to reveal any of her involvement with the situation.

"I don't know anyone who's sorry to see him go," Maureen added. "He was a real—"

"We know what he was," Toni inserted quickly.

"So what else has been going on today?" Stephanie tried to steer the conversation away from the unpleasant subject of Donald Black.

"You mean other than you and Mr. Lockwood getting

engaged, and Donald Black biting the dust? I'd say that was enough to make it one crazy Monday."

"Can you imagine what Tuesday's going to be like?" Maureen asked.

From there the five of them went to dinner at a Mexican restaurant, and by the time Stephanie got home it was close to nine o'clock. She hoped Jonas hadn't tried to get in touch with her and felt a little guilty for staying out so late. As it was, her head was swimming, so she took a quick shower and hurried to bed.

The following morning she was at her desk bright and early, hoping Jonas would stop in on his way up to his floor. She didn't know how she was going to be able to work when all she could think about was how much she loved him and how eager she was to share his life.

Before George Potter arrived, Stephanie received a call from Jan. "Can you come to my office?"

"Sure, what's up? You don't sound right."

"Just get here."

Stephanie couldn't think of a reason why her friend should sound so upset, and she hurried to her office. She took one look at Jan's red eyes and grew worried. Her friend reached for a tissue and loudly blew her nose.

"What's wrong?" Stephanie asked, taking a chair. She'd never seen Jan cry.

"Mr. Lockwood contacted me first thing this morning."

"Jonas?"

"You've been terminated."

Alarm filled Stephanie for an instant, but then she sighed and offered Jan a reassuring grin. "Of course I have. Jonas and I are getting married. I can't very well continue to work here." They hadn't talked about it specifically, but she was sure that was it.

"I don't think so," Jan said. She reached for another tissue, blinking back fresh tears.

"You're not making any sense. What did he say?"

"He said…" Jan paused to wipe her eyes. "He said to mail you your check just the way I was instructed to do with Mr. Black, and…and he asked that you give me the engagement ring. He doesn't want you on Lockwood property again. He was clear as glass on that subject."

Stephanie felt as though someone had kicked her in the stomach. For a moment she couldn't breathe. Her heart constricted with an intolerable pain.

"Steph, did you hear me?"

She nodded numbly. "Why?" The word came from deep within her throat, low and guttural.

"He…he didn't say, but he was serious, Steph. Very serious. I've never heard him more angry. You'd better give me the ring."

Ten

Stephanie's right hand covered the large diamond engagement ring protectively. "I don't understand. That doesn't make any sense."

"He was very precise when he contacted me."

Pacing the carpet in front of Jan's desk, Stephanie folded her arms around her waist and pondered her friend's words. "Call Barbara, Toni and Maureen, and ask them to get here right away."

"What?"

"Just do it," Stephanie snapped, impatient now. "And tell them to hurry."

Momentarily dumbfounded, Jan hesitated, then reached for the phone. A few minutes later their co-workers rushed into the office.

"What is it?" Maureen, the first to arrive, asked breathlessly.

Toni followed on her heels. "Hey, what's so important?"

Barbara came in last, paused, glanced around and said, "All right, I'm here, what's the big deal?"

Jan gestured toward Stephanie. "You called them here, you explain."

"Apparently," Stephanie began, swallowing past the thickening in her throat, "Jonas wants to call off the engagement."

"What?" All three newcomers cried out simultaneously in disbelief.

Barbara recovered first. "What happened?"

"I…don't know," Stephanie admitted honestly, her stomach churning as she considered the incredible situation. "I arrived at the office this morning, and Jan contacted me. She told me I had been terminated by Lockwood Industries, and I was to return the engagement ring to her."

Barbara, Toni and Maureen turned accusing eyes on Jan.

"Hey," Jan said. "It wasn't *my* fault. I'm as shocked as the rest of you."

Stephanie twisted the diamond around and around on her finger, almost believing that she would prefer to lose the appendage than surrender the ring that had been a token of Jonas's love. "You four are the self-proclaimed experts on romance. You're the ones who convinced me that Jonas and I were meant for each other. I need your advice now more than ever." Stephanie spoke quietly, doing her best to keep the emotion from her voice. "What can I do now?"

"Did he give any reason?"

"None," Jan answered. "But he was so angry…worse than I can ever remember hearing him."

"Can you think of anything?" Maureen turned to Stephanie, her brow creased in a frown that revealed the depth of her bafflement.

"Nothing. Absolutely nothing." She turned her palms to them in a gesture indicating her own confusion. Unless Donald Black had somehow convinced Jonas that she hadn't been speaking the truth…but that wasn't possible, she decided. Jonas knew her better than that. At least she prayed he did.

"Are you going to give him back the ring?" Toni asked quietly, her voice dejected and unhappy.

"I…don't know yet."

"It's obvious he doesn't want to face you," Jan said, her expression thoughtful.

"Probably because he's afraid of what would happen."

"But I would never hurt him," Stephanie returned, appalled at the suggestion that she would do anything to cause him pain.

"Not physically, silly," Barbara explained with a long sigh. "It's obvious that he loves you—that isn't going to change overnight—so breaking off the engagement is bound to be emotionally painful."

"Maybe even impossible, if he's forced to face you."

"Then that's exactly what's going to happen." For the first time Stephanie thought she could see a glimmer of hope. She wouldn't make things easy for Jonas. "I'm not going to hand over this ring without an explanation."

"You shouldn't," Maureen stated emphatically.

"He isn't going to let you leave," Toni said.

"He isn't?" Stephanie wasn't nearly as convinced as her friends.

"Oh, he might let you get as far as the door—"

"Maybe even the elevator," Jan interrupted.

"But he'll come for you once he realizes you really mean to leave."

"He'll stop me?" Stephanie was doubtful.

"Oh, yes, the hero always rejects the heroine, and then at the very last second he realizes that he couldn't possibly live without her."

"He may even quietly plead with you and say 'Don't go' in a tormented voice. You'd be crazy to walk away from him then."

"It's like that in all the best romances," Maureen said, nodding sharply.

"But Jonas hasn't read any romances." Stephanie wanted desperately to believe that what her friends said was true, but she was afraid to count on it. Jonas was too proud. Too stubborn. Too Jonas.

"He's enough of a hero to know when he's turning away from the best thing that's ever happened to him. He loves you."

Barbara's words were the cool voice of reason cutting through the fog of doubt that clouded Stephanie's troubled mind. Even Elizabeth Lockwood had told her how much Jonas needed her love. She couldn't doubt his mother.

"He must love you, or he wouldn't have asked you to marry him." Toni was equally convincing.

"So the next move is mine, right?" Stephanie glanced around at her friends' intent expressions.

"Most definitely."

The four followed Stephanie out of Jan's office, moving in single file like troops marching into battle. Down the hallway they paraded, finally coming to a halt in front of the elevator. Jan pushed the button for Stephanie, while the others offered words of encouragement.

"Fight for him," Barbara advised her. "If he's going to do this to you, then don't make it easy on him."

"Right," Toni concurred. "Let him know what he's missing."

"Good luck," Jan said as Stephanie walked into the elevator. Just before the thick steel doors glided shut her friends gave her the thumbs-up sign.

All the confidence Stephanie had felt when she stepped into the elevator deserted her the minute she faced Martha Westheimer. The woman barely looked in her direction. It was apparent the dragon was prepared for this confrontation.

For a full, intolerable minute Stephanie stood in front of the dragon's desk while Martha ignored her.

"Excuse me, please," Stephanie said in a strong, controlled tone. "I'm here to see Mr. Lockwood."

"He's in a meeting."

"I don't believe that."

"It is not my concern what you believe. Mr. Lockwood has no desire to see you."

"Now *that* I believe."

For the first time since Stephanie had known her, Martha Westheimer smiled. Well, almost smiled, Stephanie corrected herself. She wasn't completely convinced that the woman was capable of feeling amusement, much less revealing it.

"I'd like to help you, but…"

"I'll simply tell him you weren't able to stop me."

"Mr. Lockwood would know better," Martha said quietly. "If I can persevere against pesky attorneys and keep persistent salesmen at bay, one female employee is a piece of cake."

But Stephanie could see that Martha was weakening, which was in itself a sight to behold. She held her ground but didn't speak.

"He's in a rare mood," Martha whispered under her breath. "I don't remember ever seeing him quite like this."

"Is it his leg?"

"I beg your pardon?" The horn-rimmed glasses that balanced so precariously at the tip of the woman's nose threatened to slide off. Martha rescued them in the nick of time. "I don't understand your question."

"Jonas is often irritable when his leg is hurting him."

"No, it's not his leg, Ms. Coulter. It's you. First thing this morning, I asked about you. When Mr. Lockwood brought you up to his office yesterday it was apparent there'd been some trouble. You were shaking like a frightened rabbit and...well, the minute I said your name this morning, he nearly bit my head off. He said if I cared about my job I was to forget I'd ever met you. I've been with Mr. Lockwood for a good number of years, and I have never seen him like he was this morning. From the looks of it, I'd say he didn't go home last night."

A sense of urgency filled Stephanie. "It's imperative that I talk to him."

"I have my instructions, but quite honestly, Ms. Coulter, I don't believe I can go through—"

"Ms. Westheimer." Jonas's voice boomed over the intercom, startling both women. "Just how much longer am I to be kept waiting for the Westinghouse file?"

Stephanie's heart pounded frantically at the cold, hard sound of Jonas's voice. She'd thought she'd seen him in every mood imaginable. He could be unreasonable and flippant, but she had never known him to be deliberately cruel. Judging from the edge in his voice, she didn't doubt he was capable of anything today.

"Right away, sir," Martha answered quickly. She raised her head and whispered to Stephanie, "It would be better if you came back another day...perhaps tomorrow, when he's had a chance to mull things over."

"No," Stephanie countered, and shook her head for emphasis. "It's now or never." Squaring her shoulders, she picked up the file he'd requested from the corner of Martha's desk. "I'll take this to him."

Martha half rose from her chair, indecision etched on her pointed features. "I...can't let you do that."

"You can and you will," Stephanie told her firmly.

Slumping back into her chair, Martha shook her head slowly and shut her eyes. "I hope I'm doing the right thing."

With her hand on the knob of the door that led to Jonas's office, Stephanie hesitated for a second, then pushed open the door. With quick firm steps, she marched across the plush carpeting and placed the file on his desk. He was busy writing and didn't glance in her direction.

"I believe you asked for this," she said softly.

His head flew up so fast that for a moment she wondered if he'd given himself whiplash.

"Get out!"

The harsh words cut through her, but she refused to give in to the pain. "Not until you tell me what's going on. Jan Michaels gave me the most ridiculous message this morning. If you want to end our engagement, I have the right to know why."

He pointed viciously at the door. "I've had a change of heart. Leave the ring with Ms. Westheimer and get out of my sight."

She winced at the cold, merciless way he looked at

her. "It's not that simple, Jonas," she said quietly, fighting back her anger and pain. "I have a right to know what happened. This doesn't make any sense. One afternoon you love me enough to ask me to share your life, and the following morning you despise me."

Jonas lowered his gaze, and it looked for a minute as though he was going to snap the pen he was holding in half. His hands clenched and unclenched.

"Does it have anything to do with Donald Black?"

His eyes shot to hers and narrowed. "No, but perhaps I was hasty in firing the man."

She decided to let that comment slide. "Then what possible explanation could there be?"

He rose slowly from his chair and braced his hands on the side of the desk, leaning forward. His eyes were as blue as a glacier and just as cold. "An interesting thing happened on my way out of the office yesterday afternoon. I heard howls of laughter coming from a group of male employees. By pure chance I happened to overhear that Stephanie Coulter had managed to pull off the feat of the century. A mere executive assistant had won the heart of the company president. Apparently some money was riding on just how quickly you could make a fool of me."

Stephanie blanched. "Jonas, I…"

"I didn't believe it at first," he went on, his voice as sharp as a new razor blade. "At least not until I saw the betting sheet posted on the bulletin board. You did amazingly well. The odds weren't in your favor. Several of the women seemed to have underestimated you. But I noticed the men were quick to trust your many charms. But only three hundred dollars? Really, Stephanie, you sold yourself cheap." His eyes narrowed as he mentioned the money.

"I didn't have anything to do with the marriage pool."

"Not according to what I overheard. You've been in on this little setup from the beginning. You and half the office were plotting my downfall as if I was some puppet on a string. Tricking me into falling in love with you was all part of the plan, wasn't it?"

"I—"

"Don't bother to deny it. At least have the decency to own up to the truth."

"I never had any intention of falling in love with you," she admitted.

"I suppose not. All you wanted—all anyone wanted—was to see me make a fool of myself."

Stephanie inhaled sharply. "You want the truth, then fine, I'll tell you everything."

Jonas reclaimed his chair and reached for his pen. "I have no desire to hear it."

He started writing, ignoring her, but she refused to walk away from him now. He had to understand that it had never been a game with her. She'd fallen into her coworkers' plan as an unwilling victim.

"Several weeks ago, a few of the women from the office approached me. It was right after I'd worked for you when Ms. Westheimer was ill." She waited for some response, but when he didn't give her any, she continued undaunted. "They believed…that you worked so hard and demanded so much of everyone else because you needed a wife and family to fill your time. They thought you and I would be perfect together."

He snickered.

She did her best to ignore his derision. "Anyway,

I laughed at them and told them it was a crazy idea. I didn't want any part of it."

"Obviously something changed your mind."

"Yes, something did!" she cried. "Paris. I met the real Jonas Lockwood at a fountain in a French park, and I knew then that I'd never be the same. For just a fleeting instant I glimpsed the man beneath that thick facade and discovered how much I could come to love him."

"More's the pity."

"I had no intention of falling in love with you. It just…happened. Even now, I don't regret it, I can't. I love you, Jonas Lockwood. I apologize that their game got carried to that extent, but please believe me, I didn't have anything to do with the marriage pool. I didn't even know anything about it until yesterday." She paused, her chest heaving with the tension that coiled her insides like a finely tuned violin. "I'd never do anything to hurt you. Never."

He dropped his gaze again. "Okay, you've had your say, and I've listened. It's what you wanted. Now kindly do as I request and leave the ring with Ms. Westheimer. Whatever was between us, and I sincerely doubt it was love, is over."

She felt as though she'd been hit physically. Tears burned in her eyes, but she refused to give in to the emotion. "You put this ring on my finger," she said softly, slowly. "If you want it off, you'll have to remove it yourself." She held her hand out to him and waited.

Although he refused to look at her, she could sense his indecision. "If it isn't love between us, I don't know what it is," she added softly.

"I saw you last night," he said, in a voice so low that the words were barely audible. "You came out of some lounge, laughing and joking with a group of women, and I knew it was a victory celebration. You'd achieved the impossible. You'd brought me to my knees."

"Not that...never that." She didn't know how to explain that she'd simply been happy and had wanted to share her joy with her friends. Words would only condemn her now.

"Keep the diamond," he said finally. "You've earned it."

"Jonas, please—"

"Either you leave quietly, or I'll call security and have you thrown out." His tone left little doubt that the threat was real.

Stunned almost to the point of numbness, she turned away from him. Tears blinded her as she headed for the door. Her hand was on the knob when she paused, not daring to look at him. "Did you say something?" she asked hopefully.

"No."

She nodded and, leaving the door open, moved into the foyer and to the elevator. Something came over her then. A sensation so strong and so powerful that she could barely contain it. With a burst of magnetic energy she whirled around and stormed back into his office, stopping at his desk. "Well?" she cried, her hands on her hips. "Aren't you going to stop me?"

Jonas glanced up and snarled. "What are you talking about?"

"They said you'd stop me."

"Who?"

"The others. They said if you really loved me...if anything between us was real, that you wouldn't be such an idiot as to let me leave." She'd improvised a bit, but that had been the gist of their message.

"I can assure you that after yesterday I have no feelings for you. None. At this point, my only intention regarding you is to sever our relationship and be done with you once and for all."

"You fool," she said, swallowing a hysterical sob. "If your pride is worth so much to you, then fine—so be it. If you want your ring back, then here it is." She paused long enough to slip it off her finger and place it on his desk. "It's over now, and all the trust and promise that went with it: the love, the joy, the laughter, the home, the family." She sucked in her breath at the unexpected pain that gripped her heart. "Our children would have been so special."

Jonas's mouth went taut, but he said nothing.

"It may surprise you to know that you're not the only one with an abundance of pride." Although she said each word as clearly as possible, the tears rained down her face. She turned and pointed to the elevator. "It's going to tear my heart out to walk out that door, but I'm going to do it. From here on, you'll live your life and I'll live mine, and we'll probably never meet again. But I love you, Jonas, I'll always love you. Not now, and probably not soon, but someday you'll regret this. My love will haunt you, Jonas, all the way to your grave."

"I suggest if you're going to leave you do it quickly," he said tonelessly, "before security arrives."

"Stop trying to hurt me more," she said, her voice cracking. "Isn't this humiliation enough?"

Again he refused to answer her.

"Goodbye, Jonas," she said softly, her voice trembling violently. She turned and walked away from him, telling herself over and over again not to look back. It wasn't until she was in the elevator that she realized she was speaking out loud.

As the elevator carried her to the bottom floor, she felt as though she were descending into the depths of hell. She paused in the washroom to wipe the tears from her face and repair the damage to her makeup. Unable to face anyone at the moment, she took the bus directly home and contacted Jan from there.

"What happened?" Jan demanded. "Everyone's dying to know."

"The engagement is off," Stephanie announced, doing her utmost to keep her voice from cracking. "I'm going to call my parents. I'm letting go of the apartment and flying home at the end of the week. The sooner I leave Minneapolis the better."

"Steph, don't do anything foolish. It'll work out."

"It's not going to resolve itself," Stephanie said, pressing her fist against her forehead. "Jonas made that very clear, and I refuse to remain in this city any longer." Not when there was a chance she would run into him again. She could bear anything but that.

"I feel terrible," Jan mumbled, "Really terrible—I was the one who got you into this."

"I got myself into it, and no one else. I love him, Jan, and a part of me always will."

"Are you crying?"

"No." Stephanie tried to smile, but the effort was a miserable failure. "The tears are gone now. I'm not saying I didn't cry—believe me, this morning it was Waterworks International around here. But my crying jag is over. I'll recover in time. That's the best thing about being a Coulter—we bounce back."

Jan sighed with a hint of envy. "I can't believe you—you're so strong. If this were to happen to me and Jim, I'd come unglued."

Family was the sticking agent that would hold Stephanie together. Her parents would help her get through this ordeal. Now, more than at any time since she'd left home, she felt the need for their comforting love and all that was familiar. The wheat farm, the old two-story farmhouse with the wide front porch. The half-mile-long driveway with rolling fields of grain on either side. Home. Family. Love.

"Is there anything I can do for you?" Jan wanted to know.

"Nothing. If...if I don't see you before Saturday, say goodbye to everyone for me. I'll miss you all."

"Oh, Steph, I hate to see it come to this."

"I do, too, but it's for the best."

For four days Stephanie tried to pick up the pieces of her life. She packed her bags, sold what furniture she could and gave the rest to charity. None of it was worth much, since she'd bought most of it secondhand. The bookcase was the most difficult to part with, and in the end she disassembled it and packed the long boards with the rest of the things she was having trucked to Colville. The expense of doing so was worth more than three similar sets of bookshelves, but it was all that she would have to remember Jonas by, and even though she was doing everything humanly possible to purge him from her life, she wanted to hang on to the bookcase and the memory of that night together.

Late Friday afternoon, her suitcases resting in the barren apartment, she waited for Jan to pick her up and drive her to a hotel close to the airport. She half expected Maureen, Toni and Barbara to arrive with Jan, and she mentally braced herself for the drain on her emotions. Goodbyes were always difficult.

When the doorbell chimed, she took a deep breath and attempted to smile brightly.

"Hello, Stephanie." A vital, handsome Jonas stood in the doorway.

"Jonas." Her fingers clutched the door handle so tightly that she thought the knob would break off. All week she'd been praying for a miracle, but finally she had given up hope. Jonas was too proud, and she knew it.

"May I come in?"

She blinked twice and stepped aside. "As you can see, I can't offer you a seat," she said, leaning against the closed door.

He stepped into the middle of the bare room and whirled around sharply. "You're leaving?"

"I'm expecting my ride in a few minutes—I thought you were Jan."

"I see."

"You wanted something?" She tried to keep the eagerness from her voice. In her dreams, he'd had her in his arms by now.

"I've come to offer you your job back."

Her hopeful expectations died a cruel death. "No, thank you."

"Why not?"

"Surely you know the reason, Jonas."

He hesitated, ambled to the other side of the room and glanced out the window to the street below. "You're a good executive assistant."

She held her ground. "Then I shouldn't have a problem finding work in Washington."

"I'll double your salary," he said, not bothering to turn around.

She was incredulous. She could see the expression on his face; he looked weary and defeated. "Jonas, why are you really here?" she asked in a soft whisper.

He smiled then, a sad smile that didn't reach his eyes. "I'm afraid I have a mutiny on my hands."

"A what?"

"Five of my top female employees are threatening to quit their jobs."

"Five?"

"Perhaps more."

"I…I don't understand."

"For that matter, I'm having a problem comprehending it myself." He wiped a hand over his face. "This afternoon Martha Westheimer, and four others I barely know, walked into my office."

"Martha Westheimer?" Every bad thought she'd ever entertained about Jonas's executive assistant vanished in a flood of surprise and pleasure.

"Was she in on this from the beginning?" His gaze captured Stephanie's but quickly released it.

"No…just Jan, Barbara, Toni and Maureen."

His mouth formed a half smile. "They accused me of not being hero material."

"They didn't mean anything by it—they're still upset."

"I take it that being rejected as a hero makes me the lowest of the low?" He cocked his thick brows questioningly.

"Something like that." Despite the seriousness of the

conversation, she was forced to disguise a smile. "This whole thing started because Jan and the others thought I was heroine material—but they were mistaken about me, as well. I did everything wrong."

"How's that?" He turned and leaned against the windowsill, studying her.

She shrugged, lowered her gaze and rubbed the palms of her hands together nervously. "You kissed me once in your office, and I told you never to let it happen again. I was forever saying and doing the worst possible thing."

"But I did kiss you again."

This was a subject she wanted to avoid. "What else did they say?"

"Just that if I let you go I would be making the biggest mistake of my life, and that they refused to stand idly by and let it happen."

"What did they suggest you do?"

"They said if I didn't do something to prevent you from leaving they were handing in their resignations effective that minute."

Looking at him was impossible; it hurt far too much. "So that's why you offered me my old job back—you were seeking a compromise?"

"No," he said harshly. "I figured if you agreed to that, then there would be hope of you agreeing to more."

"More?"

"The ring's in my pocket, Stephanie." He brought it out and handed it to her. "It's yours."

The diamond felt warm in her palm, as though he'd been holding on to it. She raised her eyes to his, not understanding. "Jonas," she whispered past the tight knot that formed in her throat. "I can't accept this ring."

He went pale. "Why not?"

"For the same reason I refuse to go back to Lockwood Industries."

"I love you, Stephanie."

"But not enough to truly want me as your wife," she said accusingly, feeling more wretched than the day he'd fired her. "Don't worry about Jan and the others. I'll explain everything. You needn't worry about them quitting. That's the reason you're here, isn't it?"

"No," he said huskily, then paused and seemed to regain control of his emotions. "I don't want you to leave. I thought about what you said, and you're right. If you go, everything I've ever dreamed about will disappear with you. I have my pride, Stephanie, but it's been cold comfort the last few days."

"Oh, Jonas, don't tease me, I don't think I could bear it—are you saying you *want* me for your wife?"

"Yes." He raised his eyes toward heaven as if to plead for patience. "What did you think I meant?"

"I don't know. That they'd blackmailed you into proposing again, I guess."

He reached for her, drawing her soft body to his and inhaling the fresh sunshine scent of her hair. "I've been half out of my mind the last few days. To be honest, I was glad Ms. Westheimer and the others came. It gave me the excuse I needed to contact you. Right after you left it dawned on me that I'd been an idiot. I'd overreacted to that stupid marriage pool. Why should any of that silliness matter to me when I've got you?" He pressed his mouth hungrily down on hers.

Stephanie melted against him and sniffled loudly. "I love you so much."

"I know." He rubbed his chin against the top of her head. "I think we fooled the odds makers this time."

"How's that?"

"Odds were three to one that we'd get back together again."

"Three to one?"

"You know what else?"

"No," she said with a watery smile.

"There are other odds floating around the office. They say you'll be pregnant by the end of the year."

"That soon?" She wound her arms around his neck and moved her body against his, telling him without words her eagerness to experience all that marriage had to offer them.

"I say they're way off," he growled in her ear. "It shouldn't take nearly that long."

* * * * *

ALMOST AN ANGEL

One

Bethany Stone's nimble fingers flew over the computer keys. Tears blurred her soft blue eyes as she typed the few short sentences that would terminate her employment with Norris Pharmaceutical Company and J. D. Norris. This was it. The end. She'd had it up to her ears and beyond!

Any woman who would waste her life for a man who treated her like a robot deserved to be unemployed. She had played the part of a fool for three long years, perfecting the role. But no more! It was long past time for her to hold her head high, walk away and never look back.

The words from a militant protest song played loudly in her mind as she signed her name with a flourish at the bottom of the letter. She straightened. From the way Joshua David Norris treated her, she might as well have been a machine. Oh, he might miss her efficiency the first few days, but he would soon find a replacement, and then she would quickly fade from his memory. A year from now, if someone were to casually mention her name, she was convinced he would have trouble remembering who she was.

The intercom beeped unexpectedly. "Miss Stone, could I see you a moment?"

With a determination born of frustration and regret, she jerked the letter of resignation from her printer and stood. As an afterthought, she reached for her dictation pad, which he still insisted she use. Her shoulders were stiff and her back ramrod-straight as she opened the door that connected the outer office with the executive suite. She exhaled once, hard, and filled her steps with purpose as she marched into the executive office.

Joshua was scribbling notes across a yellow legal tablet with his thin scrawl. He didn't bother to glance up when she entered the room, and for a few brief moments she was given the opportunity to study the man she loved—fool that she was. He was sitting, the muscles in his broad shoulders relaxed. Not for the first time, she sensed the complexity of this man's character. He was strong and mature yet headstrong and obstinately blind. Often she'd been a witness to the way he concealed his emotions in the tight fabric of control that he wrapped around himself. In some ways she knew Joshua Norris better than he knew himself, but in others he was a complete stranger.

His hair was dark brown with faint highlights of auburn, the result of hours spent in the sun, sailing his boat on Lake Pontchartrain. His brows were thick and drawn together now in concentration as he jotted down his thoughts. The smooth contours of his handsome face were broken by a square angular jaw that revealed an overabundance of male arrogance.

His eyes were a deep rich shade of brown that reminded her of bitter chicory. She knew from experience that they could reveal such anger that she was sure one look was capable of blistering paint off a wall. And then there were those rare times when she'd seen his gaze flitter over the photo of his daughter, Angie, that rested on his desk. Bethany had seldom witnessed a gentler look. All she knew was that Angie lived somewhere in New York and was being raised by his wife's family. In all the years that Bethany had been employed by Joshua, he'd rarely mentioned his daughter. From everything she knew of the man—which was considerable, since they spent so much time together—J. D. Norris didn't seem interested in long-term relationships and created a thick outer shell that often seemed impenetrable.

Joshua dropped the pen on top of the tablet, leaned back in his chair, and pinched his thumb and index finger over the bridge of his nose.

"Miss Stone, do we have any aspirin?"

"Yes, of course." His request caught her by surprise. Quickly she crossed the room to the wet bar, amazed that he didn't even know where the aspirin were. She returned momentarily with a water glass and two tablets.

He gave her a fleeting smile of appreciation. "Thanks."

Now that she thought about it, Joshua *did* look slightly pale. "You aren't feeling well, Mr. Norris?"

He shook his head, then widened his eyes as though he regretted the action. "I've got a beast of a headache."

"If you'd like, I'll cancel your afternoon appointments."

"That won't be necessary," he informed her crisply. He tore the top sheet off the tablet and handed it to her.

"Could you have these notes typed up before you leave tonight?"

"Of course." The letter of resignation remained tightly clenched in her hand. She hesitated, wondering if she should give it to him now, then quickly decided against it. The last thing he needed was another problem. Which shouldn't have been *her* problem, of course, but old habits died hard.

His glance revealed his annoyance. "Was there something more, Miss Stone?"

"N-no." She did an abrupt about-face and left the office, closing the door behind her. Maybe she'd been too hasty. She should give him that letter, headache or not.

Ten minutes later her best friend and roommate, Sally Livingston, stuck her head inside the door. "Well, did you do it? Did you give your notice? What did he say?"

Bethany pretended to be busy, but she should have known Sally wouldn't be easily thwarted. Her friend advanced toward her desk, folded her arms and tapped her foot, waiting impatiently until Bethany looked up.

"Well?" Sally demanded a second time.

"He didn't say anything." Okay that was a lie of omission. He hadn't commented because she hadn't given him the letter.

Her roommate's brow crimped into a tight frown. "Nothing? You handed J. D. Norris your two-week notice and he didn't so much as respond?"

There was nothing left to do but confess, but still Bethany avoided looking in Sally's direction. "If you must know, I didn't give it to him."

"Bethany," Sally whispered angrily. "You promised."

"I—I wrote the letter."

"That's a start, at least."

"I was going to give it to him—honest—but he has a headache, and he looks absolutely terrible. The timing just wasn't right, and you know how important that is in these situations."

"Beth, this is crazy! The time will *never* be right—you've got to do it today, otherwise you'll end up putting it off for heaven knows how long."

"I know." Defeat weighted Bethany's voice. She'd promised Sally and herself that she wasn't going to delay this unpleasant task another day, and here she was looking for an excuse to put off the inevitable. "I'll do it Friday."

"What do you think today is?" Sally asked, sending her dark gaze straight through her.

"Oh," Bethany mumbled, and lowered her eyes. "Monday morning, then—first thing—you have my word on it."

Sally unfolded her arms and rolled her eyes. "I've heard that line before."

"All right!" Bethany cried. "You're right. I'm weak. I've got all the backbone of a…a worm."

"Less!"

Bethany paused and surveyed her friend through narrowed eyes. "What could have less backbone than a worm?"

"You!"

"But, Sally," Beth said, wishing her friend understood, "Mr. Norris isn't feeling well. I don't want to add to his troubles now. I'm sure he'll be better on Monday."

"Maybe he knows what you're planning and this is his way of generating sympathy."

Bethany knew Joshua would never do anything like that. "No, he's pale, and his head hurts. I think he might be coming down with some virus."

"It serves him right."

"Sally!" It wasn't Joshua's fault that Bethany had been silly enough to give him her heart. The man didn't so much as guess that she cared one iota about him.

It was her own fault for allowing herself to become attached to a man who chose to live his life without emotional commitments. It wasn't that he ignored her in particular. He seemed to be uninterested in women generally, least based on what she'd observed. The divorce from, and later the death of, his ex-wife had left him hard and bitter toward the opposite sex. In the long run, if she stayed on she would only get hurt even more than she already had been. She had to leave—it was best for everyone involved.

If only she knew how to crack the thick facade he had erected over the years. If she'd had a little more experience or been a bit more sophisticated, then perhaps she could have come up with a surefire plan to win his heart. But as it was, she'd simply stayed on, hoping one day Joshua Norris would look up at her and some mysterious magic would change everything. Twinkling lights would go off in the distance and little hearts would pop up around her head, and he would recognize the love she'd stored up just waiting for him to discover it.

"All right," Bethany returned forcefully, her hands knotting into tight fists of steely determination. "I'll do it."

"Today?" Sally looked skeptical.

"I'll place the letter on his desk when I leave." It was a coward's way out, but when it came to standing up to Joshua Norris, no one was going to award her a medal for velour.

"Good for you." Sally patted her across the back much as a general would before sending a raw recruit into battle. "Meet me at Charley's when you're through here."

Bethany nodded. Charley's was a popular New Orleans hangout. The two had taken to stopping there and relaxing with a glass of wine on Friday nights. A reward of sorts for making it through another difficult work week.

"I'll see you there," Bethany said. Once Joshua left the office she would simply walk inside, place her resignation on his desk and be done with it. Then there wouldn't be any time for second thoughts and looming regrets. She had to get on with her life, because clearly this was a dead end for her

It was after six by the time Bethany made her way into the crowded lounge. Sally had already found a table, and she stood up and gave a short wave. Bethany forced a smile and joined her friend. When the waitress strolled by, she pointed at Sally's wine glass and said, "Give me whatever she's having."

The woman nodded and turned away.

"So? Did you actually do it?" Sally asked, her voice low. "Did you finally hand in your notice?"

The glass of pinot noir arrived, and Bethany reached into her purse to pay for it. "Not yet."

"Not yet?" Sally echoed.

"Because *just couldn't*. I'm a weak—"

Abruptly Sally raised her hand, stopping her. "We've already determined that."

"Listen," Bethany said thoughtfully. "I've been giving some thought to my problem, and I think I may be doing Joshua Norris a disservice."

"How do you mean?"

The hum of conversation and a Dixieland band playing in the distance forced Bethany to raise her voice slightly and lean her head closer to her roommate's. "Joshua doesn't have a clue how I feel about him." At Sally's perplexed look, she hurried to add, "I should have the courtesy to at least let him know."

"Oh, Beth," Sally muttered, and shook her head. "The man has to be blind not to know how you feel. The entire company knows you love him."

Bethany paled. She actually felt all the blood rush from her face and pool at her ankles. When she spoke, her voice came out scratchy, high-pitched and weak. "Everyone knows?"

"Maybe not maintenance."

"Oh, no." Bethany took a long sip of her wine to hide her distress. This was worse than she'd ever imagined.

"Calm down, I was just joking. Not everyone knows—but enough people do."

Bethany's shoulders sagged with relief.

"What do you plan to do?" Sally asked in a husky whisper. "Saunter into his office, bat your eyelashes a couple of times and offer to bear his children?"

"No...I...I don't know yet." Bethany pushed the short dark curls from her temple.

"You've had three years to get the message across. What makes you think you can do it now?"

"I...I've never actually *told* him."

"Not outright, true, but honestly, Beth, give the matter some thought here. You're much too gentle-natured and sweet to come right out and tell J. D. Norris you have feelings for him. He's bound to give you one of those famous dark looks of his and fire you on the spot."

"I've been thinking..."

"The first time is always hardest," Sally joked. She reached for a handful of salted peanuts, munching on them one at a time.

Bethany reached for the salted nuts, too, hoping to buy herself time. "Maybe that's for the best," she finally said.

"I disagree." Sally popped another peanut into her mouth. "If you were going to fall in love, why did it have to be with him?" Her elbows rested on the tabletop, and her eyes narrowed with a thoughtful frown. "Beth, face it, the man's soured on women, soured on marriage, soured on life. He's the big bad wolf, and you're an innocent lamb. As your best friend, I refuse to stand by and let you do this to yourself."

"But...he can be wonderful." Bethany knew Joshua in ways the other employees of Norris Pharmaceutical didn't. She'd been a silent witness to his generous contributions to charity. She admired his unwavering dedication to medicine. She was sure there were times when others viewed him as harsh, but she'd never known him to be unfair or intentionally unkind. In the three years she'd worked for him, she had gotten enough glimpses of the real man inside to convince her that the exterior of indifference he wore was only a shell.

Sally chewed on a peanut as though it were rawhide, then paused, surprise widening her gaze and giving her away. "Don't look now, but…"

Instantly Bethany jerked her head around.

"I told you not to look," Sally berated her friend. "He's here."

"Who?"

Immediately Sally's dark eyes narrowed into thin slits, a sure sign she was irritated. "I thought you said your precious Mr. Norris was coming down with some dreadful virus."

Bethany's brow tightened into a frown. "He looked dreadful earlier. I got him aspirin." Sally wouldn't realize how unusual that was.

"Well," Sally said, looking properly disgusted, "he seems to have made a miraculous recovery."

"He's here?" Bethany rose halfway out of her chair before Sally jerked her back down. She felt the muscles in her throat tighten. "He's with someone, isn't he? That's the reason you don't want me to look." Already her mind was conjuring up a tall luscious blonde— someone she could never hope to compete against.

"Nope." Sally's eyes followed him. "He just sat down at the bar." Another nut was positioned in front of her mouth. "You know, now that I have a chance to get a good look at him, you're right."

"About what?"

"He is…I don't know, compelling-looking. He's got a lean hardness to him that naturally attracts women. An inborn arrogance, if you will."

Sally wasn't telling Bethany anything she hadn't already known—for years. "You're sure he's alone?"

"I just told you that."

Bethany clenched her hands together in her lap. "What's he doing now?"

"Ordering a drink. You're right about something else, too. He doesn't look the least bit like himself. Not exactly sick, though."

Bethany couldn't stand it any longer. She twisted her chair around so she could get a decent look at her employer herself. She braced herself, not sure what to expect. But when her gaze skimmed over Joshua, she stiffened and experienced a rush of concern. "Something's wrong," she whispered, surprised she'd spoken aloud.

"How can you tell?" Sally asked, her voice barely above a whisper as though the two of them were on a top secret reconnaissance mission.

"I just can. Something's troubling him. Look at the way he's leaning over his drink…how his shoulders are slouched. I wonder what happened. Something's got him worried—I can't remember the last time I saw him look so…so distressed."

Sally shook her head. "I don't know where you get that. The only reason he's slouching like that is because he wants to be left alone. Didn't you ever read a book on body language? He's letting others know he isn't in the mood for company."

"Maybe." Thoughtfully Bethany gnawed at the corner of her lower lip. "But I doubt it." Without any real plan in mind, she pushed back her chair, reached for her bag and wine glass, and stood.

"What are you doing?" Sally demanded in a tight whisper.

"I'm going to talk to him."

Sally briefly touched her arm. "Be careful, sweetie, wolves have sharp teeth."

Bethany's heart was pounding like a jackhammer as she advanced toward Joshua Norris. Luckily the stool beside his was vacant. She perched her five-foot-five frame atop it and set her glass of pinot noir on the bar, folded her hands and leaned forward. She gave him a minute to notice her and comment.

He didn't.

"Hello," she said softly.

It seemed like an eternity before he turned his head to look at her. When he did, surprise briefly widened his intense dark eyes. "Miss Stone."

She took another sip of her wine. Now that she was here, for the life of her, she couldn't think of anything to say. She tossed a glance over her shoulder, and Sally's eyes rounded as she nodded encouragingly.

"I didn't know you frequented Charley's," Bethany managed at last, amazed at how strange her own voice sounded.

"I don't." His words were clipped, and he turned his attention back to his drink, discouraging any further discussion.

"Are you feeling better?"

He turned back to her then. "Not particularly."

The bartender strolled in their direction, and Joshua motioned to the tall thin man that he wanted a refill. The man poured another shot glass of Scotch, then cast Bethany a questioning glance.

She shook her head. She had a one-glass limit, especially on an empty stomach. As it was, the alcohol was already rushing to her brain.

"I have aspirin in my purse if you need some."

"I don't." He answered without looking in her direction, as though he wished she would get up and walk away. He hadn't sought her company, and the stiff way in which he sat told her as much.

Not knowing what else to do, she took several more sips of her wine. Feeling more than a little reckless, she lightly placed her hand on his forearm. "We've worked together all this time, so I hope you feel you can trust me."

"I beg your pardon." His hard gaze cut into her.

"Won't you tell me what's wrong?"

"What makes you think anything is troubling me?"

"I've worked for you for three years. I know when something's wrong. I've seen that look in the past, and I…"

"I am well aware of the length of your employment, Miss Stone—"

"Bethany," she interrupted, her unflinching gaze meeting his. "I've worked for you all these years, and I think you should know my first name is Bethany."

His eyes formed glacial slits. "And what makes you think that I care to know your first name? Because, rest assured, I don't."

Her breath felt trapped in her lungs, and scalding color erupted in her cheeks. She'd seen Joshua be cold and insensitive before, but never intentionally like this. The look he gave her was more than embarrassing…it was humiliating. The corner of his mouth turned up in a sneer, as though he were looking at something distasteful. His eyes cut her to the quick before he dropped his attention to her fingers, which were lightly pressing against the sleeve of his jacket.

As though in slow motion, she withdrew her hand from his arm. Her whole body went numb. The uselessness of it all hit her then, more poignantly than all the lectures Sally had given her, more cutting than her own soul-searching efforts. The message in Joshua's taut gaze was sharp, hitting its mark far more effectively than he would ever guess. He didn't know who she was, not really, and he didn't care to know. The world he'd created was his own, and he wasn't ever going to invite her or anyone else inside.

Her gaze didn't waver from his as she slid off the bar stool and took one small step in retreat. "I won't bother you again." The words managed to wrestle past the stranglehold that gripped her throat muscles. What an arrogant jerk.

She didn't know where she was going. All she knew was that she had to escape. She walked past Sally's table without looking at her friend, and maneuvered her way through the crowded room and outside into the chill of the January night.

For a moment she thought she heard someone call her name, but she wasn't up to explaining what had happened to Sally or anyone else. Increasing her pace, she hurried down the crowded pavement of Decatur Street, which bordered the popular French Quarter. The road was crowded, the sidewalks busy, but she kept her head up, walking as fast as her feet would carry her. Not knowing where—not caring.

"Miss Stone. Wait."

She sucked in her breath at the sound of Joshua's impatient demand, swung her bag strap over her shoulder and pushed herself to walk faster.

"Bethany, please."

Surprisingly, once Joshua caught up with her he didn't say a word. She must have continued walking half a block with him, their steps in unison, before he spoke again.

"I owe you an apology."

"Yes, you do," she said, "You were arrogant and rude. I was only trying to help. Would it have hurt you to simply say you weren't in the mood for company?" She should have listened to Sally. His body language had said as much, but oh, no, her tender heart had wanted to reach out to him. Well, lesson learned.

Neither of them spoke for a minute, and when she looked up she noticed that they were walking past Jackson Square. Several park benches were spread across the lush green lawn in front of the statue of Andrew Jackson on horseback.

He motioned toward an empty bench. "Would you care to sit for a minute?"

She calmly took a seat, although her heart continued to beat erratically.

He sat down beside her. After what seemed like a hundred years, he spoke. "I apologize. It's Angie."

At the mention of his young daughter, alarm worked its way through Bethany, and adrenalin shot into her bloodstream. She turned so she was facing him, her hands gripping his sleeve. "Is she ill? Has she had an accident?"

"No, no." Abruptly he shook his head. "As far as I know, she's in perfect health."

She relaxed, dropped her hands and slumped against the back of the bench.

Joshua sighed, his look bleak, distressed. "What do you know about children, Miss Stone?"

"Very little, actually." She was an aunt several times over, but although she dearly loved her nieces and nephews, they lived in Texas, so she only saw them on summer vacations.

"I was afraid of that." Roughly he splayed his fingers through his hair. "Frankly, I don't know what I'm going to do."

Questions were popping up like fizz from a soda can in Bethany's mind, but after her earlier attempt to draw him out, she against a second try.

"Angie's mother and I were divorced shortly after she was born."

He paused as though he expected her to make some conventionally comforting statement. She had nothing to offer, though, so kept her half-formed thoughts to herself.

"Over the years I've visited Angie when I could," he went on, his brooding gaze seeking hers. "Heaven knows, I've tried to do everything I could moneywise."

"She's a beautiful little girl," she murmured, not knowing what else to say. Angie's photo was updated regularly, and each time Bethany looked at it she saw the promise of rare beauty in the ten-year-old.

He nodded sharply, his brow furrowed. "The thing is, I don't know anything about being a father."

"But you've been one for the past ten years," she couldn't help reminding him.

"Not really," he murmured, his facial features remaining tight. "Not a real father." He stood then, and rubbed his hand along the back of his neck. "I've never felt more inept in my life."

She was sure that the sensation was foreign to him. In all the time she'd worked for him, she'd never seen him this upset or unsure about anything.

As though forgetting his own problems for the moment, he hesitated and stared down at her. His hard gaze softened perceptibly, and a half smile teased at the edges of his mouth. "You didn't deserve my sarcasm earlier. I truly *am* sorry."

An earthquake wouldn't have been powerful enough to tear Bethany's gaze from his. In three years, this was the most personal comment he'd ever made to her. Forgetting her earlier reluctance, she asked him softly, "Won't you tell me what's happening with Angie?"

He nodded and slumped down into the seat beside her. "I talked with my mother-in-law yesterday afternoon. It seems both my in-laws have been in poor health recently."

Bethany nodded, encouraging him to continue.

"They feel it's time for Angie to come live with me. I'm supposed to pick her up at the airport in a couple of hours." He paused and inhaled sharply. His gaze sought hers. "Miss Stone…Bethany, would you consider coming with me?"

Two

The Louis Armstrong International Airport was a bee-hive of activity, just as Bethany had expected it would be. The first thing Joshua did once they'd entered the terminal was double-check the flight schedule on the television monitor positioned beside the airline reservation desk.

"The plane's on time." He sounded as though he'd been hoping for a short reprieve. After obtaining the necessary paperwork to pass security to meet his daughter, he hurriedly guided Bethany through the wide corridor to the assigned concourse. In all the time she had known him, she'd never seen him more unsettled. When it came to his business, he generally revealed so little emotion that it had become his trademark. She watched him now, amazed and also pleased at this evidence that he did indeed possess emotions.

Once they found the gate, he paced the area, his hands buried deep in his trouser pockets. After several tense minutes he parked himself beside Bethany at the huge floor-to-ceiling window and stared bleakly into the darkness.

"I appreciate your coming with me," he said. "I haven't seen Angie in almost a year." He jammed his fingers through his hair and released a harsh breath. "Do you think she'll recognize me?"

"I'm sure she will." Bethany searched for something more to say that would reassure him, but she wasn't sure he would appreciate her efforts. Joshua Norris was a difficult man to interpret. She didn't know how far she dared tread onto this carpet of unexpected trust he'd laid before her.

A series of flashing lights glowed in the distance, and she felt him tense. She checked her wrist and noted the time. "It's too early for that to be Angie's plane."

Her employer nodded and seemed to relax.

"Joshua," she whispered, unable to keep herself from speaking, "everything's going to work out fine."

At the sound of his name, his troubled gaze shot in her direction, and he frowned. His eyes revealed surprise mingled with bewilderment. "No one's called me that since I was a boy."

Color exploded in Bethany's cheeks, working its way to her ears until she was certain they glowed with the heat. She'd always thought of him as Joshua. The world knew him as J. D. Norris, but she'd found the initials too abrupt for the complex man she knew him to be. "I...apologize. I..."

"It wasn't a reprimand...Bethany, but a statement of fact." He said her name as though it felt awkward on his tongue, yet as if he had recognized she had a name other than Miss Stone. When he continued to stare at her for a long moment, she had the impression he was seeing her for the first time. She knew her clear delicate features were unlikely to attract attention. Her eyes were a pale shade of blue not unlike a thousand others'. Her cheekbones were slightly high, her nose firm and straight. But she didn't possess any one feature that would distinguish her as a great beauty. Friends had called her cute, but that was about the extent of it. She was neither short nor tall, just average height—a description that sounded so terribly boring. She was contemplating that fact when she realized that if Joshua were to take her in his arms the top of her head would just brush against his jawline. All he would need to do was bend his head to kiss her and her lips would meet his without...

With an effort she tore her gaze from his, her composure badly shaken by the brief encounter. "Are Angie's grandparents traveling with her?" she asked, purposely diverting her thoughts.

"No." Joshua abruptly shook his head and turned back to stare out the window. "It couldn't be helped. She's flying alone."

"Oh." Poor Angie. With the time difference between New York and New Orleans, the little girl would probably be exhausted—or as keyed up and full of energy as a fresh battery.

"Has her room been fixed up?"

"Room?" Joshua echoed the word as though it were something totally foreign. "I thought I'd put her in the guest bedroom for tonight.... I hadn't stopped to think beyond that. I suppose she'll need something more, won't she?" His gaze clouded.

"I'm sure the guest room will be fine for now."

"Good."

A fresh set of wing lights blinked in the distant night. "I think that's her flight now," Bethany said.

Joshua stiffened, seeming to brace himself, and nodded. "She should be one of the first ones to disembark—I arranged for a first-class ticket."

"The flight attendant will escort her off."

He exhaled sharply. "I can't tell you how glad I am that you're with me."

She couldn't have been more pleased herself. She'd been granted a glimpse of a whole new facet of Joshua Norris's personality. When it came to his daughter, he was as uncertain as any new father, which to all intents and purposes he was. It seemed completely contradictory that this same man could bring a room full of board members to silence with one shattering look. She'd witnessed glares from Joshua that were colder than a tombstone in midwinter. No one would ever guess that the man who was nervously waiting for his young daughter was the driving force behind a thriving business. She had trouble believing it herself.

A few minutes later an airline official opened the door to the Jetway, and two businessmen were the first to step into the terminal, carrying briefcases and garment bags. They were followed by a female flight attendant escorting a little girl with straight dark hair that fell to the top of her shoulders. Two pink ribbons held it away from her face, which seemed to be made up solely of round eager eyes.

"Daddy!" The girl broke away from the attendant and ran toward Joshua.

He looked startled, then fell to one knee as his daughter hurled herself into his waiting arms.

Angie tossed her arms around her father's neck and squeezed for all she was worth. Slowly, almost as if it were against his will, he closed his eyes and returned the bear hug.

Bethany felt moisture brim in her eyes at the tender scene and bit into her bottom lip, determined not to say or do anything to disturb their reunion.

Finally Joshua released his daughter and stood, claiming her hand. "Angie," he murmured, looking down on the ten-year-old, "this is Miss Stone. She works for me. She's my assistant."

"Hello." Angie's wide dark eyes stared up at Bethany.

"Hello, Angie. Welcome to New Orleans."

"Thanks." The little girl grinned and let loose with an adult-size sigh. "I can't tell you how boring that flight was. I was beginning to think I'd never get here."

"I believe your father was feeling much the same way."

Angie's smile grew wider. "I don't suppose there's a McDonald's around here? Grandma told me not to trust anything the airlines served, and I'm absolutely starved."

"Miss Stone—a McDonald's?" Joshua was looking at her as though he expected her to wave a magic wand and make one instantly appear.

"Any hamburger will do," Angie offered, her gaze growing desperate.

"There's a McDonald's a few miles away," Bethany said, checking her Blackberry.

"Thank goodness." The little girl sighed, shrugging her small shoulders. "I swear I could eat one of everything on the menu."

Come to think of it, Bethany hadn't had dinner yet, either. Her stomach growled eagerly at the mere thought of a burger.

Angie prattled on about New York and her grandparents as they moved down the concourse to the baggage claim area. In addition to her backpack, she had three gigantic suitcases.

As soon as they were seated inside Joshua's car, Angie leaned forward so her head was positioned between Bethany and Joshua.

"You're a winter, aren't you, Miss Stone?"

"A winter?" She hadn't a clue what the ten-year-old was talking about.

"Your coloring—haven't you ever been analyzed?" Angie smothered a yawn with her palm. "It was a big deal a few years ago. My grandmother says every woman should know her season."

"I guess I actually hadn't given it much thought. I need to look into that." Bethany shared a smile with Joshua.

"Oh, no need to do that. I have a gift for these things, and you're definitely a winter," Angie returned confidently. "You should wear more reds, blues, whites, those kinds of colors."

"Oh." Bethany wasn't sure how to respond. As it was, her wardrobe consisted of several bold colors, but she wore more subdued ones for the office—tans and soft blues mostly, pencil skirts, business attire.

"There's a wonderful TV series about it. You should watch that for a few fashion hints."

"Yes," Bethany said, hiding a grin. "I suppose I should."

Sitting back and buckling her seat belt, Angie turned her attention to her father. "How's the sailing going, Dad?"

"Good," he said distractedly. He seemed more concerned with getting out of the heavy airport traffic than with talking.

"I saw an interview with some guys on TV last night. You might think about studying tacking techniques if you want to be a really great sailor. Personally, I think the New Zealanders are the ones we have to watch out for in the next America's Cup."

"It wouldn't be their first win." Joshua's smiling gaze bounced off Bethany's as he briefly rolled his eyes.

Angie leaned forward again, crossing her arms over the seat and resting her chin on top of her folded hands. She hesitated for a quick moment, then said, "We're going to get along just fine, don't you think?"

"Just fine," Joshua echoed. "What I'd like right now, though, is for you to sit back and stay in your seat the way you're supposed to."

Bethany sucked in her breath. His words were clipped and far more harsh than necessary. He was right, but there were gentler ways of telling his daughter so.

"Oh, sure." Angie immediately obeyed, flopping back and tightening her seat belt. "You should have done this years ago."

"Done what?" Joshua's tone was absent-minded as he pulled to a stop to pay the parking attendant.

"Sent for me," Angie said on the tail end of a yawn.

He didn't answer for what seemed like an eternity. "You may be right," he murmured at last.

Bethany noted how his face eased into a relaxed

smile. It struck her then how rare it was for him to show pleasure at something. He ran a tight ship, as the saying went. He lived his life according to a rigid schedule, driving himself and everyone who worked closely with him to the brink of exhaustion. The control with which he molded his existence was bound to change now that his daughter had arrived. For the better, Bethany suspected.

She curved her fingers around the purse that rested on her lap. The letter of resignation neatly folded inside would stay there. Exciting things were about to happen at Norris Pharmaceutical *and* with Joshua Norris, and she planned to stick around and witness each and every one.

The living room curtain was pushed aside and Sally's eager face was reflected in the glass when the taxi deposited Bethany in front of her apartment two hours later.

"It's about time you got home!" Sally cried the minute Bethany walked inside the door. "What happened? I've been dying to talk to you. You should have phoned." She inhaled a huge breath and sank onto the deeply cushioned sofa. "But don't worry about apologizing now. Talk."

Bethany hung her jacket in the hall closet. She wasn't exactly sure where to start. "Mr. Norris followed me out of Charley's...."

"I know that much. I just hope he had the good grace to apologize. I don't know when I've seen you look more...I don't know...stricken, I guess."

"He did apologize," Bethany assured her.

"And it took him two hours?"

"No."

"The two of you had a romantic dinner together?"

"No."

Sally's shoulders sagged with disappointment. "What *did* happen?"

"Nothing, really. He told me his daughter is coming to live with him."

Sally folded her pajama-clad legs under her and leaned back, her look thoughtful. Her brows arched speculatively as she bounced her finger over her closed lips several times. "Well, that's news."

"Angie arrived tonight, and Mr. Norris asked me to go to the airport with him."

"So that's where you've been?"

"Part of the time." Bethany slipped off her low-heeled shoes and claimed the overstuffed recliner across from her roommate. "After that we went to McDonald's."

Sally grinned at that, her smile slightly off center. "How romantic."

Actually, in a weird way it had been, but she wasn't about to explain that to her friend. She was convinced it was the first time Joshua had ever been to a fast-food restaurant, and he'd looked as uncomfortable as a pond fish during a summer drought. "We went to the drive-through window, because it was obvious Angie was going to conk out any minute."

"And did she?"

"The poor kid was fast asleep by the time we arrived at his house."

"You saw Mr. Norris's house?" Sally uncrossed her

legs and leaned forward. Rumor had it Joshua Norris lived in a mansion.

Bethany answered with a short nod, remembering her first impression of the breathtaking two-story antebellum home. It was constructed of used brick in muted shades of white and red. Four stately white gables peeked out from the roof above the second floor. The front of the house was decorated with six huge brick columns that were lushly covered with climbing ivy. The house was a tasteful blend of the old South and her warm traditions with the new South and her willingness to adapt to change.

"What happened once you got there?" Sally pressed, clearly unable to hide her curiosity.

Bethany answered with a soft shrug. "I helped Angie get ready for bed, Mr. Norris brought in her luggage."

"And?"

"And then he phoned for a taxi so I'd have a way home."

He'd also thanked her and apologized again for his behavior earlier that evening. And as he did, she'd realized that he was closing himself off from her again. She could see it as clearly as if she were standing before a huge gate that was swinging shut. She'd tried to read his features, but it was impossible. She suspected that once the crisis had passed, he'd regretted having confided in her.

She didn't mention any of this to Sally, nor did she tell her roommate how Joshua had walked her to the cab once it arrived and paid her fare. He'd lingered outside for a few moments, hands buried deep in his pants pockets, his face lined with a frown that left her brooding all the way home.

"That's it?" Sally asked, looking sadly disappointed. "You were gone for hours, and that's the extent of what happened?"

"That's all there was." On the surface it didn't sound like much, and really it wasn't, but so much more had been accomplished. So much more than Bethany wished to share with her friend.

For the first time since she'd been hired as Joshua Norris's executive assistant, her employer had seen her as something more than an automaton. She chose to think he'd been pleasantly surprised by what he'd found.

Bethany was at her desk by the time Joshua arrived on Monday morning. She glanced up expectantly and was disappointed when he did nothing more than offer her a crisp good-morning, the way he'd done every day of the past three years, as he marched past her desk and into his office.

Reaching for the mail, she followed him inside. She'd taken his daughter's advice and chosen a dark blue business suit with a white silk blouse and a ribbon tie. Briefly she wondered if he would notice anything as mundane as the way she dressed. Probably not.

Following ritual, she poured him a mug of hot coffee and delivered it to his desk. He reached for the cup and took a sip before quickly leafing through the mail. He gave brisk instructions on each piece, handed back the ones she could deal with directly and kept the rest. Once he'd finished, she hesitated, standing beside his desk, uncertain.

"Yes?" he asked. "Was there something else?" He didn't so much as look up at her.

"I...wanted to ask you about Angie. How's she adjusting?"

His facade was back, and from the hard look about him, it had been heavily reinforced.

"Miss Stone, in case you've forgotten, I have a business to run. My daughter is none of your concern. Now, may I be so bold as to suggest that you do the job for which I pay you a very generous salary?"

It took Bethany a moment to quell her anger and not tell him to stuff his precious job. He wasn't paying her nearly enough to put up with his rudeness. After a moment she managed to say, "Yes, of course." Her voice was hardly more than a whisper. She found that her hands were trembling with outrage by the time she'd returned to her desk. Her legs weren't in much better shape. In fact, she had to walk around her desk two or three times before she was calm enough to sit down. She knew she should march right back into his office and hand him her resignation. But she wouldn't. She couldn't make herself do it, despite her fury.

By rote she managed to finish the morning's tasks, but by the time Sally arrived at noon, Bethany had worked herself into an uncharacteristically angry state. She shook from the force of her feelings, furious with herself for allowing Joshua to speak to her in that demeaning tone.

"He's impossible," she hissed when her friend stuck her head in the door.

"Mr. Norris?" Sally's gaze travelled from her roommate to the closed door to his office.

"Who else?" Bethany pushed back her chair so hard, she ended up six feet from the desk.

Frowning heavily, Sally stepped into the office. "Good grief, what happened?"

"I've had it!" Bethany declared, and cringed when Sally rolled her eyes toward the ceiling. Okay, so she'd been saying the same thing for weeks, but today was different. She would show Joshua Norris that she deserved respect. She refused to allow any man to talk to her the way he had. Never again. The worm had developed a backbone at last.

She reached for her purse and headed toward the door.

Open-mouthed, Sally lingered behind. "Aren't you going to let the great white shark know you're leaving?"

"No. He'll figure it out for himself."

Sally closed her mouth, then promptly opened it again. "Okay."

Bethany was halfway out the door when she glanced over her shoulder at Joshua's office. A great sadness settled over her, and she exhaled a soft sigh of regret. Her relationship with him seemed to be a case of one step forward followed almost immediately by two giant leaps back. She'd been given a rare glimpse of the man she knew him to be. It might well take another lifetime to be granted a second peek.

Unusually quiet, Sally led the way to the company cafeteria on the third floor. They ordered their lunch, then carried the bright orange trays to a round table by a window that overlooked the rambling Mississippi River.

"You're right, you know." Bethany spoke first. "I should have quit long before now." Like a romantic schoolgirl, she'd believed their relationship had shifted and he'd begun to view her as someone other than his executive assistant. Instead, their time together with Angie was an embarrassment to him, something he obviously regretted.

"I'm right about what? J. D. Norris?" Sally asked, watching her friend carefully. When Bethany didn't respond right away, she peeled open her turkey-on-wheat sandwich to remove the lettuce. She reached for the salt shaker in the middle of the table, then changed her mind and replaced it.

A long minute passed before Bethany nodded.

"Well?" Sally demanded. "Are you going to spill your guts or not?"

"Not," Bethany answered in a small voice that was filled with regret. She couldn't explain facts she herself had only recently faced. She had been pining away for three good years of her life, and just when she'd been given a glimmer of hope, she'd been forced to recognize how futile the whole situation was.

Eventually Sally would wear her down, Bethany knew. Her friend usually came up with some new way of drilling the information out of her. But she wasn't ready to talk yet. She lifted her sandwich and realized she might as well have been contemplating eating Mississippi mud for all the appeal her lunch held. She returned the sandwich to the plate untouched and pushed it aside.

"You know I've heard all this a thousand times before."

"Of course I do. But this time is different."

"Right," Sally said with a soft snicker.

"No, I really mean it," Bethany returned. "I recently read that the best time to find a job is when you're currently employed. I'm going to start applying for new positions first thing tomorrow morning."

Sally's narrowed gaze said that she wasn't sure if she could believe her friend or not. Bethany met that look with a determination that had been sadly absent in the past. This time she was serious—she honestly meant it. She was leaving Joshua Norris for good.

When Bethany returned to the office, the morning paper tucked under her arm, Joshua's door was open. He must have heard her, because he stepped out and stood at her desk as if to wait for her. Although she refused to meet his gaze, she could feel him assessing her. He left without a word a couple of minutes later.

The instant he was gone she opened the newspaper to the jobs section, carefully read the help-wanted columns and made two calls, setting up appointments.

An hour later Joshua returned, but he didn't speak to her then, either, which was just as well.

The afternoon passed quickly after that. He requested two files and dictated a letter, which she typed and returned within the half hour. No other communication passed between them, verbal or otherwise.

Finally he left for a meeting with accounting, and fifteen minutes later Bethany walked out to meet Sally for their afternoon coffee break. Apparently Sally had decided to keep her opinions to herself, because the subject of J. D. Norris didn't come up.

When Bethany returned to the office, she decided she would ask Joshua for Thursday morning off. She would tell him she had an appointment, which was true; it just wasn't the kind of appointment he would no doubt assume. The appointment was to fill out a job application. And next time she accepted a position, she was going to be certain that her employer was happily married and over fifty.

"Miss Stone. Hi."

Bethany's gaze flew to her desk, where Angie sat waiting.

The girl jumped up and smiled, looking pleased to see Bethany again. "I didn't think you'd ever get back."

"Hello, Angie." The little girl's welcoming smile would rival a Louisiana sunset. "How was your first day of school?"

The ten-year-old wrinkled up her nose. "There are a bunch of weird kids living in this town."

"Oh?"

"Not a single girl in my class has ever heard of Bobby Short or Frank Sinatra."

"What a shame," Bethany answered sympathetically.

"Anyone who knows anything about music must have heard about Bobby. Why…he's world famous. Grandma and Grandpa knew him. A long time ago they would go to the Carlisle Hotel in New York City to hear him." She crossed her arms and gave a short little pout. "I never got to go, but Grandma has his CDs."

"Do you enjoy his music?"

"Oh yes, and Frank Sinatra, too. I'm not going to tell Dad this," Angie continued, her voice dropping to a soft whisper, "because it would upset him, but the kids here have no class."

Making no comment, Bethany deposited her bag in the bottom desk drawer and took her chair.

Angie came around the other side of the computer to face her. "Do you like Britney Spears?"

Containing a smile was impossible. "Quite a bit, as a matter of fact."

The youngster seemed surprised that Bethany would openly admit as much. "I do, too, but Grandma says she's a hussy."

"And what does that mean?" A laugh worked its way up Bethany's throat but she quickly shut it down when her gaze met a pair of dark, serious brown eyes.

Angie shook her head. "I'm not sure, but I think it has something to do with getting her body pierced."

Bethany sincerely hoped the ten-year-old hadn't noticed her ears. Heaven only knew what she would think of someone who had each lobe pierced *twice*. To divert the child's attention, she turned toward her computer.

Angie dragged a chair over to the side of the desk. "Dad said I'm not supposed to bother you when you're working. The new housekeeper can't come until tomorrow, so I'm here for the afternoon."

"You won't be a bother, sweetheart."

Angie looked relieved at that. "What are you doing now?"

"I'm about to type a letter for your dad."

"Can I watch?"

"If you want." Bethany's fingers flew over the keys. She finished in a few minutes.

"You're good."

"It takes practice."

"Can I look up something on your computer? Mine is at the house."

Bethany moved aside. "Of course. If you need any help just say the word."

For the next hour Angie became Bethany's shadow. The little girl was a joy, and more than once Bethany was unable to hold back a laugh. Angela Norris was unlike any ten-year-old Bethany had ever known. Despite the fact that she'd been raised by her grandparents and had attended a small private school, she appeared utterly unspoiled. Bethany found that fact remarkable.

It was nearly five o'clock by the time Joshua returned from his meeting.

"Hi, Dad," Angie said happily. "Bethany let me use her fingernail polish. See?" She held up both hands, revealing pink-tipped fingers.

The phone rang before Joshua could respond.

"I'll get that." Bethany sucked in her breath as Angie reached for the receiver. "Mr. Norris's office, how may I help you?"

"Miss Stone?" Joshua arched his brows in a disapproving slant. "Is this your doing?"

Bethany's response was to offer him a guilty smile.

Angie pressed the receiver to her shoulder and looked at Bethany. "It's someone named Sally asking for you."

Joshua's gaze sliced into Bethany, dark with disapproval. "As soon as you're finished, Miss Stone, I'd like to see you in my office."

Three

"You asked to see me, Mr. Norris?" Bethany asked in a brisk businesslike tone, devoid of emotion. She trained her gaze on a point on the wall behind him so she wouldn't have to subject herself to his cool assessing eyes. No doubt she'd done something more to displease him. Again. It wasn't as though she hadn't been trying. All day she'd been thinking of petty ways of getting back at him for his cold treatment of her earlier.

She didn't like to think of herself as a mean person, but working with Joshua had reduced her to this level. That on its own was reason enough to find other employment.

"I wanted to apologize for Angie being here," he said.

Bethany relaxed. "She hasn't been a problem."

"Good. The housekeeper I hired starts tomorrow, so this will be the last time Angie will need to come to the office."

"I understand." Although it required willpower, Bethany kept her gaze centered on the landscape drawing behind Joshua. "Will that be all?"

"Yes." He sounded hesitant.

She turned and marched with military precision toward the door, then paused when she remembered her plan to look for another job and turned to face him again. "Mr. Norris?"

"Yes?"

"I'll need Thursday off."

"This Thursday?"

"I've got an appointment."

"All day?"

She straightened her shoulders. "That's correct."

He didn't sound pleased, but that wasn't her problem.

"All right, Miss Stone, arrange for Human Resources to send me a substitute, then."

"I'll do that, sir."

"Miss Stone," he called out impatiently. "Kindly drop the 'sir,' will you? You haven't used it in the past, and it's unnecessary to call me that now. Is that understood?"

"Perfectly, Mr. Norris."

He expelled his breath in what sounded like a frustrated sigh. "Miss Stone, is there a problem?"

She kept her face as devoid of emotion as possible. "What could possibly be wrong?" she asked in as much of a singsong sarcastic voice as she dared without invoking his full ire.

"That's my question!" he shouted.

"Then that's my answer."

His eyes rounded with surprise, and he looked as though he wanted to say something more. But when he didn't speak immediately, she quickly left the room. She'd never spoken to him in that tone before or revealed any of what she was thinking. But she wouldn't be in Joshua Norris's employment much longer, and the sense of freedom she felt amazed her.

"Miss Stone?" Angie asked, her wide eyes studying Bethany. "Is my dad upset with you?"

"No, honey, of course not."

"Good." The little girl released a long sigh that seemed to deflate her until her small shoulders sagged with relief. "He's always saying things in this deep dark voice that scares people. It used to make me want to cry, but then I realized he talks that way most of the time, and he isn't really mad."

"I know, Angie. If you'd like, you can call me Bethany."

"I can?"

"But only if we can be friends."

The ten-year-old released another one of those balloon-whooshing sighs. "After the day I've had, believe me, I could use one."

Bethany laughed at the adult turn of phrase, although she could see that the little girl was dead serious.

"It's true," Angie murmured, her dark eyes round and sad. "I don't think anyone in my new class likes me. I don't know what I did wrong, either. But I think Grandma would say I was trying too hard."

"Give it time, sweetheart."

Angie nodded and grinned. "That's something else Grandma would say."

"By the end of the week you'll have all kinds of new friends."

"Do you honestly think so?"

Bethany opened a word processing program and

brought up a fresh page. "How would you like to type a letter for me?"

"I can do that?"

"Sure. I've got some filing to do, and since you're here, you can be *my* executive assistant." She laid a form letter on the tabletop for the little girl to copy.

"I'll do my best, Miss Stone. I mean…Bethany." Angie slid the chair toward the computer, looking as efficient and businesslike as it was possible for a ten-year-old to look.

Within a couple of minutes Angie's brow was furrowed with concentration as her fingers went on a seek-and-find mission for each key on the keyboard. It took her an hour to finish the few short sentences of the letter, but when it was done, she looked as proud as if she'd climbed Stone Mountain unaided.

"You did a fine job, Angie," Bethany told her, glancing over the finished product.

"Oh, hi, Dad," Angie said, flew off her chair and went running toward her father. "Guess what? Bethany said I can be her executive assistant. I can come back tomorrow, can't I? You aren't really going to make me stay with that stuffy old housekeeper, are you? Bethany needs me here."

Bethany opened her mouth, then closed it. She'd only been trying to entertain Joshua's daughter, and now it looked as though she'd created a problem instead of solving one.

"There may be an occasional afternoon when Miss Stone could use your help," Joshua admitted thoughtfully, his gaze resting on Bethany. "But Miss Stone is quite efficient, so you shouldn't count on coming every day."

"But, Dad..."

"Miss Stone is usually able to handle all the work herself," Joshua said in a voice that brooked no argument.

"I *want* to help her, though. As often as I can, and I should be able to come every afternoon, don't you think, Bethany?"

"I said you may come occasionally," Joshua reiterated, "and that's all the argument I'm willing to listen to, Angela."

"Yes, Daddy." She didn't look pleased, but she wasn't completely deflated, either.

Considering everything, Bethany felt Joshua had offered a decent compromise. In fact, thinking it over as she left the office later, she was actually pleased with the way he had handled the situation with his daughter. He might not have had a lot of opportunity to do much parenting, but he seemed to be adapting nicely. No doubt once she found another job, Angie and Joshua would get along fine without her.

Late Thursday afternoon Bethany was sitting in front of the television, her feet propped up on the coffee table and a hot drink cupped in her hand, when her roommate let herself into the apartment.

"You look like you had a rough day," Sally commented.

"It's a jungle out there," Bethany said forcefully. Her feet ached, her spirits sagged, and she wondered if there would ever be a job that would free her heart from

Joshua Norris. She'd gone on two interviews earlier and applied for several other openings on-line.

"I take it you didn't get a job offer?"

"The woman's a mind reader."

"What'd you find out?"

"Nothing, unfortunately," Bethany admitted with a soft moan of discouragement. "I got the old 'don't call us, we'll call you' routine."

"What are you going to do?" Sally asked, the concern in her voice evident.

"What else *can* I do?" Bethany answered. "I'll stick it out with Joshua Norris until I find something suitable."

Her friend plunked herself on the sofa beside Bethany and rested her own feet on the coffee table. "Well, I've got news for *you,* too."

"What?" Bethany was in the mood for something uplifting.

"Apparently Mr. Norris didn't have a good day without you."

"Oh?"

"He went through two substitutes before noon."

"Good grief, who did H. R. send him?"

"I don't know, but the word was, Mr. Norris was in a foul mood all day."

Bethany tugged at the corner of her lower lip with her teeth. "I wonder why?"

"So does everyone else. I'll tell you one thing, though. There isn't an executive assistant in the entire company who isn't glad you're coming back tomorrow morning. Every one of them spent an anxious afternoon fearing they were going to be sent to work for him next. It's like ordering a vestal virgin to walk into the dragon's den."

"He's not that bad!" Joshua might have faults, but he certainly wasn't a tyrant. She wouldn't have fallen in love with a slave driver.

"Mr. Norris isn't bad? Wanna bet?" Sally returned forcefully. "Rumor has it that he told the first substitute she was completely useless."

Bethany gritted her teeth to keep from defending Joshua. It was apparent to her, if not to her roommate, that if her employer had called her replacement useless it was highly probable the woman had done something stupid. Bethany didn't know who H. R. had sent up to replace her, but it seemed the problem lay with them and not Mr. Norris.

"You *are* planning to go back tomorrow, aren't you?" Sally asked expectantly.

Bethany nodded; she didn't have any choice but to return. She'd envisioned walking into his office and slapping down her two-week notice, all the while smiling smugly, but that wasn't going to happen. She knew it had been foolish to expect to receive an offer on the spot, but still, she had dared to hope.

"That will save me a good deal of telephoning."

"Telephoning?"

"Yeah," her roommate said, looking pleased. "I promised I'd call the other exec assistants and let them know if you weren't going to work, because in that case, every one of them was planning to call in sick."

"But that's ridiculous."

"You weren't at the office today, Beth. You couldn't possibly know what rumors have been circulating. I swear, there isn't a woman in all of Norris Pharmaceutical who doesn't think you should be nominated for sainthood."

Bethany grinned at that. It did her ego a world of good to have others think of her as irreplaceable. Unfortunately, Joshua was the only one who mattered, and he didn't seem to care one way or the other.

The following morning proved her wrong.

Bethany was at her desk when Joshua strolled into the office. He paused just inside the door and looked relieved when he saw her. It might have been the lighting, but she actually thought she saw his gaze soften. A brief smile touched his mouth; of that, she was sure.

"Good morning, Bethany."

"Mr. Norris." She stood and was halfway into his office when she realized he'd called her by her first name. Her heart ping-ponged against her breast. For the first time in years she was a real person to him and not some kind of motor-driven robot.

By the time she delivered a cup of freshly brewed coffee to his desk and handed him the mail, she'd managed to compose herself and wipe the last traces of triumph from her face.

He leafed through the correspondence and gave his instructions the way he did each weekday morning. When he was finished, however, he paused.

"Miss Stone?"

She'd already stood, but he gestured for her to sit down again. "Yes?"

"How long have you been working for me now? Three years?"

She nodded.

"When was the last time I gave you a raise?"

"Four months ago." Her generous salary was part of the problem in finding another suitable position. Once she listed her current wages, most places were unwilling to meet or match her price. At least that was what she surmised from her experiences the day before.

"You've done an excellent job for me, Miss Stone."

"Thank you."

"I tend not to tell you that often enough."

As she recalled, he'd never said it, certainly not directly.

"We seem to work well together. Until you were gone yesterday I didn't realize how much you do to keep this office running smoothly."

"Thank you." She knew she sounded as if her vocabulary was limited to two words, but he'd taken her by surprise, and she couldn't find anything else to say that made any sense. There must have been some truth to what Sally had told her about her replacements, but she had been absent from work before. Not often, but a day or two now and again, or an annual vacation.

"You anticipate my needs," he went on, looking slightly embarrassed. "You seem to know what I'm thinking and act on it without my having to comment. I don't think I appreciated that before. It's a rare quality in an employee."

"Thank you." She hardly knew what to say.

"I feel it would only be fair to compensate you for a job well done." He paused and looked pleased with himself.

"I beg your pardon?" She wasn't sure what he meant.

"I'm giving you another raise."

He mentioned a sum that made her gasp. The amount was nearly twenty-five percent of her already more than adequate salary. "But I told you, I just received a raise last October."

Joshua arched his brows speculatively. "Does that mean you don't want this one?"

"Of course I want it."

"Good," he said briskly, turning his attention to the papers on his desk, dismissing her. "That will be all, then."

"Thank…you, Mr.…Norris," she said, getting awkwardly to her feet. A couple of the envelopes she was holding nearly slipped from her fingers, but she managed to grab them before they fell to the floor.

He grinned, and his look was almost boyish. "I believe you've thanked me quite adequately, Miss Stone."

She couldn't return to her desk fast enough. The first thing she did was call Sally, who worked in the accounting department.

"Sally," she said under her breath. "Meet me in the cafeteria."

"Now? In case you haven't noticed, it's barely after nine."

"Okay, at ten." It would kill her to wait that long, but she didn't have a choice.

"Bethany?" her friend said, sounding vaguely concerned. "We've been meeting for coffee every day at ten for three years. Why would today be any different?"

"I got a raise!" Bethany cried, unable to hold the information inside any longer.

"Another one?"

To her way of thinking, Sally didn't sound nearly as pleased as she should have been. "What you said about yesterday must have been true, because Mr. Norris seemed more than pleased to see me this morning."

"Beth, does this mean you won't be looking for another job?"

"Are you nuts? Where else would I ever make this kind of money?"

"Where else would you risk breaking your heart?" Sally asked.

The question echoed through Bethany's mind like shouts bouncing off canyon walls. The reply was equally clear: nowhere else but with Joshua Norris.

Two weeks passed, and although nothing had actually changed, everything was different. There didn't seem to be any one reason that Bethany could pin down, but she felt more at ease with Joshua. Their routine remained exactly as it had been for the last three years, but he seemed more content. He was less formal, less austere. She guessed that the changes were a result of having Angie come to live with him. The ten-year-old was such a great kid that Bethany knew her employer couldn't be around his daughter and not be affected.

Bethany was hungry for news of the little girl, but she dared not topple this fragile peace between them after that first morning when Joshua had made it clear that he didn't wish to discuss his daughter.

"Miss Stone?" He called for her when she returned from her lunch break Friday afternoon.

She reached for a pad and pencil, and stepped into his office.

Joshua was leaning back in his chair, his hands forming a steeple under his chin; his look was thoughtful. "How much do you know about fashion for ten-year-olds?"

"Fashion?" she repeated, not certain she'd heard him correctly.

"Yes. Angela recently informed me she's 'out of it' and seemed quite concerned. Apparently not wearing the latest fad is a fate worse than death."

Bethany smiled and nodded, remembering her own teen years. Ten seemed a bit young, but she could understand Angie's wanting to fit in with the other girls her age.

"Short of dying her hair orange and piercing her nose, I have very few objections to the way my daughter dresses."

Bethany nodded. She didn't particularly agree with that statement, but it wasn't her place to share her opinions on the matter with Joshua.

He straightened and looked uncomfortable. "I was wondering if it would be possible for you to take Angie shopping. She specifically asked for you, and I don't mind admitting I know next to nothing about how girls her age dress these days. Naturally I'd pay you for your time. It would mean a good deal to Angie."

"I'd enjoy it immensely."

He sighed, and then actually grinned. "You don't know how relieved I am to hear that. I had visions of Angela dragging me through the women's lingerie department."

The following morning, Bethany met Angie and Joshua in a local shopping mall. The minute Angie saw

Bethany approach, she let go of her father's hand and came running toward her as though they hadn't seen each other in years.

"Bethany, hi. I didn't think you'd ever get here."

Surprised, Bethany glanced at her wrist. "Am I late?" According to her watch, she was five minutes early.

"It seemed to take you forever," the ten-year-old said.

"We've been here ten minutes," Joshua admitted with an off-center grin that took away five years.

He looked so good that Bethany had to force her gaze back to Angie. "I take it you're excited?"

"Do the Saints play football?" Joshua asked, referring to the New Orleans football team, which had just finished an exceptionally good season.

"Dad said the sky's the limit. Are you ready?" Angie asked, her face a study in eagerness. "'Cuz I am."

"Good luck," Joshua said, and paused to look at his watch. "I'll meet you for lunch. Where would you suggest?"

Before Bethany could answer, Angie called out, "McDonald's! There's one in the food court."

"You game?" Joshua asked Bethany, looking more amused by the minute. She had trouble seeing him as the same man she worked with five days a week. For the first time in memory, he wasn't wearing a suit but was dressed casually in slacks and a light sweater that accentuated his eyes.

"McDonald's? Sure!" The last time she'd been to one had been the night they'd picked up Angie from the airport. If Joshua was game, then so was she.

By one o'clock Bethany was exhausted and Angie was just hitting her second wind. The child seemed tireless—a born shopper. It amazed Bethany how selective the ten-year-old was about her clothes. Although they'd been in at least fifteen different stores, Angie had chosen less than a dozen items. Mostly t-shirts and acid-washed jeans, and a couple of pairs of sandals and tennis shoes. Bethany did manage to talk her into one dress and a pair of dress shoes, but according to Angie she had a closet full of frilly dresses already. She needed casual clothes like the ones the other girls in her new school wore.

Joshua was sitting in a booth in McDonald's munching on a French fry when Angie and Bethany joined him.

"How's it going?" he asked.

"Bethany really knows her stuff," Angie announced, already reaching for the burger he'd ordered for her. "I knew the minute you told me she was going to take me shopping that today would be special, and it has been."

Bethany felt her heart constrict at the little girl's praise. If anyone was special, it was Joshua's precocious daughter.

Angie dabbed a French fry in the ketchup and lowered her gaze to the tabletop. "I just wish I could see Bethany more often."

Neither adult spoke. Bethany gave her attention to her own hamburger.

"Miss Stone is busy, Angie. She has other friends."

"Why do you call her Miss Stone, Dad?"

"I don't have that many other friends," Bethany said quickly. "I'd enjoy seeing Angie more often."

Joshua's eyes drifted from one female to the next, his gaze bewildered, as though he weren't certain who he should answer first. It was clear from his expression that he felt outnumbered.

"I call her Bethany, and I bet you could, too." Angie added, "Grandma told me it was all right to call an adult by their first name if *they* said it was okay. I bet Bethany wouldn't mind if you called her that instead of Miss Stone all the time. You see her every day."

"Yes, well, I suppose I could—if Miss Stone doesn't object."

"Of course I don't mind."

"And you should call Dad J.D. like everyone else," Angie continued, speaking to Bethany.

"She prefers Joshua," he explained, his eyes holding Bethany's briefly. He grinned.

"Joshua." Angie rolled the name over her tongue as if the sound of it were something rich and rare. "I like that, too. When I was born, if I'd been a boy, what would you and Mom have named me?"

"David. It's my middle name."

"Not Joshua?" Angie sounded disappointed.

"Too confusing," her father explained.

"What made you decide on Angela?" the little girl asked, closely studying her father. She was so intent that she stopped eating, a French fry hanging limply in her hand, halfway to her mouth.

"You looked like a tiny angel when the doctor first showed you to me," Joshua explained, and his gaze softened as it rested on his daughter. "I suggested the name Angela Catherine to your mother."

Angie nodded, not looking overly pleased. "I wish you'd thought I looked like a Millicent."

"Millicent?"

"Perhaps a Guinevere."

"Guinevere?" It was Bethany's turn to become an echo.

"Or even better, a Charmaine." Dramatically, the ten-year-old placed her hand over her heart, gazed into the distance and heaved an expressive sigh.

"Charmaine?" Bethany and Joshua repeated, and glanced at each other.

"Oh, yes. Those names sound pretty and smart. Angie sounds…I don't know…ordinary."

"Trust me, sweetheart, the last thing you are is conventional."

From the way Angie's eyes darted down to the table, it was apparent she didn't understand Joshua's meaning.

"That's another way of saying ordinary," Bethany explained.

"I knew that!"

Once more Bethany and Joshua shared a brief smile.

"Bethany is such a pretty name. I wouldn't have minded that name, either."

"Thank you. My father named me, too."

"He did?"

"Yes, and when I was ten I wanted to be called Dominique because it sounded sophisticated and mysterious. I used to make up stories where I was the heroine who saved all my friends from certain death."

"You did?" Angie's eyes were growing rounder by the minute. "What about you, Dad? Did you ever want to be called something else when you were ten?"

"No."

Bethany resisted the urge to kick him under the table.

Even if it was true, there wasn't any need to squelch the game.

"I believe I was eleven at the time," he answered thoughtfully. "I wanted everyone to call me Mordecai. I felt it was a name that revealed great character. When I said it, I felt stronger."

"Mordecai," Angie repeated slowly. "I like that almost as much as Joshua. Oh, Dad, this is the most fun I've had since moving to New Orleans."

Joshua grinned, and the smile Bethany had felt was so rare only hours before looked almost natural.

"Dad, can Bethany come home with us? Please? I want to show her my bedroom, and my new television and computer and everything. You don't mind, do you?"

Four

"Come see my bedroom next," Angie insisted, dragging Bethany by the hand down the long hallway. "Dad had a lady come in and decide on my colors and everything...only, I wish..." She paused and glanced over her shoulder before adding, "I like lavender much better than the yellow she picked."

Bethany paused in the doorway of the little girl's room and swallowed a soft gasp. The bedroom was elaborately decorated with ornate French-provincial-style furniture. A huge canopy bed dominated the space, with a matching desk and armoire close by. Thick canary-yellow carpeting covered the floor and was used to accent a lighter shade of sheer priscilla curtains. The bedspread had the same flowery pattern as the curtains.

"Don't you think it's simply divine?" Angie asked in a falsetto voice that Bethany was sure was an imitation of something she'd seen on TV. Angie's wide-eyed gaze made it clear she was waiting for a response.

It was all Bethany could do to nod. Yes, the room was lovely, but it didn't personify Joshua's daughter.

The little girl who now preferred acid-washed jeans and sweatshirts hadn't once been consulted regarding what she wanted in her bedroom. Bethany would stake her career on that. This room belonged to a soft, feminine, demure child, and Angie was direct, tomboyish, and full of vitality and life.

"Look at this," Angie said, stepping around her to the armoire. She opened the top doors and revealed a thirty-two-inch screen. "I can sit on my bed and watch television or play computer games as late as I want."

"What about bedtime?" Bethany immediately wished she hadn't asked. She might be curious, but it was better that she not know, because she already knew that she was going to disapprove. And she was powerless to say or do anything about it.

"Dad says I'll go to sleep when I'm tired, and I do." She flopped down across the mattress on her stomach, legs raised and crossed at the ankles. She reached for the remote control, held it out like a laser gun and pressed a button, turning on the TV. "Sometimes I fall asleep with it on, and then Dad turns it off for me before he goes to bed."

Bethany managed a weak nod.

"He's always real busy after dinner," Angie explained, her eyes a little sad. "He has a lot of homework to do...reading papers and stuff like that. You know."

Bethany did. "What do you do while your father's busy working?"

"Oh, nothing much. I come to my room and play on my computer or watch TV. Sometimes I read."

"What about homework?"

"Oh, Mrs. Larson, the housekeeper, has me do that

as soon as I get home from school," she said, and sighed expressively. "Mrs. Larson's all right, but I wish she'd let me play with the other kids, and after class is the only time I can do that."

"Have you made new friends?"

"Sure, lots—just like you said I would."

Pleased, Bethany patted the top of the little girl's head. At least that adjustment had seemed to come easily enough.

"As soon as I admitted I like Lady Gaga all the girls knew I wasn't a geek." She paused, pressed a button on the remote control and turned off the television. "The afternoon you let me paint my fingernails helped, too, I think." Her gaze dropped suggestively to her clear nails, and she let loose with a hopeful sigh and raised pleading eyes to Bethany.

"I think I just may have a bottle of that same polish in my purse. If it's all right with your father, we'll do your nails again before I leave."

"Oh, Dad won't care," Angie said, flying off the bed and throwing her arms around Bethany's waist in a bear hug.

"What won't I care about?" Joshua asked, leaning against the doorjamb, looking relaxed and amused.

His eyes sought out his daughter, then drifted, almost reluctantly, to Bethany. The warmth of his gaze did funny things to her equilibrium, and she reached out to steady herself against the bedpost.

"You won't care, will you, Dad?"

"About what, sweetheart?"

"If Bethany paints my fingernails again."

"No," he murmured, his gaze continuing to hold Bethany's. "I think that would be just fine."

"Do you want to come outside and look at the patio next?" Angie asked, her voice raised and eager. "Dad wanted to buy me a swing set, but I told him I was too old for that kind of kid stuff." She rolled her eyes for effect, and it took all Bethany's self-control not to laugh outright.

Joshua led them to the patio off the family room and gestured toward the white wicker furniture for Bethany to take a seat.

"Would you care for something to drink, Miss Stone?"

Angie slapped her hands against her thighs in a small display of disgust. "Honestly, Dad, I thought you were going to call her Bethany."

"Old habits die hard," he said, clearly trying to appease his daughter.

"I'll take a soda," Angie said, sitting beside Bethany, swinging her stubby legs.

"Bethany?"

"Iced tea, if you have it. Thanks."

He cocked one brow and grinned broadly, his eyes alight with mischief. "What, no white wine?"

Bethany quickly averted her gaze to Lake Pontchartrain, whose waters lapped lazily against the shore only a few yards away. Joshua was teasing her about the Friday night she'd approached him at Charley's, and she didn't know how to respond.

"I'll be back in a minute."

"Do you want to walk down to the water?" Angie

offered, jumping to her feet and holding out her hand to Bethany.

Bethany nodded eagerly. She'd always loved the lake and was more than willing to escape Joshua for a few moments. Questions were pounding against the edges of her mind like children beating against a locked door. She'd hungered for so long to know him better. She'd been just as anxious for him to like her. Now it was finally happening, and suddenly she was afraid. Terrified.

Sally would be furious with her for not having a witty comeback when he'd suggested the wine. He was accustomed to sophisticated women who knew how to spar verbally. Bethany could be witty, too, but it generally took a glass of wine or some time. She wasn't as quick witted as some, much to her regret. Feeling the way she did about him didn't help, either. Every time he looked at her with those warm lazy eyes, she felt light-headed and dizzy.

Angie slipped off her sneakers and socks, and tested the water with her big toe. "It's really warm."

The day was almost balmy, even though it was only the beginning of February.

"Do you think it would be all right if we waded a little bit? I think it would," Angie answered her own question and stepped out into the water until she was up to her calves.

Bethany slipped out of her sandals and followed, letting the lake lap at her toes. It was probably a silly thing to do, but she didn't care. The impulse to enjoy the water was too strong to resist.

"I love this lake," Angie said wistfully. "Dad says we'll be able to swim in a couple of months if the weather is nice, and it should be. I only wish he would let me swim alone, but he says I can't go in the water unless he's with me."

"He's right," Bethany said forcefully, frightened by the thought of Angie in the lake without an adult close by. "Don't ever go in the water alone. It's much too dangerous."

"Oh, I won't. I don't think Dad will ever go with me, though," she said regretfully. "He has too much work to do. All he does is work, work, work. I tried to talk him into reading his papers on the patio so I could play by the water, but he said no to that, too."

Bethany silently agreed with that decision. It would be much too easy for him to become involved in whatever he was working on and forget about Angie.

"Your dad's right, honey."

"I knew you'd say that," she answered with a soft pout.

Bethany laughed, enjoying the warm breeze that mussed her hair about her face. As she moved deeper the water felt cool and refreshing, and before she knew it, she had lifted the skirt of her soft pink dress and was almost knee-deep.

"Hey, look!" Angie called excitedly, waving frantically toward the house. "Dad's watching us."

Bethany twisted around and answered Joshua's wave with one of her own. In her dreams she'd often pictured a scene where they stood together by the lake with the wind whispering gently around them. She wished he would come down by the waterside and make her dream a reality. If she hadn't known better, she would have thought he was thinking the same thing, because the smile left his face and his gaze captured hers, holding it, refusing to let it go. The tender look was enough to cause her pulse rate to soar.

She wasn't sure what happened next, or how she lost her footing, but suddenly, unexpectedly, she was slipping. Her arms flew out in a desperate effort to maintain her balance. She should have known that if she was going to make a complete fool of herself it would be in front of Joshua Norris. By the time she hit the water, she'd accepted her fate.

"Bethany, Bethany, are you all right?"

Mortified, Bethany sat in the chest-deep water and buried her red-hot face in her hands, unable to answer the little girl.

"Daddy, Daddy, I think Bethany's hurt!"

Bethany heard Angie shouting as she ran toward the house. Knowing there was nothing to do but face Joshua, she stood awkwardly and walked out of the water. Her once pretty dress was plastered over her torso and thighs, and the ends of her hair dripped water. Bethany didn't understand how her hair could be wet and her shoulders dry, but they were.

Joshua stood on the shore, his hands braced against his hips, doing an admirable job, she thought, of not laughing.

"Well, Miss Stone, how's the water?"

"Fine, thanks," she said, and her voice came out an octave higher than normal.

"I've sent Angela for a towel."

Bethany nodded her thanks, and rubbed her hands up and down her chilled arms. Water pooled at her feet.

"Here, Dad," Angie said breathlessly, rushing onto

the scene, her arms loaded with a drawerful of soft thick towels.

Joshua draped one across Bethany's shoulders and held it there momentarily. "Whatever possessed you to wade in the lake?" he asked in a low growl. "For heaven's sake, it's February."

"The water was warm." The excuse sounded weak even to her own ears.

"Bethany, honestly." He pressed his forehead against hers. "Come in the house before you catch your death."

"I...I think it would be best if I just went home," she whispered, utterly miserable.

"Like this? Wet? You could catch a cold, and you must be uncomfortable, besides."

She didn't care. She was willing to suffer any discomfort in order to extract herself from this awkward situation.

"Stay," he urged, "and dry off here."

His gaze sought hers, and she found she couldn't refuse him.

With his arm cupping her shoulder, he led her toward the house. At loose ends and wanting to help in some way, Angie ran circles around them like a frolicking puppy. "Are you all right, Bethany?" she asked.

"She's fine, sweetheart," Joshua said, answering for her.

"It's all my fault."

"Bethany doesn't blame you. It was an accident, and sometimes those happen." Again he was answered for her.

Not knowing what to say or do to calm the distraught

child, Bethany held out her hand. It was immediately clasped by a much smaller one.

Joshua led her through a set of sliding glass doors at the other end of the house into what was obviously the master bedroom. Bethany hesitated, not wanting to drip water all over his pearl-gray carpet, but he urged her forward and into the large master bathroom.

"Take a warm shower," he ordered, but not unkindly, much less in the coldly unemotional voice she was accustomed to hearing from him. "Give Angie your wet things, and I'll have Mrs. Larson put them in the drier."

Bethany nodded.

"When you've finished, slip into my robe." He pointed to the thick navy blue robe that hung on the back of the door. "I'll have a hot drink waiting for you."

Again she answered him with a short nod. He left and closed the door.

"I feel terrible," Angie wailed, close to tears. "You'd never have gone into the water if it hadn't been for me."

"Sweetheart, don't worry about it. I stumbled over my own two feet." She didn't mention that she'd been looking at Joshua at the time and daydreaming.

Angie slumped down on the edge of the bathtub, looking mournful. "I will always blame myself for this," she said, sounding like a true drama queen.

"I refuse to let you," Bethany said, her teeth starting to chatter. "If you do, then I'll be forced to keep my nail polish in my purse."

"Well, actually, now that you mention it," the ten-year-old said as she nonchalantly stood and walked to the door, "it really *was* all your own fault. Are you normally this clumsy?"

"Always," Bethany muttered, and turned on the shower.

When she was finished, both Angie and Joshua were sitting in the living room waiting for her. She tightened the belt of the thick robe, which was so long on her that the hem dragged across the carpet. Her hair hung in limp strands about her face, and she felt as if she should stand on a street corner and beg for quarters.

Joshua stood when he saw her coming and made an admirable effort not to smile.

"Don't you dare laugh," Bethany warned him under her breath, at the same time reassuring Angie with a grin. She didn't know what she would do to Joshua if he did, but she would find a way to make him regret it.

"I wouldn't *dream* of laughing."

"Ha!"

"I'll pour you a cup of coffee."

She sat in a velvet wingback chair, and accepted the mug from Joshua when he brought it to her. "Thank you."

"You're quite welcome."

She had the distinct feeling he was showing his appreciation for giving him the single biggest laugh of his life.

The first sip of coffee seared its way down her throat and made her eyes widen at its potency. It was apparent the moment the liquid passed her lips that it had been liberally laced with whiskey.

"This is…Irish…coffee?" she stammered in a breathless whisper, having trouble finding her voice.

"I didn't want you to catch a chill."

"Dad was real worried about you," Angie piped in. "He said you were lucky you didn't swallow a fish."

Bethany's narrowed gaze sliced through her employer. How she wished she could say exactly what she was thinking!

"I've instructed Mrs. Larson to set the table for three this evening," he said.

Bethany had no idea it was so close to dinnertime. "I can't stay," she said hurriedly. "Really, I have to get home."

"You can't just leave," Angie said, her voice tight with disappointment. "We're having pork roast and homemade applesauce and fresh peas. But you don't have to eat the peas if you don't want. Dad makes me, but he won't make you…at least, I don't think he will."

Joshua stiffened and strolled to his daughter's side, resting his hand on her small shoulder. When he looked at Bethany, his gaze was guarded. "Miss Stone might have a date this evening, Angie. We shouldn't assume she's free."

"I…I'm not meeting anyone," Bethany said quickly. She shouldn't have been so eager to let him know that, but the truth was, she rarely dated anymore. There was no reason to, when she was already in love.

"Then you'll stay for dinner?" Angie asked eagerly.

Bethany's gaze fell to the steaming coffee. "All right," she said. She couldn't find an excuse not to, except that she'd hoped to salvage what remained of her pride. Not that there was much left—most of it had drowned in Lake Pontchartrain.

"Oh, good," Angie said gleefully. "Mrs. Larson's a terrific cook."

* * *

By the time the meal was served, Bethany's clothes were out of the drier, and she'd had time to deal with her hair. She felt infinitely better.

"I'm starved," Angie announced, claiming the chair beside Bethany and carefully unfolding the linen napkin across her lap.

"Swimming does that to me, too," Bethany added.

The corners of Joshua's mouth quivered before he burst into a full rich laugh. Soon they were all laughing.

"Rare is the woman who can find humor in her own misadventures," he announced, his face transformed by his careless smile.

Flustered, Bethany looked away, unable to hold his gaze any longer.

Before the meal was served Joshua poured her a glass of wine. She wasn't sure she should drink it on top of the laced coffee, but she decided it wouldn't hurt. A second glass followed toward the end of the meal.

Angie fell asleep on the sofa while Bethany and Joshua lingered over their second glass of wine in the living room. Candles cast flickering shadows across the wall, and the light in the room was muted, creating an intimate feeling.

"I enjoyed today," he said.

"I did, too."

"I'm grateful you were willing to take Angie shopping. It meant a good deal to us both. I want you to know I was serious about paying you for your time."

"Oh, don't, please. Being with Angie is a delight." She didn't add that spending her day with him had been equally wonderful. Thrilling, even. He was a completely different person away from the office. Having his daughter move in with him had sanded away the rough edges of his brusque personality. Her gaze shifted affectionately to the sleeping child. Knowing Angie had opened a door for Bethany that she had thought would be forever closed to her. She would be eternally grateful to the little girl.

"Angie really seems taken with you."

He said it as though he couldn't understand why, "That surprises you, doesn't it?" she asked and hated how defensive she sounded. She couldn't help it, though.

"What?" He frowned and looked confused.

"That…that anyone could be taken with me."

He looked completely shocked. "Not in the least."

She decided it was the wine that had given her the courage to speak frankly, to question him. Heaven knew she never had before…wouldn't have dared.

"You certainly can be a prickly thing," he added, frowning.

"Me?" That just went to prove how much attention he'd paid her over the years.

"I meant to compliment you when I said how much Angie liked you."

"I apologize, then."

"Fine."

A throbbing silence followed, during which she was convinced they were both searching for ways to bring the conversation back to an amicable level.

"I suppose I should think about getting home," she murmured, discouraged. The day had held such promise, but the evening had been a disaster. She should never drink wine. It went straight to her head and disassociated her tongue from her brain.

"Before you do, I'd like to ask another favor of you, if I may," he said.

Once more she could feel his reluctance, as though he didn't like to be in her debt. "I'd be happy to do anything for you...for Angie," she hurried to add.

"It's about Mardi Gras next week. Angie is looking forward to attending the festivities, and, well, you know my schedule better than anyone. Would you be willing to take her to the parade? I could meet you afterward, and we could have dinner, the three of us. That is, of course, unless you've got other plans. I certainly wouldn't want you to cancel a date with someone special."

"I'd love to take Angie to the parade."

Joshua nodded and grinned. "Bethany?"

"Yes?"

"*Is* there someone special?"

To tell him that he was the only one who mattered in her life would have been ludicrous, and even after the wine, she had the good sense to resist.

"No...not lately." She didn't know why she tagged that comment on, but she did, for better or worse.

"I see."

Bethany wasn't sure what he read into her answer—or what there was to read. "You don't have to meet us for dinner if you'd prefer to make other plans," she blurted out, then snapped her mouth closed, hardly able to believe she'd made the offer. "I mean...well, if you'd rather meet 'someone special' yourself, I'll understand."

He rotated the stem of his wineglass between his

open palms. "There hasn't been anyone for me, either," he said in a low, well-modulated voice. "Not lately, anyway." He raised his eyes to hers and grinned.

She relaxed against the back of the chair and smiled, more relaxed with Joshua than she could ever remember being. She'd often imagined quiet romantic moments such as these with him. But she'd always felt it was impossible.

"More wine?"

"No," she answered, and shook her head. "I'd better not, since I still have to drive home."

"I'll take you."

Although the thought was tempting, it would only be an inconvenience for him, and then she would need to ask Sally to drive her over to pick up her car tomorrow. Knowing Sally, and what her friend would read into her leaving her car at Joshua's…no, that just wouldn't work.

"Thank you, but no, I'll drive myself."

"What do you think of Angela's room?" he asked, and glanced proudly toward the hallway that led to the bedrooms.

She wasn't sure what to say. "It's very…yellow, isn't it?"

"You don't like yellow?"

"Oh, yes, it's a favorite color of mine."

"Then why do I hear that bit of derision in your voice?"

"No reason." It wasn't her place to tell him Angela would have preferred lavender.

"You know, Miss Stone, you don't lie the least bit convincingly."

"No, I suppose I don't."

"Now, tell me what you don't like about the very expensive bedroom I had prepared for my daughter."

"You've certainly made it appealing with all that technology." She hoped that would appease him, but one look at his frowning gaze told her differently.

"Yes. I realize she may be a bit young to appreciate some of that equipment."

"I just think—" She stopped herself in time, silently cursing the wine for loosening her tongue.

"You think what?"

"Never mind." She shook her head so hard her hair whipped across her face. She brushed her index finger across her cheek to free a maverick strand.

"Bethany, I wouldn't ask your opinion unless I wanted it." His eyes were unusually dark and solemn.

"I worry about her, that's all," she said, scooting forward a little in her chair. "You've created her own self-contained world, and I don't know if that's the best thing for a ten-year-old who's recently left the only home she's ever known."

"You think because I can afford to give her a television and a game system—"

"That's not my objection," she interrupted heatedly. Now that she'd started, the floodgate of opinion couldn't be held back. "Angie needs to be introduced to *your* world. She's got to spend time with you—not by herself in front of her own television while you watch yours. When you come home at night, she has to feel that she's more important to you than some report."

Joshua looked shocked. "I see."

"I don't mean to criticize you, Joshua, really I don't. It's just that I care so much about…about Angie." If she didn't shut up soon, she would give him more than one reason to fire her.

"Well, you've certainly given me something to think about."

She stood. It would be better if she left, before she said anything more.

"I'll walk you to your car," he murmured when she reached for her purse.

He escorted her outside and opened the driver's door. Scant inches separated them, and she moistened her dry lips, feeling the night air fill with tension. The silence seemed to vibrate between them, thick with awareness, with unspoken words. She felt it and wondered if he did too.

"There's more to you than I ever realized," he admitted. He reached out and touched her cheek, gently gliding his finger down the side of her jaw as though he were touching the most valuable thing in the world.

Bethany closed her eyes to the delicious sensation that overtook her like an unexpected weakness. Her pulse began to beat wildly. He was so close, so wonderfully close, she could feel the heat radiate from his body. She knew her lips had parted with expectation. She wanted him to kiss her. Needed him to kiss her. With her eyes still closed, she raised herself on tiptoe.

With a soft groan, Joshua settled his mouth hungrily over hers. He kissed her until she was flushed and trembling, sliding his mouth back and forth lazily across hers, soaking in her softness, savoring her gentleness. And yet he gripped her shoulders as though he wanted to push her away and couldn't find the will to do so. If it were up to her, he would go on holding and kissing her forever. It was as she'd always imagined it would be in his arms. Her whole body felt as though all the strength was draining out of her, leaving her weak and wanting, and oh, so needy.

With an indrawn breath and a shudder, Joshua dragged his lips from hers and took a step back. "Bethany," he whispered in a voice she barely recognized. "You'd better go."

She wanted to argue with him, lock her arms around his neck and tell him she didn't ever want to leave him, but that would be impossible.

"Thank you," he whispered, his voice still husky.

For one wild second she didn't know why he should thank her for anything. Then her mind cleared, and she realized he was talking about helping with Angie. If anyone should be grateful, it was her.

By taking her in his arms, Joshua had just proven that dreams actually *do* come true.

Five

Monday morning Bethany sat at her desk, her stomach a mass of nerves. The wine, she told herself. It had been the wine that had done all the talking Saturday night. In retrospect it astonished her that she could actually have told her employer how to raise his daughter. Who in heaven's name did she think she was?

She was an executive assistant. The closest she'd ever come to mothering anyone was burping her three-month-old niece. Sure, she liked kids, got along well with them, but that didn't make her an expert when it came to Joshua's relationship with his daughter.

And if the wine had been talking for her, then it might well have been responsible for Joshua's kissing her, too. She knew her employer well enough to believe that when he walked into the office this morning, he would pretend Saturday night had never happened. He'd crossed the line, no doubt regretted it, and would immediately step back, hoping she hadn't noticed—or had the good sense to forget.

But she would never forget being in Joshua's arms. It

had felt so wonderfully right and good. But instead of fulfilling a need, it had created an even greater one. The innocent emotion she'd held against her breast and nurtured had blossomed, leaving her craving so much more.

The door opened, and she held her breath as Joshua stepped into the office. He didn't glance in her direction, which was exactly what she'd expected. She'd been right. He regretted everything.

"Good morning, Miss Stone," he said tersely on his way past her.

She closed her eyes and firmly gritted her teeth. It was even worse than she'd thought. He'd barely been able to look in her direction.

Picking up the mail, she reluctantly followed him into the executive suite, pausing long enough to place the sorted correspondence on his desk. As was her habit, she delivered a cup of freshly brewed coffee and set it on the corner of his desk.

He leafed through the stack of letters, then paused and glanced in her direction. "How are you feeling, Miss Stone?"

"Fine." From the hoarse way the one word slipped past the tight constriction in her throat, it was a wonder he didn't call for a paramedic.

"Good. Then there were no lingering effects from your…swim the other day?"

"No…none—" she dropped her gaze so fast she nearly dislocated a disc in her neck "—except for a loose tongue." She felt the necessity to apologize. "Mr. Norris, I feel terrible that I took the liberty of criticizing. How you raise your daughter is none of my concern, and I sincerely hope that—"

"Miss Stone, kindly sit down."

She nearly missed the chair in her eagerness to get off her feet. Her hold on the pencil was so tense it was a credit to American craftsmanship that the wood didn't snap in two.

He reached for the coffee mug and leaned back in his chair, his look contemplative. "Ah, yes, your advice regarding Angela had slipped my mind."

Oh, no. He'd forgotten, and she'd gone out of her way to remind him! "It was the wine, you see," she said hurriedly. "I should never drink more than one glass, and I'd had two when we spoke, not to mention the Irish coffee earlier...and I can honestly say I wasn't quite myself Saturday evening."

"I see," he said with a frown. "So you have regrets?"

"Mr. Norris, please understand that under some circumstances...like those on Saturday...sometimes my tongue says things I have no intention of speaking aloud."

His frown grew darker, his brows crowding together until they formed a straight narrow line. He stiffened, seeming to shut her out completely.

She hated it when he did that, but she was powerless to do anything more than react. "I truly am sorry," she finished weakly.

"I believe you've apologized sufficiently. Shall we deal with the mail now, or is there anything else you care to confess before we get down to business?"

"The mail...of course."

Fifteen minutes later she stood, her head buzzing. She didn't exactly know where matters had gone wrong, but nothing seemed right. Joshua had been terse and impatient, issuing orders faster than she could write down his instructions. When he did look at her, his handsome face was devoid of expression.

She stood in front of the door that connected their two offices. Gathering her courage, she hesitated and turned around. She held the dictation pad to her breast like a shield of armor, her eyes infinitely sad. "Mr. Norris…one last thing."

"Yes. What is it now, Miss Stone?" he asked impatiently.

"I don't regret *everything* about Saturday night," she admitted in a raspy whisper, wanting to clear away one misconception, even at the cost of her own pride. "I can understand why *you* would prefer to forget what happened, but I don't. However, I…I promise not to embarrass either of us by ever mentioning it again."

She hurried to escape then, not waiting for a response, but several minutes later she was stunned to hear her employer whistling from behind the door.

At lunchtime she pressed the button of her intercom. "Mr. Norris, I'm leaving now."

"Miss Stone," he said hurriedly, "last year…did I do anything special for you for Assistants' Day?"

She had to think about it. "You had flowers delivered, I believe."

A soft laugh followed. "As I recall, you ordered those flowers on your own. I had nothing to do with it."

"We…we did discuss it. Briefly."

"It seems to me most employers take their assistants to lunch. Is that right?"

"I'm not sure."

"Lunch appears to be the proper protocol. If that's

the case, it seems I owe you a meal. Are you free this afternoon?"

Her mouth opened and closed several times, a bit like a trout, she was embarrassed to realize.

"Miss Stone?"

"Yes, I'm free."

"Good, I'll be finished here in about ten minutes."

She released the intercom and sat there with her mouth gaping open for a full minute before reality settled in. Joshua Norris had requested her company for lunch!

Sally stuck her head in the door. "Hey, are you coming or not? I'm hungry!"

Words square-danced on the tip of Bethany's tongue, but when she couldn't get them to cooperate with her brain, she jerked around and pointed her thumb towards Joshua's door.

"You mean the beast won't even let you leave to eat lunch?"

Bethany shook her head wildly.

"What, then? Good grief, you look like you're about to keel over. What did that monster do to you this time?" Sally walked into the room and planted her hands on Bethany's desk, her eyes afire with outrage.

"I'm taking Miss Stone to lunch," Joshua announced, standing in the suddenly open doorway. "Is that a problem, Ms. Livingston?"

Sally leaped back from Bethany's desk as though she'd been struck by lightning. "No problem. Not for me. Well, I guess I should be getting along now. Enjoy your lunch, Bethany. It was good to see you again, Mr. Norris."

"Good day, Ms. Livingston."

Bethany's friend couldn't get out of the office fast enough. "See you later," she said weakly, and waved, all but jogging in an effort to escape quickly.

Joshua leaned against the doorjamb, indolently crossed his arms and legs, his face amused. "So I'm a monster. I wonder who could have given Ms. Livingston that impression?"

Bethany stood and tightly clutched her purse to her side. "There have been times in the past, Mr. Norris, when the description was more than apt."

"Is that a fact?" He seemed to find the information more humorous than offensive. "Then I'd best repent my obnoxious ways. I made reservations at Brennan's."

"Brennan's," Bethany repeated in an excited whisper. She'd lived in New Orleans most of her life and had never eaten at the world-famous restaurant.

"You approve?"

"Oh, Joshua…Mr. Norris, I'm…I'm very pleased. Thank you."

Their table was waiting for them when they arrived. If Joshua thought she was going to order a dainty shrimp salad and a glass of iced tea, then he was in for a surprise. She informed him that her appetite had always been healthy, and started off by ordering an appetizer plate and turtle soup, and then, for the main course, Buster Crabs Béarnaise, a Brennan's specialty.

"You don't mind, do you?" she thought to ask, after the waiter had left their table.

"Of course I don't. I can see you plan to make up for all the years I didn't take you to lunch."

He was teasing her, but she didn't mind. "That's not it."

"Just where do you plan to put all that food?"

"Oh, don't worry. None of it will go to waste. I've never had a problem with my weight. None of the women in my family do until after they get pregnant, or so my mother and sisters tell me. From then on, keeping their figures is a constant battle. So I plan to enjoy all the goodies while I can." Bethany knew she was chattering, but she couldn't make herself stop. Already she felt light-headed, and the wine hadn't even been poured yet.

"So you want children?" he asked, watching her with smiling eyes.

She spread a thick layer of butter over the top of a crisp French roll. "Of course."

"You're not afraid it'll ruin your figure?"

She shrugged, pleased he hadn't noticed how thin she was. "Actually, I'm pretty much a toothpick. I'm looking forward to adding a few curves. I'm just hoping they'll show up in the right places. With my luck, my bust is likely to sink to my waistline." She paused in shock, amazed at what she'd just said and hoping that Joshua wasn't shocked.

He chuckled, and then his eyes grew warm and serious. "I don't think you need to worry, Bethany."

"I hope not," she said, and paid close attention to her roll in an attempt to calm her heart rate. She knew she shouldn't try to read anything into their conversation, but she couldn't help it. Her guess was that Angie's mother hadn't wanted children, and consequently Joshua thought all women felt the same way. It took everything in her not to announce that she would gladly bear his children. At her errant thoughts she decided to forgo the wine.

"I told Angie you'd be escorting her to the Mardi Gras parade, and she's excited, to say the least," he went on, changing the subject as if aware of her discomfort.

"I'm looking forward to it myself."

"You honestly enjoy my daughter's company, don't you?"

Bethany found that a strange question. "Yes. She's delightful."

He added a teaspoon of sugar in his coffee and stirred it vigorously. "I gave some consideration to what you said Saturday night. You may be right about me shutting Angie out of my life. It isn't easy, after living all these years alone. But I wanted to tell you that I appreciate your insight."

"You do?" She fingered the tassel on the wine list. Maybe alcohol wasn't such a detriment to her thought processes, after all. Maybe it was just the thing to burst this romance wide open.

"I'm making an effort to spend more time with Angie, and I think we're both enjoying it. I have you to thank for that."

She smiled, more pleased than she could remember being about anything in a long while.

"Unfortunately, time is at something of a premium in my life," he added in a thoughtful tone. "These next six months are crucial to the future of Norris Pharmaceutical. There's a great deal at stake."

She watched him carefully. She knew another firm had made a takeover attempt several months back, and that it had taken everything Joshua had to hold off the other company. His business was still small, but the potential for growth was huge if the firm were managed properly.

"What I'm trying to say is that for the next little while I'm not going to be able to be the kind of father I'd like to be. I'm literally not going to have the time."

She opened her mouth to tell him that time had little to do with being a good father. All Angie required was to know he loved her and that she was important to him. She needed him to listen to her problems and occasionally to laugh with her.

"Angie hasn't stopped asking about you since that first afternoon she spent at the office before Mrs. Larson, the housekeeper, arrived. She seems to like you better than anyone."

Bethany's smile grew more forced by the minute. So this lunch hadn't been an excuse to get to know each other better, as she'd imagined...as she'd hoped. It was a bribe—pure and simple. Joshua wanted her to babysit his daughter. No doubt he was willing to pay her handsomely to become a lonely ten-year-old's surrogate parent.

"I'm going to be busy for the next several weekends," he continued. "And I was wondering if you'd be willing to entertain Angela for me. Naturally I'd be more than happy to pay you for your time."

"Naturally," she repeated dully.

The waiter delivered the appetizer tray, but she knew she wasn't going to be able to swallow a single bite.

"I'm such a romantic fool," Bethany said to Sally. She should have known—she should have at least suspected—that something was up when he'd asked her to lunch. But the instant he'd mentioned children she had made assumptions. Optimism had poured into her heart as she'd wondered where the conversation was going. Well, now she knew. He was looking for a weekend babysitter.

"I can't believe I was so gullible," she continued. She hadn't told her friend the details of what Joshua had asked of her over lunch, much less her fantasies, which were simply too embarrassing to repeat.

"Honestly, Beth, no amount of money is worth this," Sally said, shaking her head.

Actually, Bethany agreed with her, but it wasn't that easy. "I can't quit now."

"Why not?"

"Angie needs me."

"J. D. Norris is using his daughter to blackmail you into staying on as his executive assistant? No wonder you're so upset."

"It isn't exactly blackmail," she said miserably. But the one who would suffer if she were to refuse to look after Angie would be Angie herself. The little girl had endured enough turmoil in the past few weeks. If Joshua was planning on using her to keep his daughter occupied and out of his hair, Bethany would do it—for Angie's sake. But she had learned her lesson when it came to her employer. She was going to guard her heart well. She was not going to be made a fool of for a second time.

"At least tell me what he pulled this time," Sally said, clearly frustrated that Bethany hadn't let her know anything beyond the basics. "If you tell me what he said, then I can hate him, too."

Bethany shook her head forcefully. She didn't know why she'd held anything back. Sally knew everything... or almost everything, anyway.

"The raise..."

"Yes?"

"The lunch..."

"Yes," Sally said, and took a step forward. "Go on."

"They weren't because Joshua is interested in me. He wants a weekend babysitter."

"What?" Sally exploded.

"He was buttering me up so I'll be willing to watch Angie over the weekend ."

Sally's eyes narrowed, and she plopped herself down on the couch and crossed her long legs, looking more furious by the moment.

"I should have known he'd never be interested in me as a woman. For one thing, that would be against company policy, and nothing's more important to him than his company."

A loyal friend, Sally gave her a gentle hug, but when she finished the fire was back in her eyes. "You're not standing still for that, are you?" she asked with grim determination. "I won't let you."

"So just what do 'I' plan to do?"

Sally tapped her finger over her closed lips as she mulled things over. "*You're* going to find yourself a man, a real man, someone who will give J. D. Norris an inferiority complex."

"And just where am I supposed to meet this paragon?"

Sally's gaze narrowed. "I think you already have. In fact, we've both met him."

"Oh, sure," Bethany muttered. If Sally had met someone so fabulous, why wouldn't she would want him for herself? "What makes you think Joshua Norris would care if I dated a hundred men?"

"He'll care," Sally said, nodding. "Trust me, by the time you're through with him, he'll care."

"Bethany, look!" Angie cried, pointing at the flambeaux carriers lining both sides of the wide cobblestone street. A golden arch of flame shot from one torch to the other. In the background a blast of music from a jazz saxophone pierced the night, followed by the unmistakable sounds of a Dixieland band.

"This is the most exciting night of my life," Angie said, and dramatically placed her hand over her heart.

Even the blue funk that Bethany had been in since her lunch with Joshua evaporated under the excitement of New Orleans during Mardi Gras.

"I've never seen so many people in my life...not even in New York." Angie shouted to be heard above the heavy noise of the milling crowd. "How's Dad ever going to find us?"

"Don't worry," Bethany answered, her voice equally loud.

"Do you think he'll like my costume?"

Bethany nodded. "He'll love it." She paused and adjusted the halo on top of the little girl's head. After hearing the story of how she'd gotten her name, Angela Catherine had insisted on dressing up like an angel, with elaborate feather wings and a golden halo. Bethany's

own outfit was far less elaborate. She'd rented an ante-
bellum-style gown, intent on doing her best imitation
of Scarlett O'Hara. Sally had advised her to flirt and
flitter, and play the part of a vamp and a tease. Not in
front of Angie, of course, but much later, for Joshua's
benefit. Bethany remained convinced such a ploy was
useless, but she didn't have any better ideas.

Just thinking about Sally's plan to make Joshua jealous was enough to cause Bethany to peel open her fancy
lace fan and cool her flushed face.

"Oh, look," Angie said next, pointing toward the
street once more. "There's a man on stilts."

"I certainly hope those are stilts," Bethany answered
with a soft laugh. "He must be all of eight feet tall."
She checked the pendant watch pinned to the bodice of
her gown and reached for Angie's hand. It was time to
leave their position on the pavement if they were going
to meet Joshua on time. "We'd better start working our
way toward the restaurant."

"But the parade isn't over."

"It won't be for hours yet, but I don't want to keep
your father waiting."

"OK," Angie agreed, although reluctantly.

"We'll still be able to see most of it." Bethany wasn't
eager to leave, either. There was so much to see and do.
Excitement arced like static electricity through the air.
People were singing and dancing in the streets. Strangers were hugging and kissing one another. Laughter
echoed all the way from the French Quarter to the exclusive Garden District.

Tightly gripping Angie's hand so as not to lose the

little girl, Bethany wove her way through the milling mass of humanity.

"Bethany, Bethany, stop!" Angie shouted, her voice filled with panic. "I lost my halo."

By the time Bethany turned around to investigate, the headpiece was gone. "Oh, dear." There was nothing she could do. The halo had apparently come loose and been quickly carted off by a masquerader who considered the golden circle fair game.

"Now I can't be an angel," Angie said, looking as if she was ready to burst into tears if something wasn't done quickly.

"I'm sure this happens all the time," Bethany said, thinking on her feet. "Real angels must have a difficult time holding on to their halos, too, don't you think? I know I would."

"What happens then?"

"Then they're considered almost-angels, and they have to work hard to regain their status as full angels," she suggested, improvising.

"Oh, I don't mind that, because it must be difficult to be perfect all the time."

"Then we'll consider Angie Norris to be almost an angel."

"Right," Angie answered, apparently appeased.

Bethany couldn't remember ever being in a larger crowd in her life. Making progress down the people-filled streets was difficult, and the restaurant wasn't even within sight.

"Look, Bethany, there's Prince Charming."

Bethany looked up in time to see a tall handsome

man astride a huge white stallion trotting down Bourbon Street. A mask covered his face.

"He's stopping!" Angie cried, her voice shrill with excitement.

Just as Angie had said, the handsome prince pulled back on the reins of the powerful stallion and came to a halt opposite them. Bethany watched in amazed wonder as he gave the horse over to a stranger, jumped down into the crowd and worked his way through the throng of partygoers until he stood in front of Bethany and Angie.

"Madam," he said softly to Bethany, "your loveliness has captured my heart."

He wore a mask, so Bethany couldn't see his face, but she would have recognized that mouth anywhere. Joshua. It had to be him. It looked like him. It even sounded like him. But he was tied up in a meeting and wouldn't be joining them for another half hour. It couldn't possibly be him. In addition, he would never do anything this wildly romantic.

"Oh, Bethany, he's so handsome. Don't you think so?"

The prince held out his palm, silently requesting her hand. By this time several people had formed a circle around them, watching the unfolding scene.

"Are you going to stand there all night, or are you going to kiss her?" a gruff male voice shouted.

"If he wants a kiss, I'm willing," a boisterous female voice added, and the crowd laughed.

Clearly trying to appease the rowdy group of merrymakers, the handsome prince took Bethany in his arms, swung her around with a flair that drew a round of applause and draped her over his forearm. Her eyes went as round as satellite dishes when he lowered his mouth to claim hers. She had half a mind to object. After all, she wasn't in the habit of kissing strange men. But this was Mardi Gras, a special once-a-year time to let down one's hair and participate in the unconventional.

The prince's mouth took hers in a warm moist kiss that was as soul-stirring as a religious revival and as deep as a bottomless sea. The kiss gentled as the fierce hunger was satisfied, and his lips moved over hers like the gentle brush of a spring sun on the hungry earth.

The crowd approved heartily.

When the prince released Bethany it was a wonder she didn't melt onto the pavement. Breathless and weak, she placed her hand over her heart, heedless to anything but the man who had held her in his arms. She blinked and took a step back.

"Wow," Angie said, her eyes round and wide. "I thought he was going to suck your lips off."

Had Bethany been any less affected she might have laughed, but even breathing was difficult…laughing would have been impossible.

Three or four women formed an impromptu line. "I've got dibs next," the first one called out, waving her fingers.

The prince, clearly being a true gentleman, kissed the hand of each woman in turn, and then, before they could object, gracefully remounted his white stallion and rode off.

"Bethany, why did he kiss you?" Angie wanted to know.

"I…I don't know." She continued to stare long after

he rode out of sight. "Angie—" she paused and looked down at the little girl "—did that man...the one who kissed me...did he remind you of anyone?"

"Oh, yes," Angie admitted. "He looked like the prince in *Cinderella*. The one who kept trying the glass slipper on all the women's feet. I always thought that was silly, you know. What woman wears glass shoes?"

"Oh." Bethany couldn't help being disappointed. It was nonsensical to think it could have been Joshua when it simply wasn't possible. The logistics were all wrong.

And yet...

Six

The noise level decreased by several decibels when Bethany and Angie left the street and entered the restaurant where they were supposed to meet Joshua. Antoine's was probably the most famous restaurant in New Orleans, having been in operation close to 150 years. Bethany secretly hoped her employer wouldn't be there. If the prince who'd kissed her *had* been Joshua, then it would have been close to impossible for him to have changed outfits so quickly and arrived at Antoine's ahead of them.

Her gaze searched the plush interior, and to her bitter disappointment she found Joshua casually sitting at a table awaiting their arrival.

"Dad, Dad, guess what I saw!" Angie went running past the maître d', weaving her way between tables to her father, then hurling her arms around his neck and squeezing for all she was worth.

The maître d' offered Bethany a strained smile and formally escorted her to Joshua's table. He paused and elegantly held out a shield-back chair for her to take a seat.

"There was a man eight feet tall," Angie was telling him, the words running together, she was speaking so fast. "And other men who tossed fire at each other, and then…*then* we met a handsome prince on a big white horse who kissed Bethany. It was soooo romantic."

Joshua's eyes widened, and when he glanced toward Bethany the edges of his mouth were quivering with the effort to hold back a smile. "It sounds like you've had quite an evening."

"Oh, yes, and, Dad, there are so many people, and everyone dresses like it's Halloween." Angie paused, and her hand flew to her hair. "I lost my halo. I was going to surprise you by being an angel because you said I looked like one when I was born, and then I lost the most important part, but Bethany said that's okay, because angels are supposed to be perfect, and well, you know me."

"I do indeed know you." He looked up and grinned in Bethany's direction. "I'm pleased to see you made it safely."

She managed a nod, still watching him closely, hoping to prove, if only to herself, that the prince who'd kissed her had been Joshua. She so desperately wanted it to be him and would always choose to believe that it had been.

"Do you usually kiss strange men on the street, Miss Stone?" he asked, seeming to read her thoughts.

"I…I…" she stammered. She couldn't very well announce that she thought the man had been him, and that was the only reason she'd allowed the prince to take her in his arms.

"It wasn't like she had much choice, Dad," Angie inserted, climbing off her father's lap and taking her own seat.

"So he forced you?"

Bethany managed a weak smile. "Not exactly."

He leaned forward, rested his elbows on the table and clasped his fingers together. "I'm curious why you would allow a complete stranger to sweep you into his arms and kiss you in front of a crowd of onlookers."

Hope fired through Bethany's blood like running water shooting off the edge of a cliff. It *had* been Joshua! It must have been, because no one had told him about the prince taking her in his arms, or that a crowd had gathered around to watch.

Boldly she raised her gaze to his. "He didn't seem the least bit dangerous," she said softly. "I…I felt that I knew him."

He cocked his thick eyebrows. "I see."

She certainly hoped he did, because her heart was pounding like a crazed pogo stick.

"Dad, is Bethany coming over Friday night?" Angie asked, sticking her head around the side of the huge menu. "You said she was."

"Bethany?" Joshua directed the question to her. From the way he turned away and started studying the menu it appeared her answer was of little consequence to him.

Despite her desire to see more of him out of the office, Bethany was aggravated. Joshua hadn't said anything to her about needing her Friday night. He'd taken it for granted that she didn't have any other plans, which fortunately she didn't, but his blatant assumption irked her.

"I suppose I could be there Friday night," she mumbled somewhat ungraciously.

"Mrs. Larson would be more than willing to stay," Joshua announced in a flat emotionless voice. "There's no need to feel obligated, especially if you have other plans."

"I'm not doing anything special." The admission took some of the bite out of her irritation.

"Oh, good," Angie said with an elaborate sigh. "Weekends are a bore, and being with you is always fun."

"Have you thought about inviting a school friend to spend the night?" Bethany asked. "We could order pizza and rent movies."

Angie slammed the menu down on top of the table, her eyes round and excited. "We could do all that?"

"Mr. Norris...Joshua?" It gave Bethany a small amount of pleasure to toss the question back into his court.

"Pizza and movies and a friend for the night?" He didn't sound overly enthused. "I suppose that won't be any problem."

"I think I'll ask Melissa over," Angie murmured thoughtfully, nibbling on her lower lip. "No, I like Wendy Miller better. She wants to be a writer, like me, and when we get tired of watching movies we could make up our own stories."

"That sounds like an excellent plan," Bethany said, pleased. "Don't you think so, Joshua?"

He mumbled something under his breath about

pizza and little girls running around the house at six in the morning, and left it at that.

The remainder of the week passed quickly. What Joshua had said about the next few months being especially busy for him and the company was true. Rarely could Bethany remember a time when he had more meetings and appointments scheduled. He was working too hard, and it showed. She wished there were some way she could lessen his load.

"Do you have the Harrison report ready?" he asked on Thursday at quitting time.

"Not yet," she admitted reluctantly, feeling guilty. The report was nearly two hundred pages in length and highly complicated. "I can stay late tonight if necessary."

"No." He shook his head. "But give it top priority first thing in the morning."

"Of course. I apologize, but there were a thousand interruptions the past couple of days." She felt obliged to explain why it was taking so long, although he didn't appear to be upset with her.

"Don't worry about it, Bethany, I understand."

Friday, Bethany skipped her lunch hour to work on the report so Joshua would have it for his meeting that evening. It was on his desk when he returned late that afternoon.

He called her into his office soon afterward and motioned for her to sit down.

"You did an excellent job with this," he told her, granting her a rare smile.

"Thank you." She was rather proud of it herself.

He hesitated and leaned back in his chair, looking anxious. "The dinner meeting this evening is with a group of financiers. I don't know what time I'll be getting back to the house. I'm afraid it could be quite late."

"Don't worry. I can stay with Angie and her friend until you get home."

"I really appreciate your help, Bethany."

She nodded, unable to voice the emotion that ran like a river deep within her heart. Helping Joshua, sharing his joys and easing his worries, was something she yearned to do every day. Since Angie's arrival their relationship had changed drastically, and yet she wanted so much more.

It was after eleven by the time Bethany heard Joshua let himself into the house. She'd been sitting in the family room reading. Both Angie and Wendy had fallen asleep at ten, exhausted from a busy week at school. They were sleeping in Angie's bedroom, and the house had been blissfully quiet since they'd gone to bed.

She set her book aside and stood, eager to talk to Joshua about what she knew had been an important meeting. She knew that the future of Norris Pharmaceutical rested on the decision of the financiers, although Joshua had never directly told her as much. Still, she would have had to be blind not to know the problems his company was currently facing.

She met him in the living room and greeted him with a warm smile. "Welcome home," she said softly, not wanting to wake the girls.

"It's good to be here." He set his briefcase down,

peeled off his suit jacket and folded it over the top of the sofa. "How did everything go with the girls?"

"Great, what about you?"

Joshua shrugged. "I won't know their decision until next week sometime."

So Joshua and Norris Pharmaceutical were going to be forced to play a waiting game.

"Are you hungry?" she asked.

He nodded, looking slightly chagrined. "Starved, as a matter of fact. I didn't have much of an appetite earlier."

Knowing the importance of his meeting, she could well believe that. She'd eaten sparingly herself. "There's plenty of pizza left."

"You'll join me?" he asked. When she nodded, he looked pleased and led the way into the kitchen. "I think I've got a couple of cold beers. Do you want one?"

"Please."

While he was searching through the refrigerator for the beer, she placed several slices of cold pizza on a plate and warmed them in the microwave. By the time they were heated he had brought out paper napkins, and set those and the two bottles of beer on the small kitchen table.

The pepperoni pizza was excellent—better than the first time around, she decided. They didn't talk much at first. He asked her a couple of questions about how her evening had gone, and she told him how the two girls had been far too keen to make up their own stories to be interested in watching a DVD.

"I've set up the television and DVD player so all Angie has to do is turn them on first thing in the morning, and they can watch then. Hopefully that'll give you an extra hour or two of peace so you can sleep in a little." She worried that he wasn't getting enough rest. Heaven knew he worked long enough hours, especially lately.

"That was thoughtful of you."

A short silence followed before he spoke again. It was clear that the meeting with the financiers continued to weigh on his mind. He told her his general feelings about how his proposal had been received, the vibes he'd felt, the mood that had persisted throughout the long dinner meeting.

She leaned back and listened attentively while he rummaged through and sorted out his thoughts. He finished, sat quietly for a moment, then downed the last of his beer.

"I suppose I should be getting home," she said, standing.

His gaze flew to his gold watch. He looked surprised when he noted the time. "I didn't mean to keep you so long, Beth."

She stopped in front of the dishwasher, turned back to him and smiled.

"Does something amuse you?"

She set their dirty plates inside. "Here you are using a nickname, when there was a time not so long ago when you didn't even know my first name."

"I knew," he whispered. He was so close behind her now that she could feel his warm breath against the side of her neck. "I've always known."

A shiver of awareness scooted down her spine, and she braced her hands against the counter as he gently cupped her shoulders, his touch so light that she thought at first she might have imagined it. His fingers gently stroked her skin as he ran his hands down the length of her arms. At the same time he tenderly drew her back so her body fitted against his full height. His movements were slow, deliberate, as though he expected her to object and was granting her ample opportunity to pull away if she so desired.

She went completely immobile. She couldn't have moved if her life had depended on it.

He rested his chin on top of her head for a short moment before he lowered his mouth to the slender curve of her neck. The instant his lips touched her sensitized skin and located the pulsing vein there, heat erupted like a fiery volcano throughout Bethany's trembling body.

She didn't know who moved first. She might have turned and slipped her arms around his waist, or his hands could have directed her. She didn't know which. It didn't matter, though, nothing did except that she was in Joshua's arms and his mouth was hungrily locked over hers. He was kissing her as if he'd thought of doing nothing else for endless hours. Again and again he dragged his lips over hers, as though the thought of releasing her so soon was too much to bear.

A helpless moan escaped her. To have him kiss her was almost like drowning, then bursting through the water's clear surface and feeling more alive than at any other time in her life.

Still holding her, he buried his face in the curve of her neck and exhaled a deep unsteady breath.

"The most important meeting of my life," he whispered, his voice husky and moist against her flushed skin. "And all I could think about was you."

"Oh, Joshua." She tucked her hands under his arms and leaned against him for support, bracing her forehead against his hard chest.

"This shouldn't be happening," he said, but there was no regret in his voice.

"I wanted it, too," she admitted, hiding her face in his chest and closing her eyes to the warm happy feeling that enveloped her.

"You've been so good for Angie," he whispered.

Some of her good feelings left, and she stiffened, fearing he was going to use her love for him to keep her as a willing babysitter. She tried to break away, but he wouldn't let her.

"What's wrong?" he asked anxiously. "Bethany, you've gone all cold on me. What did I say?"

She shook her head rather than explain.

"You're upset because I appreciate what a good friend you are to my daughter?"

He lovingly caressed the side of her jaw and lifted her chin so that she couldn't avoid meeting his gaze. "No, of course not. I love Angie."

"And she loves you." He bent forward and brushed his mouth over hers, his lips settling naturally onto hers for another swift taste.

She kept her eyes closed, still trapped in the lingering sensation, and yet her heart felt as if it were weighted down with bricks. It wasn't right that she should be in his arms and feel so terribly insecure. He should know her feelings. "I sometimes think Angie's the only reason you…you want to be around me."

The room went suspiciously quiet. The smallest noise would have sounded like a sonic boom in the silence that stretched between them. Her eyes fluttered open, but she dared not look at him, dared not meet the fiery anger she could feel radiating from him.

"You don't honestly believe that, do you?"

"What else am I to think?"

He freed her arms and took a step back from her. His eyes were dark and solemn. Sad. "If you don't know the answer to that by now, then I've failed us both."

"Failed us both?" She tossed his own words back at him. "The only time you ever want me around is to... to babysit for Angie."

The muscles in his jaw leaped as though it was an effort to control his anger. "I can't see how you could think that."

She felt miserable. Only a minute ago he'd been holding and kissing her, and now he looked as though he couldn't wait for her to get out of his house.

Rather than continue the argument, she turned toward the kitchen table and removed their crumpled napkins.

"Leave those," he said.

"I...I was just going to put them in the garbage."

"I don't want to be accused of using you as my personal maid sometime later. Believe me, I'd prefer to do the task myself."

"Okay." Swallowing hard, she dropped the napkins back on the tabletop. The only thing left for her to do was walk away. Holding her shoulders stiff and straight, she collected her purse and her book. She was almost to the front door when Joshua reached out and stopped her.

She didn't turn to look back at him.

"Beth," he said starkly. "I'm sorry."

Her head whirled around, and she saw the regret written boldly across his face.

"I'm sorry, too, Joshua." Sorry to have doubted him, sorry to have been so willing to believe the worst of him, but she couldn't help it. She might have done him a grave injustice...but she couldn't help feeling the way she did.

He kissed her again, but this one lacked the urgency or the hunger of the others. With his arm wrapped around her waist, he walked her out to her car. As she drove off, she could see his image in her rearview mirror, standing alone in the night, watching her as she pulled away.

"Okay, everything's all set," Sally announced, standing in front of Bethany's desk. She wore that off-center silly smile that indicated she was up to something.

Bethany paused with her fingers poised over the keyboard. She would play along with Sally's game for a while, until she figured out what card Sally was hiding up her sleeve, but that wouldn't take too long. "What's all set?" she asked.

"Your hot date."

"What?" Bethany exploded, and jerked her gaze toward the connecting door, grateful it was closed so Joshua wouldn't overhear their conversation. "A hot date with who?"

"Whom," her roommate corrected with a mischievous grin.

"Whom, then!"

"You honestly don't remember, do you?" Sally looked surprised, then disbelieving, then impatient. As each emotion cross her face in turn, Bethany thought it was like watching the flickering movements of an old-time silent film. "You really don't!"

"Obviously not," Bethany answered. "What are you talking about?"

With a look of disgust, Sally crossed her arms and aimed her chin toward the ceiling. "Does the name Jerry Johnson ring a bell?"

Bethany mulled it over in her mind. She knew Sally had been up to something the past couple of days, but she hadn't a clue what. "The name sounds vaguely familiar."

"Well, you *should,* since you've agreed to a date with him."

"I've what?" This nightmare was growing more vivid by the minute. "When?" Bethany demanded.

"I've arranged everything for Thursday night."

"Not *that* when," Bethany said. "When did I ever say I'd have anything to do with the man?"

Sally cast a suspicious glance towards Joshua's door. "The afternoon you sat in our living room after your lunch with Mr. Big Shot. Remember? We made plans, you and I."

The words jarred Bethany's memory. She could remember her friend telling her what a fool she was being and that she would be an ever bigger one if she continued to let Joshua Norris take advantage of her. Sally had rambled on about finding a man to make Joshua jealous, but Bethany had been too miserable to listen carefully. Now she realized her mistake. "I seem to remember you making a suggestion or two," she admitted reluctantly.

"I did more than suggest," Sally said righteously, and lowered her voice to a whisper. "I *acted,* which is more than I can say for you."

"But things are progressing between me and Joshua," Bethany answered, keeping her voice as low as possible. "I don't want to do anything to topple the cart."

"Sure, it's going just great between the two of you... now," Sally scoffed. "You're taking care of his little girl every free moment. You don't have time for anything else."

"But..."

"Just answer me one thing, Bethany. Has your precious Mr. J. D. Norris ever taken *you* out without dragging Angie along? Has it ever been just the two of you alone? Well, other than that lunch when he asked you to fill in on weekends for him?"

Her roommate had knocked away Bethany's argument as easily as if she'd toppled a stack of children's building blocks. Bethany lowered her gaze. Sally was right.

"See what I mean?" Sally muttered. "Mr. Norris is using you. He has been from the first, and as your best friend I refuse to stand by and let it happen any longer. You've got to start circulating again. I'm going to introduce you to the *right* kind of men, and I won't let you stop me."

"But, Sally..."

"I refuse to hear any more arguments. Thursday night, got it?"

"All right," Bethany agreed, but she couldn't have cared less about Jerry Johnson or Jerry anyone. She was in love with Joshua, and nothing would change the way she felt about him.

* * *

When Joshua called for her to take some dictation an hour later, Bethany briskly stepped into his office.

He smiled when he saw her, but her return smile was strained. He handed her a stack of papers. "Collate and get me fifteen copies of each of these at your convenience. There isn't any big rush."

"Is tomorrow morning soon enough?"

"That'll be fine."

She would have returned to the reception area, but he stopped her. "One minute, Miss Stone." He paused to write something across the top of a yellow legal tablet, and when he glanced up, he looked pleased about something, relaxed in a way she hadn't ever seen him. "Would you happen to be free tomorrow night, Beth?"

She felt as if a loaded logging truck had parked on top of her chest. "Thursday night?"

"That's tomorrow, yes. I realize it's short notice. Is there a problem?"

Her palms felt unexpectedly moist, and she shifted the papers she was holding to get a better grip on them. The small stack felt as though it weighed thirty pounds. "I'm sorry, Joshua…Mr. Norris, but I've already got plans."

"There's no problem. I should have asked you earlier." He frowned and went back to his task, scratching notes across the top of the pad.

"If…I hope Mrs. Larson will be able to stay with Angie, but if she can't—"

"Mrs. Larson can, so don't worry about it."

Bethany could feel her heart's thundering beat all the way to her toes.

As soon as she was back at her desk, Sally stuck her head around the door. "Have you got a moment?"

"Sally…" Bethany groaned. "What is it now?"

Her friend strolled into the office. "I've got his picture."

"Whose?"

"Jerry Johnson's." She looked as pleased as if she'd managed to smuggle secret papers out of the Kremlin. "It was in the bottom of my purse. I forgot I had it."

"Sally, honestly, I don't even want to go out with this guy."

"Don't say that until you've seen his picture." She waved the photograph under Bethany's nose, as though the blurred image would be enough to convince her how lucky she was to be dating such a hunk.

Bethany grabbed the small glossy picture from her friend's hands and studied the handsome smiling face. Jerry Johnson was attractive—okay, he was downright show stopping.

Sally leaned her hip against the side of Bethany's desk, crossed her arms and looked exceedingly proud of herself. "He knows you, too."

"Why don't I remember him?" She frowned, because he *did* look vaguely familiar.

"You only met him once," Sally said, and studied the fingernails on her right hand. "Christmas, last year, at the Dawsons' party."

Bethany could hardly remember who the Dawsons were but finally recalled they were family friends of Sally's.

"Trust me, Beth. Thursday night with Jerry Johnson is a date you won't soon forget."

"Ms. Livingston," Joshua said in a cold voice from the open doorway. "Seeing that you have nothing to do but traipse in and out of my office at all times of the day, I'm wondering just how much your work performance contributes to my company."

Sally bounced away from the desk as though she'd been sitting on a hot plate. Her eyes filled with shock as she glanced at Bethany, silently pleading for help.

"Sally was making a delivery," Bethany said, stretching the truth as far as she dared.

"Yes, I heard. The photo of your hot date."

Bethany's face flushed with brilliant color.

"I trust you two have more important business to see to on company time?"

"Yes, sir," Sally mumbled, and was gone.

"Are those papers collated yet?" Joshua demanded.

"I…no. I thought we agreed…I'll take care of that first thing in the morning."

"I need them now."

"But you said—"

"Don't argue with me, Miss Stone. I want those papers collated before you leave tonight. Is that clear?"

"Perfectly, Mr. Norris."

"Good. And the next time I see Ms. Livingston in my office talking to you on company time instead of being where she should be, she'll be looking for another job."

"If Sally leaves, then I'm going, as well."

"That decision is your own, Miss Stone." With that he spun around and returned to his office, soundly closing the door.

Seven

"Have aliens captured your brain?" Bethany demanded of her roommate. "Of all the crazy things you've pulled over the years... Couldn't you have waited until after work to bring me Jerry's photo or, better yet, have emailed it to me?"

"I know, I know," Sally said, still shaken from her earlier confrontation with J. D. Norris. "Honestly, I thought he was going to ask for my head."

"He nearly did." She didn't mention that hers would have rolled with her friend's. Joshua had been in such a bad temper that even hours after their confrontation, talking to him about the situation would have been impossible. Not that Bethany had tried. She knew her employer well enough to recognize his mood. And honor it.

"You're still going Thursday night, aren't you?" Sally asked, glancing surreptitiously toward her friend.

"Of course I'm going." But Bethany didn't feel nearly as confident as she sounded. This whole idea of dating a man she'd briefly met at a Christmas party months earlier didn't appeal to her, especially since she'd been drinking spiked eggnog at the time. Eggnog and wine were synonymous with trouble, as far as she was concerned.

Friday morning, Joshua was already at his desk when Bethany arrived. She paused between the doorway that connected their offices, surprised to see him and dismayed at the picture he presented. He looked terrible. Even from where she was standing, she could see and feel his fatigue. Dark smudges circled his eyes. His jacket had long since been discarded, his tie loosened and the top two buttons of his wrinkled shirt unfastened. One glance convinced her that he hadn't bothered to go home the night before.

"Joshua," she whispered concerned, "how long have you been here?"

Deliberately he set his pen aside, though he continued to hold on to it. "When we're at the office, Miss Stone, kindly refer to me as Mr. Norris."

"As you wish," she returned stiffly, and proceeded into the room. So that was the way it was going to be. All right, she would deal with it. Holding her back as straight as possible, she brewed a fresh pot of coffee and went back to her own desk to sort through the morning mail. When she'd finished, she returned, poured Joshua a cup of coffee and delivered it to him the way she had every morning for the past three years.

"So, Miss Stone," he said sardonically, "how did your 'hot date' go?"

His voice was so thick with sarcasm that she had to bite down on her bottom lip to keep from responding in like tones. Seeing the mood he was in, she decided against saying how her dates went was really none of his business.

"Fine, thank you." She handed him the sorted mail. "The letter you've been looking for from Charles Youngblood arrived."

"Good." He picked through the stack until he located it. "Are you planning on seeing him again?" he demanded.

"Charles Youngblood?"

"You're being deliberately obtuse. I was referring to your...date," he said impatiently.

Now he'd stepped over the line. "I hardly think that's any of your business," she snapped, her own patience a slender thread. "What happens outside this office isn't your concern."

"When your action directly affects the productivity of this company, I'd say it becomes my business."

Icy fingers wrapped themselves around Bethany's vocal cords. She couldn't have answered him had her job were depending on it, and considering the horrible mood he was in, it very well could be.

"Miss Stone, I asked you a question. I expect an answer."

It was in her mind to shout that he was demanding and unreasonable, and that she refused to discuss the details of her personal life with any employer. Instead, she squarely met his gaze and said, "My personal life is my own." With that, she turned and walked out of the office.

An hour later her hands were still trembling. If she lost her job, then so be it. The door to Joshua's office opened, and just the sound was enough to cause her to stiffen her spine, readying herself for another confrontation.

He walked over to her desk and set down the mail. A list of handwritten instructions accompanied the large stack of letters.

"Cancel my appointments for the rest of the day, Miss Stone," he said in a raspy tone.

She refused to look at him, but with her peripheral vision she saw him lean momentarily against the edge of her desk and pinch the bridge of his nose. He paused and wiped his hand down his face.

"I'm going home," he announced.

She nodded once, a quick jerky movement.

Joshua hesitated once more. "I apologize for my earlier behavior. You're absolutely right—your personal life is your own. I had no business laying into you that way."

Again she remained silent.

"If there's anything that requires my attention, you can contact me at the house. Good day, Miss Stone."

"Mr. Norris."

"J. D. Norris said all that?" Sally murmured when they got together during their break, her eyes narrowed and thoughtful.

"I've never seen him so angry and unreasonable. I'm just glad he left, because I couldn't have stood another minute.... I think I would have quit on the spot if he'd said one more word."

Sally broke off a part of her sugar-coated doughnut and paused with it in front of her mouth. "I think he could be falling in love with you, Bethany."

The sip of coffee Bethany had just swallowed jammed halfway down her throat and refused to budge. She slapped her hand over her chest and gasped. Once she'd composed herself enough to speak, she murmured, "Hardly."

"I mean it," Sally countered with a contemplative look. "He's acting like a jealous little boy, which is exactly what I thought might happen. His behavior confirms my suspicions."

"A more likely scenario is that I was a convenient scapegoat for him to vent his troubles." Bethany wasn't blind to the company's current financial problems. Having recently held off one takeover effort, Joshua had been hit almost immediately by another. His resources had been depleted by the first attempt, and he was holding on to control of the company by the thinnest of threads. Naturally, most of the information was privileged, so she wasn't at liberty to discuss it with anyone, including her best friend. A good deal of what transpired without Bethany being present. But she'd garnered enough information from the numerous transcripts she'd typed. Unfortunately, she didn't have a clue how Joshua was surviving this latest takeover bid.

"I don't know," Sally muttered, the same piece of doughnut still level with her lips. "I've been doing a lot of thinking about the way Mr. Norris has been acting these past few weeks, and it's obvious he's really into you."

"Sure he is," Bethany muttered scornfully. "Angie thinks I'm loads of fun, and he thinks I'm a soft touch when it comes to his daughter."

"Well, aren't you?"

Bethany was reluctantly forced to agree. "I...won't be able to meet you at Charley's after work," she said, almost as an afterthought.

"How come?"

"I...I've got to take some papers over to Mr. Norris's house for him to sign."

"Ah." Sally's eyes brightened, then were quickly lowered as she pretended an interest in her paper napkin. "Listen..." She paused, placed the half-eaten doughnut back on her plate and brushed the sugar granules from her fingertips. "Since you weren't really all that interested in Jerry, I was wondering..."

"Go ahead," Bethany said, having trouble disguising a smile, almost enjoying her friend's discomfort.

"Go ahead and what?"

"Date Jerry yourself. Do you honestly think I didn't know you're attracted to him? Sally, you drool every time you mention his name."

"I do?"

"I can't believe you'd fix *me* up on a date with him when you're so obviously taken with him yourself." Actually, knowing Sally's twisted way of planning things, this scheme of hers was probably the only way she'd been able to come up with to talk to him again.

"When did you figure it out?" Sally demanded.

"Not right away," Bethany was slow to admit. She'd been so caught up with what was going on between her and Joshua that she hadn't been paying attention to her friend until the obvious practically hit her over the head. After all, how many women carried a picture of a man they'd only met once in their purse for an entire year?

Not many, she would bet. Only someone as sentimental and romantic as Sally.

"So you don't mind if I—"

"Not in the least. Jerry Johnson is all yours, with my blessing."

Bethany finished the last of her duties at five and left the office to drive directly to Joshua's home on Lake Pontchartrain. Her excuse for stopping at the house was flimsy at best, but she felt terrible about what had happened that morning and longed to straighten things out—even if it meant admitting she wouldn't be seeing Jerry again.

Mrs. Larson opened the front door. "Miss Stone, how are you this evening?"

The portly widow had thick silver hair, and wore the traditional black uniform and white apron. She was kind and gentle-hearted, and on the few occasions that Bethany had met her, she'd been impressed with the older woman.

"I'm fine, thank you," Bethany answered. "How's Mr. Norris?"

Mrs. Larson's lips thinned with worry as she shook her head. "I swear, it's a miracle that man hasn't worked himself into an early grave."

"I know," Bethany said miserably. "Has he slept at all?" The more she thought about their argument that morning, the guiltier she felt for her part in it. Joshua was obviously exhausted beyond reason.

"He slept an hour or two when he came home this morning, and now he's at his desk in the den, working. Would you like me to take you to him?"

"Please." Bethany followed Mrs. Larson to the large den, which was built off the living room and faced the lake.

The older woman knocked politely, then opened the door. "Miss Stone is here to see you," she announced, and stepped aside.

Joshua half rose. "Bethany." His eyes widened with surprise. "Is there a problem? You should have phoned."

"I'm sorry to interrupt you…."

"It's no problem. Sit down."

She lowered herself into a huge overstuffed leather chair and folded her hands on her lap, watching him expectantly. If she hadn't known better, she would have sworn he was pleased to see her, and that made her feel good about her unscheduled visit.

He returned her look, his gaze expectant, and she suddenly remembered the excuse she'd invented to explain her presence. "There are some letters for you to sign, but…I seem to have left them in the car." She rushed to her feet. "I'll get them and be right back."

She all but jumped out of the chair and hurried back outside. Instead of troubling Mrs. Larson a second time after she grabbed the letters, she let herself into the house and Joshua's den.

"Taking the time to bring these over was thoughtful," he said, scribbling his name across the bottom of the first letter without bothering to read it.

"Yes…well, I felt badly about this morning," she murmured. Her face was growing warm, and she knew she was blushing. "You'd obviously been up all night and, although it really wasn't any of your concern, it wouldn't have hurt me to let you know about Jerry and me."

"Yes?" he coaxed when she didn't immediately continue. "Have you decided to continue dating Ms. Livingston's friend?" Some of the pleasure drained from his eyes. "That's understandable."

"No, Joshua...I mean, Mr. Norris. I won't be seeing Jerry again."

"You won't?" Five years disappeared from his face as his expression lightened. "Well, that's certainly your business."

"Yes, I know," she countered softly. With no excuse to linger any longer, she stood, wishing she could find a plausible reason to stay. "How's Angie?" she asked with a flash of brilliance, and reclaimed her chair.

"She's doing just fine," he answered eagerly. "Really good. She's spending the night with her friend Wendy."

Silence followed.

She stood once more.

"She seems to have made the adjustment from New York to New Orleans rather well," he said.

She sat back down, almost gleeful with relief over the excuse to stay. "Yes, I thought so."

Another moment of silence fell between them.

"I know this is spur-of-the-moment, but would you care to have dinner with me?" he asked.

"Yes." She felt excited enough about the prospect to stand up and cheer, but she restrained herself. "I'd like that a lot."

The smile he tossed her was almost boyish. He paused and glanced her way, eyeing her clothes, and frowned slightly.

"I can go home and change if you want." She was

wearing a dark blue business suit with a straight skirt
and short double-breasted jacket.

"No, you're perfect just the way you are."

"You're sure?" She was curious to know where he
was taking her. When he'd asked her to dinner, she'd
assumed at first that he meant that they would be eating there at the house.

"I'm positive," he answered, although he was dressed
far more casually than usual himself, in trousers and a
thick Irish cable-knit sweater the color of winter wheat.

After pausing to let Mrs. Larson know he was leaving, he reached for Bethany's hand and led her out to
the car. He drove into the heart of the city and parked
on a side street a few blocks off the French Quarter.

"Do you like beans and rice?" he asked.

She nodded eagerly. The popular New Orleans dish
had been elevated by the on-going interest in Cajun and
Creole cooking. The recipe had originated in the slave
quarters, and many a Southerner had grown up in a time
when each day's menu revolved around rice and beans.

"A friend of mine runs a café that serves the best
Louisiana cooking in the world." He hesitated, then
smiled. "But be warned, the food is fantastic, but the
place rates low on atmosphere."

"You needn't worry about that with me." She wondered what he would think if he were ever to join her
large family for a Sunday dinner. How would he fit in
with mismatched place settings and the ever-flowing
stream of conversation?

He slipped his arm around her waist, holding her
close to his side. "I wasn't worried that you'd disapprove, I just wanted to warn you."

"Okay, I consider myself properly warned," she told him, her eyes smiling. This was the man she was just beginning to know, the man she'd been granted rare glimpses of over the years. Excitement filled her at spending this time alone with him.

He directed her down a narrow alleyway. She had been up and down the streets of the French Quarter most of her life, but she didn't recognize this one.

"Are you sure there's a restaurant back here?" she asked.

"Positive."

The place was small and cramped, with only a handful of tables. The chairs were mismatched, and the Formica tabletops were chipped, but the smells wafting from the kitchen were enough to convince her that Joshua knew what he was talking about.

"What you doin' bringin' that skinny girl in my kitchen, J. D. Norris?" a huge black woman asked as she stepped out from behind an old-fashioned cash register.

"Bethany, meet Cleo."

The woman wiped her hands dry on the smudged apron that was tucked into the folds of her skirt. "You look like a strong wind would blow you away," Cleo announced, cocking her head to one side as she studied Bethany through narrowed dark eyes.

"Then I sincerely hope you intend to feed me."

Cleo chuckled, and her whole body shook with the action. "Honey chil', you have no idea how Cleo can feed a soul." She ambled across the room and pulled out two chairs. "Sit," she ordered. With that she started toward the kitchen, paused and looked over her shoulder. "You bring your horn?"

Joshua nodded. "It's in the car."

"It's been too long, Dizzy, much too long."

"Your horn? Dizzy?" Bethany asked once Cleo was out of sight.

"I play saxophone now and then, when the spirit moves me."

Shocked speechless, she studied him for a moment, astonished at this unknown side of the complex man she loved. There was nothing in her knowledge of Joshua that so much as hinted at any musical interest or talent. "I had no idea," she managed to say after a moment.

He grinned, as if to say there was a lot about him she didn't know, and she couldn't doubt it.

Cleo returned with plates piled high with rice and smothered with rich beans in a red sauce. "This is just for openers," she warned, setting down the food. She returned a minute later with a third plate stacked high with warm squares of corn bread oozing with melted butter.

"She doesn't honestly expect us to eat all this, does she?" Bethany asked between bites. She'd tasted beans and rice in any number of restaurants but never anything that could compare with this unusual blend of spices, vegetables and meat. No other version of the classic had ever tasted anywhere near this delicious.

"She'd be insulted if we left a crumb."

She didn't know how she managed it, but her plate was clean when Cleo returned.

The woman gave her a broad grin and nodded approvingly. "Maybe you be all right, after all," the massive woman said with a sparkle in her dark eyes.

"Maybe you be, too," Bethany returned, holding in a laugh.

Cleo let loose with a loud burst of laughter and slapped Joshua across the back. "I like her."

Joshua grinned, sharing a look with Bethany. "So do I."

"You got room for my special sweet-potato-pecan pie?" Cleo eyed them both speculatively, as if to say they were too skinny to know anything about good food.

Joshua leaned back, splayed his fingers over his stomach and sighed. "I think you better count me out. I'm stuffed to the gills. Bethany?"

"Bring me a piece."

Cleo nodded several times. "You done yourself proud, Dizzy. She don't look like much, but there's more to her than meets the eye."

The pie was thick, sweet and delicious.

Joshua watched, eyes wide, as Bethany finished off every last bite.

"You amaze me."

She licked the ends of her fingers. "I told you before, I've got a healthy appetite."

Cleo returned carrying two steaming mugs of coffee. "You takin' this pretty gal to St. Peter's?"

Joshua nodded, and Cleo looked pleased.

After he paid for their meal, he led Bethany out of the café and further down the narrow alley to another set of doors. "I hope you like jazz, because you're about to get an earful."

"I love any kind of music," she was quick to tell him, feeling closer to him than ever before. He opened the door off the alley, and a cloud of smoke as thick as a bayou fog enveloped them as they walked inside. It took a second for her eyes to adjust to the dim interior. She couldn't see much as he led her to a vacant table and pulled out a chair for her. The sounds of clicking ice, the tinny tones of an old piano and the hum of conversation surrounded her like the familiar greetings of old friends.

"What would you like to drink?" he asked, and had to lean close in order for her to hear him above the conversational roar. "A mint julep?"

She answered him with a shake of her head. "A beer, please."

He turned to leave her, but he must have forgotten something, because he hadn't gone more than a couple of steps when he turned back. She looked up expectantly, and he leaned down to press his mouth over hers in a kiss so fleeting that she hardly had time to register it.

In the front of the room was a small platform stage. A man was playing the piano, and another was setting up a drum set. Bethany watched Joshua weave a path between tables to get to the bar. He was waylaid several times as people—obviously friends—stopped to greet him. In a few minutes he returned with two frosty mugs of cold beer.

She had barely had time to taste hers when he stood and offered her his hand. She didn't understand at first, then realized he was asking her to dance. The small dance floor was crowded when they moved to the edge of it. He wrapped her in his arms, and they soon blended in with the others.

The minute he had pulled her into his embrace, a wave of warmth had coursed through her. She leaned her head back and looked up at him, realizing anew how much she loved this man.

He touched her cheek, and his fingers felt like velvet against her cool skin. His lips were only a few inches away, and she longed with everything in her for him to kiss her again.

"Beth," he whispered urgently, "don't look at me like that."

Embarrassed, she lowered her gaze, all too aware of what he must be reading in her eyes.

"No, forget I said that," he went on, and moved ever so slightly to lift her chin and direct her mouth to his.

She felt as if her bones were melting. She tasted the malt flavor of his beer as she opened her mouth to his. If his first kiss had been an appetizer, this second one was a feast. He slid his hands down her spine, molding her body intimately to his as he kissed her again. He moved his lips over hers in eager exploration until she was convinced she would faint from the sheer pleasure of being his arms.

When he broke off the kiss, she sagged against him, too weak to do anything but cling to the only solid thing in a world that was spinning out of control. He nuzzled the side of her neck and then investigated the hollow of her throat with his tongue. She was gathered as close as humanly possible against him. When he kissed her again, his mouth was so hot it burned a trail all across her face.

"Let's get out of here," he whispered in a voice so thick and raspy she could hardly understand him.

She answered with a nod.

He kept her close to his side as he led them back to their table. They were about to leave when a tall dark man with a huge potbelly and a thick dark beard stopped him.

"C'mon, Dizzy. You can't leave this place without playing the blues."

"He's right…Dizzy," she murmured, looking up at Joshua.

"Good to see you again, Fats." Joshua shook hands with the other man.

"You got your horn, brother?"

Joshua nodded reluctantly. "It's in the car."

"Get it."

Joshua looked almost apologetic as he led Bethany back to their table. "I'm sorry, sweetheart," he whispered.

She pressed her hands onto his shoulders and was so bold as to reach up and brush her lips across his. "I'm not. I want to hear you play."

The man Joshua had called Fats jumped onto the stage when Joshua reappeared, carrying his saxophone with him. Fats had brought a bass trombone. The man who'd been playing the drums reappeared carrying a trumpet. The first couple of minutes were spent checking valves and tooting a few notes. No one seemed to mind that the dancing had come to an abrupt halt. The room seemed to vibrate with a charged sense of anticipation.

Bethany sat back, watching Joshua and loving him more each minute. He stepped to the front of the stage and his gaze sought hers. The look he sent cut straight through her, and then he smiled and brought the instrument to his lips.

The blast of music split the air and was followed by shouts of encouragement from the audience. Soon the sounds of the other instruments joined Joshua: the piano, the trumpet, the trombone, each in turn.

Bethany couldn't have named the tune, didn't even know if it had a title—the players weren't following any sheet music. The melody appeared improvisational as each player in his own time bent the notes his own way, twisting and turning, soaring and landing again. She flew with them, and she wasn't alone. Every patron in the club joined the flight, ascending with the music. The men played as if they were one, yet each still separate. Bethany soaked in every note of Joshua's music as if her heart had become a sponge meant only to take in this man and his music. She experienced the bright tension of the piece as though each bar of music were meant for her and her alone. When they were finished, her eyes burned with unshed tears.

She remained in an almost dreamlike state when Joshua rejoined her. His face was close to hers, and she could see the beads of perspiration that wetted his upper lip and brow. She raised her fingertip to his cheek, needing to touch him, needing to say what was inside her and unable to find the words to explain how his music had touched her heart.

He gripped her hand with his own and kissed her fingertips.

"You liked it?" he asked, his gaze holding hers.

She nodded, and a tear escaped and ran down the side of her face. "Very much," she whispered.

"Bethany, listen." His hand continued to squeeze hers. "I'm going out of town next week."

She already knew he had a trip planned to California.

"I haven't any right to ask this of you." He stopped and tangled his fingers in her hair. "I want you to come with me."

If he'd asked for her soul at that moment, she couldn't have refused him. "I'll come," she replied.

His eyes ate her up, seeming almost to ask her forgiveness. "Angie will be with me. She wants you there, and so do I."

Eight

"When we're in California," Angie said thoughtfully, sitting beside Bethany in the first-class section of the Boeing 767, "will you call me Millicent?"

"If you like."

The little girl nodded eagerly. "At least for the first day or two. I might want to change to Guinevere or Charmaine after that."

"I may slip up now and again," Bethany admitted, doing her utmost to remain serious. There were days she couldn't keep track of who *she* was, let alone a fun-loving ten-year-old.

"That's all right," Angie said, and went back to flipping through the pages of the flight magazine. She paused abruptly and looked back to Bethany. "Do you want me to call you Dominique? I could."

Bethany hesitated, as if to give the child's offer serious consideration, then shook her head. "No thanks, sweetheart."

Joshua was sitting across the aisle from the two of them. His briefcase was open, and he was busy reviewing documents. His brow was creased in concentration, his gaze intent. Bethany was convinced he'd long forgotten both her and his daughter, and her heart ached a little with the realization.

Inhaling a deep breath, she pulled her eyes away from her employer and tried to involve herself in the plot of the murder mystery she was reading. It didn't work, although the author was one of her favorites. Instead, Sally's dire warning played back in her mind like a stubborn voice mail that refused to shut off. It was happening again, her roommate had warned. Bethany was allowing Joshua to use her as a convenient babysitter. Bethany didn't want to believe that, but...

After Friday night, when Joshua had taken her to meet Cleo and she'd heard him play the saxophone at St. Peter's, she had been convinced he felt something deep and meaningful for her. She wasn't so naive as to believe he loved her—that would have been too much to hope for so soon. But she couldn't deny that Joshua had shared a deep personal part of himself with her, and that went a long way toward making her forget she would be left solely in charge of Angie while he tended to his business meetings.

"Daddy." Angie leaned across Bethany and called to her father. When he didn't immediately respond, his daughter took to waving her hand.

Joshua obviously didn't hear or see her, too wrapped up in the report he was reading to break his concentration.

"What is it, Angie?" Bethany asked.

The girl leaned back in her seat. "How much longer?

Will we be able to go to Disneyland today? I can hardly wait to see Mickey Mouse and Snow White."

Bethany checked her watch. "It'll be another couple of hours yet before we land."

"Oh." The small shoulders sagged with disappointment. "That long?"

"I'm afraid so."

"What about Disneyland?"

"There just won't be enough time after we leave the airport and check into the hotel."

"But Dad said we—"

"We'll see Mickey and Minnie, Snow White and everyone else first thing in the morning. I promise."

It looked for a moment as though Angie was going to argue, but she apparently changed her mind and quietly settled back in her seat for a while. Then she squirmed once more.

"Is Dad going to be in meetings the whole time we're in California?"

Bethany nodded. She didn't like the idea of Joshua being constantly busy any better than Angie did. When she'd originally made the arrangements for this trip, he had requested that she schedule in a couple of days' free time so he could spend it with Angie, sight-seeing. However, once Bethany had agreed to accompany them, the days he'd set aside for vacation had quickly filled up with appointments and other business affairs. Now he would be occupied the entire five days of their visit.

Their flight landed at LAX at five that evening, but by the time their luggage had been collected and the limousine had driven them into Anaheim, it was much later. Because of the time difference, Angie was overly tired, hungry and more than a little cranky.

Bethany wasn't faring much better after the long trip. Keeping Angie occupied had drained her completely. When Joshua had first asked her to accompany him, she'd been thrilled. Now she felt abused and disappointed at the role she would be playing during the next few days. Her back was stiff, she was hungry, and she felt like Cinderella two nights after the ball, when her hair needed washing and there was a run in her tights.

Joshua had requested a hotel close to the amusement park, where Bethany and Angie planned to spend a good deal of their stay. He had reserved a large suite. By the time they were settled, Angie was close to tears. Cranky because she was hungry, grumpy because she was tired, and yet too excited to sleep.

It took Bethany the better part of an hour to convince the little girl to eat the hamburger Joshua ordered from room service. More time was spent persuading Angie that although it was still daylight, she really needed to rest. She was a little more cooperative once she took a bath, at which point she climbed into bed with hardly a complaint and was asleep within five minutes.

Bethany felt as if she'd worked straight through a double shift when she joined Joshua in the suite's living room. She plopped herself down beside him on the davenport, slipped off her shoes and sagged against the back of the sofa, more exhausted than she could remember being in a long while.

He set aside his papers and reached for her hand. His gaze revealed his appreciation—and no wonder, she thought. It had been obvious from the moment Angie started to whine that he wasn't going to be able to deal with his daughter patiently. He raised Bethany's hand to his mouth and brushed his lips over her knuckles. "I don't know what I'd do without you," he murmured.

A polite nod and a weak smile were all the response she could manage.

"I don't mean for you to work while we're here." He scooted closer and wrapped his arm around her, cupping her shoulder. "My intention had been to make this a vacation for you, as well.... I didn't realize Angie would be such a handful."

"She was just tired and cranky."

He kissed the top of her head. "I know it was completely selfish of me to ask you to make this trip."

She didn't answer. Couldn't. Sally had been telling her what a fool she was from the minute Bethany had told her she would be travelling to California with Joshua and his daughter.

"The thought of spending five days without seeing you was more than I could bear."

She desperately wanted to believe him. She tucked her head under his chin and snuggled closer, almost too exhausted to appreciate the comfort his arms offered.

"I'm being unfair to you."

Her eyes drifted shut when he raised her chin and kissed her, his mouth brushing over hers in a swift kiss. She sighed and smiled contentedly. Tenderly he smoothed wisps of hair away from her face and slowly glided his fingertips over her features.

"Such smooth skin," he whispered. "So warm and silky."

She felt as if she'd gone ten rounds with a prize

fighter, but one kiss from Joshua wiped out everything but the cozy tranquil feeling of being held in his embrace. She slipped her left arm around his middle and tipped her head back, seeking more of his special brand of comfort.

When he didn't immediately kiss her again, her lashes fluttered open. What she saw in his eyes made her heart go still. He was staring at her with such naked longing that she felt she would break out in a fever just looking at him. The words to tell him that she loved him burned on her lips, but she held them inside for fear of what voicing them would do to their relationship.

"Oh, Bethany, you are so beautiful." He whispered the words with such an intensity of emotion that she felt her heart melt like butter left sitting too long in the hot sun. She wanted to tell him that it wasn't necessary for him to say things like that to her. He owned her heart, and had for three years.

His gaze held her a willing prisoner for what seemed like an eternity as he slowly slid his hand from the curve of her shoulder upward to her warm nape. He wove his fingers into her thick dark hair, and with his hand cupping the back of her head, he directed her mouth toward his. The kiss was full and lush. Rich. The man who was kissing her wasn't the arrogant man she worked with in the office. This was the same man who'd revealed a part of himself to her she was sure few others knew existed. The same man who had soared to unknown heights on the wings of a song he'd played just for her. The same man who gazed into her eyes and revealed such need, such longing, that she would spend a lifetime basking in the pure desire she viewed there.

She was shaking so fiercely inside that she raised her hand to grip Joshua's collar in a futile effort to maintain her equilibrium. Her flesh felt both hot and cold at the same time.

When he lifted his mouth from hers, he drew several ragged breaths. "Having you with me could end up being the biggest temptation of my life," he whispered in a raspy voice. He captured her hand and flattened her palm over his heart. "Feel what you do to me."

"I don't need to feel…I know, because you're doing the same thing to me."

"Bethany…listen, this isn't the right time for either of us and—"

She cut him off, not willing to listen to his arguments. All she longed to do was savor the sweet sensations he'd aroused in her with a single kiss. She slipped her hands around his neck and offered him a slow seductive smile as she gently directed his mouth back to hers.

His eyes momentarily widened with surprise.

She answered him with a smile, her lips parting, deepening the kiss.

"Bethany, oh, my sweet, sweet Bethany." He closed his eyes like a man enduring the worst kind of torture.

The distinctive ring of his cell didn't penetrate her consciousness at first. But he reacted almost immediately, jerking his head up and groaning aloud.

"Yes?"

It wasn't until he spoke that she realized he had left her and gone to find his phone. She blinked a couple of times, her eyes adjusting to the glaring light. Ill at ease, she sat upright and tried to catch her breath.

"The flight was on time. Yes…yes, first thing in the morning. I'm looking forward to it. I've got those figures you asked to see. I think you'll be impressed with what's been happening the past couple of months. Yes, of course, eight. I'll be there."

He spoke in crisp clear tones, and no one would have guessed that only a few moments earlier he'd been deeply kissing her. The transformation from lover to businessman was as slick as black ice on a country road.

It took her several minutes to gather her composure enough to stand. Her knees felt shaky, and she was sure desire lingered in her expression. She brushed the hair out of her face, her hands trembling. He was sitting with his back to her, intent on his conversation. As far as he was concerned, she could have been back in New Orleans. He had completely forgotten she existed.

She didn't wait until he was finished with his call. With her heart pounding like a battering ram against her rib cage, she walked across the floor, opened the door to the darkened bedroom she would be sharing with Angie and slipped inside. The little girl was sound asleep, and Bethany didn't bother to turn on any lights. She undressed silently, and found her way into the bathroom to brush her teeth and wash her face. Then she eagerly slipped between the clean sheets. Within minutes she felt herself sinking into a black void of slumber, but not before she heard Joshua's footsteps outside the bedroom door. He paused, then apparently thought better of waking her and walked away.

Angie was wearing Mickey Mouse ears and carrying a series of colorful balloons, two huge stuffed animals and other accumulated goodies when Bethany opened the door to their suite late the following afternoon.

"Hi, Dad." Angie flopped down in a chair and let out a giant whoosh of air. "Boy, am I tired."

Joshua grinned and sent a flashing query to Bethany. "How did you survive the day?"

"Great—I think. Only there isn't enough money in the world to get me back on some of those rides."

"Bethany screamed all the way through Big Thunder Mountain," Angie announced in a tattletale voice. "I thought she had more guts than that."

"At least I didn't hide my eyes when I rode through the Matterhorn."

"The abominable snowman frightened me," Angie announced, accepting the ribbing good-naturedly.

Joshua leaned back in his chair and grinned at them. "It looks to me like you both had a great time."

"Did we ever! We saw Donald Duck and Goofy and Snow White."

"Did Bethany happen upon another Prince Charming?" Joshua asked. His gaze met hers, and it was filled with curiosity.

"Unfortunately, no."

"A shame," he muttered, looking appropriately disappointed.

"The only white stallion I encountered was connected to an old-fashioned fire truck," she told him, sharing his amusement. "I didn't have time to investigate further."

He chuckled.

"How did your meeting go?" She was all too aware that the future of Norris Pharmaceutical rested on the outcome of this trip. She was worried for Joshua and prayed everything would go his way.

"It went well." But he didn't elaborate.

"I'm starved."

Bethany nearly fell out of her chair at Angie's sudden announcement. "You just ate two hot dogs, cotton candy and a bag of peanuts."

"Can I help it?" the girl asked. "I'm a growing child—at least that's what Mrs. Larson keeps telling me."

"And I'm one pooped adult." The thought of leaving the comfort of the suite on a food-seeking expedition so soon after getting back didn't thrill Bethany.

"Is anybody interested in taking a swim?" Joshua asked, diverting his daughter's attention.

"Me!" Instantly Angie was on her feet, eager to participate in anything that involved her father.

Bethany shook her head, too exhausted to move for the moment. "Maybe later—give me a few minutes to recuperate first." Her feet were swollen, although she'd worn a comfortable pair of shoes. Her back ached, and her head continued to spin from all the rides Angie had insisted they go on.

"I'm ready anytime you are, Dad," Angie said, and ran into the bedroom to change.

Joshua walked over to Bethany's side and bent down to lightly kiss her lips. "You look exhausted."

She smiled and nodded. "I'm too old to keep up with a ten-year-old."

"Go ahead and rest. I'll keep Angie occupied for the next hour or so."

"Bless you." She wasn't teasing when she'd told Joshua how exhausted she was. The energy level of one small girl was astonishing. They'd arrived at Disneyland when the amusement park opened that morning and then had stayed for the full day. On the monorail ride back to the hotel, Angie had casually announced that she intended to return to the park the following morning and then had wondered what there was to do that evening. All Bethany could think about was soaking in a hot bath and taking a long uninterrupted nap.

"We're off," Joshua said, coming out of his bedroom. He was wearing swimming trunks and had a thick white towel draped around his neck. He made such an attractive virile sight that Bethany nearly changed her mind about accompanying the two of them.

"Bye, Bethany," Angie said, and waved, looking happy and excited. "Rest up, okay? Because there are still a whole lot of things to do."

Opportunities for the little girl to spend time alone with her father were rare. Bethany was pleased that Joshua was making the effort to fit Angie into his busy life.

The door closed, and, with some effort, Bethany struggled to climb out of the chair. With her hand pressing against the small of her back, she made her way into the bedroom, deciding to forgo a soak in the tub and instead rest her eyes a few minutes.

The next thing she knew an hour had slipped away, and she could hear whispered voices.

Angie stuck her head in the bedroom door and announced to her father, "Bethany's asleep," then withdrew.

Bethany's mouth formed a soft smile as she bunched up the feather pillow beneath her head and pulled the blanket more securely over her shoulders. She'd been having such a pleasant dream that she wanted to linger in the warm bed and relive it. In her mind, Joshua had been telling her how much he loved her. The scent of orange blossoms wafted through the air, and she was convinced she could hear the faint strains of the "Wedding March."

"Dad," Bethany heard Angie whisper. "Have you ever thought about getting married again?"

Bethany's eyes popped open.

"No," Joshua muttered, and the tone of his voice told her that he found the subject matter distasteful.

"I've been thinking a lot about what it would be like to have a mother," Angie continued, apparently undaunted by the lack of enthusiasm in her father's voice.

Bethany lifted herself up on one elbow, wondering what she should do. If she were to make some kind of noise, then Angie and Joshua would know she was awake and end their talk. However, if she lay there and listened, she was going to regret it and feel guilty about eavesdropping when their discussion clearly wasn't meant for her ears.

"Angie, listen to me. I—"

"You're supposed to call me Millicent," she interrupted, impatience ringing in her young voice.

"Millicent, Guinevere, whoever you choose to be at this moment, I don't think my remarrying is a subject you and I should be discussing."

"Why not?"

Joshua seemed to have some difficulty answering, because only silence filtered into the bedroom where Bethany lay listening. She knew she should let them know she was awake. Obeying her conscience, she made a soft little noise that apparently went undetected.

"I've been thinking about what it would be like if you married Bethany," Angie continued. "I like her a whole bunch. She's a lot of fun."

"Bethany's too young," Joshua answered shortly. "I'm nearly eleven years older than she is and—"

"Oh puh-lease," Angie said dramatically. "I saw you kiss her once, and you didn't seem to think she was too young for that!"

"When?" Joshua demanded.

"A long time ago. I forget exactly when, but you did, and I saw you with my own two eyes."

Too young! Bethany mouthed the words in astonished disbelief. It was obvious that Joshua was pulling excuses out of a hat in an effort to appease his daughter.

"You *did* kiss her, didn't you?"

"Yes," Joshua muttered.

"And you liked it?"

"Angie." He paused, and Bethany could hear his sigh of frustration. "All right…Millicent, yes I *did* like it." The admission was ungracious, but it filled Bethany with joy, anyway.

"Then I think you should marry her."

"A whole lot more than liking the way someone kisses has to happen before a man considers marriage," Joshua explained with gruff impatience.

"It does?" Angie questioned. "Like what?"

"Things that a man doesn't discuss with his ten-year-old daughter."

"Oh," Angie muttered.

"Now for heaven's sake, don't say anything to Bethany about this or it'll make her uncomfortable." He paused, and in her mind Bethany could see him pacing the floor. "You haven't talked to Bethany about this, have you?"

"No," Angie admitted reluctantly. "I wanted to discuss it with you first. You told me I could talk to you about anything, and I thought I should let you know that if you wanted to marry Bethany I'd approve: She'd make a great mother."

"Whatever you do, Angela, don't say anything to her!"

"I won't." Bethany heard Angie make a disparaging sound, but she wasn't sure what had prompted it. "Do you want more children, Dad?"

"What?" The word seemed to explode from him.

"You know, another kid, like me?"

"I...I hadn't given it much thought. What makes you ask that?" It was clear from his tone of voice that Angie's questions were exasperating him.

"I don't know," Angie admitted, "except that if you and Bethany were to get married, then you'd probably have more children, and I'd like that. I want a little sister and then a little brother."

"Did Bethany put you up to this?" Joshua's low voice was filled with suspicion.

Bethany was so outraged that she nearly flew out of bed to argue in her own defense. How dare Joshua Norris think she would use his daughter to achieve her own ends. The very thought was despicable! If he believed for one second that she would resort to such underhanded tactics, then he didn't know her at all, and that hurt more than anything else he'd said.

"Bethany doesn't know anything yet. I told you, I wanted to talk to you first."

"I see," Joshua muttered.

"You *will* think about marrying her, won't you, Dad?"

A year seemed to pass before Joshua answered. "Maybe."

Bethany's face was so hot she was sure she was running a fever. Her heart constricted, and she closed her eyes, wishing with everything in her that she'd been asleep and oblivious to this rather unpleasant conversation.

After lingering in the bedroom for another forty minutes, Bethany opened the door and stepped into the living area, only to discover that Angie and her father were engrossed in a television movie.

"I didn't think you were ever going to wake up," Angie announced. "I'm starved, but Dad said we had to let you sleep."

"I'm sorry to keep you waiting," she said, having trouble sounding normal. "You should have gone without me. I wouldn't have minded." The way she was feeling now, she didn't know that she could maintain her composure and not let Joshua know what she'd innocently overheard.

Angie didn't seem to notice a change in Bethany's attitude, but Joshua certainly did. He studied her, and his gaze narrowed. "Are you feeling all right?"

"I'm fine," she said, and to prove it she smiled brilliantly in his direction.

"Good. I hope your healthy appetite is in place, because I've picked out an excellent Italian restaurant for dinner tonight."

"That sounds great," Angie said, reaching out to claim Bethany's hand. "Come on, let's go, Dominique."

The remainder of their days ran together, they were so filled with activities. Angie and Bethany visited Knott's Berry Farm, Universal Studios and every other tourist attraction they could find. In the evenings Joshua took charge of his daughter, finding ways of entertaining her and relieving Bethany of the task. There were plenty of opportunities for Bethany to spend time alone with Joshua, but she avoided them as much as she could without, she hoped, being obvious.

The final night of their stay, Angie fell asleep in front of the television. Joshua carried the little girl into the bedroom and gently laid her on top of the mattress.

Bethany pulled the covers over the small shoulders and bent down to plant a swift kiss on the smooth brow. Joshua followed suit.

"I think I'll turn in myself," Bethany murmured, avoiding his eyes.

He arched his brows in surprise. "It's only a little after nine."

"It's…it's been a long day."

"Come on, I'll order us some wine. We have a lot to celebrate."

"Then the meetings went well for you?"

He grinned and nodded.

She was relieved for his sake. Now perhaps his life

could return to normal, and he could go back to keeping regular hours instead of working day and night.

He had a chilled bottle of Chablis sent to their room. The waiter opened it for them and poured.

"I have a one-glass limit," Bethany said, feeling awkward.

"You had more the other night, as I recall."

"Sure, but I'd just swan dived into Lake Pontchartrain, too, if you'll remember."

A smile broke out across his handsome features. "I'm not likely to forget."

They sat in the living room with the lights dimmed, looking out over the flickering lights of the city. Neither spoke for a long time.

"I want you to know how grateful I am that you accompanied me and Angie," Joshua started off by saying. "Since Angie's come to live with me, things have changed between us, haven't they?"

She stared into her wine and nodded.

"I always thought of you as an efficient executive assistant, but bit by bit I've come to learn you're a warm, caring, nurturing woman."

"Thank you."

"I know you're attracted to me, Beth, and I haven't made any secret of the way I feel about you."

Her brain filled with an agitated buzzing. He was going to ask her to marry him. She knew it as clearly as if he'd removed a diamond ring from his pocket and waved it under her nose. Angie had specifically requested her for a mother and Joshua was simply complying with his daughter's wishes.

She glanced up and tried to hold back the emotions that were clamoring for release.

His intense gaze held hers.

"I know this must seem rather sudden, Beth, but I'd very much like you to consider marrying me."

Nine

"Bethany?"

With deliberately calculated movements, she set aside her glass of Chablis. Her mind was spinning like a child's toy top, wobbling precariously now as the momentum was slowing. Her heart was shouting for her to accept Joshua's proposal, but her head knew it would be wrong, especially since she'd heard him declare he had no intention of marrying again. All she could think was that over the last few days Angie had pleaded, whined and convinced Joshua against his better judgment to propose.

"For a moment there I actually thought I could do it," she whispered, feeling both miserable and elated at the same time.

Joshua's face sobered. "I don't understand."

She raised her hand to his face and lovingly pressed her palm against the side of his jaw. "I don't expect you to. I'm honored, Joshua, that you would ask me to be your wife, but the answer is no."

"No?" He looked positively stunned. "You didn't

even take time to think it over. You're turning me down? I thought…I'd hoped…"

She hung her head. "I want so much more out of marriage than to be a replacement mother for a lonely little girl."

Joshua's brow creased into a deep dark frown. "What gives you the impression I'm asking you to be my wife because of Angie?"

"Joshua, please…"

"I want to know why," he demanded, his words as stiff and cold as frozen sheets.

If he was looking for an argument, she wasn't going to provide one. She stood and offered him a sad but strong smile. "At least you didn't lie and tell me how much you love me. I've always admired that inherent streak of honesty in you. It's been ego shattering at times, but I've come to appreciate it." She swallowed tightly and then whispered, "Good night."

"Bethany." He ground out her name from between his teeth. "Sit down. It's obvious, if only to me, that we've got a great deal to discuss."

She shook her head. If they talked things over, she would be forced to tell him that she'd overheard his exchange with Angie. To admit as much would be humiliating to them both.

"Good night, Joshua."

He clenched his jaw, and a muscle leaped at the side of his face. She knew he was struggling to hold back his anger. She looked away, determined to leave the room with her pride, even if nothing else, intact.

The return to New Orleans was as much of an ordeal for Bethany as the flight to California had been five days earlier. At least this time Angie slept a good portion of the way. Once again Joshua sat across the aisle from her, but he might as well have been on a different airplane for all the attention he paid her. The silent treatment was exactly what she had expected, but it still hurt. His protective shield was securely fastened in place, and with no apparent regret or effort he'd shut her out of his heart and his life. Whatever possibility there had ever been for her to find happiness with Joshua Norris was now lost. He wouldn't ask her to marry him again and no doubt was sorry he'd done so the first time.

When they landed, Joshua saw to their luggage with only a few clipped instructions to Bethany to wait with Angie for his return.

"Did you and my dad have a fight?" Angie asked, tucking her small hand in Bethany's and studying her carefully.

"Not an argument." Bethany knew it would be wrong to try to mislead Joshua's daughter into believing everything was as it had been earlier in the week, but she had no idea what to say.

"How come ever since we left California you look like you want to cry?"

The best answer Bethany could come up with was a delicate shrug, which she knew wasn't going to appease a curious ten-year-old.

"Dad's been acting weird, too," Angie murmured thoughtfully, glancing toward her father, who was waiting for their suitcases to appear on the carousel. "He hardly talks to you anymore." She paused, as though waiting for Bethany to respond, and when she didn't, Angie added, "Dad and I had a long talk, and we decided that it would be a good idea if you two got married." She slapped her hand over her mouth. "I wasn't supposed to tell you that."

"I already know," Bethany said, feeling more miserable by the minute.

"You *are* going to marry Dad, aren't you?" Eyes as round as oranges studied her, waiting for her response.

"No." The lone word wavered and cracked on its way out of Bethany's mouth. She loved Angie almost as much as she did Joshua, but she couldn't marry him to satisfy his little girl.

"You *aren't* going to marry my dad?" If Joshua had looked stunned when she'd refused his proposal, it was a minor reaction compared to the look of disbelief Angie gave her. "You really aren't?"

"No, sweetheart, I'm not."

"Why not?"

Bethany brushed the soft curls away from the distraught young face and squatted down to wrap her arms around Angie, who wanted to be called Millicent. "I love you both so much," she whispered brokenly.

"I know that." Ready tears welled in Angie's eyes. "Don't you want to be my new mom?"

"More than anything in the world."

"I don't understand…"

Bethany didn't know any way to explain it. "Your father will find someone else, and…"

"I don't want anyone else to be my mother. I only want you."

Fiercely Bethany hugged the little girl close, and Angie's tears soaked through her silk blouse. "I…have to go now," Bethany whispered unevenly, watching Joshua make his way toward them, carrying their suitcases. "Goodbye, Millicent."

"But, Bethany, what about…?"

Remaining there and listening to Angie's pleas was more than Bethany could bear. She lifted her suitcase out of Joshua's hand without looking at him and hurriedly walked away.

"Bethany, don't go!" the little girl cried. "Don't go… please, don't go."

The words ripped through Bethany's heart, but she didn't turn around. Couldn't. Tears streaked her face as she rushed outside the terminal and miraculously flagged down a taxi.

"You honestly refused Joshua's proposal?" Sally demanded, pacing in front of Bethany like an angry drill sergeant. "You were delirious with fever at the time and didn't know what you were saying. Right?"

"No, I knew full well what turning him down would mean."

"Are you nuts, girl?" Sally asked, slapping her hands against the sides of her legs and stalking like a caged panther. "You've been in love with him for years."

"I know."

"How can you be so calm about this?" Sally slapped her thighs a second time.

Bethany shrugged, not exactly sure herself. "I wouldn't even mention it except I'm going to be looking for another job right away. And I knew as soon as you realized what I was doing, you'd hound me with questions until I ended up confessing everything, anyway."

"He fired you!"

"No," Bethany whispered. But she couldn't continue to work with Joshua. Not now. It would be impossible for them both.

"I thought you were crazy about the guy?"

"I am." Crazy enough to want the best for him. Crazy enough to want him to find his own happiness. Crazy enough to love him in spite of everything. For Joshua to marry her to provide a mother for his little girl wouldn't be right. "When he first asked me, I honestly thought I could do it. The words to tell him how much I wanted to share his life were right there on the tip of my tongue, but I had to force myself to swallow them." It had been the most difficult task of her life, but she didn't feel noble. Her emotions ran toward sad and miserable. Perhaps someday she would be able to look back and applaud her own gallantry. But not now, and probably not for a long time.

"But why would you refuse him?" Sally was looking at her as though it would be a good idea to call in a psychiatrist.

"He doesn't love me."

"Are you so sure of that?" Her roommate eyed her carefully, clearly unconvinced.

"I'm positive."

"Well, big deal! He'd learn to in a year or so. Some of the greatest marriages of all time were based on something far less than true love."

"I know that, but the risk is too high. He might come to love me later, but what if he doesn't? What if he woke up a year from now and realized he loved another woman? I know him. I know that he'd calmly accept his fate and let the woman he really loved walk out of his life."

"What about *your* life?"

Bethany ran her hand down her skirt, smoothing away an imaginary wrinkle. The deliberate movement gave her time to examine her thoughts. "I'm not being completely unselfish in all this. Yes, I love him, and yes, I love Angie, but I have a few expectations when it comes to marriage, too. When and if I ever marry, I want my husband to be as crazy in love with me as I am with him. When he looks at me, I want him to feel that his life would be incomplete without me there to share it with him."

"So you've decided to give J.D. your two week-notice first thing Monday morning?"

Bethany nodded. "You should be glad, Sal. You've been after me to do it for months."

"I don't feel good about this," Sally muttered, folding her arms over her chest, her brow furrowed with a frown. "Not the least bit."

Monday morning, Bethany had her letter of resignation typed before Joshua arrived at the office and had left it on his desk, waiting for him.

She gave him a minute to find it before entering his inner sanctum. He was sitting at his desk reading it when she delivered his coffee and handed him the morning mail.

"I hope two weeks is sufficient notice?" she asked politely, doing her utmost to remain outwardly calm and composed.

"It's plenty of time," he said without looking in her direction. "I'd like you to review the resumes yourself, decide on two or three of the most qualified applicants and I'll interview those you've chosen."

"I'll contact personnel right away."

"Good."

She turned to leave, but he stopped her. "Miss Stone."

"Yes?"

His gaze held hers for an agonizingly long moment. "You've been an excellent executive assistant. I'm sorry to lose you."

"Thank you, Mr. Norris." She hesitated before turning and walking out of his office. She longed to ask him about Angie but knew it would be impossible. She hadn't contacted the little girl, believing a clean break would be easier for them both. But she hadn't counted on it being this difficult, or on how much she would miss the little ray of sunshine who was Joshua's daughter.

A week passed, and Bethany was astonished that she and Joshua could continue to work together so well, even though they rarely spoke to each other, except for a few brief sentences that were required to accomplish the everyday business of running the office. She was miserable, but she knew she was right, and however painful it was now, the hurt would eventually go away.

Following Joshua's instructions, she reviewed all the applications personnel sent up. She chose three who she felt would nicely fill her role. Joshua interviewed all three and chose a matronly woman in her early fifties. For the next week Bethany worked closely with the woman so the transition would be as smooth as possible.

On her last day Joshua called her into his office,

thanked her for three years of loyal service and handed her a bonus check. She gasped when she saw the amount, pressed her lips together and calmly said, "This is too much."

"You earned it, Miss Stone."

"But…"

"For once, Miss Stone, kindly accept something without arguing with me."

It wouldn't do much good, anyway, so she nodded and whispered brokenly, "Thank you, Mr. Norris."

"Have you found other employment?" he asked her unexpectedly, delaying her departure.

She shook her head. She hadn't taken the time to look. With everything else going on in her life, another job didn't seem all that important.

"I wish you the very best, Miss Stone."

"You, too, Mr. Norris." She couldn't say anything more, fearing her voice would crack. As it was, tears hovered just below the surface. "Thank you again."

"Goodbye, Bethany."

She lowered her gaze and worried the corner of her lower lip. "Goodbye, Joshua."

With that, she turned and walked out of his life.

"Well, did you get the job?" Sally asked one afternoon.

The whole day had been gorgeous and sunny, and Bethany knew she should be like everyone else in the city and enjoy this unusual display of summerlike weather. Instead, she was inside, reading a book.

Shaking her head, she said, "They offered the position to someone else." Amazingly, she couldn't have cared less.

"You don't look all that disappointed."

"Sally, I don't know what's wrong with me," she said on the tail end of a drawn-out sigh. "I don't care if I ever find another job. All that interests me is sleeping, and if I'm not doing that, I'm reading. I've read more books in the past month than I did all last year."

"You're escaping."

"Probably." All she knew was that it didn't hurt as much when her face was buried in a good book—as long as it wasn't a romance. True love wasn't exactly her favorite topic at the moment. Murder mysteries appealed to her far more. Bloody battered bodies—that sort of thing.

Sally looked at her watch and gasped. "I've got to change and get ready," she said, and hurried toward her bedroom.

"For what?" Bethany asked, following her friend.

Sally blushed. "Jerry and I are going on a picnic."

"You've been out with him every night for the past week."

"I know," Sally admitted, and sighed sheepishly. "I'm in love, and I'll tell you right now—if Jerry Johnson proposed to me, I'd accept." She grew serious. "Tell me, honestly, Bethany, are you okay?"

"I'll be fine," she said, feigning a smile. "I've got everything I need. I stopped off at the library on my way back to the apartment. I've got enough reading material to last most people a lifetime, though at the rate I've been going I'll be done in a week." Her small attempt at humor fell decidedly flat.

Ever the true friend, Sally rolled her eyes toward the ceiling and mumbled something under her breath about misguided love and Bethany not knowing what was good for her.

The apartment felt empty with Sally gone. Bethany figured she might as well get used to it. The way her roommate's romance was progressing, Sally could well end up marrying her attorney boyfriend before the end of the summer.

At about seven, the doorbell rang. Bethany climbed off the sofa to answer it, unsure who it could be.

She pulled open the door and then nearly sagged against it. "Joshua?" She had never been more shocked to see anyone in her life.

"Is this a bad time? I know I should have phoned, but I was detained and…" He let the rest of what he was saying dwindle off.

"No, I'm not doing anything important. Please come in." She stepped aside to let him enter the apartment.

She hurried to get ahead of him and picked up an empty soda can and a banana peel, feeling embarrassed and foolish. "Sit down." She gestured toward the couch. "Can I get you something to drink?"

"No, thank you."

She deposited the rubbish in the kitchen and rushed back into the living room, holding her hands behind her back in nervous agitation. "Is something wrong at the office? I mean…I'd be happy to help in any way I can."

"Everything's fine."

Alarm filled her when she realized there could only be one reason why Joshua would come to her. "It's Angie, isn't it? She's had an accident—"

"No. Angie's doing very well. She misses you, but that's to be expected."

Relief flooded through her, and she sagged into the chair across from him.

He sat uncomfortably close to the end of the sofa. "The purpose of my visit is to see if you'd found another job."

"Not yet...." She couldn't very well announce that she'd taken to job hunting the way a cat does to a bath. If she spent the rest of her life reading and eating bananas, she would be content.

"I see." He braced his elbows against his knees and laced his fingers together. "I thought I might be able to help."

"Help?" It came to her then. The purpose behind his visit should have been as clear as Texas creek water. Anyone but a blind fool would have figured out that Joshua wanted to hire her as a babysitter for Angie. If he couldn't convince her to marry him, then he would no doubt be willing to pay her top dollar for her child-rearing services.

"Yes, help," Joshua said, ignoring her look of outrage. "I have certain connections, and I may be able to pull a few strings for you, if you'd like."

"Strings?" Bethany repeated. So he hadn't come because of Angie. She narrowed her gaze suspiciously, not knowing what to believe.

"Is something wrong?"

"No," she returned quickly.

"I understand Hal Lawrence of Holland Mills is looking for an executive assistant, and I'd be happy to put in a good word for you."

"That would be thoughtful."

"I'll call him first thing in the morning, then."

"Thank you." She continued to watch him closely, unsure what to make of his offer.

He stood, but she could tell he was reluctant. "I was wondering…" he said after an awkward moment.

"Yes?" she prompted, tilting her head back so far that she nearly toppled in her effort to look up at him.

He jammed his hands inside his pants pockets, then jerked them out again. "What makes you so certain I don't love you?"

Briefly she toyed with the idea of asking him outright what he *did* feel for her.

"Bethany," he said softly, "I asked you a question."

"I wasn't asleep," she answered weakly, her voice trapped and unstable.

"Asleep?" he demanded. "What are you talking about?"

"The first day in California," she continued, refusing to meet his impatient gaze. "I overheard Angie ask you if you'd ever thought of remarrying."

"Ah," he whispered, sounding almost relieved.

She didn't like his attitude. "Perhaps more important, Joshua Norris, I heard your answer."

"You're basing everything on that?"

"As I recall, you seemed to think I'd put her up to asking. That was the worst of it…that you assumed I would use Angie that way."

"I knew you wouldn't do that—you must have misunderstood me."

"Perhaps." She was willing to concede that much.

"Even if I hadn't heard you talking to Angie...that night you ordered the wine..."

"Yes?" He was clearly growing impatient with her, shifting his weight from one foot to the other.

"You didn't tell me how you felt then, either. I may have been too willing to jump to conclusions, but it seems to me that if you honestly love me then that would've been the time to tell me."

"Did it ever occur to you that a man wouldn't ask a woman to marry him without feeling something for her?"

"Oh, I'm sure you do...did," she corrected stiffly. "I haven't worked with you all these years without knowing how you operate. Unfortunately, I want more."

He paced back and forth a couple of times before sitting down again. He leaned forward, braced his elbows on his knees and exhaled sharply.

"The word *love* frightens me," he said after a moment, his gaze leveled on the worn carpeting. "I loved Angie's mother, but it wasn't enough. Within a year after we were married, Camille was discontented. I thought a baby would keep her occupied, but she didn't want children. I should have listened to her, should have realized then that nothing I would ever do would be enough. But I was young and stupid, and I loved her too much. Angie was unplanned, and Camille had a terrible pregnancy. When she was about five months along, she moved to New York to be with her family. She never cared for Angie, had never wanted to be a mother. Whatever instincts women are supposed to have regarding children were missing in her. Her mother was the one who took care of Angie from the very first.

"Camille insisted she needed a vacation to recover after Angie's birth and stayed with her parents, while I took what time off I could to fly between the two cities.

"Angie was only a few months old when Camille asked for the divorce. She was in love with another man." He paused and wiped a hand over his face, as if the action would clean the slate of that miserable portion of his life. "Apparently Camille had been involved with him for months after she moved to New York— even before Angie was born."

The pain in his eyes was almost more than Bethany could stand. She stood, walked over to the sofa and sat beside him. He clasped her hand in his.

"She died in a freak skiing accident a few months later."

"Oh, Joshua, I'm so sorry." She closed her eyes and pressed her forehead against his shoulder.

"Why?" he asked, almost brutally.

"Because…because she broke your heart."

"Yes, she did," he admitted reluctantly. "I'd assumed I was immune to love until Angie came to live with me. I felt safe from emotional attachments."

A tear rolled down the side of her pale face.

He paused and gently wiped the moisture from her cheek. He gripped her shoulders then, turned her in his arms and firmly planted his mouth over hers. His kiss was unlike any they'd shared in the past. His mouth moved urgently in a ruthless plundering, as if to punish both of them for the misery they'd caused each other. He slid his hands from her shoulders to her back, crushing her into his chest. This was a trial by fire, and she felt herself losing control, surrendering all she was, all she would ever be, to Joshua. Like a hothouse flower peeling open its petals, she blossomed under his expert lovemaking.

When he'd finished, her body was aflame and trembling. He straightened and sucked in deep gulps of air. His gaze was narrowed and clouded.

"Honestly, Bethany, if this isn't love, I don't know what is."

With that, he stood and walked out.

She was too weak to do anything more than lift her hand to stop him. Her voice refused to go higher than a weak whisper when she called out to him.

The door shut, and she sat there for a full minute, too stunned to do anything except breathe. Gradually the beginnings of a smile formed. A shaky kind of hopeful happiness took control of her. Joshua had never been a man to express his emotions freely. Maybe, just maybe, she'd misjudged him. He'd swallowed his considerable pride and come to her, and although he hadn't admitted that he loved her in words, he'd come so close as to make no difference. In thinking back to his proposal, she felt she hadn't given him the opportunity to tell her how he felt.

An hour later the phone rang. She reached for it and was pleasantly surprised to hear Joshua answer her greeting.

"Oh, Joshua, I'm so pleased you called. I've been thinking ever since you left and—"

"Bethany, have you heard from Angie?"

"No," she admitted, a little hurt by the cutting tone of his voice.

"You're sure she hasn't called you?"

"Of course I'm sure." His implication that she would lie to him was strong, and she didn't like it.

"Joshua, what's going on?"

A long moment passed before he spoke. "Angie's missing. Mrs. Larson saw her after school, but she hasn't been seen by anyone since."

The memory of the little girl telling her how much she enjoyed swimming and how she wished her father would go with her more often rang in Bethany's mind like a funeral gong.

"Joshua," she whispered through her panic. The evening was gorgeous. Sally and Jerry were on a picnic. "Could Angie have gone to the lake?"

Ten

Bethany didn't bother to ring the doorbell to Joshua's Lake Pontchartrain home. She barreled through the front door, breathless and so frightened she could barely think clearly. Her mind continued to echo Angie's words about wanting to swim alone in the lake like ricocheting bullets, and the fear Bethany experienced with each beat of her heart was debilitating.

"Joshua?" she called, stepping into the living room.

He walked out of his den, and his eyes held a look of agony. "She hasn't been seen or heard from since right after school. At least there's no evidence she went down to the lake. At least none that Mrs. Larson or I could find…."

Tears blurred Bethany's vision as she rushed across the room and into his arms. She wasn't sure what had driven her there—whether it was to lend comfort or receive it. Perhaps both. His chest felt warm and solid as she pressed her face into it and breathed in deeply in an effort to regain her equilibrium.

He held on to her desperately, burying his face in

the gentle slope of her throat, drinking in her strength, her courage, her love.

The thought passed through her mind that perhaps this was the first time Joshua had ever truly needed her.

"I think she may have run away," he confessed in a voice that was thick with emotion. "She told me once she'd thought about it. There's no other plausible explanation."

"But why?"

He dropped his arms and momentarily closed his eyes. "I'm rotten father material. From the first, I've done everything wrong. I love Angie, but I'm just not a good parent. Heaven knows I've—"

"Joshua, no!" Bethany reached for his hand, holding it between her own and pressing it to her cheek. "That's not true. You've been wonderful, and if you've made mistakes, that's understandable…really. No parent is perf—" She stopped speaking abruptly, cutting off the last word. Her eyes grew round as the horror of her actions struck her…the consequences of refusing Joshua's proposal. "It's me, isn't it? Angie's been upset because I haven't talked to her since…since the California trip, hasn't she? I bet she assumed I turned you down because of her, and, Joshua…oh, Joshua, that just isn't true." She took a step away from him and folded her hands over her middle as the reality burned through her. "That's…that's why you came to see me today, isn't it? You were worried then that something like this would happen, and you thought…" Everything was so amazingly clear now.

"No," he said gruffly, regretfully. "I'm not going to lie. Angie and I *did* discuss the matter before I proposed and…and after, but she accepted your decision…." He paused and looked away, his expression tight and proud. "In fact, she took it better than I did." He turned away and raked his hand impatiently through his hair. "Telling you this no doubt confirms the worst."

"Confirms the worst," she repeated. "I don't understand."

"You chose to believe I asked you to be my wife because I was looking for a mother for Angie."

She hadn't been able to help thinking exactly that, of course. But it wouldn't have mattered if Joshua truly loved her. She looked at him, her soul in her eyes. "It was true, though, wasn't it? About wanting me to be a mother to Angie?"

His shoulders sagged a little, and a sad smile briefly lifted the edges of his mouth but didn't catch. "I can't say the way Angie loves you didn't weigh into my decision, and I suppose that condemns me all the more. But my daughter loves Mrs. Larson, too, and the thought of marrying her never once entered my mind."

Bethany's heart began to do a slow drumroll.

"I know you probably don't believe this, but I *do* love you, Bethany. I have for weeks."

His words had the most curious effect on her. She stared at him, her blue eyes as wide as the Mississippi River. She was too stunned to react for a wild second, and then she calmly, casually, burst into tears.

It was clear from the way Joshua he forward and then quickly retreated that he didn't know what to do.

"Then why didn't you once so much as hint at the way you felt?" she asked, tears still streaming.

"I did," he countered. "Every way I knew how."

"But…"

"You weren't exactly a fountain of information yourself," he told her.

"You knew how I felt. You couldn't have missed it."

"Yes," he admitted reluctantly. "I caught on the evening we bumped into each other at Charley's…the night Angie arrived."

That soon. She gulped at the information. Her thoughts were interrupted when a glimpse of color flashed in her peripheral vision. She turned abruptly to see the tail of a flowered summer shirt disappear into Joshua's sloop.

Angie.

"Joshua…" She folded her fingers around his forearm and pointed toward the sailboat moored at the end of the long dock at the edge of the lake. "I just saw Angie."

"What?" He was instantly alert. "Where?"

"She's hiding in the sailboat."

"What on earth! Why would she do that?"

"I…don't know."

"Well, I intend to find out. Right now." He jerked open the French patio door hard enough to practically pull it off its hinges.

"Joshua…" She ran after him. "Calm down."

"I'll calm down once she's been properly disciplined."

Bethany was forced to run to keep up with his long strides.

He marched onto the dock like an avenging warlord. "Angela Catherine!" he shouted, and his voice was furious.

The top of a small brown head appeared, followed slowly by a pair of dark eyes.

"Angie! How could you have worried us this way?" Bethany cried, and covered her mouth with her hand, both relieved and upset.

"Hi, Dad." Hesitantly Angie stood and lifted her hand to greet him. "Hi, Bethany."

"Come out of that boat this minute, young lady," Joshua demanded.

"Okay." As though she'd recently returned from a world tour, Angie retrieved a pillowcase stuffed full of her clothes and tossed it to her father. She handed Bethany another, this one crammed to the top with a week's supply of snack foods. Finally she made a show of climbing over the side of the boat and onto the dock.

Bethany had to give the child credit for sheer courage.

"I suppose I'm going to get the spanking of my life," Angie said, calmly accepting her punishment. "I don't mind. Really." She squared her shoulders and offered her father a brave smile.

"Go to your room and wait for me there," Joshua ordered.

"Okay." The girl glanced from her father to Bethany and back again. "Can I ask Bethany something first?"

Joshua expelled his breath in a burst of impatience and nodded.

"Are you going to marry my Dad and me?"

"Angela Catherine, go to your room." Joshua pointed in the direction of the house. "Now!"

The girl's head dropped. "All right."

The two adults followed Angie through the patio

doors. Bethany deposited the pillowcase full of food in the kitchen, then followed Joshua into the family room. Standing there, she rubbed her palms back and forth as she gathered her thoughts.

"I was right," he said, looking pale and troubled. "Angie *did* run away."

"I don't think she was planning to go far."

He sat on the edge of the sofa and dragged his hands over his face. "But why?" He tossed the question to her and seemed to expect an answer.

"I...I don't know."

"Angie and I have been closer than ever the past few weeks," he said, and every feature of his handsome face revealed his bewilderment. "I can hardly believe she would do this."

Unable to understand it herself, Bethany sat beside him, her legs weak with relief that they'd found the little girl.

"I'm not cut out for this parenting business. I've done everything wrong from the minute that child was born," he muttered, his discouragement palpable.

"I sincerely hope you don't mean that," she whispered, and rested her head against the outside curve of his shoulder.

He turned to her then, his gaze narrow and curious.

"I'd like us to have a family someday," she whispered, gladly answering the question in his eyes.

"You would?" His voice was taut, strangled.

"Yes," she answered with a short nod. "Two, I think. Three, if you want."

"Bethany, oh, Bethany." His eyes went dark, the pupils dilating as he continued to stare at her. "You mean it, don't you?"

"Of course I mean it! I love you so much."

His eyes closed, as though he had paused to savor each syllable of each word. "Then you *do* plan to marry me?"

"I'd prefer to do it before the children are born," she answered with a soft teasing smile.

He pulled her into his arms and kissed her with hungry desperation, rubbing his mouth back and forth over hers, sampling her lips as a man would enjoy an expensive and rare delicacy.

She wound her arms around his neck and leaned into him, offering him everything. He broke off the kiss, but his lips continued a series of soft nibbles down the side of her face.

"That night at Charley's…" he whispered.

"Yes…?"

"Having you come up to me at the bar, your eyes so full of concern, your love so open…it shook me to the core. I'd worked with you all that time, and I'd never seen you as anything more than an excellent executive assistant."

"I know," she said with a tinge of remembered frustration. She ran her fingers through his hair and down the side of his face to his neck, reveling in the freedom to touch him. "I was ready to give you my notice then. Everything felt so hopeless."

"I think I realized that, too…and for a time I thought it would be for the best if you *did* find other employment. Then you were gone that one day, and the office seemed so empty and dark without you. I thought if you left, nothing would ever be the same in my life again, and I couldn't let you go."

"Oh, Joshua."

"My reasoning wasn't so selfless," he admitted. "I didn't intend to fall in love with you...that took me by surprise. The day you fell in the lake, I knew it was useless to pretend anymore. Oh, my beautiful, adorable Bethany, what a sight you made that afternoon, with water dripping at your feet."

She groaned at the memory.

"But you held your head high and walked out of that water as though drenching yourself had been your intention all along. I stood on the shore and knew right then and there it wasn't going to do the least bit of good to fight my love for you any longer. I was hooked for all the days of my life."

"The prince..." She lifted her face to watch him, needing to know if the man who'd swept her into his arms at the Mardi Gras parade had been Joshua.

"Yes?"

"It *was* you, wasn't it?"

He looked sheepish when he nodded. "I can't believe I did something so crazy.... It's not like me, but I wanted to kiss you again, needed to, because I didn't know if I'd ever get the chance given what was happening with the com—"

"But why?" she interrupted.

He took her hand and lifted it to his mouth. "You were aware of only a fraction of what was going on with the business at the time. I nearly lost it, Bethany, nearly lost everything. I was in the middle of the biggest financial struggle of my life. The timing for falling in love couldn't have been worse."

"Telling me you loved me would have gone a long way, Joshua Norris."

He grinned. "Now, perhaps…but not last month. Everything I had in the world was on the line. I had to deal with the financial issues before I could pursue our relationship."

"I could have helped." She wasn't sure how, but surely there would have been some way.

"You couldn't—there wasn't anything you could have done. I was sure if I lost Norris Pharmaceutical, I'd be losing you, too."

"How can you say that? I would never have left you.…"

"I know that. Now." He held her face between his hands and kissed her again. "I died a thousand deaths when I heard Sally arrange that date for you."

"She…she was convinced you were using me."

Joshua leaned his forehead against hers. "As a babysitter? There wasn't a single moment I needed you to watch Angie—they were all excuses to have you close, to spend time with you. I thanked God for that excuse. I was so afraid I was going to lose you to someone else while I was forced to deal with the second takeover bid. I invented reasons to keep you close."

"But in California, when Angie suggested you marry me, you didn't sound pleased with the prospect."

"I wish you'd been asleep that day," he admitted with a frown. "Everything was still up in the air—I'd only met one day with Hillard and his group. I loved you then, Bethany, but a man can't come to a woman without something to offer her."

"But it really did sound as if you thought I'd put Angie up to that conversation."

He grinned. "If I *did* suggest that, then it was with a prayer and a smile, because I wanted you so much, and I was hoping you wanted me, too. I could hardly stand the wait myself. The day the negotiations were finalized, I asked you to marry me. Delaying it even a minute longer was intolerable."

"But you didn't tell me you loved me, and…"

"Bethany, I was a nervous wreck. Surely you noticed? I'd been as jumpy as a toad all evening, waiting to get you alone, and then, when I finally managed it, you didn't seem the least bit inclined to want my company. All day I'd been rehearsing what I wanted to say, and instead I blurted out the question like a complete idiot. You could have bowled me over with a Ping-Pong ball when you refused."

"I thought…"

He interrupted by sliding his mouth over hers. "I know exactly what twisted thoughts you'd been harboring…and I'll admit my pride took a beating that night and all the nights that followed. It wasn't easy to come to you this afternoon, but I've grown to accept that my life isn't going to be worth anything if I can't share it with you."

"Oh, Joshua." Tenderness filled her eyes, and a precious kind of sweetness pierced her heart. She found his mouth with hers and kissed him with all the love she'd been holding in for so long.

"And then I blew everything a second time and came home to discover Angie was missing."

At the mention of his daughter, Bethany straightened. "I think we should talk to her. Together."

"All right," he agreed, standing. His hand was linked with hers as he led her down the hallway to the bedrooms.

Joshua rapped at Angie's bedroom door and then let himself inside. Angie sat on the edge of the mattress, her head bowed and her hands clasped in her lap.

"All right, young lady, what do you have to say for yourself?"

"Nothing."

The word was so soft Bethany had to strain to hear it.

"Surely you know how worried Bethany and I would be?"

Angie nodded several times, still not looking at them.

"If you knew that, then what possible reason could you have had for doing something like that?"

Her small shoulders jerked up, then sagged.

"Are you unhappy, sweetheart?" Bethany asked.

The little girl shook her head. "I like living here better than anyplace in the world."

"Then why would you want to run away?" Joshua demanded.

A short pulsating silence followed. Finally Angie said, "So Bethany would come."

"I beg your pardon?" He advanced a step toward his daughter.

"So Bethany would come," Angie repeated a little louder.

"I heard you the first time, but I don't understand your reasoning."

"When you talked to me last week, you said we might have been hoping for too much with Bethany, because she didn't want to marry you, and I knew that was wrong. I knew she loved you and I know she loves me, so I figured if something bad happened, then she'd come and you two would talk, and then maybe she'd want to marry us."

Bethany gasped at the logic, because that was essentially what *had* happened.

"Your intentions may have been good, but what you did was very wrong."

"I know." For the first time Angie raised her eyes to meet her father's. "Can you let me know how many swats I'm going to get? If you tell me that, I can hold on and not cry."

Joshua seemed to be contemplating that when Angie went on.

"I saw Bethany from the sailboat, and she looked real worried, and then I saw you talking and I could hardly wait to hear what you said, so I snuck out of the boat and came to the patio to listen." A smile as wide as the Grand Canyon broke out across her face. "I wasn't sure, but it sounded like Bethany wants us."

"Oh, sweetheart, I've always wanted you." Bethany wasn't sure if Joshua would approve of her comforting Angie, but she wrapped her arms around the little girl and hugged her close.

"So are you going to marry us?"

Bethany nodded eagerly.

"Oh, good!" Angie beamed at her father and added,

"You can give me as many swats as you want, and I bet I won't even feel them."

Bethany was just preparing to move into the role of stepmother, and she didn't want to cross Joshua, but she couldn't bear the thought of Angie being spanked. She tried to tell him as much with her eyes.

He answered her with a look of his own, cleared his throat and announced, "Seeing as everything's worked out for the best, I believe we can forgo the spanking."

"We can?" Angie all but flew off the bed. Her arms groped for Joshua's waist, and she hugged him with all her might.

"However, you caused Bethany, Mrs. Larson and several others a good deal of concern. You're grounded for the next two weeks, young lady."

Some of the delight drained out of Angie's eyes. She sank her teeth into her lower lip and nodded. "I won't ever do it again, I promise. I...I thought it would be fun, but it wasn't. I was bored to tears."

"Good. I sincerely hope you've learned your lesson."

"Oh, I did." She slipped one arm around Bethany's waist and the other around her father, and stood between the two adults. "We're going to have such a good life together."

"I think so, too," Bethany agreed.

"Especially after the other kids arrive," Angie said, looking vastly pleased with herself. "I want a sister first, okay? And then a brother."

Joshua's gaze reached out to Bethany and wrapped her in an abundance of warmth. "I'm more than willing to do my part to complete the picture."

Bethany couldn't have looked away to save the world

from annihilation. Joy welled up inside her, and she nodded. "Me, too."

Angie released a long slow sigh. "Good. Now when can I tell my friends about the wedding? I was thinking Saturday the fifteenth would be a good choice, don't you? At the reception, we'll serve Big Macs and macadamia nuts."

"Sounds good to me," Joshua said with an indulgent chuckle.

"I couldn't think of anything I'd like more," Bethany added.

"Now, about the honeymoon…"

Joshua's gaze didn't leave Bethany as he spoke. "That's one thing I plan to take care of myself."

"Anything you say, Dad." Angie looked up at Bethany and winked. "We're going to be so happy."

And they were.

* * * * *

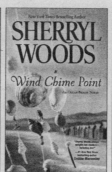
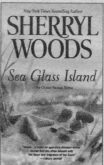

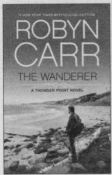
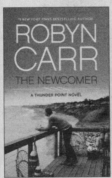
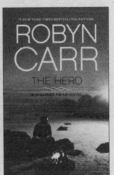

New York Times Bestselling Author
BRENDA NOVAK

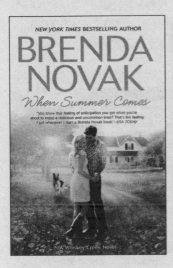

NEW YORK TIMES BESTSELLING AUTHOR
BRENDA NOVAK
When Summer Comes

"You know that feeling of anticipation you get when you're about to enjoy a delicious and uncommon treat? That's the feeling I get whenever I start a Brenda Novak book."—USA TODAY

A Whiskey Creek Novel

One day, Callie Vanetta receives devastating news…

She needs a liver transplant. But her doctors warn that the chances of finding a compatible donor aren't good.

Determined to spend whatever time she has left on her own terms, she keeps the diagnosis to herself and moves out to her late grandparents' farm. She's always wanted to live there. But the farm hasn't been worked in years and she begins to fear she can't manage it, that she'll have to return to town.

One night, a stranger comes knocking at her door…

He's an attractive and mysterious drifter by the name of Levi McCloud, and he offers to trade work for a few nights' shelter. The arrangement seems ideal until what was supposed to be temporary starts to look more and more permanent. Then Callie realizes she does have something to lose—her heart. And although he doesn't yet know it, Levi stands to lose even more.

Available wherever books are sold.

HARLEQUIN® MIRA®
™ www.Harlequin.com

MBN1423

REQUEST YOUR FREE BOOKS!

2 FREE NOVELS
FROM THE ROMANCE COLLECTION
PLUS 2 FREE GIFTS!

YES! Please send me 2 FREE novels from the Romance Collection and my 2 FREE gifts (gifts are worth about $10). After receiving them, if I don't wish to receive any more books, I can return the shipping statement marked "cancel." If I don't cancel, I will receive 4 brand-new novels every month and be billed just $5.99 per book in the U.S. or $6.49 per book in Canada. That's a savings of at least 25% off the cover price. It's quite a bargain! Shipping and handling is just 50¢ per book in the U.S. and 75¢ per book in Canada.* I understand that accepting the 2 free books and gifts places me under no obligation to buy anything. I can always return a shipment and cancel at any time. Even if I never buy another book, the two free books and gifts are mine to keep forever.

194/394 MDN FVU7

Name	(PLEASE PRINT)
Address	Apt. #
City	State/Prov.	Zip/Postal Code
Signature (if under 18, a parent or guardian must sign)	

Mail to the Harlequin® Reader Service:
IN U.S.A.: P.O. Box 1867, Buffalo, NY 14240-1867
IN CANADA: P.O. Box 609, Fort Erie, Ontario L2A 5X3

Want to try two free books from another line?
Call 1-800-873-8635 or visit www.ReaderService.com.

* Terms and prices subject to change without notice. Prices do not include applicable taxes. Sales tax applicable in N.Y. Canadian residents will be charged applicable taxes. Offer not valid in Quebec. This offer is limited to one order per household. Not valid for current subscribers to the Romance Collection or the Romance/Suspense Collection. All orders subject to credit approval. Credit or debit balances in a customer's account(s) may be offset by any other outstanding balance owed by or to the customer. Please allow 4 to 6 weeks for delivery. Offer available while quantities last.

Your Privacy—The Harlequin® Reader Service is committed to protecting your privacy. Our Privacy Policy is available online at www.ReaderService.com or upon request from the Harlequin Reader Service.

We make a portion of our mailing list available to reputable third parties that offer products we believe may interest you. If you prefer that we not exchange your name with third parties, or if you wish to clarify or modify your communication preferences, please visit us at www.ReaderService.com/consumerchoice or write to us at Harlequin Reader Service Preference Service, P.O. Box 9062, Buffalo, NY 14269. Include your complete name and address.

DEBBIE MACOMBER

32988	OUT OF THE RAIN	___ $7.99 U.S.	___ $9.99 CAN.
32971	92 PACIFIC BOULEVARD	___ $7.99 U.S.	___ $9.99 CAN.
32970	8 SANDPIPER WAY	___ $7.99 U.S.	___ $9.99 CAN.
32969	74 SEASIDE AVENUE	___ $7.99 U.S.	___ $9.99 CAN.
32968	6 RAINIER DRIVE	___ $7.99 U.S.	___ $9.99 CAN.
32967	44 CRANBERRY POINT	___ $7.99 U.S.	___ $9.99 CAN.
32946	311 PELICAN COURT	___ $7.99 U.S.	___ $9.99 CAN.
32929	HANNAH'S LIST	___ $7.99 U.S.	___ $9.99 CAN.
32918	AN ENGAGEMENT IN SEATTLE	___ $7.99 U.S.	___ $9.99 CAN.
32911	THE MANNING SISTERS	___ $7.99 U.S.	___ $9.99 CAN.
32884	SUSANNAH'S GARDEN	___ $7.99 U.S.	___ $9.99 CAN.
32861	204 ROSEWOOD LANE	___ $7.99 U.S.	___ $9.99 CAN.
32860	16 LIGHTHOUSE ROAD	___ $7.99 U.S.	___ $9.99 CAN.
32858	HOME FOR THE HOLIDAYS	___ $7.99 U.S.	___ $9.99 CAN.
32856	A GIFT TO LAST	___ $7.99 U.S.	___ $9.99 CAN.
32828	ORCHARD VALLEY BRIDES	___ $7.99 U.S.	___ $9.99 CAN.
32822	CHRISTMAS IN CEDAR COVE	___ $7.99 U.S.	___ $9.99 CAN.
32806	1022 EVERGREEN PLACE	___ $7.99 U.S.	___ $9.99 CAN.
32798	ORCHARD VALLEY GROOMS	___ $7.99 U.S.	___ $9.99 CAN.
32783	THE MAN YOU'LL MARRY	___ $7.99 U.S.	___ $9.99 CAN.
32743	THE SOONER THE BETTER	___ $7.99 U.S.	___ $9.99 CAN.
32702	FAIRY TALE WEDDINGS	___ $7.99 U.S.	___ $9.99 CAN.
32701	WYOMING BRIDES	___ $7.99 U.S.	___ $8.99 CAN.
32602	THE MANNING GROOMS	___ $7.99 U.S.	___ $7.99 CAN.
32569	ALWAYS DAKOTA	___ $7.99 U.S.	___ $7.99 CAN.
32506	CHRISTMAS WISHES	___ $7.99 U.S.	___ $9.50 CAN.
32474	THE MANNING BRIDES	___ $7.99 U.S.	___ $7.99 CAN.
32362	COUNTRY BRIDES	___ $7.99 U.S.	___ $9.50 CAN.
31299	YOU...AGAIN	___ $7.99 U.S.	___ $9.99 CAN.
31251	1105 YAKIMA STREET	___ $7.99 U.S.	___ $9.99 CAN.
28827	THE SHOP ON BLOSSOM STREET	___ $7.99 U.S.	___ $9.99 CAN.
28810	BACK ON BLOSSOM STREET	___ $7.99 U.S.	___ $9.99 CAN.
28803	A GOOD YARN	___ $7.99 U.S.	___ $9.99 CAN.
28629	50 HARBOR STREET	___ $7.99 U.S.	___ $9.99 CAN.
26/93	MARRIED IN SEATTLE	___ $7.99 U.S.	___ $7.99 CAN.
23662	BE MY VALENTINE	___ $7.99 U.S.	___ $9.50 CAN.

(limited quantities available)

TOTAL AMOUNT	$ _____
POSTAGE & HANDLING	$ _____
($1.00 for 1 book, 50¢ for each additional)	
APPLICABLE TAXES*	$ _____
TOTAL PAYABLE	$ _____

(check or money order—please do not send cash)

To order, complete this form and send it, along with a check or money order for the total above, payable to Harlequin MIRA, to: **In the U.S.:** 3010 Walden Avenue, P.O. Box 9077, Buffalo, NY 14269-9077; **In Canada:** P.O. Box 636, Fort Erie, Ontario, L2A 5X3.

Name: _____
Address: _____ City: _____
State/Prov.: _____ Zip/Postal Code: _____
Account Number (if applicable): _____
075 CSAS

*New York residents remit applicable sales taxes.
*Canadian residents remit applicable GST and provincial taxes.

HARLEQUIN® MIRA®
™ www.Harlequin.com

MDM0213BL